BEST CANADIAN
Christmas Stories

THE ✝ LUNG ASSOCIATION™
L'ASSOCIATION PULMONAIRE

*Proceeds from the sale of this book will be donated to the
Canadian Lung Association Christmas Seal Campaign*
Donate online: info@lung.ca
Donate by telephone: 1-888-566-LUNG (5864)

BEST CANADIAN
Christmas Stories

Edited by
Don Bailey & Bob Hilderley

QUARRY PRESS

Canadian Cataloguing in Publication Data is available.

ISBN 978-1-55082-358-5

Text designed and typeset by Laura Brady.

Cover art by Danielle Marchand, 2003 Christmas Seal,
courtesy of The Lung Association.

Cover designed by Susan Hannah.

Printed and bound in Canada. For bulk orders, call 613.548.8429.

Published by Quarry Press Inc
PO Box 1061
Kingston, Ontario K7L 4Y5 Canada
www.quarrypress.com

Contents

Preface

Christmas is celebrated by most of us in North America four days after the winter solstice. We are relieved to be moving from the darkest time of the year toward the light. We celebrate the lengthening days and reflect on how we have filled our time over the past year. Regrets are acknowledged and new dreams are born in an atmosphere of hope.

Christmas is a time to exchange gifts with those we care for, to reach out to those we have overlooked. It is a season to renew passions that have become buried and forgotten under the everyday grind of surviving. During the Christmas season most of us strive to be better human beings. We accommodate relatives whom we abhor around our feast tables. We tolerate the rude and the loud, the selfish and the silly. Some of us become physically demonstrative, hugging ancient aunts who have halitosis capable of melting plastic.

Christmas is an emotional territory, a kind of promised land, where expectations are sometimes raised to unrealistic heights. For some it is a time of great joy and delight, but for others it brings disappointment and sorrow.

Christmas is also a time to tell stories, especially so, it would seem, in Canada. Perhaps it is the cold north wind outside or the warm hearth inside that inspires these Christmas stories. Our best-known authors have written stories celebrating the occasion. Many of these occasional tales are comic, even raucous; some are ironic, if not acerbic; and a few are sad, dark tales with only a glimmer of light shining through. That and a smile. Some follow the conventions of science fiction, fantasy, and mystery writing to refresh our view of the season. Christmas becomes a time for laughter and comfort, a time for forgiving our foes and making friends, for re-affirming family rituals, for redemption. It is a time for unexpected visitors and unqualified hospitality. It is a time to love.

In this collection, we have tried to select writing that represents the many moods that are inspired by the Christmas season. We know that you will find something in these stories to warm your heart and assuage your soul. Merry Christmas.

DON BAILEY (1942–2003)
BOB HILDERLEY

Big Blue Spruce

Brian Doyle

"In the good old days," my father is saying, "we used to go out and cut down our own Christmas trees. None of this sissy stuff buying a tree for Christmas. We'd get out the axe and the saw and find our own tree back then. None of this wasting good money buying a tree. Yessir, we'd cut our own, we would!"

My mother is boiling cranberries, mixing cookie dough, simmering chocolate, stirring mince, smashing walnuts, slicing ginger, pouring molasses, whipping cream, sifting flour, chilling jelly between the windows, rolling pastry, separating eggs, measuring sugar, rendering butter, all, it seems at the same time.

It is 1947.

"Don't listen to him," my mother says.

Not too long ago, I got into trouble by listening to my father. Trouble at school. I got a three in history. Three out of a hundred.

"That's almost nothing," my father said, and laughed all afternoon. Then he told me that when he was in school, back in the good old days, he was an excellent student, top of his class, all the way through until Grade 4, when he began to drink very heavy.

It was my father's fault that I got almost nothing in history.

The teacher told us that Columbus discovered America in 1492 when he sailed the ocean blue.

"Tell the teacher she's full of it," my father told me. "Leif Ericson, the Viking, came to Labrador 500 years before that snivelling Columbus ever set sail in those sissy girlie ships, the Nina, the Pinta, the Santa Maria. Columbus didn't discover anything – it was already discovered – there were lots of people here already in North America. He just bumped into it – he didn't 'discover' it!"

The next day, I told the teacher.

I said: "Miss Gilhooly, you're full of it! A Viking came to Canada 500 years before. Columbus didn't discover anything – it was already discovered. He just bumped into it by mistake!"

"Who's filling your head with this impudent nonsense?" Miss Gilhooly said.

"My father," I said. "He was at the top of his class all the way through school right up to Grade 4 when he began to drink very heavy!"

The teacher told me that she was breaking all the rules to give me three, and that I didn't deserve it.

My father is in a pretty good mood.

The Civil Service (I used to think it was the Silver Service) just got a raise. Twenty dollars a month. And two months' back pay. He has 60 dollars extra this month for Christmas.

While he is talking about the good old days, I am helping my mother by licking the bowl and keeping my special Down syndrome sister out of everything. I do this by showing her how to squeeze her rubber duck, making it whistle and quack. That is an easy way to mind her. She can do this all day long and be happy.

We stop our cooking and run to the door to meet the bread man. He stands in the hall with his basket strapped to him. He smells like ginger snaps and snow and doughnuts with icing sugar on. His basket is heavy with Christmas fruitcake tied with red ribbon.

My special sister gives him a big hug.

My special sister gives everybody who shows up at our door a big hug, Christmas or not.

She hugs the mailman, the vegetable man, the iceman, the grocery man, coal man, wood man, milk man, meter man, my father's drunk friends home from the war, the rag picker, the priest, the police . . .

Everybody except Horrors Leblanc.

She doesn't like Horrors because of what happened one time with his hair.

Horrors is a man from Alcoholics Anonymous who comes over to our house once a week or so to smell my father. He always says he is over for a little visit and a chat, but we know he is smelling my father. He stands very close to him when they talk and you can see Horrors' nostrils moving.

The first time he came over, my special sister went to hug him, but ran howling up the stairs instead. Horrors had taken off his hat and his hair came off with it and dropped on the floor. My special sister stared at it there on the floor and then when Horrors picked it up and slapped it back on his head, she let out a howl and ran, terrified, up the stairs.

My mother gets turning the egg beater so fast you can't see her hand. It is a blur. She talks over the whirl of the beater about what is on the front page of the paper today. There is a picture of a boy. The caption says, "Died Seeking Christmas Tree."

In a village somewhere in Canada, a boy and his little brother went to cut a tree for their school Christmas party and never came back. Searchers found their stiff huddled bodies. Their boots were frozen in ice and their soaked clothing was hard as concrete.

While my mother and father are talking about that, Horrors Leblanc is at the door and my special sister goes howling up the stairs.

My mother and I watch as Horrors takes off his hat. His hair isn't too bad today. Just on a bit crooked is all.

My father and Horrors sit down and get talking about the good old days.

Horrors works with my father in the Silver Service. In the Customs and Excise Branch (I used to say Customers and Exercise). Their office is in the Connaught Building (my father calls it the Cannot Building) on Sussex Street (my father calls it Such and Such Street).

Back in the good old days, they're saying, when you worked real work, it was men's work, cutting pulpwood up the Gatineau River in the bush. Not like now, working in the Silver Service in the Customers and Exercise Branch in the Cannot Building on Such and Such Street. Nossir! Back in those days, for Christmas dinner it was sow belly, beans, bread, and tea and now they hear that these days up the Gatineau they have hundreds of turkeys for the roast pan and gravy and fruitcake and pudding and rum and Christmas decorations and everything from soup to nuts and now the cry is, "Come and get it or we'll throw it out!"

"They even have cook instructors goin' round the camps with new recipes, if you please!" says Horrors Leblanc. When he says "if you please," he tilts his head hard a few times from side to side and purses his lips – his imitation of a sissy. My mother and I watch to see when his hair will fly off.

"They're even flyin' in altar boys for the Christmas High Mass, can you imagine!" says my father. "Altar boys in the bush!"

"Everything's goin' to pot," says Horrors Leblanc.

It is the housing shortage after the war. We live in Air Force barracks at Uplands Airport. Next to us and the airport is the Ottawa Hunt and Golf Club.

"Do you know why they call it the Hunt and Golf Club?" my father asks Horrors.

"Because they spend all summer long hunting for their balls?" Horrors says.

I walk along the snow-swept runways of the airport towing my toboggan with the axe and bucksaw tied on.

The golf course forests bob in the distance.

I know this golf course inch by inch. I caddied the 18 holes there last summer nearly a hundred times.

I can see in my mind's eye the very tree I will cut. She is to the right of the green at the end of fairway No. 1.

Her skirts are rich and she tapers at the top to a perfect point for the star. Her branches are fat and full with long sharp needles. She has a bluish tint. A bluish silvery glow. Presents will flow from under her. My special sister will watch herself reflected in her glittering decorations.

My father will say, "That's my boy!"

"Good King Wenceslas" is playing over and over in my head.

I used to sing "Good King Wences Last Looked Out." I couldn't understand why King Wences, a good king, "last" looked out. Why was this the last time he looked out?

And what was he looking out on? He was looking on something called the Feast of Stephen. I thought the feast of Stephen was a field or a meadow or a fairway or something like that.

". . . and the snow lay round about . . ."

The service road along fairway No. 1 is plowed and there are tire tracks, but nobody is around.

The gentle slopes of the golf course are lathered in creamy

untouched white. Ahead is green No. 1. I can see the exact place where the flag would be in the summer.

"...deep and crisp and even..."

My tree, shining silvery blue there in the pale sun.

I push the snow away from her trunk and kneeling, I begin hacking with the axe.

The trunk seems quite a bit bigger than I thought it would be.

About halfway through, the head flies off the axe and plunges out into the deep snow in the sand trap.

I know it will be useless to look for it. They'll find it in the spring.

I finish off the tree with the bucksaw. When I am almost through, the tree twists and jams the saw blade, then turns and rolls silent onto her side, breaking the smooth crust of the deep snow.

The only sound is the snapping of the bucksaw blade.

But now there's another sound – an engine.

I get off my knees, stand up and turn. There on the service road is the groundskeeper getting out of his small flatbed truck.

"What are ya doin' son, are ya crazy!"

I tell him about the good old days and how my father used..."

"Well, good old days or not," says the groundskeeper, "the police are comin'."

The policeman, Constable Kealey, it turns out, knows my father from away back in the good old days. "So you're Jimmy Malarkey's son, Jimmy!" Constable Kealey and the groundskeeper put the tree on the flatbed and me in the police car and the toboggan and the bladeless bucksaw and the axe handle in the trunk and both truck and police car drive to my place and park in front and we get out and go up and Constable Kealey knocks on our door.

It feels lonesome, standing there outside while somebody knocks on your own door.

"How did you plan on getting this tree inside your house?" Constable Kealey asks me while he knocks on the door a second time. "Do you realize how big it is?"

I look at the tree lying there on the flatbed truck. Standing out on the golf course in the great expanse of fairway and forest, it didn't look large at all. But now, here . . . it is at least three times as tall as our front door.

"You could always cut a hole in your roof," says the grounds-keeper who has a big wart on his nose and seems to me to be a sarcastic sort of person.

When the door opens, I can hear singing.

It sounds like my father and Horrors Leblanc.

"Bring me bread and bring me wine.

Bring me pine logs hither . . .

Thou and I shall see him dine . . ."

My special sister hugs Constable Kealey and then the grounds-keeper and then me. My mother says, "It's the police," and my father and Horrors come into the hall to see what all the commotion is. Horrors is carrying a bottle of De Kuyper gin.

After Constable Kealey and my father shake hands as hard as they can – long time, no see, Jimmy, long time – everybody sits down in the little living room to drink De Kuyper gin. They decide that no charges will be laid and that my father will pay $50 damages to the golf club and we can keep the tree.

"There goes my raise," says my father, who has fallen off the wagon. "And he's taken Horrors Leblanc with him," says my mother.

"I'll drink to that!" says Horrors Leblanc.

"The $50 will pay for transplanting another blue spruce in the same spot so's the look of the first fairway won't be entirely spoiled," the groundskeeper says, looking right at me and raising his glass.

The wart on his nose is a lot bigger than when I first saw it. And is it glowing? Is it the De Kuyper gin that makes it glow like that?

The house smells like shortbread and chocolate and sage.

"When we find the axe head in the spring," the groundskeeper sneers at me, "do you want us to polish it up and send it over to ya, special delivery?"

After Constable Kealey and my father talk about the good old days for a bit and then promise to get together real soon to talk some more about the good old days, the two visitors leave, everybody shouting "Merry Christmas!" at everybody else.

Before he goes out the door, the groundskeeper turns to me. "There's a nice 300-year-old oak tree right by the club house. Would you like to come over and cut that down for us? It's only just standing there doin' nothin'!"

My mother stands behind me and puts her hands on my shoulders to protect me from his words.

After they are gone, my father and Horrors Leblanc discuss what to do with the blue spruce. If they cut it exactly in half, they think, one half of it will probably fit in the house somehow.

The bottom half would be very, VERY bushy, awful flat on the top, the tree would be almost square when you think of it and would pretty well fill up the whole room.

"Be no room for Santa to come in . . ." Horrors says, off in another world, his hair almost off now.

"The top half will be better," my father decides. "We could decorate it up real nice. Point will just touch the ceiling!"

My mother is ironing the wrinkles out of some of last year's wrapping paper, sorting out ribbon, decorating small boxes for homemade candy, organizing the big box of Christmas balls and decorations, untangling and testing the Christmas tree lights, curling boughs into wreaths and plucking cotton batting into wisps for snow, all, it seems, at the same time.

Horrors Leblanc is asleep sitting on the couch, his hair clutched to his chest.

My special sister peeks in from the hall, looking at Horrors, afraid to come in. My father is talking.

"In the good old days, we used to make our own decorations. None of this store-bought stuff. We'd get bells from the horses' harnesses. We'd collect real pine cones. We'd use rowanwood berries and hawthorn branches. We'd catch chickadees and nut-hatches and use their feathers. We'd cut sumac and pussy willows and loganberries. We'd cut the tails off raccoons, foxes, deer . . . we'd use milkweed . . . one time we even went to the barber shop and got bags of white hair from when the old men would get their beards trimmed – used it for fake snow . . . we'd . . ."

"Don't listen to him, Jimmy Junior," my mother says.

And so I try not to.

The Christmas Log

by Mary Alice Downie

"Once upon a time, my children ..." the grandmother began.

At this moment there was a stir among the listeners in the farmhouse kitchen. Everyone moved in his place. The father coughed; the little ones leaned forward with elbows on knees and chins in hands.

"Once upon a time, my children," repeated the grandmother. "There was an old château, very old indeed, very gloomy and solitary. It stood on the rocky flank of a hill crowned by a forest of giant oaks. Its real name was the castle of Kerfoël but it was better known as the Devil's Tower. It was said that in the old days the Devil had built a forge and furnace in the highest room on the turret. There he made gold for the lords of the domain. They in turn belonged to him from generation to generation.

There must have been an evil source for their wealth. From the top of that gloomy tower one could see nothing but barren moors, with here and there a menhir. These big fair-stones that stand up like men are called Satan's distaffs.

I must tell you, my children, that this story took place in France in the old province of Brittany, where *my* grandmother came from when our people settled in this land of Canada.

At the time of my story, the lord of Kerfoël and owner of the Devil's Tower was named Robert. He had been crippled from birth and was bandy-legged and club-footed as well, but he was still as strong as a giant. He had an evil reputation, for apart from his deformity, he was both ill-tempered and wicked. He hunted wild boar in the woods, even on Sundays. He harried the peasants, blasphemed the name of God, and was never seen in church. He ate meat on Fridays and he laughed at funerals.

People whispered that they had seen him far away on the moors at night, limping along on his twisted leg in company with the menhirs. They said that these stones followed him as obediently as dogs in the moonlight. No one knew where he was going. In short, the Count Robert de Kerfoël was a wretched sinner who feared neither God nor Satan.

His mother had died of a broken heart because of his sinful ways. His father had died without confession in a corner of the forest where his body had been found half-devoured by wolves. The son was to finish more miserably still."

Not a finger moved; every word, every syllable was snapped up as the grandmother continued her story.

"You have seen the man in the moon, haven't you, my children?"

"Yes, Me'mère."

"A lame man."

"Who is going down hill."

"With a bundle of straw on his shoulders."

"No, a faggot."

A log, little ones, a burning log. You can see him at night when the stars glitter in the sky and there is a full moon. He is especially clear on Christmas night when the rosy light from the church windows mingles with the pale radiance that falls from Heaven on the snow-covered hills. You have seen him, haven't you?"

"Yes, yes, Me'mère."

"With the log on his shoulder."

"Yes, and with his crooked leg."

"Well, listen now. In Brittany, the valiant land of Brittany, they did not celebrate Christmas as we do here with midnight mass and afterwards a glass of liquor and a branch of croquignole sprinkled with powdered sugar. There it was the peasants' day, the feast of the poor and the country festival above all others. The folk gathered in the châteaux and farmhouses and waited, young and old, with all manner of rejoicing, for midnight mass.

First they had the *Christmas log*. It was dragged into the hall, baptized with a glass of wine from the last vintage and burnt in the great chimney place. After that they sang the old carols and feasted with cider and crusty little cakes called nieulles.

Then they danced. How they danced! Not waltzes or quadrilles or cotillions as they do in the Governor's mansion in Quebec. In Brittany the boys and girls danced the bourrèe and the cariole to the sound of the binioux, which is something like the bagpipes that the Scotch play in their misty hills.

As you can easily imagine, my pets, Christmas was not celebrated in this way at the Devil's Tower. The people at the château on that night went to church and then returned to gather silently around the hearth. The old game-keeper Le Goffic would tell a tale or sing an old carol in a very low voice for fear of being overheard by the master. Season after season went by in sadness and fear without a moment's gaiety or joy.

One morning it happened that Count Robert sent for his

steward Yvon Kerouak and they had a long talk. Then he ordered his best horse saddled. He set off without saying a word to a living soul. Where did he go? No one knew.

Months followed weeks and years months. There was no news of him. People supposed him dead and made the sign of the cross when they heard the name of the Count de Kerfoël. He must have been the victim of some dreadful punishment. He would surely never be seen again in this life, or if it pleased God, in the other either.

Twenty years went by. The steward, the housekeeper and the other servants had grown grey. Old Le Goffic counted over eighty years.

Everyone was convinced that Count Robert would never return. The inhabitants of the old château began to lead a quieter life and merry times were as frequent at the Devil's Tower as anywhere else.

Christmas Eve was a special time of gaiety and feasting under the battlements of the old tower. One year the inhabitants of the château decided to celebrate with exceptional splendor. A huge log was cut from one of the giant oaks in the park and prepared for the ceremony. At eight o'clock that night, all the neighbors, the binioux-player in the lead, crowded into the great hall of the château. It was illuminated by pine branches and the lively blaze of the Christmas log itself in the hearth.

The merrymakers shouted with laughter. Their goblets rang as they toasted each other and then swallowed the foaming cider, while the long snuffling notes of the binioux droned on.

Suddenly: "Noël! Noël!" they all cried so loudly that the leaded panes of the old Gothic windows tinkled in response. The Christmas log caught fire. It crackled and spread showers of sparks.

"The baptism! The baptism!" they cried.

"Uncle le Goffic! To you the honors of the ceremony."

"Come, baptize the Christmas log, Uncle le Goffic."

"Uncle le Goffic! Uncle le Goffic!"

Then all fell on their knees, while the old game-keeper, bare-headed, advanced towards the fireplace. The light shone like a glory around his long white hair.

"In the name of the Father and of the Son and of the Holy Ghost," he said. His knotted trembling hand dropped the wine like a string of rubies on the massive log.

Before they could answer "amen" a wild gust of wind swept aside the flames on the hearth. There in the open doorway stood the squat figure of Count Robert de Kerfoël!

The people stood, dumb and horrified. Count Robert glanced about ferociously and advanced with drawn sword through the terrified peasants.

"Par la mort Dieux! How long has my château been the scene of such mummeries!" He turned to his old groom and pointed to the blazing fire. "Joel! Remove this emblem of a cursed superstition."

Despite their fear, the peasants cried aloud.

"The Christmas log?"

"Yes, the Christmas log. Out with it! Do you hear me, Joel?"

"My Lord Count," Joel replied, kneeling in terror. "The Christmas log is sacred. I would die rather than touch it."

"By all the devils!" screamed the count, half-maddened with rage. "Who commands here?"

"My Lord Count," said the steward. "The Christmas log is hallowed. It would be a sin to touch it."

"It would be a sin," repeated the others like an echo.

"Stupid idiots!" cried Count Robert. He seized two jugs of cider and emptied them over the burning log. With his own hands he pulled it from the fireplace and heaved it onto his shoulder. He paid no attention to the fire-brands that singed his hair and shrivelled his skin.

"My Lord Count," warned the old game-keeper, shivering from head to foot. "The Christmas log has been baptized. Beware of God's hand, my Lord Count!"

"Sacrilege!" cried several among the crowd. The Count, limping dreadfully, staggered across the threshold. His back was bent under the weight of the smoking log. He disappeared into the darkness outside, blaspheming horribly.

"Let us kneel and pray!" cried old le Goffic.

Too late. An inhuman cry sounded in the night. Count Robert de Kerfoël, last Lord of the Devil's Tower, was never seen again.

Ever since that night, my children, in clear weather, on the shining disk of the moon you can see a man with a twisted knee. He stoops under a strange burden and those who see well enough say that it is a half-burnt log still flaming here and there. The unfortunate Count Robert is condemned to carry that heavy burden on his shoulder until the day of the last judgment."

The Trapper's Christmas Eve

Robert Service

It's mighty lonesome-like and drear.
Above the Wild the moon rides high,
And shows up sharp and needle-clear
The emptiness of earth and sky;
No happy homes with love a-glow;
No Santa Claus to make believe:
Just snow and snow, and then more snow;
It's Christmas Eve, it's Christmas Eve.

And here am I where all things end,
And Undesirables are hurled;
A poor old man without a friend,

Forgot and dead to all the world;
Clean out of sight and out of mind ...
Well, maybe it is better so;
We all in life our level find,
And mine, I guess, is pretty low.

Yet as I sit with pipe alight
Beside the cabin-fire, it's queer
This mind of mine must take to-night
The backward trail of fifty year.
The school-house and the Christmas tree;
The children with their cheeks a-glow;
Two bright blue eyes that smile on me ...
Just half a century ago.

Again (it's maybe forty years),
With faith and trust almost divine,
These same blue eyes, abrim with tears,
Through depths of love look into mine.
A parting, tender, soft and low,
With arms that cling and lips that cleave...
Ah me! it's all so long ago,
Yet seems so sweet this Christmas Eve.

Just thirty years ago, again ...
We say a bitter, *last* good-bye;
Our lips are white with wrath and pain;
Our little children cling and cry.
Whose was the fault? it matters not,
For man and woman both deceive;
It's buried now and all forgot,
Forgiven, too, this Christmas Eve.

_____

And she (God pity me) is dead;
Our children men and women grown.
I like to think that they are wed,
With little children of their own,
That crowd around their Christmas tree...
I would not ever have them grieve,
Or shed a single tear for me,
To mar their joy this Christmas Eve.

Stripped to the buff and gaunt and still
Lies all the land in grim distress.
Like lost soul wailing, long and shrill,
A wolf-howl cleaves the emptiness.
Then hushed as Death is everything.
The moon rides haggard and forlorn...
"O hark the herald angels sing!"
God bless all men — it's Christmas morn.

One More Wiseman

by David Helwig

The only warning I got was a telegram from Montreal. It said "ARRIVING TOMORROW LOVE JACOB." Just that after five years.

The last time I'd seen him was in England, in a London Tube station, Tottenham Court Road I think it was. We were taking trains going in different directions, and as we separated, Jacob grinned back at me. He was wearing a heavy overcoat that made him look like a bear, and his teeth were very white in the middle of his dark beard.

"I'll see you tonight," he said.

The next day I got a telegram from Rome. It said "COME TO ITALY LOVE JACOB." Then two years of silence while I poked away at England and finally packed my life in a bag and came back to Toronto. Then three more years, happy enough, I suppose, with a job that was not too demanding and not too rewarding, a few friendships, and most recently, an arrangement of sorts with Laura, something that could have ended in marriage but hadn't.

Laura had been a widow for a year and a half now, and I had known her for about a year. We had spent gradually more time together as the months went on. I let things happen, but never seemed to act, to be in control. Her dead husband was a presence that I could not exorcize. I had never known him, Laura never mentioned him. And I did not ask. So his presence continued to haunt us. The only honest one, I sometimes thought, was Laura's nine-year-old daughter Cathy, who disliked me because I was not her father and she would allow no replacement. Laura and I went on, politely, foolishly, as friends. I didn't tell her that I loved her, didn't ask her to marry me. I don't know quite what I was waiting for, but I was still waiting.

Now Jacob was about to arrive in my quiet world. Over the last three years I had received two letters from him, one saying that he was separating from his wife and another two days later asking whether he'd ever written to say he was married. It was three days before Christmas when I got his telegram, and I assumed he was planning to stay with me over the holiday. The next morning I decided I would get some extra food and liquor in, to be ready to celebrate his return.

Jacob, my old friend, how to tell about him, where to start? I think I met him when we were both ten years old. It seems to me that he was a fat, grinning ten-year-old boy with a thick dark beard, standing on a street-corner, in the snow maybe, and laughing. It was always hard for me to keep the facts straight in my mind where Jacob was concerned.

His father, who had left Austria for political reasons, directed the United Church choir in which Jacob and I sang, I in a remarkably high soprano and Jacob in a rough but powerful contralto.

His mother was a round smiling woman who baked buns and bread and cookies and cakes and pies and pastries and loved to see us eat them. She kept Jacob almost as round as she was herself by filling him with her food.

And Jacob, my friend for years. He had a brown sweater with a hawk on it. He had an old short wave radio. The biggest collection of Captain Marvel comic books in town. A single copy of a sunbathing magazine full of naked women. When we got to the age for real girls, he would tell me everything, and I would tell him nothing.

Holding Jacob's telegram in my hand, I looked out the window of my apartment and saw a Christmas wreath in a lighted window across the road. I remembered how we had loved Christmas. When we sang carols in church, Jacob insisted on singing the melody instead of the dull contralto harmonies that the hymn book offered him. And I, not to be outdone, would invent soaring descants. We would look across the choir loft at each other and only keep from laughing because we loved the singing, especially the wild joyful carols, *Joy to the World* or *O Come All Ye Faithful*.

As I stood there, I decided I'd better phone Laura. I was expected to spend Christmas Eve and Christmas Day with them, and I thought I should tell her (did I mean warn her?) about Jacob's coming.

I phoned, and as I knew she would, she said to bring him with me, perhaps a bit apprehensive or not really happy about it, but determined to do the right thing. I like to talk to Laura on the phone, she has a nice voice, but this time I let the conversation die quickly because I didn't want to say too much about Jacob or try to make her imagine him. I have lots of funny stories about him, but he becomes unreal in the stories, and there's some kind of disloyalty in telling them. Anyway she'd meet him soon enough. Let her judge for herself. I had a suspicion she wouldn't like him. He certainly wasn't like any of her friends. I put on a record and sat staring out the window, wondering what Jacob had been doing for the last five years, what I was going to do for the next twenty-five.

In the morning I found myself a bit puzzled about when he might arrive, and whether I should make any attempt to meet him. He might be coming by train or plane, even by car for all I knew. There was nothing to do but tape a note on the door saying I'd be back at five-thirty and set off to work.

It was a busy morning and at noon I forgot to buy extra groceries, but I left early and arrived home just before five-thirty with my arms full of food and liquor. As I walked up to the door of my apartment, I could hear music from inside, *Gottes Zait ist die allerbaste Ziet* sung by a choir and a loud extra baritone. My arms were full, and I wasn't sure I could get my key without putting everything down so I knocked on my own door and waited.

The door opened and Jacob's familiar bearded face smiled at me. He had the same bright, scrubbed look that I remembered, and the same tattered clothes.

"Jerry," he said, "it's great, goddamit it's great."

I could see he wanted to shake my hand or throw his arm around my shoulders, but he couldn't really get at me for the bags. I went into the kitchen to put them down.

"How did you get in?" I said. "I didn't think the caretaker would ever open up for you."

"That's a funny thing," he said. "I was standing there at the door looking at your note and figuring how much trouble I'd have getting anyone to let me in or even finding out where you work when I noticed the lock was made by a company in Germany that I used to work for. That particular design has a weakness. If you know about it you can take it apart from outside. I put it back together after I got in."

"Same old Jacob," I said.

Then suddenly I didn't know what to say anymore. It was five years and I was different. I didn't know where to start.

"It's great," Jacob said again.

"Do you want a drink?" I said.

"Yeah," he said, "I want a drink."

We drank and talked a bit and then drank some more and then ate, and within a couple of hours, it had all come back so that we didn't have to think of things to talk about. He was surprised that I'd never got married. I was surprised that he had. I wanted to tell him something about Laura, but I held off for a long time. When I did mention her, he wanted me to describe her, and I tried, said she was small but not really small, had brown hair with a bit of grey coming now, and then gave up and told him to wait and see. He let it go at that, and we talked about other things, his family, my family, five years of time, and as we got drunker and more relaxed, sat in the dark listening to music and talking less. Sometime after midnight Jacob suddenly stood up and turned to me.

"This Laura," he said, "she's a widow, not young and innocent, so you must go to bed together, eh? I mean there's nothing wrong with you is there?"

"Dammit Jacob," I said, "why don't you mind your own business? Of course we go to bed together sometimes, and of course there's nothing wrong with me. Is there anything wrong with you?"

"Not a damn thing," he said. "But what I want to know is why you don't marry her?"

"I don't know why. Maybe we don't want to get married." I was shouting a little.

"Don't get touchy," he said.

"I'm not," I said. "I'm just going to bed."

I had an extra bedroom that I used for a study, and the bed

there was made up so I only had to turn on the light and point to it before I wandered back to my own room and fell into bed. The last thing I remember was hearing Jacob talking to himself.

I didn't wake till almost eight o'clock. I got organized in a hurry and left Jacob a note saying I'd be home about four. There was a party at the office, but I planned to leave early.

When I got home that afternoon, it was later than I'd expected, and I only had time to wash up before we drove to Laura's for dinner. During the short drive over, Jacob asked more questions about her and I tried to answer them. He didn't seem to be listening to what I was saying.

When we got to the house, it was Cathy who answered the door, very polite and mature, giving away nothing. I wondered, as I often did when I saw her, whether she ever cried over silly things. Laura came in, wearing an apron, and apologized for not meeting us at the door. Because I'd been trying to describe her to Jacob the night before, I kept noticing things I could have mentioned: she has brown eyes and a funny mouth, she looks good in an apron though I don't know why, she's good at covering how she feels. I introduced her to Jacob and tried not to notice how they reacted to each other. I kept telling myself that it didn't matter. Two days from now Jacob would disappear and not come back for years. Still I caught myself listening to them. They didn't have much to talk about, but they seemed to want to be friends. I gave Laura the bottle of wine I had brought, and we all had a drink before she went back to the kitchen.

After we'd spent a few minutes sitting around, Jacob had the bright idea of asking Cathy to show him the house. At first she didn't want to, but before long she started to enjoy it. As we followed her about, Jacob carried the wine bottle with him and drank from it every couple of minutes. The part that Cathy enjoyed most was showing us the cellar. She had to ask her mother if she could go down, and I guess because it was an unusual thing her excitement started to show. She even relaxed enough to tell us how old the house was and that there was an old cistern under the kitchen. Jacob wanted to see that too, and the pair of them got quite involved over it. I could see that Cathy was starting to like Jacob, and I felt a bit jealous. After they were through with the cistern, Jacob wanted to see the furnace and the fuel tank.

"For God's sake, Jacob," I said, "you don't want to see the furnace."

"Of course I do," Jacob said with a big smile. "When I see a house I want to see everything. Don't you think that's right Cathy?"

"I guess so," she said, but I'm not sure she really agreed.

Jacob had a good poke around the furnace and we went back upstairs. Cathy had already eaten, and Laura got her off to bed before she served the dinner. It was a fine meal, and Jacob did it credit. He made me think of his mother's huge meals as he crouched behind his plate chewing happily, warm and content, like a stove that took in food for its fuel and gave out some rare spiritual host. Every now and then he would wink at me, and I was puzzled, but assumed that he was just expressing his delight in Laura and the food.

It was with the coffee that I started to feel cold, and by the time we had done the dishes, I was shivering and so was Laura. She went to turn up the thermostat, but when she did, nothing happened.

"Must be something wrong with the furnace," Jacob said. He seemed pleased. "I'm beautiful on furnaces," he said and headed downstairs.

"Does he know what he's doing?" Laura whispered to me.

I shrugged. There was some soft noise from the cellar, then a loud noise and the sound of Jacob running upstairs.

"Bit of a problem," he said. "I punched a hole in the fuel line somehow. I don't think there's anything to set it off, but maybe we better get out anyway. We can drive over to Jerry's place after we phone the firemen and the furnace people."

"Jacob," I said, "did you really?"

He nodded his head.

"Laura better get Cathy."

Laura looked as though she didn't know whether to be mad or scared, but she went to get Cathy. When she was gone, Jacob turned to me with a big smile.

"Beautiful eh?" he whispered.

"You didn't do that on purpose?"

He nodded.

"I figured what's nicer than to have all your friends at your place for Christmas. You and Laura and Cathy are all too well-organized."

"You're out of your goddam head."

He grinned. I could hear Laura coming. Cathy had wrapped herself in a blanket and was walking along still half asleep. I went to the kitchen phone and found the number of the Fire Department. They wanted to know how the fuel line got broken. Then I got the number of the heating company and phoned them. They asked if I'd phoned the firemen and then wanted to know how the fuel line got broken.

Cathy hadn't said anything, but she looked a bit frantic so Laura took her out to the car. Jacob offered to stay till the firemen and heating people came. We left him there and drove to my apartment. Almost every house we passed on the way had some kind of colored lights up. Even without snow everything looked nice, but I didn't think I'd mention that to Laura.

We got Cathy up to my apartment and I suggested that Laura make her some hot chocolate before she went to bed.

"Are we going to sleep here?" Cathy said.

Laura nodded.

"Just for tonight," she said.

When Laura went to the kitchen, Cathy sat in silence. Could see she was trying not to cry.

"Don't worry," I said, "We'll leave a note. Santa Claus will find you."

"I don't believe in Santa Claus," she said.

Laura came in with the hot chocolate.

"Cathy and you can have my big bed," I said. "Jacob can have the little bedroom, and I'll sleep here on the couch."

We didn't say anything while Cathy drank her chocolate and even when Laura had taken her off to the other room and put her in bed, we were silent, everything made strange by the child sleeping near us in a bed that was not her own. Still, I was happy in a way that we were there, ready to admit Jacob's wisdom, or maybe only one part of it, for I could see that Laura was worried and afraid that her house might be in flames. She kept fiddling with the back of her hair. I'd never seen her do that before.

"Do you want me to phone back to your place?" I said, "and see if everything's all right?"

"Would you mind? I'm pretty nervous."

I dialed her number. For a long time nobody answered, but finally Jacob came. He said everything was under control, that they had all the oil out of the basement, but that the fuel pipe wouldn't be fixed for a few hours at least.

I hung up and gave Laura the message.

"I'm sorry about this," I said. "Jacob always makes a little bit of chaos wherever he goes."

"In two weeks I'll laugh about it," Laura said. "Afterwards I'll think how refreshing it was, but right now I'm not sure I'm up to it." She reached out and took my hand.

I kissed her on the top of the head and went to put on a record.

"We'll have to go and get Cathy's presents," she said.

"Wait till Jacob gets back, then we'll go. We'll leave him to babysit."

"Do you think we'd dare?"

"I suppose not."

I sat down beside Laura on the couch. For an hour and a half we sat and waited for Jacob, and as we waited, we talked. It was strange, different from any other time. I even asked about her husband. Once or twice I called Laura's house looking for Jacob, but there was no answer. It was after eleven when the phone rang. It was Jacob.

"Where are you?" I said.

"At a police station."

"What in hell are you doing there?"

"They thought I was trying to steal a dog."

"What dog?"

"At the pound. I thought I'd get a dog for Cathy for Christmas."

"She doesn't want a dog."

"She'd love one. A great kid like that should have a dog, but when I went to the pound it was closed. I could hear dogs inside, and I figured if I could get one I could pay after holidays. But when I climbed over the fence I got stuck and they saw me and now they won't let me explain."

"All right," I said. "I'll come." I found out where he was and hung up.

When I tried to explain to Laura, I started to giggle and then she started and I never got the whole story out. I wanted to keep Laura with me, so I got a teenager from down the hall to stay with Cathy and we drove to the police station.

The cops weren't too difficult about it. They hadn't charged him with anything, and one of them was a man I'd met a couple of times, a friend of a friend, so eventually we got Jacob out after I'd given my word that I'd keep him out of trouble. They thought he was just drunk.

As we drove home, everything started to seem unreal to me. I guess I was probably tired. I pulled into the parking lot and we all got out.

"Oh Jerry," Laura said, "I just remembered the presents."

"Back to the car," I said.

"It isn't far is it?" Jacob said. "We can walk. It will wake me up. You should always go out walking Christmas Eve."

I looked at Laura.

"It's a nice night," she said.

"Let's go," I said, and we started out. It was cold, but we walked quickly and kept warm that way as we passed through the streets and parking lots that lay between my apartment and her house. Within a few minutes we were there.

We walked up the steps to the dark house and stood at the door while Laura looked for her key.

"Don't you have a key?" Jacob said to me.

"No."

Laura fumbled a little harder in her bag.

"Why not?" Jacob said.

"Here it is," she said. She got the door open. The house still smelled of oil, and it seemed as cold inside as out. Jacob beat his arms as he walked up and down the hall making a roaring noise. Laura stood at the door of the living room.

"I guess we'll just take the presents," she said.

"No," Jacob said, "we have to take the tree. We can't have Christmas without a tree."

"How can we take it?" I said.

Jacob looked at me. He was really surprised.

"Of course we can take it," he said. "We'll take off the decorations while Laura gets the presents packed."

I was too tired to argue. We began to take the decorations off. Jacob whistled happily, but I kept thinking that my eyes were going to close on me. Once or twice I stopped to watch Laura as she packed up the presents. It didn't take her long, and when she had finished, she sat down in a chair and closed her eyes. Sitting there, she looked small and old, vulnerable and desirable.

We had the tree stripped in a few minutes but had trouble getting the decorations packed away. I dropped a silver ball and broke it, then dropped another one.

"Out with you," Jacob said. "You take the tree and Laura take the presents and get on your way. I'll finish packing these and be right behind you."

"Okay," I said. I tried to pick up the tree and dropped it. Tried again and got a face full of needles. Jacob manoeuvred me and the evergreen and got us in some kind of order. He pushed me out the door and helped Laura get the parcels settled in her arms.

"I'll be right along," he said.

Laura and I walked down the street and started across a parking lot. We didn't speak, just walked. The high buildings stood guard over our mad pilgrimage through the crackling cold, and above us a thousand stars gave their silent fire to the night. My face hurt from the scratching of spruce needles against my skin. Loaded down, we walked slowly, and there was no sound but the sound of our feet on the cold ground. Then, from behind us somewhere in that huge silence, came Jacob's voice, loud and raucous, but still a courageous noise in the face of winter, singing *O Come All Ye faithful*. We stopped and listened.

"Laura," I said. "I don't agree with Cathy. I believe in Santa Claus. I can hear him singing to me."

She, my poor tired friend, tried to smile at me, or as much of me as she could see through the branches of that big spruce.

"Laura," I said, "I want to marry you."

In the distance I could still hear Jacob singing. Then I joined in.

Upon a Midnight Clear

by Margaret Laurence

I would bet a brace of baubles plus a partridge in a pear tree that when Charles Dickens wrote *A Christmas Carol* no one wanted to identify with Scrooge, before he became converted to Christmas. How very different now. One is likely at this time of year to run into all kinds of people who view themselves as the Good Guys and who actually try to make you feel guilty if you celebrate Christmas. "It's become totally commercial," they virtuously say. "*We* don't have anything to do with it."

All I can reply, borrowing a word from Scrooge, is *Humbug*. Sure, okay, the stores may less-than-subtly put out their Christmas displays immediately after Halloween; the carols may be used to advertise fur coats or washing machines; the amount of phoniness surrounding Christmas in our culture may be astronomical. But Christmas itself remains untouched by all this crassness. It's still a matter of personal choice, and surely it's what happens in your own home that counts. In our house, Christmas has always been a very important time.

My background and heritage are strongly Christian, although I reserve the right to interpret things in my own way. In my interpretation, what Christmas celebrates is grace, a gift given from God to man, not because deserved, just because given. The birth of every wanted and loved child in this world is the same, a gift. The birth of *every* child should be this way. We're still frighteningly far from that, but maybe this festival can remind us. Christmas also reaches back to pre-Christian times – an ancient festival celebrating the winter solstice. *The Concise Oxford Dictionary* defines solstice very beautifully – "Either time (summer, winter) at which the sun is farthest from the equator and appears to pause before returning." For countless centuries in the northern lands, this time of year was a festival of faith, the faith that spring would return to the land. It links us with our ancestors a very long way back.

Christmas when I was a child was always a marvelous time. We used to go to the carol service on Christmas Eve, and those hymns still remain my favorites. *Hark the Herald Angels Sing, Once in Royal David's City*, and the one I loved best, *It Came Upon a Midnight Clear*. It couldn't have been even near midnight when we walked home after those services, but it always seemed to me that I knew exactly what "midnight clear" meant. I had no sense then that there could be any kind of winter other than ours. It was a prairie town, and by Christmas the snow would always be thick and heavy, yet light and clean as well, something to be battled against and respected when it fell in blinding blizzards, but also something which created an upsurge of the heart at times such as those, walking back home on Christmas eve with the carols still echoing in your head. The evening would be still, almost silent, and the air would be so dry and sharp you could practically touch the coldness. The snow would be dark-shadowed and then suddenly it would look like sprinkled rainbows around the sparse streetlights. Sometimes there were northern lights. My memory, probably faulty, assigns the northern lights to *all* those Christmas eves, but they must have appeared at least on some, a blazing eerie splendor across the sky, swift-moving, gigantic, like a message. It was easy then to believe in the Word made manifest. Not so easy now. And yet I can't forget, ever, that the child, who was myself then, experienced and recognized it.

We always had the ceremony of two Christmas trees. One was in the late afternoon of Christmas Day, and was at the home of my grandparents, my mother's people, at the big brick house. There would be a whole congregation of aunts and uncles and cousins there on that day, and we would *have the tree* (that is how we said it) before dinner. One of my aunts was head of the nursing division in Saskatchewan's public health department, and was a distinguished professional woman. I didn't know that about her then. What I knew was that each Christmas she came back home with an astounding assortment of rare and wonderful things from what I felt must be the center of the great wide world, namely Regina. She used to bring us those packages of Swiss cheese, each tiny piece wrapped in silver paper, and decorations for the table (a Santa with reindeer and sleigh, pine-cone men painted iridescent white with red felt caps), and chocolate Santas in red and gold paper, and chocolate coins contained in heavy gold foil so that they looked like my idea of Spanish doubloons and pieces of eight, as in *Treasure Island*.

The dinner was enormous and exciting. We had *olives* to begin with. We rarely had olives at any other time, as they were expensive. My grandfather, of course, carved what was always known as The Bird, making the job into an impressive performance. He was never an eminently lovable man, but even he, with his stern ice-blue eyes, managed some degree of pleasantness at Christmas. The children at dinner were served last, which seems odd today. One of my memories is of myself at about six, sighing mightily as the plates were being passed to the adults and murmuring pathetically, "Couldn't I even have a crust?" My sense of drama was highly developed at a young age.

When the dishes were done – a mammoth task, washing all my grandmother's Limoges – we would make preparation to go home. I always had my own private foray into the kitchen then. I would go to the icebox (yes, icebox, with a block of ice delivered daily) and would tear off hunks of turkey, snatch a dozen or so olives, and wrap it all in wax paper. This was so I could have a small feast during the night, in case of sudden hunger, which invariably and improbably occurred each Christmas night.

The day of Christmas, however, began at home. The one I recall the best was the last Christmas we had with my father for he died the next year. We were then living in my father's family home, a red-brick oddity with a rose window, a big dining room, a dozen nearly hidden cupboards and hidey-holes, and my father's study with the fireplace, above which hung a sinister bronze scimitar brought from India by an ancestor. I was nine that year, and my brother was two. The traditions in our family were strong. The children rose when they wakened (usually about 6 a.m. or earlier) and had their Christmas stockings. In those days, our stockings contained a Japanese orange at the toe, some red-and-white peppermint canes, a bunch of unshelled peanuts, and one or two small presents – a kaleidoscope or a puzzle consisting of two or three interlocked pieces of metal which you had to try to prise apart, and never could.

As my memory tells it to me, my very young brother and myself had our Christmas stockings in our parents' bedroom, and Christmas had officially begun. We were then sent back to bed until the decent hour of 7:30 or 8:00 a.m., at which time I could get dressed in my sweater and my plaid skirt with the straps over the shoulder, while my mother dressed my brother in his sweater and infant overalls. We then went down for breakfast. In our house, you always had breakfast before you had The Tree. This wasn't such a bad thing. Christmas breakfast was sausage rolls, which we never had for breakfast any other time. These had been made weeks before, and frozen in the unheated summer kitchen. We had frozen food years before it became commercially viable. I guess our only amazement about it when it came on the market was that they could do it in summer as well. After breakfast, we all went into the study, where we had to listen to the Empire Broadcast on the radio, a report from all those pink-colored areas on the world map, culminating in the King's speech. The voice seemed to go on forever. I don't recall how my brother was kept pacified – with candy, probably – but I recall myself fidgeting. This was the ritual – the Empire Broadcast *before* The Tree, a practice which now seems to me to have been slightly bizarre, and yet probably was not so. Our parents wanted to hear it, and in those days it wasn't going to be repeated in capsule form on the late night news. I guess it also taught us that you could wait for what you wanted – but that's a concept about which I've always felt pretty ambiguous.

At last, at last, we could go into The Living Room for The Tree. The Living Room, I should say, was the only formal room in that house. We did not live in it; it was totally misnamed. It was For Best. It was the room in which my mother gave the afternoon teas which were then required of people like the wives of lawyers in towns like ours. The Living Room had a lot of stiff upholstered furniture, always just so. It was, as well, chilly. But it was the place for The Tree, and it seemed somehow the right place, something special.

And there it was, The Tree. *Oh*.

I could see now why we'd been so carefully kept out of the room until this moment. There, beside The Tree, were our presents. For my brother, a rocking horse, two horses cut out of wood and painted white with green flecks, joined by a seat between them. Our dad had made it, for he was a very good amateur carpenter. And for me – wow! A desk. A small desk, found in an attic, as I later learned, and painted by our dad, a bright blue with flower patterns, a desk which opened up and had your own private cubbyholes in it. My own desk. My *first*. That remains the nicest present that anyone has ever given me, the present from my parents when I was nine.

It was only many years later that I realized that the rocking horse and the desk had been our presents then because no one could afford to buy anything much in that depression and drought year of 1935. And it wasn't until long afterwards, either, that I realized how lucky and relatively unscathed we'd been, and how many people in this country that year must have had virtually no Christmas at all.

One other aspect of my childhood Christmases was Lee Ling. He was the man who ran our town's Chinese restaurant, and he lived without his family for all the time he was there. In those days Chinese wives were scarcely allowed into this country at all. My father did Lee's legal work, and every Christmas Lee gave us a turkey, a large box of chocolates, and a box of lichee nuts. You might possibly say that Lee did it because he hoped to get on the right side of the lawyer. My father wasn't like that, and neither was Lee. The point of this story, however, is that Lee Ling continued at Christmas to give our family a turkey, a box of chocolates, and a box of lichee nuts after my father died, for years, until Lee himself died. To me, that says something valuable about both Lee Ling and my father.

Much later on, when my own children were young and growing up, our Christmas became patterns which reflected my own Christmases many years ago, but with our own additions. We had ten Christmases in our house in England, Elm Cottage, before my children became adults and I moved back home to Canada to stay. Christmas in that house was always something very good and warm, and there were usually a lot of young Canadian visitors there with us at that time.

As in my childhood, the Christmas stockings were opened early in the morning. The difference was, with us, that my kids always made a Christmas stocking for me as well, their own idea. The stockings had candies, including the same kind of chocolate coins, but they also had a variety of joke presents, sometimes kids' books when my kids were no longer children, because we've always liked good children's books and we frequently give them to one another.

Some of the traditions continued. In our house, you always have breakfast before you have The Tree. But in our time, The Tree was in my study, not a "special" place, and we frequently went in wearing housecoats and dressing-gowns and bearing large mugs of coffee. The presents were distributed one at a time so everyone could look at each. We made it last about two hours. I don't think gifts need to be meaningless. I love opening presents from people who care about me, and I love giving presents to people I care about, hoping I've chosen something they will really like, something that fits their own personality, something that will be a symbol of my feeling for them.

Our dinner at Elm Cottage was always fairly hectic. I was in charge of what we called The Bird, as it had been called in my own childhood. I twittered and worried over that turkey, wondering if I put it in the oven soon enough, or if I was going to overcook it to the point of total disaster. It always turned out fine, an amazing fact when one considers that our stove was so small as to be almost ridiculous and that even cramming a 15-pound turkey into it all was a major task. The turkey, I modestly admit, was accompanied by some of the best sage-and-onion stuffing in the entire world. Our friend Alice always made her super cranberry sauce, which included walnuts and orange, and was the best I've ever tasted. Our friend Sandy always used to do the plum pudding, which she cleverly heated on a small electric burner set up in the hall, as there wasn't room on the stove. My daughter had been the one to organize the cake, a month before, and everyone had given it a stir for luck. It was a very co-operative meal.

Yes, the women did prepare all the food. But the men carved The Bird, served the dinner, and did the dishes. It always seemed to me that our efforts meshed pretty well. Our friend Peter once said that Elm Cottage was a scene of "agreeable anarchy." I think it was, and that phrase certainly describes our Christmas dinners, at which we never had less than a dozen people, and sometimes more.

After dinner, we would move to The Music Room, which was our version of The Living Room, except that we really lived in it. It had a good stereo and a feeling that people could come in and sit around the fireplace and play their guitars and sing their own songs. This used to happen a lot, and always at Christmas. We made new traditions. One of my own favorites was a ritual which said that at some point in the evening our friend Ian would play and sing two songs for me. Corny and out-of-date they may be, but I like them. They were *She Walks These Hills in a Long Black Veil* and *St. James Infirmary Blues*.

Those Christmases at Elm Cottage had a feeling of real community. For me, this is what this festival is all about – the sense of God's grace, and the sense of our own family and extended family, the sense of human community.

Never Smile
Before Christmas

by Lesley Choyce

S arah MacNeil wished that her mother could be happier. But
there was nothing she seemed to be able to do about it. Sarah
was afraid that maybe her mother was the unhappiest mother in
the whole world. But when twelve-year-old Sarah woke up on
a sunny summer morning in Nova Scotia, she found it hard to
believe that anyone could be unhappy here.

Her bedroom looked out over a blue sparkling inlet. Sea gulls
swooped up and down and a great blue heron walked gingerly
through the shallows. Off towards the ocean, she could see the
outline of Far Enough Island. Sarah thought that there was something magical about Far Enough Island because nobody lived
there and she had never set foot on it. The island was always there

in her bedroom window, full of interesting possibilities.

Jeremiah was scratching at her door. Good old Jeremiah. He was her pure black Labrador retriever, and the best friend she ever had in the world.

"Sarah, get up and let your dog out!" her mother yelled from the kitchen.

Sarah jumped up from bed and let Jeremiah into her room. Jeremiah dove at her and knocked her down on the floor, licking her nose and slobbering all over her face.

"What's going on up there?" her mother yelled again.

"Nothing," Sarah answered. Good old Jeremiah. "Dad didn't let you go on the boat again today, did he?" she said to her dog.

Jeremiah just rolled over on the floor and scratched his back by wiggling back and forth, upside down on the floor.

Sarah changed into her clothes in seconds and ran outside, with Jeremiah right on her heels. Without even saying good morning to her mother, she raced at top speed to the end of the wharf, stopping at the very last second before she would have toppled over into the icy water. Jeremiah galloped along behind her but forgot to stop at the end of the wharf. He just kept running straight out over the end, his feet kicking at the empty air. Then he splashed down hard into the water, surfaced, and turned around to swim back to the shore.

Sarah laughed and laughed. It was one of her games she liked to play with Jeremiah in the summer. He probably could have stopped if he wanted to, but Sarah knew he was a good swimmer and Jeremiah always seemed so happy after she had tricked him into flying off the end of the wharf. Now he was on the shoreline, shaking himself, water flying in a million directions.

Out past Far Enough Island, Sarah could see her dad's boat coming back from sea. That seemed strange. It was way too early for that.

Sarah walked back to the house and went into the kitchen where her mother was worrying over a pile of papers at the kitchen table. Jeremiah bounded past her and shook himself in the middle of the kitchen floor.

"Get that mangy beast out of there!" Sarah's mother went off like a canon.

"Sorry, I'll clean it up," Sarah said. The last thing she needed was to get her mother mad at her. Sarah grabbed a towel and began to mop the water drops off everything, including her mother. She grabbed poor Jeremiah by the collar and skidded him across the floor and out the door. Jeremiah looked very hurt that he was being thrown out.

"Why is Daddy headed back in so soon?" she asked her mother. She was used to her father's boat arriving back from fishing at around eleven or twelve o'clock. She saw that it was only nine-thirty.

"The fish are gone. There are hardly any left," Sarah's mother said, her voice like dry gravel.

"But there's millions of fish in the sea."

"Well, not around here, there's not. Get yourself some cereal for breakfast."

"Sure." Sarah filled a bowl to the very top.

"Sarah, that's too much. Don't waste it. Money doesn't grow on trees, you know."

Sarah poured half of it back into the box. Why didn't money grow on trees, she wondered. In fact, it should. Her parents were always worrying about money and Sarah couldn't see why. They weren't exactly poor.

Jeremiah had managed to stand up outside the door and turn the doorknob with his paw. He had it open a crack just big enough so that he could stick his nose through. He looked so funny that Sarah thought she was going to burst out laughing and spit her cereal all over the floor. Instead, she held it in. But she couldn't help having a big funny lopsided grin on her face as she tried to chew her cereal.

Her mother looked up at her. She was very annoyed about something. But it couldn't just be Sarah. Sarah was just being herself.

"Why are you smiling like that?" she asked.

Sarah shrugged her shoulders.

"Well, never smile without a good reason. You should know that. People will think there's something wrong with you. Never smile before Christmas. That's what my mother used to say." She let out a deep sigh. "And even then there's not always something to smile about."

Jeremiah had arrived in the middle of the night, six years before. It was during the worst hurricane Nova Scotia had seen in fifty years.

"What was that?" six-year-old Sarah asked. Sarah, her mother and her dad were sitting around the kitchen table. They had on a smelly kerosene lantern because the storm had knocked down a power line.

"That was just the wind," her mother said. Her mother looked frightened by the storm and her father was holding her hand.

"It'll calm down by morning," Sarah's father said, trying to be reassuring.

"What if you lose the boat?"

"I have her tied up real good. She won't go anywhere. That ole boat wouldn't know where else to go."

"Be serious," Sarah's mother said. She was staring deep into the flame.

"Stop worrying," he said.

"That's easy for you to say," Sarah's mother snapped back.

"There, I heard it again," Sarah said. "It sounded like someone crying."

"It's just your imagination," her mother explained.

"No, it wasn't," Sarah insisted. She ran to the back door and threw it open. A torrent of wind and rain blew into the room. The wind blew out the lamp and they were thrown into total darkness.

"Now what?" Sarah's mother groaned, always expecting the worst.

"Just be calm," her father said. "I'll find the flashlight. Sarah, close the darned door!"

The door slammed shut hard and Sarah's father fell over a chair in the dark as he tried to find the flashlight. Outside the wind howled.

Her father found the flashlight and flicked it on. There was little Sarah sitting on the wet floor by the door. In her arms was a little black puppy.

"Well, I'll be darned," her father said. "Where'd he come from?"

"I don't know, but he found us now," Sarah answered. "We're keeping him."

Her father was re-lighting the old kerosene lantern. "Well, I don't know. Your mother was never very fond of dogs. Besides, he probably belongs to someone. What do you think dear?" he asked his wife.

Sarah was so busy hugging the little squirmy puppy that she didn't even look up to see her mother crying and shaking her head up and down. "Yes," she said. "We'll keep him until we find his real home."

Now the storm had picked up even more strength. The waves pounded at the wharf. The wind tore at the wooden shingles on the roof until it had set some of them free.

"It's going to be a long night," her father said.

"This is the best night of my life," Sarah said.

No one ever lay claim to the puppy so Sarah's mother said she could keep it.

"What do you want to name him, Sarah?" she asked.

Sarah thought long and hard. "I don't know. There are so many good names. You pick one."

"I always liked the name, Jeremiah," her mother said. "I think maybe if you had a brother, I might have called him Jeremiah." Her mother looked at her with sad, gentle eyes.

"But maybe you should save that name in case I do have a brother."

"No, I don't think that will happen. I want you to use the name for the puppy."

Those were the years when the fishing was good. Sarah's dad went to sea during the good weather and nearly filled the boat with cod and hake and haddock and flounder. He sold it to the fish plant further up the inlet and came home with money in his pockets.

Her dad seemed to like getting up at five-thirty in the morning when it was still dark and going off to sea in his boat alone. It's good to get back up the inlet before the winds come up," he'd explain. But Sarah's mother worried about him out there all alone. She always expected the worst to happen. Even in the good times.

"Stop your frettin'," he'd say. "I'm very careful." He had a big, wonderful smile on his face.

"Never smile before Christmas," his wife chided him. "You never know what can go wrong. You don't want to tempt fate with all that over-confidence."

But her dad kept smiling anyway.

Sarah didn't have many friends because she lived such a long way from town and from school. It took a half hour in their old Chevy pick-up truck to drive down the muddy gravel road to get her to school. Sarah had tried to keep track of the number of potholes.

"Three thousand and seventy five."

"What?" her mother asked.

"Three thousand and seventy-five potholes to school and back."

"And next year there'll be four thousand and seventy five," her mother answered.

Jeremiah would ride in the back of the pick-up and sniff at the air. He looked strong and proud riding back there. And when Sarah would come home from school, they would go hiking along the beaches where Sarah would imagine them having all sorts of adventures.

Even though Jeremiah never hurt another animal, he loved to chase any living thing he came across – spruce grouse, weasels, otters, or ducks. Sarah would try to stop him, but Jeremiah just had too much wild energy that had to be released.

That was until one day when he got too close to a porcupine. Jeremiah howled with regret. He was only playing when he ran up close and nipped at the porcupine's fur which turned out not to be fur at all but hundreds of sharp needles.

Jeremiah howled in pain. Sarah ran to him and found his mouth filled with porcupine needles and blood. Sarah thought Jeremiah might die. She didn't know what to do. Jeremiah didn't seem to want to follow her. He was acting crazy from the pain. Sarah tried to pick him up but he was almost as big as she was.

She heard an engine from a boat coming from the inlet and ran to the stony beach. There was her father just rounding Far Enough Island and headed home. She stood on the shore and waved and yelled for almost twenty minutes until her dad was close enough to see her. He pulled his boat in close and jumped into the shallow water.

"What is it?"

"It's Jeremiah. He chased a porcupine. Now I think he's going to die."

Sarah's father ran into the woods with her and found Jeremiah lying in a pool of blood. He wasn't moving.

Sarah's father picked him up and ran him to the boat. "Come on, honey," he said to Sarah. "We have to get the boat up the inlet to town before the tide gets too low."

On the boat, Sarah's father roared the engine and they charged towards town.

Sarah knew that her father would never take the boat up the tricky inlets unless it was a dire emergency. It was too easy to hit a rock or get stuck on a sand bar. And the boat was his life. It was what her father needed to make enough money for them to live.

"Sit up front and look for logs or rocks or shallow water," he yelled. "Just hold on good."

Sarah had to lie down on the bow of the boat with both hands braced on the wood railing. She yelled to her father to go right or left whenever she saw something ahead. The tide was dropping and the water seemed to keep getting more shallow.

Jeremiah lay very still in the back on top of the fish. He was breathing but his eyes looked funny.

"Is he going to die, Daddy?" Sarah asked.

"No," he shouted. "Just keep the look out."

Sarah knew that if they got stuck, they'd never get Jeremiah to the vet in time. She watched the water ahead very carefully, shouting when she saw a grassy shallow or a rock ahead.

At the vet's, the woman gave Jeremiah a needle. "This way he won't feel any pain," she said.

Sarah thought she meant she was putting him to sleep for good. "No! You can't" she screamed.

Her father pulled her back and the vet smiled. "No. It's not that. He's not going to die." When she pulled out the needle, she took a pair of pliers and began to gently remove the porcupine quills. Sarah counted twenty in all.

"He's a very lucky dog to have two friends like you," the vet said.

Sarah's dad had to phone her mother to come pick them up. The tide was too low to get the boat back down the inlet towards the sea, towards home.

"You could have wrecked the boat!" her mother said to them in the truck. Jeremiah was asleep across her dad's lap.

"I couldn't just let him die, could I?" her father said. He seemed really mad at her for saying it. Sarah just remained quiet.

"Well, it's just an old dog," her mother said. "If you wrecked the boat, then what would we do for money?"

"It's not just an old dog," Sarah said, angry now at what her mother said. She didn't understand at all.

Her mother stopped the truck and slapped her across the face. Sarah felt it like a hot burn across her cheek. Sarah raised her arm to hit her mother back but her father grabbed onto her wrist, firm but gently.

"You shouldn't have slapped her," he said.

Sarah's mother turned off the truck. She threw the keys at Sarah's father. Then she got out, slammed the door, and began walking.

"I'm walking home. You drive home just the two of you. I'm the only one who does all the worrying around here. Get on with you."

Sarah's father tried to stop her but it did no good. He lay Jeremiah on the seat and slid over to drive.

"Why is she like that?" Sarah asked.

"It's hard to explain," her father said. "Her mother was very cruel to her. And I think she always hoped I'd be something more than a fisherman."

"What's wrong with being a fisherman?"

"Well, sometimes you have good times and sometimes you have bad times. And you know her father drowned."

"Yeh, but you can swim."

"Sure, I can swim good," he said, even though it was a lie, but it was one he had repeated over and over so many times that he half believed it.

Sarah's father couldn't get out to sea the next day to fish because his boat was tied up in town and he had missed the high tide in the middle of the night. So he lost a day's fishing, which cost the family needed money.

Just like Sarah's mother had predicted, things did get worse. It seemed that every year there were fewer and fewer fish. The weather was getting stormier and colder early in the fall. With less fish and fewer days in the season, the fish plant closed down and there was no place to sell what little catch there was. Her father lost his boat to the bank because he couldn't keep up payments. He took a job at a garage in town fixing cars, but he hated it.

"At least it's money coming in," her mother would say. "But I know it's gonna get worse before it gets better. If it ever gets better."

Sarah didn't like school very much, and now that her father was working in town, she had to hang around the gas station until five o'clock when he got off work so he could drive her home.

She missed her long walks along the beach with Jeremiah in the afternoons. She hated the garage, which always smelled of cigarettes and grease and gasoline. Men and boys stood around and talked tough. Her father was always telling them to use good language when Sarah was around, but it didn't do any good.

And she really missed waking up in the morning and seeing her father's boat way off out to sea toward Far Enough Island. She missed how happy her father had been coming home to the wharf with a boatload of fish.

"Since you're not fishing any more, we might as well sell the place and move to town. It would be better for Sarah and it would be better for us," her mother said in a sour voice.

"Jeremiah would hate it in town," Sarah said.

"Then we'd just have to find Jeremiah a new home. He costs us an arm and a leg to feed anyway. And we need to save all the money we can. Hard times might be ahead."

Sarah's father looked down at the floor and didn't say a thing. But the next day when he took Sarah to town, he said he didn't want her to go to school, that he needed her help. First they went to the bank and he took out almost all their saved money. Then they drove over to Old Man Fogerty's little run-down wharf on a narrow channel of the inlet.

Old Man Fogerty was eighty-five-years old. "She's a good boat," he said. "Old but good. You treat her well, she'll last you a few years."

The boat was certainly old. But it didn't look so good.

"All it needs is a little paint," her father said. "With a little luck I'll be able to afford better in a couple of years."

Her father handed over the money.

"You bought it? What will mother say?" Sarah asked.

"I don't know. I just know I'm fed up with the garage and I don't want to move to town. Now lie down up front there and help me steer out the channel to home before the tide slips."

So Sarah helped steer her dad and his new boat home.

The engine made loud coughing noises. It sputtered and stalled several times but eventually they made it. When they pulled up, there was Sarah's mother on the wharf with her arms folded and a dirty look on her face. When Jeremiah spotted them he came racing down the boards and launched himself out off the wharf before her mother could stop him. He jumped halfway to the boat before splashing down and swimming the rest of the way. Sarah's dad helped him up over the side and as Jeremiah shook the water off, he sprayed Sarah and her dad until they were soaked.

It should have been a very funny scene. But Sarah's mother wasn't laughing at all.

Sarah's father worked night and day at fixing up the boat.

"It's too old," Sarah's mother said.

"Fogerty says there's life in her yet."

"I don't trust you out there alone in that old boat. Something could happen."

"Why don't you take Jeremiah along," Sarah said. "Just for company."

"He'd only get in the way," her father said. "A dog's not much good on a boat."

"But he likes the water."

Sarah's mother scowled. "Yes, why not take the dog with you. Get him out from being underfoot."

Sarah's father nodded okay. He didn't mind having a little dog company on board if it gave his wife one less thing to complain about.

It was getting late in the year for a good start but the fish had come back now and there was plenty to catch.

Sarah was in school when her father came back each day with the boat, but she knew things were going well.

She missed Jeremiah jumping up and licking her in the face every morning, but she did get to play with him after school. And she liked the idea of good old Jeremiah being out there with her father every day, out beyond Far Enough Island. The only problem was that Jeremiah now always smelled like fish and he wasn't allowed into the house anymore, except when Sarah sneaked him in when her mother wasn't home.

"I knew everything would work out," her father told the family one night at dinner. "I got the boat. The cod are back. I'm even getting a pretty good price from the new buyer. I'll have a newer boat soon."

"I think it's Jeremiah on the boat that brings good luck," Sarah said. Sarah and her father looked at each other and beamed.

Sarah's mother wasn't convinced. "It's always calmest just before the storm," she said. "Season's not over yet. Just wait. Never smile before Christmas, that's what I'd say."

But things were going well. And everyone should have been happy, only Sarah's mother couldn't convince herself things were going to be all right.

Then one morning that started out bright and cheery, the wind switched and a heavy fog pulled up the inlet.

It was a Saturday and Sarah was not in school. Her mother stared out the window and began to wring her hands together. "I hope he gets back in here soon."

"He'll be okay. He knows the inlet out there. Don't worry," Sarah said.

But she worried.

Her father might have high-tailed it shoreward before the fog if he wasn't having trouble with the engine. But the old contraption was giving him problems. Water in the carburetor. He was stalled and drifting, still trying to fix it, when the fog pulled in tight so that he couldn't see a thing. Then the wind stopped and it was dead still.

Jeremiah was nervous, nosing around the boat, wondering why it was quiet and they weren't moving.

Sarah's father had the lid off the engine and was pouring gasoline down the carburetor. He tried the ignition. It back-fired a couple of times. Then suddenly it coughed a long flame out the mouth of the carburetor, knocking her father off balance and back onto the slimy pile of the day's catch. Before he could turn off the ignition, gasoline was leaking out of the fuel line and the flame had caught it on fire.

Sarah's father grabbed a heavy tarp and threw it across the engine. But it too caught fire. Jeremiah was barking loud and fiercely as if the fire was a living thing and he was going to fend it off.

The fire began to creep out onto the floorboards. It was headed towards the gas tank. Sarah's father tried to sneak past it towards the small cabin to grab for a life vest, but a new, more violent burst of flame roared up from below the deck, knocking him overboard. In the water, he flailed his arms. He kept telling himself that he did know how to swim. He had told that to his wife so often that he truly believed it. The water was cold. It was like sharp knives sticking into his arms and legs.

On the boat, Jeremiah continued to bark. What should he do, Sarah's father wondered. Should he get back in the boat or try to swim away from it. He tried to stay calm, kept himself floating, and tried to think it through.

"Here, Jeremiah. Jump!" he yelled.

Jeremiah launched into the water and swam towards him.

Now the entire boat was aflame. Within minutes it would be down. There was no explosion, just the crackle of wood.

All too soon, the water was up to the gunwales and the flame diminished to nothing as the boat sank beneath. Still hanging onto Jeremiah to keep him afloat, Sarah's father swam back towards where the boat had gone down, hoping to find a plank, some sort of wood to hold onto and keep him up. He found a section of the hull that had been left floating. It wasn't much but it was enough to keep his head above water. Around them was a sickly pool of oil and gas and black ash. The fog was now so dense he couldn't see more than ten feet in any direction. Jeremiah pulled himself up onto a section of deck that was afloat. At first he began to whine. But then he shook himself and began to bark loudly.

"I'm sorry old boy," Sarah's father said. "I don't know what good barking will do you. You might as well save your breath."

But Jeremiah went on barking louder and louder. It was like he had gone crazy and couldn't stop himself.

Sarah's father felt so cold and weak from being on the water that he grew discouraged. He could think of no plan of action. He felt helpless and doomed. The dog barked on and he wished he could make Jeremiah shut up.

After what seemed to be an hour, he thought he heard a boat engine. It was far off in the fog but coming closer.

"Keep barking!" he now shouted to Jeremiah, but Jeremiah was floating away from him.

The boat was coming closer. Sarah's father convinced himself he had to move. He let go of the wood and began to swim towards the engine noise. Then he heard Jeremiah splash into the water and swim up to him. "Over here!" he yelled. But as he did so, his mouth filled with water. He felt himself sink under. He reached out with his hands and there was Jeremiah. He grabbed the collar, pulled the dog under with him, but Jeremiah kicked his legs and kept swimming.

The boat was nearly on top of them.

"Cut the engine quick," someone shouted. Arms were reaching down. Sarah's father was fighting to stay above water. He knew he was pushing down on Jeremiah. It was the only thing keeping him from sinking altogether. He knew he was probably drowning the dog. But he couldn't help it.

Then the arms had grabbed him. He was being hauled up into a boat. He was flat on the deck and his lungs were heaving. He was gasping for air.

"Anyone else out here?" a man's voice asked frantically.

"A dog," Sarah's father said. "Jeremiah. Did you get the dog?"

"I didn't see no dog but that's why I came this way. I heard some fool dog barking his head off. But if he was out there he's not around now," the man said.

Sarah's father pulled himself up to the gunwale and looked over the side. There was nothing to see. No Jeremiah, nothing but a thick ugly fog.

They circled around for twenty minutes but saw and heard nothing.

"He saved my life," Sarah's father said and sunk back onto the floor.

"I told you things would get worse. I felt it in my bones. We're just a family of bad luck."

"That's not true," Sarah shouted back at her mother. "If it wasn't for Jeremiah, Dad would be dead by now."

Her dad hung his head down. "That's right. I have to go look for him. I'll get Hopper to loan me his boat."

"Not in this weather, you're not!" Sarah's mother insisted.

"I suppose you're right. One swim in the sink is one too many."

"But we need to look for him!" Sarah screamed. "He might be alive."

"He couldn't swim all the way back here," her father said.

"But he might have made it to the island. He could have, you know?"

Her father shook his head. "It's unlikely. I don't know how close to the island we were. Besides, how could he find it in all that fog?"

"He's just dead and that's all there is to it," her mother said. "Now let's just leave it at that."

But by morning the sun was out. "I'm going looking for him. Hopper said I could borrow his boat." Sarah's father had a life jacket on. Just then Sarah burst out of her room. She had one on as well. "I'm going too," she announced.

Her father put an arm around her and gave her a hug. "Sure. We'll both look for him."

Her mother looked furious. "Sure, get both of you drowned now! That's all I need."

Sarah's father walked up to her and took her by the shoulder, kissed her on the cheek, and whispered something in her ear. "Please, we'll be careful," Sarah said. "We won't go past the island. We just have to look once."

They were gone most of the day. Sarah and her father walked all around the island and looked everywhere along the beaches. But there was no sign of Jeremiah.

"I'm sorry, honey," her father said.

Sarah tried not to cry but she couldn't help it. "He was my only real friend," she said, and the tears kept coming all the way home. But when she entered the kitchen and saw how happy her mother was to have the two of them home safe, she brightened a little.

They had a big dinner without any arguing at all, and her father promised to try to get his job back at the garage.

After that the weather turned very cold for so early in the year. All the fishermen pulled up their boats weeks before they normally would. Raging northeast storms pummelled the coast. Then came snow in October. Sleet and ice and snow. Schools were closed. Sarah's father got fired from his garage job and went on unemployment.

Sarah's mother always wore a frown on her face. "We should have just packed up and moved long ago. Now's the time. Let's get away from here."

But Sarah didn't want to move. She kept remembering those happy sunny days walking the shoreline with Jeremiah and discovering all sorts of things. She still couldn't believe he was gone. Some mornings she'd wake up and expect him to come bounding into her room, smelling of fish and mud. But she kept reminding herself that if it wasn't for Jeremiah, she wouldn't have a father.

It was Christmas morning and things had been so rotten around Sarah's house for so long that she knew even today was going to be rotten.

The only thing that would make it better was a miracle. Her parents argued all the time about money and about moving. Sarah, herself, would get so tired of it all that she'd just scream, "Shut up!" and run out of the living room and lock herself in her bedroom.

It had been a strange December. The harbor froze up early and the ice grew thick across the shallows and even out into the channel.

"It's a sign of worse things to come," her mother said. "I've never seen anything like it."

They could no longer afford oil for the furnace so her father spent much of his time each day cutting spruce logs and hauling them home for firewood, splitting them and stoking the stoves.

The ice had crept all the way out the inlet almost to Far Enough Island. It was the first time that had happened this early, Old Man Fogerty said, since 1915. It was going to be a long, cold, sad winter.

"But today is Christmas," her mother said. "And I'm not going to worry about a thing. Today I want all of us to be happy!"

She wasn't very convincing but she tried. She had always said it was the one day that she refused to worry about anything. She woke Sarah early in the morning, even before the sun was up, with a peck on the cheek.

"Merry Christmas, Sarah."

But Sarah woke up thinking about Jeremiah and all the other Christmases he had been there. She remembered how he had torn up the wrapping paper to get at his presents – dog bones and leather chew toys. He had been so funny and cute. And now she would never, ever see him again.

Her mother tried singing to Sarah to cheer her up, but it didn't do any good.

The presents were opened and Sarah tried to act surprised and happy but nothing there interested her.

Her father tried to be cheerful, but he was a lousy faker.

By the end of the day, her mother's good humor had worn off and they all sat around tired and depressed.

"This is the worst Christmas of my life," Sarah finally said out loud. "I never want to have another Christmas as long as I live." She sulked off to her room, slammed her door, and went to bed.

The day after Christmas was something else. The ice storm had stopped. The sun was shining brightly and Sarah flipped open the shade on her window. All the trees were coated in ice and the inlet was like one sheet of pure, clear glass. The wharf was like some magical creation coated in crystal. And off in the distance, Far Enough Island, with all the trees glazed with ice, appeared like a magical kingdom.

Sarah just wanted to keep looking out her window. She didn't want to go down to her family and face all the gloom and worry. If only she could just stare out her window like this forever and see the world as a gleaming magical place, everything would be all right.

And then, off in the far distance, she saw a small black speck that arrested her attention. Out towards Far Enough Island something was moving on the ice. An otter, she decided. She should get her father's binoculars and watch him.

She quietly slipped out of her bed and into her parents' bedroom. They were still asleep. But by the window were the binoculars. She returned with them to her room.

At first she couldn't relocate the animal in the glare of ice. But then she found it. Maybe it wasn't an otter, after all. It was larger than an otter, for sure. And it had longer legs. It was running. Running towards her.

Her eyes began to tear up. She couldn't focus properly. She wiped her face. Yes, whatever it was, it was running. And it was black. It kept slipping and falling on the ice. But it was running towards her from the island. She closed her eyes and pinched herself to make sure she was awake. She had had dreams like this before. And always when she opened her eyes, she was alone, and the image was gone.

She re-opened her eyes. The pinch had hurt. She was awake. She put the binoculars to her eyes again.

It was him. The ice now stretched from Far Enough Island all the way to her shore. He was on his way home.

Sarah ran downstairs and on outside into the bright cold air. She yelled "Jeremiah!" out across the vast expanse of ice.

Then she heard the first bark. It was his unmistakable bark. She started to run towards him, out across the frozen yard, but slipped and fell. Everything was covered with ice and it was almost impossible to take a step.

Her shout had awakened her father and mother. They were beside her now, her father helping her up.

"He was there after all," her father said, his eyes fixed on the black animal still making his difficult way across the ice. "He had made it to the island and he was too tired or injured for us to find him. And now that the inlet has frozen up all the way to the island, he's coming back."

"Today is the day for all of us to smile," Sarah's mother said.

All three of them, still in their night clothes, began a slow slippery walk across the icy yard towards the inlet, towards Jeremiah. Sarah wanted to run, but her parents held her back. When they reached the wharf, there was Jeremiah, his feet going every which way as he scratched the ice to make his way home.

Sarah knelt down on the cold glassy surface and felt the hot, familiar breath of Jeremiah. She let him lick her face and bark loud as a canon shot right in her ear.

With a lot of slipping and sliding, they all found their way back into the warm kitchen where Jeremiah was treated to all the leftover Christmas dinner he wanted.

And as soon as Sarah had calmed down enough to allow her brain half a chance to think, she realized by looking at her mother and her father and at Jeremiah that things were going to get better after this. It wouldn't matter if the fish never came back or the money was tight or if the whole world froze solid. There would always be this moment that would make every one of them smile, any time of the year, long before Christmas.

The Santa Claus Trap

by Margaret Atwood

Once upon a time there was a man named Mr. Grate,
Whom the thought of Christmas filled
With an indescribable and fungoid hate.

He hated Christmas trees and presents
And carols and turkeys and plum
Puddings, and he thought Santa Claus and his reindeer
Were not only dumb

But ought to be banned and not allowed
Into the country, and dogs
That barked and children who laughed

Too much made him furious,
And he wished they would all fall down
Holes or drown in bogs.

Mr. Grate, although he was quite rich,
Lived in one miserable little room
Which he never cleaned with a vacuum cleaner
Or swept with a broom
So that it was all covered with dust and dirt
And spiderwebs and old pieces of cheese
And so was Mr. Grate,
And if you ever came near him
You would begin to cough and sneeze,

But nobody ever did, because he never went outside,
But stayed in,
And counted his money, and wrote nasty letters to the editor,
And sometimes drank a bottle of gin

All by himself, or a glass of lemonade without any sugar,
Because he liked it sour,
And he peered out the window and hated everybody,
By the hour.

He had round eyes like an owl's
And his face was all squizzled up
And covered with frowns and scowls.

One day in December, Mr. Grate thought up a horrible plot,
"Everyone," he said to himself –he talked out loud a lot –
"Has a lot of nice things, much nicer than anything *I've* got,

And every Christmas they give each other presents,
And nobody ever gives *me* none,
And not only that, but I never have any fun,

And Santa Claus comes and fills their stockings
And panti-hose and socklets
With oranges and licorice sticks and bubble gum
And chocolates.

But what if Santa Claus were to suddenly disappear,
And all that ever gets found is his empty sled and reindeer?
What if I could kidnap Santa Claus and keep him in a sack
And say I would never give him back

Unless the children sent ME all their candy
And jellybeans and maybe a teddy bear?
Not only would I get even with them and give them a scare,
But I'd have all the stuff, and maybe I'd even be a millionaire.

I'll keep Santa Claus in a cupboard
And feed him on water and crumbs,
While I sit outside and laugh myself silly
And stuff myself with candy apples and bubble gums!"

And for the first time in a long long while,
Mr. Grate began to laugh and chuckle,
But it wasn't a nice laugh, and he turned all red and purple
And rolled around on the floor
And had to loosen his belt buckle.

After that he got up again and set to work.
"The thing is," he said to himself,

"Santa Claus is obviously a jerk

All he ever does is give things to people –
It's really shocking –
And he can't seem to resist an unfilled stocking.

Therefore, all I have to do is get a lot of stockings,
And hang them all over the room as a kind of bait,
And build a trap in the fireplace which will catch him
When he comes down the chimney,
And then I'll just sit and wait."

So first Mr. Grate went to a Sale,
And bought a whole armful of stockings
And socks and mukluks and several rubber boots,
Pushing old ladies out of his way
And scowling and frowning at the men
Who were ringing bells, dressed up in Santa Claus suits,

And then he went to a junk yard and bought all kinds of junk:
Some pieces of old cars, a wringer washing machine,
Several rolls of barbed wire,
Some string and rubber bands, a wrench, a lever, a gear,
And a box full of old tin cans
Which unfortunately also contained a dead skunk,

But that's life, said Mr. Grate to himself
As he carted all these things home
In a U-Haul he'd rented.
And when he got them back to his room, he started to build
The most complicated trap that has ever been invented.

The trap was foolproof and full of pulleys and levers,
And anyone who came down the chimney and stepped into it
Would be grabbed by mechanical hands
And rollered on rollers and tangled in wires and zoomed
Right into a sack in Mr. Grate's closet,
And it looked as if Santa Claus was doomed,

EXCEPT

Next door to Mr. Grate lived some twins,
A girl named Charlotte and a boy named William.
Charlotte's favorite flower was the Rose,
And William's was the Trillium.

They were both very curious
And they were always looking in people's windows
And back yards and bureau drawers or over their shoulders.
Charlotte was somewhat self-contained,
But William was bolder.

And one day, when Mr. Grate was building his trap and
Talking out loud to himself
About his plan to hold Santa Claus ransom,
Charlotte just happened to be standing on William's shoulders
And looking through his transom.

She overheard the whole plan, and she was so dismayed
She almost fell off,
And then she almost gave them away,
Because even Mr. Grate's transom was so dusty
It made her cough,

But luckily Mr. Grate was hammering something
At the time, and didn't hear.
Charlotte climbed down and whispered in William's ear,
"William, I have just heard the most terrible thing,
And Christmas is going to be ruined this year!"
These words of Charlotte's filled William's heart with fear.

The twins hurried back to their own house,
And sat down at the kitchen table,
And while they were eating some peanut butter sandwiches
To keep up their strength,
Charlotte repeated what she had heard, as well as she was able.
"But that's terrible!" said William, "If Santa Claus is caught
In the trap, and tied up with a large knot,

No children in the entire world
Will get anything in their stockings, you see!
And – I hardly need to point out –

That includes you and me.
I feel that this could turn into a major catastrophe."

"Don't be so obvious," Charlotte said.
"The main thing is, how can we stop him?"
"Well," said William,
"I could go over there with my baseball bat and bop him
On the head." "You aren't big enough,"
Charlotte said, she was practical.
"We have to think of a plan that is both feasible and tactical,

By which I mean something we can do ourselves
That will actually work."

But the possibility of no Santa Claus
Filled them with depression, gloom and murk.

And they found it hard to even think about it,
It made them so sad.
"Some people are naughty," said Charlotte,
"but Mr. Grate is *bad*."

For days they did nothing but sigh and mutter
And eat sandwiches made of peanut butter.

Once they went to spy on Mr. Grate,
But the trap was even bigger,
And Mr. Grate was rubbing his hands
And looking at it, with a nasty snigger.

The sight of the enormous trap
Made Charlotte and William feel helpless and small,
And they seemed unable to think of anything to do at all.

They knew they couldn't tell the police or any grownups,
Because no one would believe them anyway,
And it was too late to write Santa Claus to warn him,
Because Christmas was due now any day.

"Is this the end?" said William, feeling doleful.
"Do not give up," said Charlotte, looking soulful.

AT LAST

They had a brilliant idea, and being twins
They had it both at once, because

75

Twins often do. "I know!" they cried together.
"We'll make a false Santa Claus!

We'll make it out of red potato sacks, and fill it full of rocks,
And let it down Mr. Grate's chimney on a rope,
And it will snarl up the trap and possibly break it, because
Of the rocks." This idea filled them with hope.

"Come on," said William, "let's get going,
We have no time to waste!"
So, pausing only to eat one more small sandwich each
And to put on their winter coats
And their mittens, boots and hats,
They rushed out the door in considerable haste.

"Where are they going?"
Their mother called after them as they ran down the street.
"We're going to save Santa Claus!" they called back, and
Not realizing the seriousness of the situation,
She said, "Isn't that sweet."

It was Christmas Eve, and Mr. Grate
Had hung up his stocking, or I should say
His stockings, because he had about a hundred of them
Dangling all over his room,
In every color you can think of,
Red, green, yellow, purple, blue, and gray,
And the total effect would have been rather joyous and gay

If it hadn't been for the sinister machine
Lurking near the fireplace in the corner.
"All right, Santa Claus," muttered Mr. Grate,

"Once down that chimney and you're a goner!"

He was sitting in his one dingy old chair,
Hugging himself and chortling,
When up on his roof he heard an odd sound,
Part scuffling and part snortling.

"It must be a reindeer!" cried Mr. Grate, and jumped up
To give the final touch to his arrangement of socks.
(It was actually Charlotte and William,
Having a little trouble with the rocks.)

"Now Santa will slide down the chimney
With a nice, round, fat kind of slither,
And I'll have him safe in my closet,
And all the children of the world will be thrown into a dither,

And serve them right," said Mr. Grate.
He could hardly wait.

But imagine his surprise
When instead of a round little man landing
With a comfortable plop in his trap, there was a loud crash!
Followed by a thud and a rattle and a smash!

Someone – or something – dressed red
Had come down the chimney, though it wasn't light

Enough to see clearly, and Mr. Grate's trap had spun into action
But it was throwing out sparks left and right!

Its mechanical arms were getting all snarled up

In the barbed wire,
And its washing machine wringer was out of control,
Spinning higher and higher,
And something seemed to be wrong
With the sack that Santa was supposed to fall into –
It had caught on fire!

Suddenly all the fuses blew,
And a thin, tiny, eerie voice came wafting
Down the chimney flue:
"Mr. Grate! Mr. Grate!

REPENT

Before it is too late!"

This was actually Charlotte,
Which Mr. Grate had no way of knowing.

"It's ghosts!" he cried.
"I've got to get out of here, even though it's snowing!"

He ran towards the door, but because
There were now no lights in the entire place,
He tripped over something and fell flat on his face.

Then something else grabbed him from behind,
And one of the gears that wasn't broken began to grind,

And then there was an unpleasant ZAP
And Mr. Grate was caught in his own trap!
"Help, Help," he cried, and began to struggle,

Which only made the tangle worse,
"I'm perishing! I'm expiring!
I need a doctor and also a nurse! O curse

The day I decided to trap poor Santa Claus!
Please, someone, bring some wire clippers and tinsnips,
And wrenches, and saws
And get me out!"

Charlotte and William, on the roof, heard his feeble shout.
"I believe it's worked," Charlotte said. "He seems to be caught,
Which is more than we expected.
Should we let him out, or not?"

Mr. Grate was lying all covered with barbed wire
And bits of cheese from the floor,
And feeling decidedly sorry for himself,
And also rather battered and sore,
When Charlotte and William climbed
Through the transom over his door.

(They didn't have a key, and the door itself was locked.)
"Well," said Charlotte, looking down at Mr. Grate,
Where he lay clinking and clanking,
"In my opinion you deserve a good spanking."

"In *my* opinion," said William,
"You deserve a good kick in the behind."
"But," said Charlotte, intervening –
She felt one should be polite, if at all possible –
"This is Christmas and we are going to be kind.

We'll get you out of the trap *this* time,
If you promise not to do it again, and make amends."
"But why did you think of such an evil thing to do
In the first place?" said William.
"Boohoo," said Mr. Grate, "I don't have any friends,

Or a teddy bear, or *anything*,
And everyone else was having such a good time,
Especially at Christmas, and my room is all covered with grime,
And no one invites me to dinner,
And I never get anything in my stocking but pieces of coal,
Or sometimes a hole,
Or a rotten potato, and once, in a good year, a single Smartie,
And it's a long long time since I even went to a birthday party!"

"There, there," said Charlotte, wiping away his grubby tears,
While William was snipping him out of the trap
With a pair of shears,

"I understand perfectly. You just wanted some attention."
(Which had been said to her on several occasions
When she herself has been rather surly,
But these we won't mention.)

"You can come back to our house for Christmas.
I'm sure our Mum won't mind, if we ask,
And we'll even help you clean up your room."
Which they did, and it was an unpleasant task . . .

But in Mr. Grate's closet they found a couple of suits
That weren't too dirty,
And when they had washed his face and shined his boots

He looked quite presentable,
And was so pleased he actually smiled
And allowed his fingernails to be cut and his moustache filed,

And off they all went to Charlotte's and William's house,
And had a wonderful Christmas dinner
With lots of trimmings,
And when Mr. Grate got up from the table
He was certainly not thinner.

And after that day, though he was not
A completely different person, and still
Didn't like dogs much, and was known to spill

A few bits of cheese on the carpet now and then,
He was much nicer than before,
And played Monopoly with Charlotte and William,
So that they were quite glad he lived next door.

And he changed the spelling of his name to Mr. Great,
And often said things like "It's never too late."

"And although he didn't manage
To *catch* Santa Claus," said Charlotte one day,
"At least he found him."
Which is true, when you think about it, in a way,

And also he had found not only one friend
But two. Which is a pretty good place to say

THE END.

The Three Christmases

by Marian Engel

Rufus and Geraldine stood staring out the window of their new house. It was eight o'clock on Christmas Eve, and snow was at last falling. The flakes were fluffy and soft against the dark night sky.

The houses across from them all looked the same. They had wide front windows, dark verandas, and high gables. Some of them had Christmas tree lights along their verandas.

Rufus and Geraldine stared at them and sighed. They had just moved into their house. They knew that the street had lots of other children on it, but they had not met any of them yet. "I wish we had lights," Geraldine said.

Rufus was thinking about something else. "What did you like best?"

"About what?"

"Daddy's apartment, silly."

"Oh." Geraldine saw herself in the white and silver place again, where everything was new, so new she was scared to touch it. "I know what you liked best."

"No you don't."

"Yes I do. It was when the waiter lit the sauce for the pancakes."

Rufus sighed and shook his head. "I'm growing out of that stuff," he said. "What I really liked was looking at all the lights. He's so high up it's like being in an airplane."

Their father had invited them to his new apartment for Christmas Eve dinner. Instead of living with them, now, he lived in a penthouse in an apartment building on the waterfront, and ordered his meals wheeled on a cart to him by a waiter in a uniform. He had treated them to a splendid supper – and delivered them home promptly because, he said, "Your baby sitter will be waiting for you."

They didn't dare tell him that there was no baby sitter, that they were going home to an empty house full of unpacked boxes, to an unmade Christmas.

What had happened was this: six months before, their parents had had a dreadful quarrel and it was not like one of their own quarrels because it did not get made up. It ended when their father went off to get his own apartment and their mother bought this little house. The day they moved, it rained and rained. Then they found that the furnace didn't work properly, and it took days to get that fixed. They still went to their old school, but on the bus, which took a cold, long time. Their mother was proud of her own little house, but they weren't ... much. It seemed narrow and mean to them.

Their mother was out. She had experimented with baby sitters for them, but they were experts at hassling baby sitters, and she couldn't get one any more. She had finally yelled at them, "Well, stay by yourselves, then, until I get back. I have to work for a living, and this is my busy season." She played the cello and there were a lot of concerts at Christmas time.

So they stood in their window and sighed. Their mother kept telling them everything would be all right – one day.

"I wish we had a tree," Rufus said.

"I do too," sighed Geraldine.

"I saw a guy selling trees up the street and around the corner."

"Yes, but what would we do with it? Where's the stand?"

Rufus looked despairingly at the boxes that stood around them. He knew all those boxes: he had brought them home from the supermarket himself, six a day, after school. "It might be in one of them."

"Where are the decorations?"

"In the blue suitcase, where they are every year, silly."

"But where's that, Rufus? She can never find anything."

"I saw the movers put it in the basement. Have you got any money, Geraldine?"

"Aside from Daddy's cheque I've got two dollars and forty-three cents."

"Good. I've got four-sixty. We should be able to get a tree for that: I mean, on Christmas Eve the guy wants to go home, he'll sell us one cheap. Hurry on. Get your coat."

"We're not supposed to go out again after we get home."

"She'll never know, stupid. Anyway, we're doing her a favor."

Geraldine was twelve and Rufus was eleven. She was better at rules than he was, but he was strange because wherever you set him down, he immediately learned his way around. In no time at all they were both on a corner and he was beating a man down on the price of a small Scotch pine.

Earlier in the day, it had been freezing cold. Now the soft white snow seemed to be warming the world. They carried their bargain tree down the street that was new to them. They passed doors that were open to let visitors in.

They got to their own house. It was a job getting the tree in the door until they remembered you did it backwards, so the branches of the tree slid smoothly into the house's stomach.

Then Rufus plunged into the boxes to hunt for the tree stand, while Geraldine braved the depths of the basement to hunt for the blue suitcase. When she lugged it up the stairs, he had found the stand, his old blue quilt, all the books he wanted to read in the next ten years, and the spice rack. The living room was a mess.

They opened the ornament boxes and looked at the silver and red and blue balls that were so delicate that you could stick your fingers through them. They found the birds with spun glass tails that had been their grandmother's. The lights (but the Santa Claus bulb had gone out), the hooks, the old tinsel, the felt stockings.

It took ages to get the stand on the tree, to get the tree up and straight. They had to clear boxes away to make a place for it. They bickered about how to put up the lights, but they got them on. Rufus spent a lot of time moving bulbs around so no two of the same color would be together. Geraldine put the star on the top of the tree and made sure the glass birds had a place where they could be seen.

They stood back and looked at it. It was beautiful. It was like a sparkling necklace of city they could see from their father's balcony.

Geraldine said softly, "It makes the house feel warm."

Rufus said nothing. He began stacking boxes. He had never wanted to be neat before in his life, but he didn't want mess interfering with the view of their tree.

Geraldine let Rufus work. After all, she'd had to do a lot of picking up after him. She looked out the window and twisted her hair and wondered how she'd spend her father's cheque. He said he was giving them money so he wouldn't get in a present competition with their mother. It was a good idea. She wanted a microscope so she could see the insides of small things.

Outside the window, the street was quieter. She could see, as well as the houses across the street, the reflection of their Christmas tree in the glass. And she noticed something else; a tiny little fir tree in their tiny little front yard, something she hadn't had time to notice before. A cold-looking sparrow was perched on top of it.

"Rufus, did you know we have a little Christmas tree of our own?"

"That thing in the front yard?"

"Yeah. Could we decorate that, do you think?"

"We don't have any outdoor lights."

But she knew what they did have, and in minutes they were popping corn and stringing cranberries. How they found the string and the darning needles that they had been looking for for days was a kind of miracle, but they did, so she strung while Rufus popped, and popped while Rufus strung, and in the end they hard garlands and garlands for the birds.

And Rufus had a super idea: he also found the candles. "We can't burn the house down, can we, if they're outside?"

Geraldine glanced at the clock. It was eleven. The concert should be over. Their mother should have been home. Maybe she'd stopped off for a drink somewhere. She was kind of irresponsible. She wasn't bringing any presents, she had said. Buying them a house was all she could do. Musicians didn't make much money. "Let's go outside and do it," she said.

They put on their coats and took strings of popcorn and cranberries and a box of white candles their mother called mouse candles and matches outside. There was no way to attach the candles to the weak little branches of the silly little fir tree, so they set them in a circle around its base. There were twelve of them, and they knelt down and took turns lighting them.

Everything was very quiet. It was as if the sky was breathing snow at them. They sat on their haunches and watched the candles flicker as the snowflakes hit them. "It makes me want to sing *Silent Night*," Geraldine said, "in spite of the fact that I would never sing it at school."

"Ssh," said Rufus.

They were startled when they heard a car drive up. Their mother appeared like a ghost behind them, her arms full of parcels. Someone they didn't know took her cello into the house for her, but she stood over the little fence staring at them.

Funny; she didn't say, "You should be in bed." Later, in the kitchen, she didn't say, "How the heck did you kids manage to make such a goldurned mess?" She just stood there with a lovely smile on her face while the car drove off, and then said, "Merry Christmas, children," and, "It's beautiful."

Finally it got cold out there and they went inside where she admired the tree. Then she wiped off the kitchen table and put her parcels down. "I guess you're too old to hang up your stockings."

"No, never!" they cried.

"Well, I'm too old . . . tonight. Did you have a good time with Daddy?"

"Yes," they said, in careful voices. They didn't want to get into a conversation about Daddy on Christmas Eve.

Neither did she. "Look, it's late," she said. "You get into your pyjamas, and I'll fill the stockings, and then you barrel down the stairs and we can pretend it's morning and open everything." It was after midnight.

Which they did. Geraldine even futilely brushed her teeth. And they brought down the things they had made for her – an ash tray in pottery class, a bookmark in sewing, a birdhouse in carpentry.

They leapt into their presents. They had not expected presents, but these were deliciously wrapped in real ribbon and fancy paper. There were boxes of tiny things wrapped to make them look bigger. "It's the year of the mortgage," she said. Staplers. Good erasers. A dozen ball-point pens for each of them. A set of Narnia books, even if they had read them before. A really good pair of scissors for Geraldine. A vise-grip wrench for Rufus, who was always taking apart his bicycle, even in winter. Little china animals for them both.

"You'll buy your big things out of Daddy's cheque," she said. "And I do love the things you have made."

Then she sat down at the piano and played long soft music until they felt very sleepy indeed.

Outside the window, the light was changing. "Isn't it funny," Geraldine said, "the dawn is coming, and we've already had three Christmases."

Rufus yawned and counted. She was right. They had had three: their father's (and he would never forget the cart, and the pan of pancakes going up in flames, boom, like that), their mother's (Geraldine's scissors would be useful for models), and their own.

Outside, all the candles had gone out.

"Up to bed," their mother said. "We're going to Gran's tomorrow."

"Four Christmases?" Geraldine asked sleepily.

"Well," said their mother, "we've had a rough year, but there's an old expression."

"Good night, Mum," they said, "and Merry Christmas."

Blue Christmas, an Inspector Banks Story

by Peter Robinson

A *three-day holiday.* Banks sat down at the breakfast table and made some notes on a lined pad. If he was doomed to spend Christmas alone this year, he was going to do it in style. For Christmas Eve: Alastair Sim's *A Christmas Carol,* black-and-white version, of course. For Christmas Day: *Love, Actually.* Mostly it was a load of crap – no doubt about that – but it was worth it for Bill Nighy, and Keira Knightley was always worth watching. For Boxing Day: *David Copperfield,* the one with the Harry Potter actor in it, because it had helped him through a nasty hangover one Boxing Day a few years ago, and thus are traditions born.

Music was more problematic. Bach's *Christmas Oratorio* and Handel's *Messiah,* naturally. Both were on his iPod and could be played through his main sound system. But some years ago, he had made a Christmas compilation tape of all his favourite songs: from Bing's "White Christmas" to Elvis's "Santa Claus is Back in Town" and "Blue Christmas," The Pretenders' "2000 Miles," and Roland Kirk's "We Free Kings." Unfortunately, that had gone up in flames along with the rest of his music collection. Which meant a quick trip to HMV in Eastvale that afternoon to pick up a few seasonal CDs, so he could make a playlist. He had to go to Marks and Spencer, anyway, for his frozen turkey dinner, so he might as well drop in at HMV while he was in the Swainsdale Centre. As for wine, he still had a more than decent selection from his brother's cellar – including some fine Amarone, Chianti Classico, Clarets, and Burgundies – which would certainly get him through the next three days without any pain. Luckily, he had bought and given out all his Christmas presents earlier – what few there were: money for Tracy, a Fairport Convention boxed set for Brian, chocolates and magazine subscriptions for his parents, and a silver-and-jet bracelet for Annie Cabbot.

Banks put his writing pad aside and reached for his coffee mug. Beside it sat a pristine copy of Sebastian Faulks' *Human Traces*, which he fully intended to read over the holidays. There should be plenty of peace and quiet. Brian was with his band in Europe and wouldn't be able to get home in time. Tracy was spending Christmas with her mother, Sandra; stepdad, Sean; and their baby, Sinead; and Annie was heading home to the artists' colony in St. Ives, where they would all no doubt be having a good weep over *A Junkie's Christmas*, which Annie had told him was a Christmas staple among her father's crowd. He had seen it once himself, and he had to admit that it wasn't bad, but it hadn't become a tradition with him.

All in all, then, this Christmas was beginning to feel like something to be got through with liberal doses of wine and music.

Even the weather was refusing to cooperate. The white Christmas everyone had been hoping for since a tentative sprinkle in late November had not materialized, though the optimists at the meteorological centre were keeping their options open. At the moment, though, it was uniformly grey and wet in Yorkshire. The only good thing that could be said for it was that it wasn't cold. Far from it. Down south, people were sitting outside at Soho cafés and playing golf in the suburbs. Banks wondered if he should have gone away, taken a holiday. Paris. Rome. Madrid. A stranger in a strange city. Even London would have been better than this. Maybe he could still catch a last-minute flight.

But he knew he wasn't going anywhere. He sipped some strong coffee and told himself not to be so maudlin. Christmas was a notoriously dangerous time of year. It was when people got depressed and gave in to their deepest fears, when all their failures, regrets, and disappointments came back to haunt them. Was he going to let himself give in to that, become a statistic?

He decided to go into town now and get his last-minute shopping over with before it got really busy. Just before he left, though, his phone rang. Banks picked up the receiver.

"Sir? It's DC Jackman."

"Yes, Winsome. What's the problem?"

"I'm really sorry to disturb you at home, sir, but we've got a bit of a problem."

"What is it?" Banks asked. Despite having to spend Christmas alone, he had been looking forward to a few days away from Western Area Headquarters, if only to relax and unwind after a particularly difficult year. But perhaps that wasn't to be.

"Missing person, sir."

"Can't someone else handle it?"

"It needs someone senior, sir, and DI Cabbot's on her way to Cornwall."

"Who's missing?"

"A woman by the name of Brenda Mercer. Forty-two years old."

"How long?"

"Overnight."

"Any reason to think there's been foul play?"

"Not really."

"Who reported her missing?"

"The husband."

"Why did he leave it until this morning?"

"He didn't. He reported it at six o'clock yesterday evening. We've been looking into it. But you know how it is with missing persons, sir, unless it's a kid. It was very early days. Usually they turn up, or you find a simple explanation quickly enough."

"But not in this case?"

"No, sir. The husband's getting frantic. Difficult. Demanding to see someone higher up. And he's got the daughter and her husband in tow now. They're not making life any easier. I've only just managed to get rid of them by promising I'd get someone in authority to come and talk to them."

"All right," Banks said, with a sigh. "Hang on. I'll be right in."

Major Crimes and CID personnel were thin on the ground at Western Area Headquarters that Christmas Eve, and DC Winsome Jackman was one who had drawn the short straw. She didn't mind, though. She couldn't afford to visit her parents in Jamaica, and she had politely passed up a Christmas dinner invitation from a fellow member of the potholing club who had been pursuing her for some time now, so she had no real plans for the holidays. She hadn't expected it to be particularly busy in Major Crimes. Most Christmas incidents were domestic, and as such, they were dealt with by the officers on patrol. Even criminals, it seems, took a bit of time off for turkey and Christmas pud. But a missing-person case could turn nasty very quickly, especially if she had been missing for two days now.

While she was waiting for Banks, Winsome went through the paperwork again. There wasn't much, other than the husband's report and statement, but that gave her the basics.

When David Mercer got home from work on December 23 at around six o'clock, he was surprised to find his wife not home. Surprised because she was always home and always had his dinner waiting for him. He worked in the administration offices of the Swainsdale Shopping Centre, and his hours were fairly regular. A neighbor had seen Mrs. Mercer walking down the street where she lived on the Leaside Estate at about a quarter past four that afternoon. She was alone and was wearing a beige overcoat and carrying a scuffed brown leather bag, the kind with a shoulder strap. She was heading in the direction of the main road, and the neighbor assumed she was going to catch a bus. She knew that Mrs. Mercer didn't drive. She said hello, but said that Mrs. Mercer hadn't seemed to hear her, had seemed a bit "lost in her own world."

Police had questioned the bus drivers on the route, but none of them recalled seeing anyone matching the description. Uniformed officers also questioned taxi drivers and got the same response. All Mrs. Mercer's relatives had been contacted, and none had any idea where she was. Winsome was beginning to think it was possible, then, that someone had picked Mrs. Mercer up on the main road, possibly by arrangement, and that she didn't want to be found. The alternative – that she had been somehow abducted – didn't bear thinking about, at least not until all other possible avenues had been exhausted.

Winsome had not been especially impressed by David Mercer

– he was the sort of pushy, aggressive white male she had seen far too much of over the past few years, puffed up with self-importance, acting as if everyone else were a mere lackey to meet his demands, especially if she happened to be black and female. But she tried not to let personal impressions interfere with her reasoning. Even so, there was something about Mercer's tone, something that didn't quite ring true. She made a note to mention it to Banks.

The house was a modern Georgian-style semi with a bay window, stone cladding, and neatly kept garden, and when Banks rang the doorbell, Winsome beside him, David Mercer opened it so quickly he might have been standing right behind it. He led Banks and Winsome into a cluttered but clean front room, where a young woman sat on the sofa wringing her hands and a whippet-thin man in an expensive, out-of-date suit paced the floor. A tall Christmas tree stood in one corner, covered with ornaments and lights. On the floor were a number of brightly wrapped presents and one ornament, a tiny pair of ice skates, which seemed to have fallen off. The radio was playing Christmas music faintly in the background.

"Have you heard anything?" David Mercer asked.

"Nothing yet," Banks answered. "But if I may, I'd like to ask you a few more questions."

"We've already told everything to her," he said, gesturing in Winsome's direction.

"I know," said Banks. "And DC Jackman has discussed it with me. But I still have a few questions."

"Don't you think you should be out there on the streets searching for her?" said the whippet-thin man, who was also turning prematurely bald.

Banks turned slowly to face him. "And you are?"

He puffed out what little chest he had. "Claude Mainwaring, solicitor. I'm Mr. Mercer's son-in-law."

"Well, Mr. Mainwaring," said Banks, "it's not normally my job, as a detective chief inspector, to get out on the streets looking for people. In fact, it's not even my job to pay house calls asking questions, but as it's nearly Christmas, and as Mr. Mercer here is worried about his wife, I thought I might bend the rules just a little. And believe me, there are already more than enough people out there trying to find Mrs. Mercer."

Mainwaring grunted as if unsatisfied with the answer; then he sat down next to his wife. Banks turned to David Mercer, who finally bade him and Winsome to sit, too. "Mr. Mercer," Banks asked, thinking of the doubts that Winsome had voiced on their way over, "can you think of anywhere your wife might have gone?"

"Nowhere," said Mercer. "That's why I called you lot."

"Was there any reason why your wife might have gone away?"

"None at all," said Mercer, just a beat too quickly for Banks' liking.

"She wasn't unhappy about anything?"

"Not that I know of, no."

"Everything was fine between the two of you?"

"Now, look here!" Mainwaring got to his feet.

"Sit down and be quiet, Mr. Mainwaring," Banks said as gently as he could. "You're not in court now, and you're not helping. I'll get to you later." He turned back to Mercer and ignored the slighted solicitor. "Had you noticed any difference in her behavior before she left, any changes of mood or anything?"

"No," said Mercer. "Like I said, everything was quite normal. May I ask what you're getting at?"

"I'm not getting at anything," Banks said. These are all questions that have to be asked in cases such as these.

"Cases such as these?"

"Missing persons."

"Oh God," cried the daughter. "I can't believe it. Mother: a missing person."

She used the same tone as she might have used to say "homeless person," Banks thought, as if she were somehow embarrassed by her mother's going missing. He quickly chided himself for being so uncharitable. It was Christmas, after all, and no matter how self-important and self-obsessed these people seemed to be, they *were* worried about Brenda Mercer. He could only do his best to help them. He just wished they would stop getting in his way.

"Has she ever done anything like this before?" Banks asked.

"Never," said David Mercer. "Brenda is one of the most stable and reliable people you could ever wish to meet."

"Does she have any close friends?"

"The family means everything to her."

"Might she have met someone? Someone she could confide in?"

Mercer seemed puzzled. "I don't know what you mean. Confide? What would Brenda have to confide? And if she did, why would she confide in someone else rather than in me? No, it doesn't make sense."

"People do, you know, sometimes."

"Not Brenda."

This was going nowhere fast, Banks thought, seeing what Winsome had meant. "Do you have any theories about where she might have gone?"

"Something's happened to her. Someone's abducted her, obviously. I can't see any other explanation."

"Why do you say that?"

"It stands to reason, doesn't it? She'd never do anything so irresponsible and selfish as to mess up all our Christmas plans and cause us so much fuss and worry."

"But these things – abductions and the like – are much rarer than you imagine," said Banks. "In most cases, missing persons are found healthy and safe."

Mainwaring snorted in the background. "And the longer you take to find her, the less likely she is to be healthy and safe," he said.

Banks ignored him and carried on talking to David Mercer. "Did you and your wife have any arguments recently?" he asked.

"Arguments? No, not really."

"Anything that might upset her, cause her to want to disappear?"

"No."

"Do you know if she has any male friends?" Banks knew he was treading on dangerous grounds now, but he had to ask.

"If you're insinuating that she's run off with someone," Mercer said, "then you're barking up the wrong tree. Brenda would never do that to me. Or to Janet," he added, glancing over at the daughter.

Banks had never expected his wife, Sandra, to run off with another man, either, but she had done. No sense in labouring the point, though. If anything like that had happened, the Mercers would be the last people to tell him, assuming that they even knew themselves. But if Brenda had no close friends, then there was no one else he could question who might be able to tell him more about her. All in all, it was beginning to seem like a tougher job than he had imagined.

"We'll keep you posted," he said, and then he and Winsome headed back to the station.

Unfortunately, most people were far too absorbed in their Christmas plans – meals, family visits, last-minute shopping, church events, and what have you – to pay much attention to local news stories as they did the rest of the time, and even that wasn't much. As

Banks and Winsome whiled away the afternoon at Western Area Headquarters, uniformed police officers went from house to house asking questions and searched the wintry Dales landscape in an ever-widening circle, but nothing came to light.

Banks remembered, just before the shops closed, that he had things to buy, so he dashed over to the Swainsdale Centre. Of course, by closing time on Christmas Eve, it was bedlam, and everyone was impatient and bad-tempered. He queued to pay for his turkey dinner because he would have had nothing else to eat otherwise, but just one glance at the crowds in HMV made him decide to forgo the Christmas music for this year, relying on what he had already and what he could catch on the radio.

By six o'clock, he was back at home, and the men and women on duty at the police station had strict instructions to ring him if anything concerning Brenda Mercer came up.

But nothing did.

Banks warmed his leftover lamb curry and washed it down with a cold beer. After he finished the dishes, he made a start on *Human Traces*, then opened a bottle of claret and took it with him into the TV room. There, he slid the shiny DVD of *A Christmas Carol* into the player, poured himself a healthy glass, and settled back. He always enjoyed spotting the bit where you could see the cameraman reflected in the mirror when Scrooge examines himself on Christmas morning, and he found Alastair Sim's over-the-top excitement at seeing the world anew as infectious and uplifting as ever. Even so, as he took himself up to bed around midnight, he still had a thought to spare for Brenda Mercer, and it kept him awake far longer than he would have liked.

The first possible lead came early on Christmas morning when Banks was eating a soft-boiled egg for breakfast and listening to a

King's College Choir concert on the radio. Winsome rang to tell him that someone had seen a woman resembling Mrs. Mercer in a rather dazed state wandering through the village of Swainshead shortly after dawn. The description matched, down to the coat and shoulder-bag, so Banks finished his breakfast and headed out.

The sky was still like iron, but the temperature had dropped overnight, and Banks thought he sniffed a hint of snow in the air. As he drove down the dale, he glanced at the hillsides, all in shades of grey, their peaks obscured by low-lying cloud. Here and there, a silver stream meandered down the slope, glittering in the weak light. Whatever was wrong with Brenda Mercer, Banks thought, she must be freezing if she had been sleeping rough for two nights now.

Before he got to Swainshead, he received another call on his mobile again from Winsome. This time she told him that a local train driver had seen a woman walking aimlessly along the tracks over the Swainshead Viaduct. When Banks arrived there, Winsome was already waiting on the western side along with a couple of uniformed officers in their patrol cars, engines running so they could stay warm. The huge viaduct stretched for about a quarter of a mile across the broad valley, carrying the main line up to Carlisle and beyond into Scotland, and its twenty or more great arches framed picture-postcard views of the hills beyond.

"She's up there, sir," said Winsome, pointing as Banks got out of the car. Way above him, more than a hundred feet up, a tiny figure in brown perched on the edge of the viaduct wall.

"Jesus Christ," said Banks. "Has anyone called to stop the trains? Anything roaring by her right now could give her the fright of her life, and it's a long way down."

"It's been done," said Winsome.

"Right," said Banks. "At the risk of stating the obvious, I think we'd better get someone who knows about these things to go up there and talk to her."

"It'll be difficult to get a professional, sir, on Christmas Day."

"Well, what do you . . .? No. I can read your expression, Winsome. Don't look at me like that. The answer's no."

"But you know you're the best person for the job, sir. You're good with people. You listen to them. They trust you."

"But I wouldn't know where to begin."

"I don't think there are any set rules."

"I'm hardly the sort to convince someone that life is full of the joys of spring."

"I don't really think that's what's called for."

"But what if she jumps?"

Winsome shrugged. "She'll either jump or fall if someone doesn't go up there soon and find out what's going on."

Banks glanced up again and swallowed. He thought he felt the soft, chill touch of a snowflake melt on his eyeball. Winsome was right. He couldn't send up one of the uniformed lads – they were far too inexperienced for this sort of thing – and time was of the essence.

"Look," he said, turning to Winsome. "See if you can raise some sort of counselor negotiator, will you? In the meantime, I'll go up and see what I can do."

"Right you are, sir." Winsome smiled. Banks got back in his car. The quickest way to reach the woman was drive up to Swainshead station, just before the viaduct, and walk along the tracks. At least that way, he wouldn't have to climb any hills. The thought didn't comfort him much, though, when he looked up again and saw the woman's legs dangling over the side of the wall.

"Stop right there," she said. "Who are you?"

Banks stopped. He was about four or five yards away from her. The wind was howling more than he had expected – whistling around his ears, making it difficult to hear properly – and it seemed colder up there, too. He wished he was wearing some-thing warmer than his leather jacket. The hills stretched away to the west, some still streaked with November's snow. In the dis-tance, Banks thought he could make out the huge rounded moun-tains of the Lake District.

"My name's Banks," he said. "I'm a policeman."

"I thought you'd find me eventually," she said. "It's too late, though."

From where Banks was standing, he could only see her in pro-file. The ground was a long way below. Banks had no particular fear of heights, but even so, her precarious position on the wall unnerved him. "Are you sure you don't want to come back from the edge and talk?" he said.

"I'm sure. Do you think it was easy getting here in the first place?"

"It's a long walk from Eastvale."

She cast him a sidelong glance. "I didn't mean that."

"Sorry. It just looks a bit dangerous there. You could slip and fall off."

"What makes you think that wouldn't be a blessing?"

"Whatever it is," said Banks, "it can't be worth this. Come on, Brenda, you've got a husband who loves you, a daughter who needs –"

"My husband doesn't love me, and my daughter doesn't need me. Do you think I don't know? David's been shagging his sec-retary for two years. Can you imagine such a cliché? He thinks I don't know. And as for my daughter, I'm just an embarrassment to her and that awful husband of hers. I'm the shop-girl who mar-ried up, and now I'm just a skivvy for the lot of them. That's all I've been for years."

"But things can change."

She stared at him with pity and shook her head. "No, they can't," she said and gazed off into the distance. "Do you know why I'm here? I mean do you know what set me off? I've put up with it all for years – the coldness, the infidelity – just for the sake of order, not rocking the boat, not causing a scene. But do you know what it was?"

"No," said Banks, anxious to keep her talking. "Tell me." He edged a little closer so he could hear her voice above the wind. She didn't tell him to stop. Snowflakes started to swirl around them.

"People say it's smell that sparks memory the most, but it wasn't, not this time. It was a Christmas ornament. I was putting a few last-minute decorations on the tree before Janet and Claude arrived, and I found myself holding these tiny, perfect ice skates I hadn't seen for years. They sent me right back to a particular day when I was a child. It's funny because it didn't seem like just a memory. I felt as if I was *really* there. My father took me skating on a pond somewhere in the country; I don't remember where. But it was just getting dark, and there were red and green and white Christmas lights and music playing – carols like "Silent Night" and "Away in a Manger" – and someone was roasting chestnuts on a brazier. The air was full of the smell. I was . . . My father died last year."

She paused and brushed tears or melted snowflakes from her eyes with the back of her hand. "I kept falling down. It must have been my first time on ice. But my father would just pick me up, tell me I was doing fine, and set me going again. I don't know what it was about that day, but I was so happy, the happiest I can ever remember. Everything seemed perfect, and I felt I could do anything. I wished it would never end. I didn't even feel the cold. I was just all warm inside and full of love. Did you ever feel like that?"

Banks couldn't remember, but he was sure he must have. Best to agree, anyway. Stay on her wavelength. "Yes," he said. "I know what you mean." It wasn't exactly a lie.

"And it made me feel worthless," she said. "The memory made me feel that my whole life was a sham, a complete waste of time of any potential I once might have had. And it just seemed that there was no point in carrying on." She shifted on the wall.

"Don't!" Banks cried, moving forward.

She looked at him. He thought he could make out a faint smile. She appeared tired and drawn, but her face was a pretty one, he noticed. A slightly pointed chin and small mouth, but beautiful hazel eyes. "It's all right," she said. "I was just changing position. The wall's hard. I just wanted to get more comfortable."

She was concerned about comfort. Banks took that as a good sign. He was within two yards of her now, but he still wasn't close enough to make a grab. At least she didn't tell him to move back. "Just be careful," he said. "It's dangerous. You might slip."

"You seem to be forgetting that's what I'm here for."

"The memory," said Banks. "That day at the pond. It's something to cherish, surely, to live for?"

"No. It just suddenly made me feel that my life's all wrong. Has been for years. I don't feel like *me* anymore. I don't feel anything. Do you know what I mean?"

"I know," said Banks. "But this isn't the answer."

"I don't know," Brenda said, shaking her head. "I just feel so sad and so lost."

"So do I," said Banks, edging a little closer. "Every Christmas since my wife left me for someone else and the kids grew up and moved away from home. But it does mean that you feel something. You said before that you felt nothing, but you do, even if it is only sadness."

"So how do you cope?"

"Me? With what?"

"Being alone. Being abandoned and betrayed."

"I don't know," said Banks. He was desperate for a cigarette, but remembered that he had stopped smoking ages ago. He put his hands in his pockets. The snow was really falling now, obscuring the view. He couldn't even see the ground below.

"Did you love her?" Brenda asked.

The question surprised Banks. He had been quizzing her, but all of a sudden, she was asking about him. He took that as another good sign. "Yes."

"What happened?"

"I suppose I neglected her," said Banks. "My job . . . the hours . . . I don't know. She's a pretty independent person. I thought things were okay, but they weren't."

"I'm sure David thinks everything is fine as long as no one ruffles the surface of his comfortable little world. Were you unfaithful?"

"No. But she was. I don't suppose I blame her now. I did at the time. When she had a baby with him, that really hurt. It seemed . . I don't know . . . the ultimate betrayal, the final gesture."

She had a baby with another man?"

"Yes. I mean, we were divorced, and they got married and everything. My daughter's spending Christmas with them."

"And you?"

Was she starting to feel sorry for him? If she did, then perhaps it would help to make her see that she wasn't the only one suffering, that suffering was a part of life and you just had to put up with it and get on with things. "By myself," he said. "My son's abroad. He's in a rock group. The Blue Lamps. They're doing really well. You might even have heard of them."

"David doesn't like pop music."

"Well . . . they're really good."

"The proud father. My daughter's a stuck-up, social-climbing bitch who's ashamed of her mother."

Banks remembered Janet Mainwaring's reaction to the description of her mother as missing: an embarrassment. "People can be cruel," he said.

"But how do you cope?"

Banks found that he had edged closer to her now, within a yard or so. It was almost grabbing range. That was a last resort, though. If he wasn't quick enough, she might flinch and fall off as he reached for her. "I don't know," he said. "Christmas is a difficult time for all sorts of people. On the surface, it's all peace and happiness and giving and family and love, but underneath . . . You see it a lot in my job. People reach breaking point. There's so much stress."

"But how do *you* cope with it alone? Surely it must all come back and make you feel terrible?"

"Me? I suppose I seek distractions. *A Christmas Carol. Love, Actually* – for Bill Nighy and Keira Knightley – and *David Copperfield*, the one with the Harry Potter actor. I probably drink too much as well."

"Daniel Radcliffe. That's his name. The Harry Potter actor."

"Yes."

"And I'd watch *Love, Actually* for Colin Firth." She shook her head. "But I don't know if it would work for me."

"I recommend it," said Banks. "The perfect antidote to spending Christmas alone and miserable."

"But I wouldn't be alone and miserable, would I? That's the problem. I'd be with my family and miserable."

"You don't have to be."

"What are you suggesting?"

"I told you. Things can change. You can change things." Banks leaned his hip against the wall. He was so close to her now that he could have put his arms around her and pulled her back, but he didn't think he was going to need to. "Do it for yourself," he said.

"Not for them. If you think your husband doesn't love you, leave him and live for yourself."

"Leave David? But where would I go? How would I manage? David has been my life. David and Janet."

"There's always a choice," Banks went on. "There are people who can help you. People who know about these things. Counsellors, social services. Other people have been where you are now. You can get a job, a flat. A new life. I did."

"But where would I go?"

"You'd find somewhere. There are plenty of flats available in Eastvale, for a start."

"I don't know if I can do that. I'm not as strong as you." Banks noticed that she managed a small smile. "And I think if I did, I would have to go far away."

"That's possible, too." Banks reached out his hand. "Let me help you." The snow was coming down heavily now, and the area had become very slippery. She looked at his hand, shaking her head and biting her lip.

"*A Christmas Carol?*" she said.

"Yes."

"I always preferred *It's a Wonderful Life.*"

Banks laughed. "That'll do nicely, too." She took hold of his hand, and he felt her grip tightening as she climbed off the wall and stood up. "Be careful now," he said. "The ground's quite treacherous."

"Isn't it just?" she said, and moved towards him.

The Errors of Santa Claus

by Stephen Leacock

I t was Christmas Eve.

The Browns, who lived in the adjoining house, had been dining with the Joneses.

Brown and Jones were sitting over wine and walnuts at the table. The others had gone upstairs.

"What are you giving to your boy for Christmas?" asked Brown.

"A train," said Jones, "new kind of thing – automatic."

"Let's have a look at it," said Brown.

Jones fetched a parcel from the sideboard and began unwrapping it.

"Ingenious thing, isn't it?" he said. "Goes on its own rails. Queer how kids love to play with trains, isn't it?"

"Yes," assented Brown, "how are the rails fixed?"

"Wait, I'll show you," said Jones, "just help me to shove these dinner things aside and roll back the cloth. There! See! You lay the rails like that and fasten them at the end, so – "

"Oh, yes, I catch on, makes a grade, doesn't it? Just the thing to amuse a child, isn't it? I got Willie a toy aeroplane."

"I know, they're great. I got Edwin one on his birthday. But I thought I'd get him a train this time. I told him Santa Claus was going to bring him something altogether new this time. Edwin, of course, believes in Santa Claus absolutely. Say, look at this loco-motive, would you? It has a spring coiled up inside the fire box."

"Wind her up," said Brown with great interest, "let's see her go."

"All right," said Jones, "just pile up two or three plates or some-thing to lean the end of the rails on. There, notice the way it buzzes before it starts. Isn't that a great thing for a kid, eh?"

"Yes," said Brown, "and say! See this little spring to pull the whistle. By God, it toots, eh? Just like real!"

"Now then, Brown," Jones went on, "you hitch on those cars and I'll start her. I'll be engineer, eh!"

Half an hour later, Brown and Jones were still playing trains on the dining-room table.

But their wives upstairs in the drawing room hardly noticed their absence. They were too much interested.

"Oh, I think it's perfectly sweet," said Mrs. Brown, "just the loveliest doll I've seen in years. I must get one like it for Ulvina. Won't Clarisse be perfectly enchanted?"

"Yes," answered Mrs. Jones, "and then she'll have all the fun of arranging the dresses. Children love that so much. Look! There are three little dresses with the doll, aren't they cute? All cut out and ready to stitch together."

"Oh, how perfectly lovely," exclaimed Mrs. Brown. "I think the mauve one would suit the doll best – don't you? – with such golden hair – only don't you think it would make it much nicer to turn back the collar, so, and put a little band – so?"

"What a good idea!" said Mrs. Jones, "do let's try it. Just wait, I'll get a needle in a minute. I'll tell Clarisse that Santa Claus sewed it himself. The child believes in Santa Claus absolutely."

And half an hour later Mrs. Jones and Mrs. Brown were so busy stitching dolls' clothes that they could not hear the roaring of the little train up and down the dining table, and had no idea what the four children were doing.

Nor did the children miss their mothers.

"Dandy, aren't they?" Edwin Jones was saying to little Willie Brown, as they sat in Edwin's bedroom. "A hundred in a box, with cork tips, and see, an amber mouthpiece that fits into a little case at the side. Good present for dad, eh?"

"Fine!" said Willie, appreciatively. "I'm giving father cigars."

"I know. I thought of cigars, too. Men always like cigars and cigarettes. You can't go wrong on them. Say, would you like to try one or two of these cigarettes? We can take them from the bottom. You'll like them, they're Russian – away ahead of Egyptian."

"Thanks," answered Willie. "I'd like one immensely. I only started smoking last spring – on my twelfth birthday. I think a feller's a fool to begin smoking cigarettes too soon, don't you? It stunts him. I waited till I was twelve."

"Me too," said Edwin, as they lighted their cigarettes. "In fact, I wouldn't buy them now if it weren't for dad. I simply had to give him something from Santa Claus. He believes in Santa Claus absolutely, you know."

And while this was going on, Clarisse was showing little Ulvina the absolutely lovely little bridge set that she got for her mother.

"Aren't these markers perfectly charming?" said Ulvina, "and don't you love this little Dutch design – or is it Flemish, darling?"

"Dutch," said Clarisse, "isn't it quaint? And aren't these the dearest little things – for putting the money in when you play. I needn't have got them with it – they'd have sold the rest separately

– but I think it's too utterly slow playing without money, don't you?"

"Oh, abominable," shuddered Ulvina, "but your mamma never plays for money, does she?"

"Mamma! Oh, gracious, no. Mamma's far too slow for that. But I shall tell her that Santa Claus insisted on putting in the little money boxes."

"I suppose she believes in Santa Claus, just as my Mamma does."

"Oh, absolutely," said Clarisse, and added, "What if we play a little game! With a double dummy, the French way, or Norwegian Skat, if you like. That only needs two."

"All right," agreed Ulvina, and in a few minutes they were deep in a game of cards with a little pile of pocket money beside them.

About half an hour later, all the members of the two families were down again in the drawing room. But of course nobody said anything about the presents. In any case they were all too busy looking at the beautiful big Bible, with maps in it, that the Joneses had bought to give to Grandfather. They all agreed that, with the help of it, Grandfather could hunt up any place in Palestine in a moment, day or night.

But upstairs, away upstairs in a sitting room of his own, Grandfather Jones was looking with an affectionate eye at the presents that stood beside him. There was a beautiful whiskey decanter, with silver filigree outside (and whiskey inside) for Jones, and for the little boy a big nickel-plated Jew's harp.

Later on, far in the night, the person, or the influence, or whatever it is called Santa Claus, took all the presents and placed them in the people's stockings.

And, being blind as he always had been, he gave the wrong things to the wrong people – in fact, he gave them just as indicated above.

But the next day, in the course of Christmas morning, the situation straightened itself out, as it always does.

Indeed, by ten o'clock, Brown and Jones were playing with the train, and Mrs. Brown and Mrs. Jones were making dolls' clothes, and the boys were smoking cigarettes, and Clarisse and Ulvina were playing cards for their pocket money.

And upstairs – away up – Grandfather was drinking whiskey and playing the Jew's harp.

And so Christmas, just as it always does, turned out all right after all.

An Irish Jig

by *Eric Wright*

I t had been raining on and off all day, but this was Ireland and they were prepared for it. They had no intention of letting a few showers interfere with their holiday.

They arrived at the hotel in Dublin in plenty of time to take the small nap their age required, and to make plans for the evening. "There's a place called Bewley's that advertises light suppers," Mrs. Grantham said. "It's on our way. If the rain's stopped, we could walk there and be at the theatre in plenty of time." They had been lucky enough to get two tickets for a new play by Brian Friel at the Abbey Theatre. They had seen two of his earlier plays and enjoyed them very much.

When they were rested, the sky was clear and they had a lovely walk to Bewley's, across the green, past the Shelbourne Hotel, which they promised themselves to stay in one day.

"Ireland!" Mrs. Grantham said. "It's just like I imagined."

The light supper was excellent: fish cakes followed by an apple tart. The play, though, was not the holiday entertainment they were looking for but a dramatization of a terrible incident in the ongoing civil struggle. They left at the first intermission.

"A bit grim," Mr. Grantham said. "Still, we've seen the Abbey Theatre."

Although the streets were wet with a recent shower, the rain had stopped, and they decided to walk back to the hotel to see what Irish television had to offer. The sky stayed clear and starry until they reached their hotel.

The hotel consisted of two large houses, back-to-back on parallel streets, joined by an inner courtyard fashioned out of the two gardens. The path across the courtyard was covered with a corrugated plastic roof but not enclosed, and the whole courtyard was bricked in by walls six feet high. At night, they had been told, only the front door was open, and so they had to walk round to the next street, through the other house, across the courtyard and along the corridor to reach their room.

Mr. Grantham fiddled with the door key for a long time until his wife took the key from him and jiggled with it herself before giving up. "You'll have to go back to the desk and tell them to come and unstick this lock," she said. "I'll wait here. Don't hang about."

When he returned, he was accompanied by the night manager, a youth in his late teens, who took his turn at jiggling the key. "It's not responding," he said looking at them for help.

"Call the landlord," Mrs. Grantham said.

"He's in Sligo, at his holiday cottage. I'll get my arse in a sling if I phone him there."

"Then call a locksmith."

"This time of night, he'll want 50 pounds!"

"At least," Mr. Grantham agreed. You'd better call Sligo first and get an okay."

"Sure I had," the manager said. "Would you wait in the lounge while I call, then?"

"We'll stay here," Mrs. Grantham said.

The landlord in Sligo gave his permission, a locksmith was named and found, one who owed the landlord a favour for business put in his way, and half-an-hour later they were in the room. "The inside bolt was on," the locksmith explained as he withdrew his probe. "It's supposed to keep out burglars."

The four of them stood there for a couple of minutes. Then Mrs. Grantham said, "I didn't close the curtains like that." She crossed the room and took her suitcase from the closet and opened it. "I knew someone had been in the room," she said. "I've been robbed." She peered into a wallet that she had kept in the case. "All my English money is gone, and the Canadian."

"Ah, no," the manager said. "You've mislaid it surely."

Mr. Grantham opened his own case, which he had hidden under the bed. "Mine's gone, too," he said. "Just the money. They've left the travellers' cheques and the passports. You'd better call the police."

When the garda arrived, he noted everything down, saying about the failure to take the passports, "It'll be just kids, then." He walked to the window, looked out, and added, "They came over the wall, onto the covering over the walkway, up the drainpipe and in. Easy. I could have done it meself, once." He patted his stomach and looked up at the window, which was locked from the inside. "Did you just lock that, sir?"

Mrs. Grantham said, "No. I left it open a bit because it was so warm."

"So he came in through the window, locked it shut after him, then left through the door. Right?"

Mrs. Grantham said, "I only left it open about six inches."

"Be a little fella, then," the policeman said.

The locksmith said, "How did he get out and lock the door after him as well as the window?"

"That we have to sort out," the garda said. "What we have here is a real Locked Room Mystery. I know all about them."

Mrs. Grantham crossed the room and sat on the window seat under the window. "Perhaps if he locked the window first, then shut the door hard behind him, the bolt sort of slid shut. What do you think, constable?" She looked at her husband. "I'm enjoying this." She took a peppermint from her purse and sucked on it while the garda thought.

"I think I've got it," he said. "I saw it done in Toronto by a book writer. A demonstration. What he did was tie a piece of thread round the knob of the bolt, and pass the thread through the keyhole. Then he closed the door – it fit very loose like this one – and pulled on the thread to jerk the bolt along. He didn't tie the thread, you understand, just wrapped it around the stem of the knob three or four times, enough to take the strain. Then when he'd slid the bolt across, he could pull a little bit harder and unravel the thread. Yes, that's the way of it. Perfect."

"And unbelievable," Mr. Grantham said. "You saw the locksmith free up the bolt. There was still so much old paint on that bolt you'd need a hammer to move it."

"Oh, now, George, it's a lovely solution. Don't spoil it. Now officer, we'll have to claim our money from the insurance people. We'll need your corroboration."

"I'll send you a copy of my report, ma'am. Might take a month or so. We're very busy with all the holiday traffic."

"Where do we start?"

"You'll have to make a statement in the morning. Down at the station."

"We're leaving on the 8 o'clock ferry from Dun Laoghaire," she said, flaunting her pronunciation.

"Then you could write when you get home, from Canada. My sergeant will take it up eventually."

"What are the odds, do you think, of our ever seeing our money again?" Mr. Grantham asked.

"Well, it's not a lot you've lost, is it, sir? It won't interfere with your holiday, I shouldn't think." He put away his notebook. "I'll say goodnight, then. There's a man on the night shift fancies himself as a bit of a book writer. Mysteries. He'll be interested in this."

The night manager waited for the door to close, then said, "The owner told me there'll be no charge for the room. He's very upset it should happen to a guest in the hotel."

They shook his hand as he backed out of the door.

Mr. Grantham said, "With a hundred off for the room I think we should write the rest off to experience."

"No need for that," his wife said. "Bolt that door, and get hold of that poker." She pointed to the fire irons in the hearth. Then she slipped off the window seat and opened the lid. "Out you come," she said.

A scruffy, underfed boy, perhaps 13 years old, poked his head above the edge of the box, looked warily at Mr. Grantham, who stepped back to let him get out. The boy uncoiled himself and slid out on to the floor, where he stayed crouched.

"Don't think of running," Mr. Grantham said, waving the poker. "You'd have me and two sets of bolts and locks to get through. You'd never make it."

"How did ye know I was in there, missus?" the boy croaked, straightening himself up.

"It was the only answer. I eliminated the impossible, including the garda's silly idea about the bolt, and I was left with the improbable truth that you were still here. Besides I saw you lift the lid a bit when we first came in. Now, 400 pounds, please."

The boy put his hand down his sock and pulled out a flat wad of bills. He tried for a smile. "You'll be making a profit now, will ye not? I heard him give you a free room. And you can claim on the insurance."

"It's everybody's lucky night," Mrs. Grantham said. "In a minute we will turn our backs and you will make a run for it, through the back door."

"You're never going to let us go?"

"Yes. Before you do, though, I want to know why you closed the window again. You might have got away while we were trying the door."

"True enough. But it started to rain and was blowin' the curtain in so someone outside could see in. I had to have a light on. So I closed the window to close the curtains. Then I couldn't lift it up."

"Why did you bolt the door?"

"So I wouldn't be disturbed. In case. I didn't expect you for another hour. That would be normal for folks on a holiday, wouldn't it?"

"Go on now. Go."

"Could you spare me a little something before I go?" He pointed at the money in her hand. "I haven't got a copper. I'll nivver say a word."

She laughed and gave him a 20 pound note.

"You're a dascent skin, missus so you are."

When the boy had gone, Mr. Grantham asked, "Why?"

"Do you want to spend tomorrow morning filling out forms in a police station? Miss our ferry? Wait heaven knows how long for the next ferry? Arrive late and pick our way across Wales in the dark?"

"All right, all right. But you didn't have to tip the little bastard."

"I didn't have to, no. I just thought he'd earned it."

A Crow Girls' Christmas

by Charles de Lint and MaryAnn Harris

"We have jobs," Maida told Jilly when she and Zia dropped by the professor's house for a visit at the end of November.

Zia nodded happily. "Yes, we've become veryvery respectable."

Jilly had to laugh. "I can't imagine either of you ever being completely respectable."

That comment drew an exaggerated pout from each of the crow girls, the one more pronounced than the other.

"Not being completely respectable's a good thing," Jilly assured them.

"Yes, well, easy for you to say," Zia said. "You don't have a cranky uncle always asking when you're going to do something useful for a change."

Maida nodded. "You just get to wheel around and around in your chair and not worry about all the very serious things that we do."

"Such as?" Jilly asked.

Zia shrugged. "Why *don't* pigs fly?"

"Or why is white a colour?" Maida offered.

"Or black."

"Or yellow ochre."

"Yellow ochre is a colour," Jilly said. "Two colours, actually. And white and black are colours, too. Though I suppose they're not very *colourful*, are they?"

"Could it be more puzzling?" Zia asked.

Maida simply smiled and held out her tea cup. "May I have a refill, please?"

Jilly pushed the sugar bag over to her. Maida filled her tea cup to the brim with sugar. After a glance at Zia, she filled Zia's tea cup as well.

"Would you like some?" she asked Jilly.

"No, I'm quite full. Besides, too much tea makes me have to pee."

The crow girls giggled.

"So what sort of jobs did you get?" Jilly asked.

Zia lowered her teacup and licked the sugar from her upper lip. "We're elves!" she said.

Maida nodded happily. "At the mall. We get to help out Santa."

"Not the *real* Santa," Zia explained.

"No, no. He's much too very busy making toys at the North Pole."

"This is sort of a cloned Santa."

"Every mall has one, you know."

"And *we*," Zia pronounced proudly, "are in charge of handing out the candy canes."

"Oh my," Jilly said, thinking of the havoc that could cause.

"Which makes us very important," Maida said.

"Not to mention useful."

"So pooh to Lucius, who thinks we're not."

"Do they have lots of candy canes in stock?" Jilly asked.

"Mountains," Zia assured.

"Besides," Maida added. "It's all magic, isn't it? Santa never runs out of candy or toys."

That was before you were put in charge of the candy canes, Jilly thought, but she kept her worry to herself.

Much to everyone's surprise, the crow girls made excellent elves. They began their first daily four-hour shift on December 1, dressed in matching red-and-green outfits that the mall provided: long-sleeved jerseys, short pleated skirts, tights, shoes with exaggerated curling toes, and droopy elf hats with their rowdy black hair poking out from underneath. There were bells on their shoes, bells at the end of their hats, and they each wore brooches made of bells that they'd borrowed from one of the stores in the mall. Because they found it next to impossible to stand still for more than a few seconds at a time, the area around Santa's chair echoed with their constant jingling. Parents waiting in line, not to mention their eager children, were completely enchanted by their happy antics and the ready smiles on their small dark faces.

"I thought they'd last fifteen minutes," their uncle Lucius confided to the professor a few days after the pair had started, "but they've surprised me."

"I don't see why," the professor said. "It seems to me that they'd be perfectly suited for the job. They're about as elfish as you can get without being an elf."

"But they're normally so easily distracted."

The professor nodded. "However, there's candy involved, isn't there? Jilly tells me that they've been put in charge of the candy canes."

"And isn't that a source for pride." Lucius shook his head and smiled. "Trust them to find a way to combine sweets with work."

"They'll be the Easter Bunny's helpers in the spring."

Lucius laughed. "Maybe I can apprentice them to the Tooth Fairy."

The crow girls really were perfectly suited to their job. Unlike many of the tired shoppers that trudged by Santa's chair, they remained enthralled with every aspect of their new environment. The flashing lights. The jingling bells. The glittering tinsel. The piped-in Christmas music. The shining ornaments.

And, of course, the great abundance of candy canes.

They treated each child's questions and excitement as though that child was the first to have this experience. They talked to those waiting in line, made faces so that the children would laugh happily as they were having their pictures taken, handed out candy canes when the children were lifted down from Santa's lap. They paid rapt attention to every wish expressed and adored hearing about all the wonderful toys available in the shops.

Some children, normally shy about a visit to Santa, returned again and again, completely smitten with the pair.

But mostly, it was all about the candy canes.

The crow girls were extremely generous in handing them out, and equally enthusiastic about their own consumption. They stopped themselves from eating as many as they might have liked, but did consume one little candy cane each for every five minutes they were on the job.

Santa, busy with the children, and also enamored with his cheerful helpers, failed to notice that the sacks of candy canes in the storage area behind his chair were dwindling at an astonishing rate. He never thought to look because it had never been an issue before. There'd always been plenty of candy canes to go around in the past.

On December 19, at the beginning of their noon shift, there were already lines and lines of children waiting excitedly to visit Santa and his crow girl elves. As the photographer was unhooking the cord to let the children in, Maida turned to Zia to ask where the next sack of candy canes was just as Zia asked Maida the very same question. Santa suggested that they'd better hurry up and grab another sack from the storage space.

Trailing the sound of jingling bells, the crow girls went behind his chair.

Zia pulled aside the little curtain.

"Uh-oh," she said.

Maida pushed in beside her to have a look herself. The two girls exchanged worried looks.

"They're all gone," Zia told Santa.

"I'll go to the stockroom for more," Maida offered.

Zia nodded. "Me, too."

"What stockroom?" Santa began.

But then he realized exactly what they were saying. His normally rosy cheeks went as white as his whiskers.

"They're all gone?" he asked. "*All* those bags of candy canes?"

"In a word, yes."

"But where could they all have gone?"

"We give them away," Maida reminded him. "Remember?"

Zia nodded. "We were supposed to."

"So that's what we did."

"Because it's our job."

"And we ate a few," Maida admitted.

"A very very few."

Santa frowned. "How many is a few?"

"Hmm," Zia said.

"Good question."

"Let's see."

They both began to count on their fingers as they talked.

"We were very very careful not to eat more than twelve an hour."

"Oh so very careful."

"So in four hours –"

" – that would be forty-eight – "

" – times two – "

" – because there are two of us."

They paused for a moment, as though to ascertain that there really were only two of them.

"So that would be . . . um . . ."

"Ninety-six – "

" – times how many days?"

"Eighteen – "

" – not counting today – "

" – because there aren't any today – "

" – which is why we need to go to the stockroom to get more."

Santa was adding it all up himself. "That's almost two thousand candy canes you've eaten!"

"Well . . . almost," Maida said.

"One thousand seven hundred and twenty-eight," Zia said.

"If you're keeping count."

"Which is *almost* two thousand, I suppose, but not really."

"Where *is* the candy cane stockroom?" Maida asked.

"There isn't one," Santa told her.

"But –"

"And that means," he added, "that all the children here today won't get any candy canes."

The crow girls looked horrified.

"That means us, too," Zia said.

Maida nodded. "We'll also suffer, you know."

"But we're ever so stoic."

"Ask anybody."

"We'll hardly complain."

"And never where you can hear us."

"Except for now, of course."

Santa buried his face in his hands, completely disconcerting the parent approaching his chair, child in hand.

"Don't worry!" Maida cried.

"We have everything under control." Zia looked at Maida. "We do, don't we?"

Maida closed her eyes for a long moment, then opened them wide and grinned.

"Free tinsel for everyone!" she cried.

"I don't want tinsel," the little boy standing in front of Santa with his mother said. "I want a candy cane."

"Oh, you do want tinsel," Maida assured him.

"Why does he want tinsel?" Zia asked.

"Because ... because ..."

Maida grabbed two handfuls from the boughs of Santa's Christmas tree. Fluttering the tinsel with both hands over her head, she ran around the small enclosure that housed Santa's chair.

"Because it's so fluttery!" she cried.

Zia immediately understood. "And shiny!" Grinning, she grabbed handfuls of her own.

"Veryvery shiny," Maida agreed.

"And almost as good as candy," Zia assured the little boy as she handed him some. "Though not quite as sugary good."

The little boy took the tinsel with a doubtful look, but then Zia whirled him about in a sudden impromptu dance. Soon he was laughing and waving his tinsel as well. From the line, all the children began to clap.

"We want tinsel, too!" one of them cried.

"Tinsel, tinsel!"

The crow girls got through their shift with great success. They danced and twirled on the spot and did mad acrobatics. They fluttered tinsel, blew kisses, jingled their bells, and told stories so outrageous that no one believed them, but everyone laughed.

By the end of their shift, even Santa had come around to seeing "the great excellent especially good fortune of free tinsel."

Unfortunately, the mall management wasn't so easily appeased, and the crow girls left the employ of the Williamson Street Mall that very day, after first having to turn in their red-and-green elf outfits. But on the plus side, they were paid for their nineteen days of work and spent all their money on chocolate and fudge and candy and ice cream.

When they finally toddled out of the mall into the snowy night, they made chubby snow angels on any lawn they could find, all the way back to the Rookery.

"So now we're unemployed," Zia told Jilly when they came over for a visit on the twenty-third, shouting, "Happy eve before Christmas Eve!" as they trooped into the professor's house.

"I heard," Jilly said.

"It was awful," Maida said.

Jilly nodded. "Losing a job's never fun."

"No, no, no," Zia said. "They ran out of candy canes!"

"Can you imagine?" Maida asked.

Zia shook her head. "Barely. And I was there."

"Well, I'm sorry to hear that," Jilly said.

"Yes, it's a veryvery sorrysome state of affairs," Maida said.

"And we're unemployed, too!"

"Lucius says we're unemployable."

"Because now we have a record."

"A permanent record."

"Of being bad bad candy cane-eating girls."

They both looked so serious and sad that Jilly became worried. But then Zia laughed. And Maida laughed too.

"What's so funny?" Jilly asked.

Zia started to answer, but she collapsed in giggles and couldn't speak.

Maida giggled, too, but she managed to say, "We sort of like being bad bad candy-cane-eating girls."

Zia got her fit of giggles under control. "Because it's like being outlaws."

"Fierce candy cane-eating outlaw girls."

"And that's a good thing?" Jilly asked.

"What do you think?" Maida asked.

"I think it is. Merry Christmas, Maida. Merry Christmas, Zia."

"Merry Christmas to you!" they both cried.

Zia looked at Maida. "Why did you say, 'Merry Christmas toot toot'?"

"I didn't say 'toot toot.'"

"I think maybe you did."

"Didn't."

Zia grinned. "Toot toot!"

"Toot toot!"

They pulled their jingling bell brooches out of their pockets, which they'd forgotten to return to the store where they'd "found" them, and marched around the kitchen singing "Jingle Bells" at the top of their lungs until Goon, the professor's housekeeper, came in and made them stop.

Then they sat at the table with their cups of sugar, on their best behavior, which meant they only took their brooches out every few moments, jingled them, and said "toot toot" very quietly. Then, giggling, they'd put the brooches away again.

The Turkey Season

by Alice Munro

When I was fourteen I got a job at the Turkey Barn for the Christmas season. I was still too young to get a job working in a store or as a part-time waitress; I was also too nervous.

I was a turkey gutter. The other people who worked at the Turkey Barn were Lily and Marjorie and Gladys, who were also gutters; Irene and Henry, who were pluckers; Herb Abbott, the foreman, who superintended the whole operation and filled in wherever he was needed. Morgan Elliott was the owner and boss. He and his son, Morgy, did the killing.

Morgy I knew from school. I thought him stupid and despicable and was uneasy about having to consider him in a new and possibly superior guise, as the boss's son. But his father treated him so roughly, yelling and swearing at him that he seemed no more than the lowest of the workers. The other person related to the boss was Gladys. She was his sister and in her case there did seem to be some privilege of position. She worked slowly and went home if she was not feeling well and was not friendly to Lily and Marjorie, although she was a little, to me. She had come back to live with Morgan and his family after working for many years in Toronto, in a bank. This was not the sort of job she was used to. Lily and Marjorie, talking about her when she wasn't there, said she had had a nervous breakdown. They said Morgan made her work in the Turkey Barn to pay for her keep. They also said, with no worry about the contradiction, that she had taken the job because she was after a man, and that the man was Herb Abbott.

All I could see when I closed my eyes, the first few nights after working there, was turkeys. I saw them hanging upside down, plucked and stiffened, pale and cold, with the heads and necks limp, the eyes and nostrils clotted with dark blood; the remaining bits of feathers – those dark and bloody, too – seemed to form a crown. I saw them not with aversion but with a sense of endless work to be done.

Herb Abbott showed me what to do. You put the turkey down on the table and cut its head off with a cleaver. Then you took the loose skin around the neck and stripped it back to reveal the crop, nestled in the cleft between the gullet and the windpipe.

"Feel the gravel," said Herb encouragingly. He made me close my fingers around the crop. Then he showed me how to work my hand down behind it to cut it out, and the gullet and windpipe as well. He used shears to cut the vertebrae.

"Scrunch, scrunch," he said soothingly. "Now, put your hand in."

I did. It was deathly cold in there, in the turkey's dark insides.

"Watch out for bone splinters."

Working cautiously in the dark, I had to pull the connecting tissues loose.

"Ups-a-daisy." Herb turned the bird over and flexed each leg. "Knees up, Mother Brown. Now." He took a heavy knife and placed it directly on the knee knuckle joints and cut off the shank.

"Have a look at the worms."

Pearly-white strings, pulled out of the shank, were creeping about on their own.

"That's just the tendons shrinking. Now comes the nice part!"

He slit the bird at its bottom end, letting out a rotten smell.

"Are you educated?"

I did not know what to say.

"What's that smell?"

"Hydrogen sulfide."

"Educated," said Herb, sighing. "All right. Work your fingers around and get the guts loose. Easy. Easy. Keep your fingers together. Keep the palm inwards. Feel the ribs with the back of your hand. Feel the guts fit into your palm. Feel that? Keep going. Break the strings – as many as you can. Keep going. Feel a hard lump? That's the gizzard. Feel a soft lump? That's the heart. O.K.? O.K. Get your fingers around the gizzard. Easy. Start pulling this way. That's right. That's right. Start to pull her out."

It was not easy at all. I wasn't even sure what I had was the gizzard. My hand was full of cold pulp.

"Pull," he said, and I brought out a glistening, liverish mass.

"Got it. There's the lights. You know what they are? Lungs. There's the heart. There's the gizzard. There's the gall. Now, you don't ever want to break that gall inside or it will taste the entire turkey." Tactfully, he scraped out what I had missed, including the testicles, which were like a pair of white grapes.

"Nice pair of earrings," Herb said.

Herb Abbott was a tall, firm, plump man. His hair was dark and thin, combed straight back from a widow's peak, and his eyes seemed to be slightly slanted, so that he looked like a pale Chinese or like pictures of the Devil, except that he was smooth-faced and benign. Whatever he did around the Turkey Barn – gutting, as he was now, or loading the truck, or hanging the carcasses – was done with efficient, economical movements, quickly and buoyantly. "Notice about Herb – he always walks like he had a boat moving underneath him," Marjorie said, and it was true. Herb worked on the lake boats, during the season, as a cook. Then he worked for Morgan until after Christmas. The rest of the time he helped around the poolroom, making hamburgers, sweeping up, stopping fights before they got started. That was where he lived; he had a room above the poolroom on the main street.

In all the operations at the Turkey Barn it seemed to be Herb who had the efficiency and honour of the business continually on his mind; it was he who kept everything under control. Seeing him in the yard talking to Morgan, who was a thick, short man, red in the face, an unpredictable bully, you would be sure that it was Herb who was the boss and Morgan the hired help. But it was not so.

If I had not had Herb to show me, I don't think I could have learned turkey gutting at all. I was clumsy with my hands and had been shamed for it so often that the least show of impatience on the part of the person instructing me could have brought on a dithering paralysis. I could not stand to be watched by anybody but Herb. Particularly, I couldn't stand to be watched by Lily and Marjorie, two middle-aged sisters, who were very fast and thorough and competitive gutters. They sang at their work and talked abusively and intimately to the turkey carcasses.

"Don't you nick me, you old bugger!"

"Aren't you the old crap factory!"

I had never heard women talk like that.

Gladys was not a fast gutter, though she must have been thorough; Herb would have talked to her otherwise. She never sang and certainly she never swore. I thought her rather old, though she was not as old as Lily and Marjorie; she must have been over thirty. She seemed offended by everything that went on and had the air of keeping plenty of bitter judgments to herself. I never tried to talk to her, but she spoke to me one day in the cold little washroom off the gutting shed. She was putting pancake makeup on her face. The colour of the makeup was so distinct from the colour of her skin that it was as if she were slapping orange paint over a whitewashed, bumpy wall.

She asked me if my hair was naturally curly.

I said yes.

"You don't have to get a permanent?"

"No."

"You're lucky. I have to do mine up every night. The chemicals in my system won't allow me to get a permanent."

There are different ways women have of talking about their looks. Some women make it clear that what they do to keep themselves up is for the sake of sex, for men. Others, like Gladys, make the job out to be a kind of housekeeping, whose very difficulties they pride themselves on. Gladys was genteel. I could see her in the bank, in a navy-blue dress with the kind of detachable white collar you can wash at night. She would be grumpy and correct.

Another time, she spoke to me about her periods, which were profuse and painful. She wanted to know about mine. There was an uneasy, prudish, agitated expression on her face. I was saved by Irene, who was using the toilet and called out, "Do like me, and you'll be rid of all your problems for a while." Irene was only a few years older than I was, but she was recently – tardily – married, and heavily pregnant.

Gladys ignored her, running cold water on her hands. The hands of all of us were red and sore-looking from the work. "I can't use that soap. If I use it, I break out in a rash," Gladys said.

"If I bring my own soap in here, I can't afford to have other people using it, because I pay a lot for it – it's a special anti-allergy soap."

I think the idea that Lily and Marjorie promoted – that Gladys was after Herb Abbott – sprang from their belief that single people ought to be teased and embarrassed whenever possible, and from their interest in Herb, which led to the feeling that somebody ought to be after him. They wondered about him. What they wondered was: How can a man want so little? No wife, no family, no house. The details of his daily life, the small preferences, were of interest. Where had he been brought up? (Here and there and all over.) How far had he gone in school? (Far enough.) Where was his girlfriend? (Never tell.) Did he drink coffee or tea if he got the choice? (Coffee.)

When they talked about Gladys's being after him they must have really wanted to talk about sex – what he wanted and what he got. They must have felt a voluptuous curiosity about him, as I did. He aroused this feeling by being circumspect and not making the jokes some men did, and at the same time by not being squeamish or gentlemanly. Some men, showing me the testicles from the turkey, would have acted as if the very existence of testicles were somehow a bad joke on me, something a girl could be taunted about; another sort of man would have been embarrassed and would have thought he had to protect me from embarrassment. A man who didn't seem to feel one way or the other was an oddity – as much to older women, probably, as to me. But what was so welcome to me may have been disturbing to them. They wanted to jolt him. They even wanted Gladys to jolt him, if she could.

There wasn't any idea then – at least in Logan, Ontario, in the late forties – about homosexuality's going beyond very narrow confines. Women, certainly, believed in its rarity and in definite boundaries. There were homosexuals in town, and we knew who they were: an elegant, light-voiced, wavy-haired paperhanger who called himself an interior decorator; the minister's widow's fat, spoiled only son, who went so far as to enter baking contests and had crocheted a tablecloth; a hypochondriacal church organist and music teacher who kept the choir and his pupils in line with screaming tantrums. Once the label was fixed, there was a good deal of tolerance for these people, and their talents for decorating, for crocheting, and for music were appreciated – especially by women. "The poor fellow," they said. "He doesn't do any harm." They really seemed to believe – the women did – that it was the penchant for baking or music that was the determining factor, and that it was this activity that made the man what he was – not any other detours he might take, or wish to take. A desire to play the violin would be taken as more a deviation from manliness than would a wish to shun women. Indeed, the idea was any manly man would wish to shun women but most of them were caught off guard, and for good.

I don't want to go into the question of whether Herb was homosexual or not, because the definition is of no use to me. I think that probably he was, but maybe was not. (Even considering what happed later, I think that.) He is not a puzzle so arbitrarily solved.

The other plucker, who worked with Irene, was Henry Streets, a neighbour of ours. There was nothing remarkable about him except that he was eighty-six years old and still, as he said of himself, a devil for work. He had whiskey in his thermos, and drank it from time to time through the day. It was Henry who had said to me, in our kitchen, "You ought to get yourself a job at the Turkey Barn. They need another gutter." Then my father said at once, "Not her, Henry. She's got ten thumbs," and Henry said he was just joking – it was dirty work. But I was already determined to try it – I had a great need to be successful in a job like this. I was almost in the condition of a grownup person who is ashamed of never having learned to read, so much did I feel my ineptness at manual work. Work, to everybody I knew, meant doing things I was no good at doing, and work was what people prided themselves on and measured each other by. (It goes without saying that the things I was good at, like schoolwork, were suspect or held in plain contempt.) So it was a surprise and then a triumph for me not to get fired, and to be able to turn out clean turkeys at a rate that was not disgraceful. I don't know if I really understood how much Herb Abbott was responsible for this, but he would sometimes say, "Good girl," or pat my waist and say, "You're getting to be a good gutter – you'll go a long ways in the world," and when I felt his quick, kind touch through the heavy sweater and bloody smock I wore, I felt my face glow and I wanted to rest my head against his wide fleshy shoulder. When I went to sleep at night, lying on my side, I would rub my check against the pillow and think of that as Herb's shoulder.

I was interested in how he talked to Gladys, how he looked at her or noticed her. This interest was not jealous. I think I wanted something to happen with them. I quivered in curious expectation, as Lily and Marjorie did. We all wanted to see the flicker of sexuality in him, hear it in his voice, not because we thought it would make him seem more like other men but because we knew that with him it would be entirely different. He was kinder and more patient than most women, and as stern and remote, in some ways, as any man. We wanted to see how he could be moved.

If Gladys wanted this, too, she didn't give any signs of it. It is impossible for me to tell with women like her whether they are as thick and deadly as they seem, not wanting anything much but opportunities for irritation and contempt, or if they are all choked up with gloomy fires and useless passions.

Marjorie and Lily talked about marriage. They did not have much good to say about it, in spite of their feeling that it was a state nobody should be allowed to stay out of. Marjorie said that shortly after her marriage she had gone into the woodshed with the intention of swallowing Paris green.

"I'd have done it," she said. "But the man came along in the grocery truck and I had to go out and buy the groceries. This was when we lived on the farm."

Her husband was cruel to her in those days, but later he suffered an accident – he rolled the tractor and was so badly hurt he would be an invalid all his life. They moved to town, and Marjorie was the boss now.

"He starts to sulk the other night and say he don't want his supper. Well, I just picked up his wrist and held it. He was scared I was going to twist his arm. He could see I'd do it. So I say, 'You *what*?' And he says, 'I'll eat it.'"

They talked about their father. He was a man of the old school. He had a noose in the woodshed (not the Paris green woodshed – this would be an earlier one, on another farm), and when they got on his nerves he used to line them up and threaten to hang them. Lily, who was the younger, would shake till she fell down. This same father had arranged to marry Marjorie off to a crony of his when she was just sixteen. That was the husband who had driven her to the Paris green. Their father did it because he wanted to be sure she wouldn't get into trouble.

"Hot blood," Lily said.

I was horrified, and asked, "Why didn't you run away?"

"His word was law," Marjorie said.

They said that was what was the matter with kids nowadays – it was the kids that ruled the roost. A father's word should be law. They brought up their own kids strictly, and none had turned out bad yet. When Marjorie's son wet the bed she threatened to cut off his dingy with the butcher knife. That cured him.

They said ninety per cent of the young girls nowadays drank, and swore, and took it lying down. They did not have daughters, but if they did and caught them at anything like that they would beat them raw. Irene, they said, used to go to the hockey games with her ski pants slit and nothing under them, for convenience in the snowdrifts afterward. Terrible.

I wanted to point out some contradictions. Marjorie and Lily themselves drank and swore, and what was so wonderful about the strong will of a father who would ensure you a lifetime of unhappiness? (What I did not see was that Marjorie and Lily were not unhappy altogether – could not be, because of their sense of consequence, their pride and style.) I could be enraged then at the lack of logic in most adults' talk – the way they held to their pronouncements no matter what evidence might be presented to them. How could these women's hands be so gifted, so delicate and clever – for I knew they would be as good as dozens of other jobs as they were at gutting; they would be good at quilting and darning and painting and papering and kneading dough and setting out seedlings – and their thinking so slapdash, clumsy, infuriating?

Lily said she never let her husband come near her if he had been drinking. Marjorie said since the time she nearly died with a hemorrhage she never let her husband come near her, period. Lily said quickly that it was only when he'd been drinking that he tried anything. I could see that it was a matter of pride not to let your husband come near you, but I couldn't quite believe that "come near" meant "have sex." The idea of Marjorie and Lily being sought out for such purposes seemed grotesque. They had bad teeth, their stomachs sagged, their faces were dully and spotty. I decided to take "come near" literally.

The two weeks before Christmas was a frantic time at the Turkey Barn. I began to go in for an hour before school as well as after school and on weekends. In the morning, when I walked to work, the street lights would still be on and the morning stars shining. There was the Turkey Barn, on the edge of a white field, with a row of big pine trees behind it, and always, no matter how cold and still it was, these trees were lifting their branches and sighing and straining. It seems unlikely that on my way to the Turkey Barn, for an hour of gutting turkeys, I should have experienced such a sense of promise and at the same time of perfect, impenetrable mystery in the universe, but I did. Herb had something to do with that, and so did the cold snap – the series of hard, clear mornings. The truth is, such feelings weren't hard to come by then. I would get them but not know how they were to be connected with anything in real life.

One morning at the Turkey Barn there was a new gutter. This was a boy eighteen or nineteen years old, a stranger named Brian. It seemed he was a relative, or perhaps just a friend, of Herb Abbott's. He was staying with Herb. He had worked on a lake boat last summer. He said he had got sick of it, though, and quit.

What he said was, "Yeah, fuckin' boats. I got sick of that."

Language at the Turkey Barn was coarse and free, but this was one word never heard there. And Brian's use of it seemed not careless but flaunting, mixing insult and provocation. Perhaps it was his general style that made it so. He had amazing good looks: taffy hair, bright-blue eyes, ruddy skin, well-shaped body – the sort of good looks nobody disagrees about for a moment. But a single, relentless notion had got such a hold on him that he could not keep from turning all his assets into parody. His mouth was wet-looking and slightly open most of the time. His eyes were half shut, his expression a hopeful leer, his movements indolent, exaggerated, inviting. Perhaps if he had been put on a stage with a microphone and a guitar and let grunt and howl and wriggle and excite, he would have seemed a true celebrant. Lacking a stage, he was unconvincing. After a while he seemed just like somebody with a bad case of hiccups – his insistent sexuality was that monotonous and meaningless.

If he had toned down a bit, Marjorie and Lily would probably have enjoyed him. They could have kept up a game of telling him to shut his filthy mouth and keep his hands to himself. As it was, they said they were sick of him, and meant it. Marjorie took up her gutting knife. "Keep your distance," she said. "I mean from me and my sister and that kid."

She did not tell him to keep his distance from Gladys, because Gladys wasn't there at the time and Marjorie would probably not have felt like protecting her anyway. But it was Gladys Brian particularly liked to bother. She would throw down her knife and go into the washroom and stay there ten minutes and come out with a stony face. She didn't say she was sick anymore and go home, the way she used to. Marjorie said Morgan was mad at Gladys for sponging and she couldn't get away with it any longer.

Gladys said to me, "I can't stand that kind of thing. I can't stand people mentioning that kind of thing and that kind of – gestures. It makes me sick to my stomach."

I believed her. She was terribly white. But why, in that case, did she not complain to Morgan? Perhaps relations between them were too uneasy, perhaps she could not bring herself to repeat or describe such things. Why did none of us complain – if not to Morgan, at least to Herb? I never thought of it. Brian seemed just something to put up with, like the freezing cold in the gutting shed and the smell of blood and waste. When Marjorie and Lily did threaten to complain, it was about Brian's laziness.

He was not a good gutter. He said his hands were too big. So Herb took him off gutting, told him he was to sweep and clean up, make packages of giblets, and help load the truck. This meant that he did not have to be in any one place or doing any one job at a given time, so much of the time he did nothing. He would start sweeping up, leave that and mop the tables, leave that and have a cigarette, lounge against the table bothering us until Herb called him to help load. Herb was very busy now and spent a lot of time making deliveries, so it was possible he did not know the extent of Brian's idleness.

"I don't know why Herb don't fire you, Marjorie said. "I guess the answer is he don't want you hanging around sponging on him, with no place to go."

"I know where to go," said Brian.

"Keep your sloppy mouth shut," said Marjorie. "I pity Herb. Getting saddled."

On the last school day before Christmas we got out early in the afternoon. I went home and changed my clothes and came into work at about three o'clock. Nobody was working. Everybody was in the gutting shed, where Morgan Elliott was swinging a cleaver over the gutting table and yelling. I couldn't make out what the yelling was about, and thought someone must have made a terrible mistake in his work; perhaps it had been me. Then I saw Brian on the other side of the table, looking very sulky and mean, and standing well back. The sexual leer was not altogether gone from his face, but it was flattened out and mixed with a look of impotent bad temper and some fear. That's it, I thought; Brian is getting fired for being so sloppy and lazy. Even when I made out Morgan saying "pervert" and "filthy" and "maniac," I still thought that was what was happening. Marjorie and Lily, and even brassy Irene, were standing around with downcast, rather pious looks, such as children get when somebody is suffering a terrible bawling out at school. Only old Henry seemed able to keep a cautious grin on his face. Gladys was not to be seen. Herb was standing closer to Morgan than anybody else. He was not interfering but was keeping an eye on the cleaver. Morgy was blubbering, though he didn't seem to be in any immediate danger.

Morgan was yelling at Brian to get out. "And out of this town – I mean it – and don't you wait till tomorrow if you still want your arse in one piece! Out!" he shouted, and the cleaver swung dramatically towards the door. Brian started in that direction but, whether he meant to or not, he made a swaggering, taunting motion of the buttocks. This made Morgan break into a roar and run after him, swinging the cleaver in a stagy way. Brian ran, and Morgan ran after him, and Irene screamed and grabbed her stomach. Morgan was too heavy to run any distance and probably could not have thrown the cleaver very far, either. Herb watched from the doorway. Soon Morgan came back and flung the cleaver down on the table.

"All back to work! No more gawking around here! You don't get paid for gawking! What are you getting under way at?" he said, with a hard look at Irene.

"Nothing," Irene said meekly.

"If you're getting under way get out of here."

"I'm not."

"All right, then!"

We got to work. Herb took off his blood-smeared smock and put on his jacket and went off, probably to see that Brian got ready to go on the suppertime bus. He did not say a word. Morgan and his son went out to the yard, and Irene and Henry went back to the adjoining shed, where they did the plucking, working knee-deep in the feathers Brian was supposed to keep swept up.

"Where's Gladys?" I said softly.

"Recuperating," said Marjorie. She, too, spoke in a quieter voice than usual, and "recuperating" was not the sort of word she and Lily normally used. It was a word to be used about Gladys, with a mocking intent.

They didn't want to talk about what had happened, because they were afraid Morgan might come in and catch them at it and fire them. Good workers as they were, they were afraid of that. Besides, they hadn't seen anything. They must have been annoyed that they hadn't. All I ever found out was that Brian had either done something or shown something to Gladys as she came out of the washroom and she had started screaming and having hysterics.

Now she'll likely be laid up with another nervous breakdown, they said. And he'll be on his way out of town. And good riddance, they said, to both of them.

I have a picture of the Turkey Barn crew taken on Christmas Eve. It was taken with a flash camera that was someone's Christmas extravagance. I think it was Irene's. But Herb Abbott must have been the one who took the picture. He was the one who could be trusted to know or to learn immediately how to manage anything new, and flash cameras were fairly new at the time. The picture was taken about ten o'clock on Christmas Eve, after Herb and Morgy had come back from making the last delivery and we had washed off the gutting table and swept and mopped the cement floor. We had taken off our bloody smocks and heavy sweaters and gone into the little room called the lunchroom, where there was a table and a heater. We still wore our working clothes, overalls and shirts. The men wore caps and the women kerchiefs, tied in the wartime style.

I am stout and cheerful and comradely in the picture, transformed into someone I don't ever remember being or pretending to be. I look years older than fourteen. Irene is the only one who has taken off her kerchief, freeing her long red hair. She peers out from it with a meek, sluttish, inviting look, which would match her reputation but is not like any look of hers I remember. Yes, it must have been her camera; she is posing for it, with that look, more deliberately than anyone else is. Marjorie and Lily are smiling, true to form, but their smiles are sour and reckless. With their hair hidden, and such figures as they have bundled up, they look like a couple of toughs and jovial but testy workmen. Their kerchiefs look misplaced; caps would be better. Henry is in high spirits, glad to be part of the workforce, grinning and looking twenty years younger than his age. Then Morgy, with his hangdog look, not trusting the occasion's bounty, and Morgan very flushed and bosslike and satisfied. He has just given each of us our bonus turkey. Each of these turkeys has a leg or a wing missing, or a malformation of some kind, so none of them are saleable at the full price. But Morgan has been at pains to tell us that you often get the best meat off the gimpy ones, and he has shown us that he's taking one home himself.

We are all holding mugs or large, thick china cups, which contain not the usual tea but rye whiskey. Morgan and Henry have been drinking since suppertime. Marjorie and Lily say they only want a little, and only take it at all because it's Christmas Eve and they are dead on their feet. Irene says she's dead on her feet as well but that doesn't mean she only wants a little. Herb has poured quite generously not just for her but for Lily and Marjorie, too, and they do not object. He has measured mine and Morgy's out at the same time, very stingily, and poured in Coca-Cola. This is the first drink I have ever had, and as a result I will believe for years that rye-and-Coca-Cola is a standard sort of drink and will always ask for it, until I notice that few other people drink it and that it makes me sick. I didn't get sick that Christmas Eve, though; Herb had not given me enough. Except for an odd taste, and my own feeling of consequence, it was like drinking Coca-Cola.

I don't need Herb in the picture to remember what he looked like. That is, if he looked like himself, as he did all the time at the

Turkey Barn and the few times I saw him on the street – as he did all the times in my life when I saw him except one.

The time he looked somewhat unlike himself was when Morgan was cursing out Brian and, later, when Brian had run off down the road. What was this different look? I've tried to remember, because I studied it hard at the time. It wasn't much different. His face looked softer and heavier then, and if you had to describe the expression on it you would have to say it was an expression of shame. But what would he be ashamed of? Ashamed of Brian, for the way he had behaved? Surely that would be late in the day; when had Brian ever behaved otherwise? Ashamed of Morgan, for carrying on so ferociously and theatrically? Or of himself, because he was famous for nipping fights and displays of this sort in the bud and hadn't been able to do it here? Would he be ashamed that he hadn't stood up for Brian? Would he have expected himself to do that, to stand up for Brian?

All this was what I wondered at the time. Later, when I knew more, at least about sex, I decided that Brian was Herb's lover, and that Gladys really was trying to get attention from Herb, and that that was why Brian had humiliated her – with or without Herb's connivance and consent. Isn't it true that people like Herb – dignified, secretive, honourable people – will often choose somebody like Brian, will waste their helpless love on some vicious, silly person who is not even evil, or a monster, but just some importunate nuisance? I decided that Herb, with all his gentleness and carefulness, was avenging himself on us all – not just on Gladys but on us all – with Brian, and that what he was feeling when I studied his face must have been a savage and gleeful scorn. But embarrassment as well – embarrassment for Brian and for himself and for Gladys, and to some degree for all of us. Shame for all of us – that is what I thought then.

Later still, I backed off from this explanation. I got to a stage of backing off from the things I couldn't really know. It's enough for me now just to think of Herb's face with that peculiar, stricken look; to think of Brian monkeying in the shade of Herb's dignity; to think of my own mystified concentration on Herb, my need to catch him out, if I could ever get the chance, and then move in and stay close to him. How attractive, how delectable, the prospect of intimacy is, with the very person who will grant it. I can still feel the pull of a man like that, of his promising and refusing. I would still like to know things. Never mind facts. Never mind theories, either.

When I finished my drink I wanted to say something to Herb. I stood beside him and waited for a moment when he was not listening to or talking with anyone else and when the increasingly rowdy conversation of the others would cover what I had to say.

"I'm sorry your friend had to go away."

"That's all right."

Herb spoke kindly and with amusement, and so shut me off from any further right to look at or speak about his life. He knew what I was up to. He must have known it before, with lots of women. He knew how to deal with it.

Lily had a little more whiskey in her mug and told how she and her best girlfriend (dead now, of liver trouble) had dressed up as men one time and gone into the men's side of the beer parlour, the side where it said "Men Only," because they wanted to see what it was like. They sat in a corner drinking beer and keeping their eyes and ears open, and nobody looked twice or thought a thing about them, but soon a problem arose.

"Where were we going to go? If we went around to the other side and anybody seen us going into the ladies', they would scream bloody murder. And if we went into the men's somebody'd be sure to notice we didn't do it the right way. Meanwhile the beer was going through us like a bugger!"

"What you don't do when you're young!" Marjorie said.

Several people gave me and Morgy advice. They told us to enjoy ourselves while we could. They told us to stay out of trouble. They said they had all been young once. Herb said we were a good crew and had done a good job but he didn't want to get in bad with any of the women's husbands by keeping them there too late. Marjorie and Lily expressed indifference to their husbands, but Irene announced that she loved hers and that it was not true that he had been dragged back from Detroit to marry her, no matter what people said. Henry said it was a good life if you didn't weaken. Morgan said he wished us all the most sincere Merry Christmas.

When we came out of the Turkey Barn it was snowing. Lily said it was like a Christmas card, and so it was, with the snow whirling around the street lights in town and around the coloured lights people had put up outside their doorways. Morgan was giving Henry and Irene a ride home in the truck acknowledging age and pregnancy and Christmas. Morgy took a shortcut through the field, and Herb walked off by himself, head down and hands in his pockets, rolling slightly as if he were on the deck of a lake boat. Marjorie and Lily linked arms with me as if we were old comrades.

"Let's sing," Lily said. "What'll we sing?"

"'We Three Kings'?" said Marjorie. "'We Three Turkey Gutters'?"

"'I'm Dreaming of a White Christmas.'"

"Why dream? You got it!"

So we sang.

A Christmas Story

by Roy Bonisteel

U sually when you live on a mixed farm you can count on a few dollars from at least one source, even if other crops or pursuits fail. But the fall of 1944 found our family approaching Christmas with no cash. We had enough to eat and we could certainly count on a plump turkey or chicken for the festive dinner, and of course we had our own Christmas tree. It was just that there was no money for the extras. Despite this, my father told my mother to go ahead and buy what she needed, since the friendly merchants in Trenton would give us credit until after the holidays. Our ace-in-the-hole was the woodlot. As soon as we got a few inches of snow we would go into the woods and cut enough firewood to pay off our debts.

A week before Christmas the snow started. Big fat flakes that just kept piling up until the fence tops disappeared. Two days before Christmas the snow plow came down our dead-end road and turned around in the barnyard. It was a large wooden V loaded with boulders and pulled by a four-horse team. The driver gave the horses a rest while he stomped the snow off his boots and came into the kitchen for a cup of hot coffee.

"They've got it a lot worse back around Stirling," he said. "Some drifts over eight feet high. By the way, are you selling any wood this year? Sam Barton told me to ask if I saw you. He's right out and looks like he might have a pretty cold Christmas." Sam Barton lived on the ninth concession with his wife and four children. He worked the old Homer place on shares and often bought a few cords of wood from us, usually later on in the New Year.

On the afternoon before Christmas, my older brother Bert and I piled two stacks of dry, split wood, each eight feet by four feet by four feet, on to the stake body of the old Fargo truck and started out through the still-falling snow on the ten-mile trip to the Barton place. The truck's heater never worked well, but we were bundled up warmly and the cab was small enough that body heat was sufficient. Bert played a mean harmonica, and while my singing voice left a lot to be desired, I knew all the words to most songs. As we made our way slowly through the thickening snow we tortured every tune on the current hit parade and assaulted every Christmas carol that came to mind.

It was almost five and we had turned on the Fargo's one good headlight by the time we spotted the Barton mailbox and drove up the snow-filled ruts of the lane. Sam and his wife and the four noisy youngsters made us feel like the relief of Dunkirk as they greeted us warmly and began to unload our precious cargo. When we had finished, Sam asked Bert how much he owed.

"Same as last year. Dad said not to charge any more just because it's dry. That's twelve dollars a cord and a dollar for gas."

I was thinking that twenty-five dollars would certainly help

Mom pay off what she owed for Christmas presents when I heard
Sam say, "To tell the truth, I'm a little short this year. All I can
spare is twenty dollars."

Bert hesitated. Mrs. Barton looked embarrassed and hopeful at
the same time. She said, "Let me give you a nice capon. It's already
dressed and ready for the oven. My chickens were the only thing
we had any luck with this year!"

"That'll be just fine, ma'am," said Bert.

I waited until we were out of the driveway and turned towards
home before I said, "Dad's going to be some mad that you're short
five dollars. And the last thing in the world we need is a chicken."

"What was I supposed to do?" asked Bert. "Put the wood back
on the truck?"

The snow was still falling in earnest and a cold east wind
had started piling drifts diagonally across the road. The truck,
now without its weighty ballast, was skidding dangerously as
the wheels carved new tracks behind the pale glow of our single
headlight. The windshield and windows were becoming thick
with frost and we took turns scraping clear a small peep-hole on
the driver's side.

It was at the corner of the fifth concession, still about five miles
from home, that we went off the road. The back wheels swerved
over the edge of a hidden culvert and we slid silently and deeply
into the snow-filled ditch.

"The Creighton place is a little over a mile west," said Bert.
"He'll have a tractor to pull us out."

We had trudged only about a hundred yards through the storm,
and I was thinking what a cold, miserable Christmas Eve it had
turned into, when we saw a light coming from the window of a
small house off to the side of the road.

"Who lives there?" I shouted over the wind.

"I don't know." Bert stopped and peered through the trees that lined the front yard. "I think it used to be an old tenant house, but somebody has fixed it up. Let's give it a try."

We were just about to knock on the door when Bert said, "Look!" Through the curtainless window I saw the strangest sight I had seen in my fourteen years. An old man, bald except for a grey fringe over his ears and wearing faded red long johns, was dancing spryly around the room – with a dog. A handsome, well-groomed collie had both front paws planted firmly on the man's shoulders and was awkwardly but purposefully striding back and forth. We could hear the music and could see a wind-up phonograph in the corner of the room.

Bert and I looked at each other, then back down the road, where the truck was fast becoming invisible, and finally knocked on the door. We heard the music stop and slippered feet shuffle to the door. It was opened wide and we felt the warmth of a roaring wood fire hit us as the man beckoned us quickly inside.

Bert said, "Our truck has slid into the ditch at the corner. I was wondering if you had a tractor I could borrow to pull it out."

"Sure have, young feller. Got a small Allis-Chalmers in the shed behind the house should do the trick. Take off those coats and sit for a minute first. You must be frozen. Don't worry about your boots."

As he motioned us to a slip-covered hobo couch to one side of the fireplace, I took off my coat and glanced around the room. It was small but neat. In the centre was a kitchen table and two curved-back chairs. A rocking chair was pulled up near the fire. A large kitchen cupboard dominated the far wall, and the other three were hung with framed calendar prints of mountain ranges, seascapes, and floral arrangements.

"How about a hot drink?" he asked. Without waiting for an answer, he took an earthen jug and some glass tumblers from the cupboard and put them on the table. Grabbing the poker from the hook over the fireplace, he pushed it deep into the red coals below the burning logs. He turned and smiled at us.

"Wasn't expecting company. Not many people stop in here. My own fault, I guess. Rose and I never made many friends out here. Oh well, it's too late now." He stood with one hand on the poker and stared at a small photograph over the mantel. It showed a laughing woman with thick long hair, head thrown back, eyes bright and full of humor.

"We moved here over three years ago from the Maritimes when I retired from the shipyard. Always wanted to get a small farm. Rose had a real green thumb. Grew vegetables. Didn't make much, but we were sure happy!"

The end of the poker was glowing red now. He removed it slowly and plunged it into the jug on the table. A hiss of steam erupted and filled the room with the smell of apple cider. He poured us each a glass full and took his to the rocking chair. The first swallow of the warm liquid seemed to bounce off my empty stomach and brought tears to my eyes. I felt little tingles in my brain and realized that it certainly wasn't this year's crop. I glanced sideways at Bert and saw him smiling appreciatively. He was not the stranger I was to hard cider. The old man finished his drink in one long, thirsty gulp and absently poured himself another. He poked the fire needlessly.

"She died. Died two years ago. Just like that." He snapped his fingers but no sound came. "Not a day goes by but I miss her. Like an ache it is. Sure miss her at Christmas. It was a special time for us. Didn't pay much attention to the religion part of it, but the love part was sure there. Maybe it's the same, I don't know. We'd make presents for each other, decorate the place with some crepe paper and always had a roast goose or chicken. I can make a real good stuffing.

"I got good memories. Some minister came by after and said

not to worry because Rose wasn't dead, she was living on in heaven. I guess he meant well. I know Rose is dead and the only place she lives on is in my memories. Maybe that's what heaven is – memories."

A log fell in the fire and sent a shower of sparks up the chimney. This seemed to rouse him from his reveries and he noticed that both his glass and Bert's were empty. I was still taking small sips from mine and thinking the warm room was making me woozy. "There's plenty more," he said.

"Thanks, but I'd better get the truck out," answered Bert. Then, with a glance at the old man, he said to me, "You stay here and keep warm. I can yank it out by myself."

"Be careful of the crank, it kicks sometimes," he said as Bert buttoned his coat and went out the door. With his glass refilled, he sat down by the fire and in a minute continued talking. His dog yawned and stretched closer to the fire.

"She was an English girl. Met her on Christmas Eve at a dance in Liverpool during the last war. I couldn't dance worth a hoot, but she showed me how. Would you mind putting that music back on?"

I went over to the phonograph and gave the handle a couple of turns then dropped the arm over the edge of the record. The music started as I returned to the couch.

"That piece is called *Greensleeves*. It's an English tune. We danced to it that first night. It's a waltz, you know. Rose taught me how to make a box pattern with my feet. One-two-three . . . one-two-three. We laughed so much. We got married while I was still in the navy, then after the war we came to Canada. Got off the boat in Halifax and decided to stay there. Lots of good years. Never had kids. Didn't seem to matter. Had each other.

The music stopped and the needle made a scraping sound in the last groove. He started to sing in a low, halting voice:

Alas, my love! Ye do me wrong
To cast me off discourteously:
And I have loved you so long,
Delighting in your company.

I went over to the machine, lifted the arm and turned off the turntable.

"I heard they made a Christmas carol out of that piece," he said. "Makes sense. It's always been a Christmas song to me."

He was humming now and staring into the fire. I heard the tractor come up beside the house and sputter to a stop in the shed. Bert came through the door in a blast of cold air. The old man didn't even look up. I put on my coat.

"Thank you very much," my brother said. "We really appreciate your help." There was no reply from the figure by the fire that rocked and hummed. Bert took from under his mackinaw the fat capon and set it on the table beside the cider crock. "Goodbye," we both said as we backed out the door. The dog thumped his tail twice on the floor in acknowledgement.

The snow was tapering off and by the time we got to the second concession it had stopped completely. Neither of us spoke on this final leg of our journey. As we started down our own dead-end road, the moon broke through and shot blue shadows over the snow drifts. I could see the lights ablaze from every window of our farmhouse as we drew near and I thought of Christmas Day, just a couple of hours away. With the snowfall ended, my other brothers and sister and my aunts and uncles would be able to come. There would be laughter and games and shouts of joy as we opened our almost-paid-for presents. Loved ones, together.

As we turned up the lane towards the yellow lamplight spilling over the snow, Bert had his harmonica out again. He was softly playing *What Child Is This?*

To Everything There is a Season

by Alistair MacLeod

I am speaking here of a time when I was eleven and lived with my family on our small farm on the west coast of Cape Breton. My family had been there for a long, long time and so it seemed had I. And much of that time seems like the proverbial yesterday. Yet when I speak on this Christmas, I am not sure how much I speak with the voice of that time or how much in the voice of what I have since become. And I am not sure how many liberties I may be taking with the boy I think I was. For Christmas is a time of both past and present and often the two are imperfectly blended. As we step into its newness we often look behind.

We have been waiting now, it seems, forever. Actually, it has been most intense since Hallowe'en when the first snow fell upon us as we moved like muffled mummers upon darkened country roads. The large flakes were soft and new then and almost generous, and the earth to which they fell was still warm and as yet unfrozen. They fell in silence into the puddles and into the sea where they disappeared at the moment of contact. They disappeared, too, upon touching the heated redness of our necks and hands or the faces of those who did not wear masks. We carried our pillowcases from house to house, knocking on doors to become silhouettes in the light thrown out from kitchens (white pillowcases held out by whitened forms). The snow fell between us and the doors and was transformed in shimmering golden beams. When we turned to leave, it fell upon our footprints, and as the night wore on obliterated them and all the records of our movements. In the morning everything was soft and still and November had come upon us.

My brother Kenneth, who is two and a half, is unsure of his last Christmas. It is Hallowe'en that looms largest in his memory as an exceptional time of being up late in magic darkness and falling snow. "Who are you going to dress up as at Christmas?" he asks. "I think I'll be a snowman." All of us laugh at that and tell him Santa Claus will find him if he is good and that he need not dress up at all. We go about our appointed tasks waiting for it to happen.

I am troubled myself about the nature of Santa Claus and I am trying to hang on to him in any way that I can. It is true that at my age I no longer really believe in him, yet I have hoped in all his possibilities as fiercely as I can; much in the same way, I think, that the drowning man waves desperately to the lights of the passing ship on the high sea's darkness. For without him, as without the man's ship, it seems our fragile lives would be so much more desperate.

My mother has been fairly tolerant of my attempted perpetuation. Perhaps because she has encountered it before. Once I overheard her speaking about my sister Anne to one of her neighbours. "I thought Anne would believe forever," she said. "I practically had to tell her." I have somehow always wished I had not heard her say that as I seek sanctuary and reinforcement even in an ignorance I know I dare not trust.

Kenneth, however, believes with an unadulterated fervor, and so do Bruce and Barry, who are six-year-old twins. Beyond me there is Anne who is thirteen and Mary who is fifteen, both of whom seem to be leaving childhood at an alarming rate. My mother has told us that she was already married when she was seventeen, which is only two years older than Mary is now. That, too, seems strange to contemplate and perhaps childhood is shorter for some than it is for others. I think of this sometimes in the evenings when we have finished our chores and the supper dishes have been cleared away and we are supposed to be doing our homework. I glance sideways at my mother, who is always knitting or mending, and at my father, who mostly sits by the stove coughing quietly with his handkerchief at his mouth. He has "not been well" for over two years and has difficulty breathing whenever he moves at more than the slowest pace. He is most sympathetic of all concerning my extended hopes, and says we should hang on to the good things in our lives as long as we are able. As I look at him out of the corner of my eye, it does not seem that he has many of them left. He is old, we think, at forty-two.

Yet Christmas, in spite of all the doubts of our different ages, is a fine and splendid time, and now as we pass the midpoint of December our expectations are heightened by the increasing coldness that has settled down upon us. The ocean is flat and calm and along the coast, in the scooped-out coves, has turned to an icy slush. The brook that flows past our house is almost totally frozen and there is only a small channel of rushing water that flows openly at its very centre. When we let the cattle out to drink, we chop holes with the axe at the brook's edge so that they can drink without venturing onto the ice.

The sheep move in and out of their lean-to shelter, restlessly stamping their feet or huddling together in tightly packed groups. A conspiracy of wool against the cold. The hens perch high on their roosts with their feathers fluffed out about them, hardly feeling it worthwhile to descend to the floor for their few scant kernels of grain. The pig, who has little time before his butchering, squeals his displeasure to the cold and with his snout tosses his wooden trough high in the icy air. The splendid young horse paws the planking of his stall and gnaws the wooden cribwork of his manger.

We have put a protective barricade of spruce boughs about our kitchen door and banked our house with additional boughs and billows of eel grass. Still, the pail of water we leave standing in the porch is solid in the morning and has to be broken with the hammer. The clothes my mother hangs on the line are frozen almost instantly and sway and creak from their suspending clothespins like sections of dismantled robots: the stiff-legged rasping trousers and the shirts and sweaters with unyielding arms outstretched. In the morning we race from our frigid upstairs bedrooms to finish dressing around the kitchen stove.

We should extend our coldness half a continent away to the Great Lakes of Ontario so that it might hasten the Christmas coming of my oldest brother, Neil. He is nineteen and employed on the "lake boats," the long flat carriers of grain and iron ore whose season ends any day after December 10, depending on the ice conditions. We wish it to be cold, cold on the Great Lakes of Ontario, so that he may come home to us as soon as possible. Already his cartons have arrived. They come from different places: Cobourg, Toronto, St. Catharines, Welland, Windsor, Sarnia, Sault Ste. Marie. Places that we, with the exception of my father, have never been. We locate them excitedly on the map, tracing their outlines with eager fingers. The cartons bear the lettering of Canada Steamship Lines, and are bound with rope knotted intricately in the fashion of sailors. My mother says they contain his "clothes" and we are not allowed to open them.

For us it is impossible to know the time or manner of his coming. If the lakes freeze early, he may come by train because it is cheaper. If the lakes stay open until December 20, he will have to fly because his time will be more precious than his money. He will hitchhike the last sixty or hundred miles from either station or airport. On our part, we can do nothing but listen with straining ears to radio reports of distant ice formations. His coming seems to depend on so many factors which are out there far beyond us and over which we lack control.

The days go by in fevered slowness until finally on the morning of December 23 the strange car rolls into our yard. My mother touches her hand to her lips and whispers "Thank God." My father gets up unsteadily from his chair to look through the window. Their longed-for son and our golden older brother is here at last. He is here with his reddish hair and beard and we can hear his hearty laugh. He will be happy and strong and confident for us all.

There are three other young men with him who look much the same as he. They, too, are from the boats and are trying to get home to Newfoundland. They must still drive a hundred miles to reach the ferry at North Sydney. The car seems very old. They purchased it in Thorold for $200 because they were too late to make any reservations, and they have driven steadily since they began. In northern New Brunswick their windshield wipers failed, but instead of stopping they tied lengths of cord to the wipers' arms and passed them through the front window vents. Since that time, in whatever precipitation, one of them has pulled the cords back and forth to make the wipers function. This information falls tiredly but excitedly from their lips and we greedily gather it in.

My father pours them drinks of rum, and my mother takes out her mincemeat and the fruitcakes she has been carefully hoarding. We lean on the furniture or look from the safety of sheltered doorways. We would like to hug our brother but are too shy with strangers present. In the kitchen's warmth, the young men begin to nod and doze, their heads dropping suddenly to their chests. They nudge each other with their feet in an attempt to keep awake. They will not stay and rest because they have come so far and tomorrow is Christmas Eve and stretches of mountains and water still lie between them and those they love. After they leave, we pounce upon our brother physically and verbally. He laughs and shouts and lifts us over his head and swings us in his muscular arms. Yet in spite of his happiness he seems surprised at the appearance of his father, whom he has not seen since March. My father merely smiles at him, while my mother bites her lip.

Now that he is here there is a great flurry of activity. We have left everything we could until the time he might be with us. Eagerly I show him the fir tree on the hill which I have been watching for months and marvel at how easily he fells it and carries it down the hill. We fall over one another in the excitement of decoration.

He promises that on Christmas Eve he will take us to church in the sleigh behind the splendid horse that until his coming we are all afraid to handle. And on the afternoon of Christmas Eve he shoes the horse, lifting each hoof and rasping it fine and hammering the cherry-red horsehoes into shape upon the anvil. Later he drops them hissingly into the steaming tub of water. My father sits beside him on an overturned pail and tells him what to do. Sometimes we argue with our father, but our brother does everything he says.

That night, bundled in hay and voluminous coats, and with heated stones at our feet, we start upon our journey. Our parents and Kenneth remain at home, but all the rest of us go. Before we leave we feed the cattle and sheep and even the pig all that they can possibly eat, so that they will be contented on Christmas Eve. Our parents wave to us from the doorway. We go four miles across the mountain road. It is a primitive logging trail and there will be no cars or other vehicles upon it. At first the horse is wild with excitement and lack of exercise and my brother has to stand at the front of the sleigh and lean backwards on the reins. Later he settles down to a trot and still later to a walk as the mountain rises before him. We sing all the Christmas songs we know and watch for the rabbits and foxes scudding across the open patches of snow and listen to the drumming of partridge wings. We are never cold.

When we descend to the country church we tie the horse in a grove of trees where he will be sheltered and not frightened by the many cars. We put a blanket over him and give him oats. At the church door the neighbours shake hands with my brother. "Hello, Neil," they say. "How is your father?"

"Oh," he says, just "Oh."

The church is very beautiful at night with its festooned branches and glowing candles and the booming, joyous sounds that come from the choir loft. We go through the service as if we are mesmerized.

On the way home, although the stones have cooled, we remain happy and warm. We listen to the creak of the leather harness and the hiss of runners on the snow and begin to think of the potentiality of presents. When we are about a mile from home the horse senses his destination and breaks into a trot and then into a confident lope. My brother lets him go and we move across the winter landscape like figures freed from a Christmas card. The snow from the horse's hooves falls about our heads like the whiteness of the stars.

After we have stabled the horse we talk with our parents and eat the meal our mother has prepared. And then I am sleepy and it is time for the younger children to be in bed. But tonight my father says to me, "We would like you to stay up with us a while," and so I stay quietly with the older members of my family.

When all is silent upstairs Neil brings in the cartons that contain his "clothes" and begins to open them. He unties the intricate knots quickly, their whorls falling away before his agile fingers. The boxes are filled with gifts neatly wrapped and bearing tags. The ones for my younger brothers say "from Santa Claus" but mine are not among them any more, as I know with certainty they will never be again. Yet I am not so much surprised as touched by a pang of loss at being here on the adult side of the world. It is as if I have suddenly moved into another room and heard a door click lastingly behind me. I am jabbed by my own small wound.

But then I look at those before me. I look at my parents drawn together before the Christmas tree. My mother has her hand upon my father's shoulder and he is holding his ever-present handkerchief. I look at my sisters, who have crossed this threshold ahead of me and now each day journey farther from the lives they knew as girls. I look at my magic older brother who has come to us this Christmas from half a continent away, bringing everything he has and is. All of them are captured in the tableau of their care.

"Every man moves on," says my father quietly, and I think he speaks of Santa Claus, "but there is no need to grieve. He leaves good things behind."

The Man with the Notebook

by Norman Levine

If you saw him by himself sitting in the park or in the corner of a pub you would have noticed the clerical appearance of his face, the soft eyes, the grey straight hair, and the glasses. About his features there was an overall mildness. You felt certain that he had never raised his voice, no matter what the occasion, and that he would be prompt to apologize if he so much as brushed against another person.

He lived by himself in a room in Bayswater. Every morning he would wash, dress, go down to the first step and pick up his morning paper. Then come back and prepare breakfast in the kitchen at the end of the passage. He would have a raw orange, bacon, two cups of black coffee. After reading the paper he would wash the dishes, make the bed, clean the room. Then pick up a small inexpensive dark-green notebook from his desk and go out.

His favourite walk was to Kensington Gardens. In the early
morning he would walk past the deserted playground, watch the
birds – the fat wood pigeons with their small heads – avoid the
water that lay in the hollows of the path, until he reached the
Round Pond. Here he would sit on one of the benches, take out
his notebook and write at the top of a clean page: *Day cloudy.
Wind moderate.* Then he would put the notebook down, smoke his
pipe, and watch.

He came to the Gardens to observe people. The nannies, in
grey uniform with white collars, pushing expensive prams. The
well-dressed men and women taking their dogs for their morning
walk. The business men going through the park to work. But, if,
like today, he came early and few people were about, he would take
his notebook and write of the landscape around him. *Trees without leaves. Sun getting warm. Water in pond, green, blue, grey. Groups
of young birds at edge preening themselves. Ducks asleep. Flycatchers
on a wire fence – sun catches the weeds in front of them and reflects the
green to the underneath part of their bodies.* And he tried even with
this warming-up exercise to see in the familiar landscape something fresh – like this morning's flycatchers.

From the Gardens he walked to Hyde Park and got on a bus
that took him to Picadilly, Trafalgar Square, the East End, or to one
of the railway stations, a street market, or along the Embankment
– a choice that followed a list drawn up every month. And once
there he would mix with people, go into a café, a pub, watch and
listen. And write down what he saw and heard.

In the late afternoon he would return to his room and type out
what he had written that day. And from these notes, over the next
three days, he would put together a sketch built around a particular person in each of the places. On Thursday night he would
type out the 1,500 words and send them to a weekly journal. On

the following Saturday he received a copy of the sketch as it had appeared and a cheque for thirty guineas. The editor of the journal, not long out of university, was a firm believer in taking things "directly from life." When he had read two of the early sketches, sent in by chance, he accepted them. And, after he had published five more, contracted the old man to send a sketch a week. This arrangement had now gone on for more than two years. The old man was always punctual with his story. And the weekly cheque removed the financial insecurity he had experienced before.

He saved all his clippings, pasting them neatly in large leather-bound volumes. And in the evenings he often would sit and read about the different people he had written. Occasionally he wondered where some of them might be. For though his livelihood depended on being with people, watching them, listening to what they said – he had few friends.

This uneventful life would have continued had not the government requisitioned the site where he lived for the construction of an office building. He disliked not so much the idea of leaving his room, or that part of London, but the fact that his routine would be upset. When his editor suggested that he move to a cottage, in a small fishing village in Cornwall, which he knew to be vacant, he was glad that the decision was made by somebody else.

From his window he could look out at a kind of valley with a lot of narrow streets and stone cottages with chimneys belching out smoke around tea-time. And though the cottage was small and damp it was much better than his room in Bayswater. He could now work in one room, sleep in another, and eat in still another. And the longer he lived in the village the more he grew to like it.

He liked the way people recognized him when he walked in the streets, said "Good Morning," or spoke about the weather. He liked it even more when they began to tell him the local gossip. He became a familiar sight along the front, the High Street, in the pubs. People referred to him as the man with the notebook. And after he had been there six months accepted him into their communal life. The editor continued to be satisfied with his writing.

He had lived in Cornwall seven months and his morning began with the usual walk down the slope to get his paper, then to the fishmonger by the front. The fishmonger, a small ex-sailor, knew what his customers wanted. Their conversation, apart from fish, was negligible. The fishmonger selected a long thin mackerel from a wicker basket, cut and flicked off the head to the pail below. The fishmonger said: "Did you know Bill Stevens is dead?"

"No," the old man said. "No, I didn't."

It was by the bandstand on the front that he first saw him. A row of chairs was placed near the bank for the feeble-minded who came to hear the music. And Bill Stevens stood by the rails beside them. Otherwise he spent all his time walking. He was 93. A small neat man in a grey double-breasted suit, very light blue eyes, always wearing a fedora, carrying a cane, and walking out his days.

He came across Stevens often when he was out. And they always stopped and talked. Stevens told him what this place was like when he was a boy. When winter was the busy time, not summer. And the visitor such a rare thing that if one came it was news and his name and where he was staying appeared in the local paper. Fishermen, at the start of the season, were blessed at the Slipway. And coffins were carried through the streets. When the pallbearers tired, they stopped, and small stools would be placed on the road. The coffin put on the stools. And everyone rested.

The old man put it all in, in his sketch of *Mister Bill*, as he called it. He had liked Stevens. He had written about him. Now he was dead. As he drank his second cup of black coffee he went to his book of clippings and re-read *Mister Bill*. He wondered if in his way he had made Bill Stevens alive for thousands of people who had never seen him.

In a couple of weeks' time he had forgotten about the funeral.
Though it was only the start of February – snowdrops were out
and the crocuses beginning – the place was getting ready for the
summer season. The harbor rails were repainted silver; the summer cafés and restaurants redecorated; the holes in the streets
repaired. The sand that the winter tides had swept up to the walls
was bulldozed back into the sea. And the few remaining fishermen were repainting their boats and bringing out the mended
gear from storage.

The old man enjoyed this activity and recorded it in his
notebook.

But this sensation of feeling part of this village changed
abruptly when he realized, with the death of the pier car-park
attendant, that all the funerals since he arrived in this village were
the funerals of people he had written about.

Most of the early sketches from Cornwall were descriptions
of the sea, the village, the harbor. He had written about few people: *The Town Crier; The Man with the Heavy Eyelids; Lack, the
Fisherman; Mister Bill; The Pier Car-Park Attendant.* But all these
people, soon after he had written about them, died.

At first he thought it was coincidence. After all, he wrote
mainly about old people.

He went to the notebook, read over the beginning of the week's
sketch that he was working on.

*The bell was tolling at ten on the Monday morning and I knew that
someone was being buried. This was Mister R's daughter. Our landlady
said that when she was being born he told the hospital to ring him
up. If it was a boy, they were to say, 'Strawberries;' if it was a girl, to
say 'Peaches'. He came running down the hill to tell the landlady. 'It's
peaches,' he said. 'It's peaches.'*

That was as far as he had gone with it and he knew he would
go no farther.

For the next two days he was depressed. *I am reluctant to leave this cottage and be seen in the streets*, he wrote in his notebook. *Therefore I wake up just before six. Then I go out for my walk and get to see what the place is like. I do some window shopping. Walk around the front. Along the pier. Watch the gulls, the black backs, the sparrows. And I am back to the cottage by seven.*

The next day, because a gale was blowing, he felt safe enough to go out at noon.

There are five French crabbers in the Bay, he wrote in his notebook, *facing the land, anchored and swaying violently. In front of them about a dozen gannets are diving for sand eels. They rarely go higher than the masts of the crabbers. I watch from a shelter by the ladies' lavatory. They come low across the water, turn into the wind, climb sharply, drift across, then plummet down, entering with a splash.*

But these were the reflexes of a writing animal. The human was no longer observed or noted down.

After another day of trying to come to terms with himself he decided to satisfy his conscience by deliberately writing about someone young and healthy for his next sketch.

He chose his next door neighbour's son. A young man in his twenties. He worked in the post office by the Methodist Chapel. It seemed odd to see him – looking like something from a physical fitness poster – sit on a high stool and give out stamps in the small post office. His girlfriend was a waitress in a café along the front during the summer and a telephone operator in the winter.

The old man went to the post office with his notebook. It was not an easy job. For not only was he under a strain, but the young seemed to wear a mask for him. His first draft of *Hal*, as he named him for the sketch, was not of a young man, but that of an old person. He tried again. Not knowing what he was after he wrote too much. Besides describing the restless eyes, the trace of boredom already showing in the mouth, the power of the body; he noted down every poster, every announcement and warning that was on the walls. He decided that he would write *Hal* as a paradox; the young man, full of vitality – and the drabness of his surrounding and lightness of work.

He sent off the sketch on the Thursday night. He did not return to the cottage but walked aimlessly by the harbor in the light rain. He was not certain whether he believed that there was a link between the recent deaths and his writing – or whether, getting old, he wanted to give his work some kind of recognition.

They found his neighbour's son on Monday morning. He was lying at the bottom of the courtyard. Apparently he visited his girlfriend by scaling the side of the house, going across the gable roof, and then entered her room through the bedroom window which she left open. The policeman thought he probably lost his footing and fell some thirty feet on to concrete. The scandal that this accident revealed helped to talk out the tragedy. But to the old man Hal's death was no accident. And neither were the others.

He spent Monday and Tuesday by himself. He ate sparingly and didn't bother to wash up or tidy the room. In the evenings he took down his leather-bound books.

His first sketch was of Konrad. A Polish actor he met by chance in Soho. They spent the afternoon drinking and Konrad told him how he was liberated.

One night British come in farmyard. Next S.S. I stay with the cows. I have big P on left breast. I saw British soldier come. I could cry I was so happy.

> *Young blonde with dictionary in hand.*
> *Wer sind Sie?*
> *I am a Pole.*
> *Do you speak English.*

A little.

Sind Sie ein Pole?

Ya.

Wohnen Sie in Warsaw?

Yes.

Come in.

Everybody was drunk singing Hurrah Konrad. I meet my best friend. You need suit. What do you need? Here drink, and took from his blouse a bottle. Ah Konrad, freedom. Drink. Let's get drunk. British soldiers give whisky, cigarettes, everybody drinking, kissing, eating, all cans of petrol filled with spirits. Sometimes German planes come and machine gun. All women drunk. All suits given away free. Fifteen nationalities in camp. No organization. Everybody drinking, dancing.

Who is drunk can't leave camp.

Good, now I'm imprisoned by the British. That is fine. Das ist liberation. Good. Let's drink. Germans in barns. DPs in house. Germans cook for us. All DP camps drunk. Fifteen nationalities, fifteen camp leaders, fifteen committees. Loudspeakers going all day from five until twelve at night.

Viva holiday.

We have revolvers. We shoot. Ping. A place is cleared. We throw grenades. Give prizes.

He liked the *Konrad* sketch and the other early ones. *Jerome*, the debt collector who looked like a professor. He met him in Lyon's in the Strand. He worked for a firm that bought up old debts at a discount then employed *Jerome* to collect them. The third sketch was *Doris.* He met her at Waterloo Station. She was pushing a tea trolley. She told him how she made her money by bringing her own packages of tea and putting these into the tea-urn, and selling them, instead of British Rail . . .

"Obituary notices," he said to himself. "That's what I was writing."

He knew he would not have a sketch ready that week. The editor said nothing, and reprinted an early one. But after it happened twice he received a telegram asking if he was ill. He replied that he was but he would try to send him something soon.

Weeks passed. The cheques stopped arriving. He tried to write of places he had never seen. But he knew that they were not right. He had always used the notebook and these attempts, to write imaginative pieces, he knew were lifeless. When, in desperation, he sent one of these off, the editor promptly returned it, at the same time reminding him that he was one of the best writers "in the naturalistic tradition," and that was what he wanted.

He believed it would be more human if he went to people who were already dying. He visited the small hospital. There was one old woman. The doctor told him that she was dying. He looked at her. Her teeth had fallen underneath the bed. She asked him to pick them up for her . . .

Summer passed. He would lie in his bed during the day, not wanting to get up. Sometimes at night he went out and wandered in the back streets worrying what he could possibly write about to bring in some money. He felt certain that what he had done, especially in the village, was wrong. But he did not know why. He wanted to write but not to harm anyone.

I am reluctant to leave my cottage, he wrote on New Year's Day in the notebook. *When I do, I'm afraid of running into someone I know. He will show surprise and say, I thought you were away. And I say, Yes. It stops a lot of questions. I keep away from certain streets because I owe money to two grocers, the paper place, the tobacconist, the butcher, the milkman, the coal-merchant. On Christmas Day, as a gesture, I went by the side streets and alleys to the old pier and sat down on the bench by a couple. They must have been in their fifties or sixties. They were on holiday. She took hold of the man's hand and began clumsily to stroke it. She had a small fattish hand. And there is something desperate about her action. They talk about the far shore fields, of traveling in a car there some time ago.*

'What's the time?' the man says suddenly.

She leaves go the man's hand to look at her wrist. 'Nearly two.'

'Why is it so early?' he says, 'it's been early all day!'

I get up and quickly walk away from them. I can't use them, I can't use them, I can't use them . . . And I realize I am walking through the streets talking to myself . . .

It would be easy. Perhaps not easy but possible, even at this late stage, to turn this into a happy ... if not happy at least a suitable ending. But that would be going against the way it happened. No. The old man died. On a particularly cold night, late in January, weak from hunger and cold. And when they found him, he had burned the leather-bound books in an attempt to keep warm.

But I can't help feeling that if your sympathy is with the old man that it isn't misplaced. He wanted, what seems on the surface (he was always sound on externals) a simple request: to go through life without hurting anyone. He reminds me of some sensitive people I know who can't do certain things – like borrow money, identify a corpse – so others have to do it for them. As if the others haven't got feelings. It was only toward the end that the old man ... and had he been able to make something of his last entry ... but if he had (he would have had to be made of sterner stuff – it's a tough game) he might have found out that it is hard to write – or live for that matter – without hurting someone. Even if it would only be himself.

Turning on the Christmas Blights

A Camilla Macphee Story

by Mary Jane Maffini

"The trouble with humbug, if you ask me, is that it doesn't go far enough." Not that my opinion of the Christmas season and all the twaddle surrounding it meant a dog's dropping to Alvin Ferguson. He ignored me and sailed across the tide of rush-hour traffic on Wellington Street – beaky nose high, long ponytail flowing in the winter wind. As Alvin is a human tsunami of seasonal enthusiasm, I found myself swept after him. Not without a certain amount of resentment.

"You can't cross on a red," I shouted as a westbound STO bus narrowly missed my butt.

"Rules," Alvin shouted back over his bony shoulder, "are made to be broken."

His plan was to join the thousands of frost-bitten citizens gathered on Parliament Hill to watch the annual Christmas Lights Across Canada ceremony. It was a good plan if you like lights or Christmas or ice-cold feet. And Alvin would be lucky if his seven visible earrings didn't contribute to frostbite on a grand scale.

The overcast December night combined with an icy mist made it hard to see even at this early hour. Even so, I couldn't pretend to lose Alvin. Not with that scarf. His recent knitting binge had yielded a six-foot-long red and green number, which was wrapped four times around his neck. In case red and green was a tad too subtle, he had thoughtfully woven gold LED Christmas lights into the final product. Or Christmas blights, as I thought of them. I assumed there was a small battery pack attached somehow, too. Of course, I wouldn't have given a flying fig what he was wearing if he hadn't made me the twin scarf. He claimed it was an early Christmas gift.

Besides being way too noticeable from a mile away, it was also pretty scratchy on the neck. I took mine off and stuffed it into the pocket of my parka. We'd been getting way too many stares.

Alvin sniffed. "What are you doing that for? If you don't like your gift, I'll take it back."

"It's not that, Alvin . . ." But he had already snatched the scarf out of my pocket and stomped off ahead. Why is everyone I know such a drama queen? And why are people with more stuff than they need obsessed with heaping gifts on other people who are drowning in possessions? Alvin wasn't alone in this. I'd already had my annual snarl at my friend Merv about that. Merv, the morose Mountie, is crabby and miserable all year long, which is part of what I like about him. Up until this December, he's been worse than usual, something to do with one year left before retiring from the RCMP and still on Hill patrol on the long winter nights. But come December and he gets all misty-eyed. Gift swap, indeed. I just said no to that. What was he thinking?

I puffed up the hill and tried to catch up to Alvin, who had joined a jumbled line going somewhere. "Too bad you didn't knit Christmas socks instead. It's minus seventeen and dropping by the minute." I stamped my feet to keep warm. "Let's just get it over with."

"The lights don't come on for another forty-five minutes, Camilla."

"Forty-five minutes? I'll be dead by then. Do we have to keep standing in this lineup?"

"We're getting hot chocolate. Traditional. And even better – free," Alvin snapped. "Lighten up, Camilla."

Yeah right. "Why are those people grinning? What's wrong with them? New teeth?"

Alvin reached for his hot chocolate. "They're volunteers, Camilla. Happy to be out here, meeting members of the community and getting in the spirit of the season."

"I guess," I said, accepting a cup of steaming hot chocolate from a frighteningly happy fellow.

"Trust me," Alvin said.

"It's too dark and I can't see over all these people," I grumbled as we headed back to battle the crowds.

Alvin said, "Let's not get separated."

I wouldn't want you to think I kowtow to the world's most irritating office assistant, code name Alvin, but the truth was I'd lost a bet with him over who would win the Liberal leadership race. For payback, I had to be dragged along to the ceremony and make nice.

"Come on, Camilla, we need torches."

This will teach me to gamble on something as futile as politics, I reminded myself as I followed him to a tent staffed with still more smiling volunteers. Where did they find these people?

"Great scarf," the volunteer said to Alvin as she handed each of us a candle stuck in a plastic glass. My glass was red and Alvin's was green. "Very twinkly."

Alvin said, "Take it, Camilla. You use the bottom of the candle as a holder and the plastic keeps the flame from going out. Cool, isn't it?"

"If you say so." It was actually very cool, and the sight of thousands of bobbing little lanterns made for a pretty sight on the frigid, dark Hill.

"You can humph all you want, Camilla. This is fun. Let's find a bonfire."

Around us, hundreds of cheerful families prattled on in English and French, jostling for places in the hot chocolate lineup or a space near the many bonfires. "Toasted marshmallows," Alvin said, elbowing his way through past a couple of guys in Sens sweaters.

"Watch out," I said as a young man in a puffy maroon ski jacket jostled my arm. Hot chocolate spilled down the front of my old brown parka.

He said, "Excuse me, ma'am. Let me help with that."

"Back off," I said.

His eyes widened, with surprise at first, then a flicker of recognition. "Sorry," he said, turning away.

I tapped him on the shoulder. "Hey, not so fast. I know you."

He turned and said in low voice, "Maybe not, because what you don't know won't hurt you."

"Don't you threaten me."

I stepped forward but he was gone, melted into the crowd of happy families, hand-holding lovers, cocoa-swilling babies, and gleeful volunteers. The maroon jacket was dark enough to blend with the night. I staggered after him, waving my little candle torch like a deranged tree decoration.

"Rollie!" I called.

Perhaps he'd dodged behind the beaver-tails hut? I checked, but except for a few people trying to have a quiet smoke, it was deserted.

Maybe he'd scurried toward the front where we'd soon be hearing Christmas carols by local choirs and seasonal drivel from politicians. Was he lurking behind one of the dozens of Christmas trees that had sprung from the snow on the hill? Wherever he was, I intended to find him.

Alvin yelled in my ear. "Do you want your toasted marshmallow or not? I only have two hands."

I whirled. "I just saw Rollie the Roach."

"Did you say 'Rollie the Roach'? Who's that? Can you take this thing?" Alvin thrust the marshmallow at me. "It's not like I'm your mother, you know."

"Rollie is the slickest little pickpocket this town has ever known. Pulling the old distraction game: Bump into some poor mark, spill something on them, wipe it off, and pick their pockets. That little creep makes more than a bank robber on a good day."

"What? That guy you were just talking to? A pickpocket? Here? Where? Let met at him."

"He got away. That must be obvious, Alvin, even to you. Damn. He could lift dozens of wallets here."

"But," Alvin sputtered, "it's Christmas!"

"Of course, it's Christmas. Best time of year for these guys. Bonanza. Fat wallets. Credit cards he can use or sell to scammers. He'll make a fortune. Then, if he's not too exhausted from all this pickpocketing, he'll break into people's homes while they are at midnight Mass and steal the kids' gifts."

"Someone has to stop him!"

"Not much chance of that."

"How do you even know this guy, Camilla?"

"I was his legal-aid lawyer on more than one occasion. For my sins. But mostly for his."

"Really?"

"Eventually, I had to fire him as a client."

"Why?"

"Long story. Client privilege while it lasted. Do you know the little rat told me what I didn't know wouldn't hurt me?"

Alvin scowled. "That's pretty bold. And he didn't even look like a crook. That jacket probably cost like five hundred plus. Even that cap was more than I can afford."

"Pickpockets usually look pretty well-dressed. Less suspicious. Clothes are the tools of the trade. He probably ripped it off a retailer or maybe some poor devil standing around tonight shivering. Do you think you can recognize him?"

"Pretty distinctive jacket."

"Was it? I'm not too much into that snowboarder style. And if we don't find him fast, he'll probably slip into something else. Would you recognize him if he was wearing different clothing?"

Alvin frowned in concentration. "I think so. I'm good at faces and I got a clear look at his. You made him nervous, that's for sure. But we have to stop him!"

"Well, I know that, Alvin. But I can't see him anymore. The thing is he's probably not working alone. He likes company. He likes to vary the approach. They'd play all the old scams, distraction, compassion. One minute, he'll jostle some unsuspecting mark, the next he'll . . . Oh, hold on."

I dashed around a couple of kids and grabbed the collar of a young man who was just apologizing to a sweet-faced, white-haired lady in a beaver coat. He turned pale at the sight of me. His hand dropped.

"Bunny," I said. "How could you?"

Bunny Mayhew stared at his feet and fidgeted. He'd probably stolen that baby-blue jacket because it went with his eyes.

I cleared my throat.

He bent down, stood up again, and said to the woman in the fur coat, "Sorry, ma'am. You seemed to have dropped this."

She took the wallet from his hand. Her face lit up like one of our candle torches. "Why, thank you."

"Better check the clasp on your purse, ma'am," he said.

"Bless you. You're too kind," she said, fishing out a twenty and pressing it into Bunny's hand. "Merry Christmas."

At least, he had the grace to look sheepish. As soon as she'd turned away, I snatched the twenty from his larcenous fingers. "This is going right in the first Salvation Army kettle I see. Or have you already plundered that, too?"

Bunny protested. "What do you think I am, Camilla? You think that I'd steal from the Sally Ann?"

"I know you're a thief, Bunny. But I believed you confined your habit to works of art. And furthermore, I thought you'd promised to settle down and straighten up. What's Tonya going to say?"

"It's not my fault."

I rolled my eyes. "Trust me, she won't be saying that."

"No, it's really not, Camilla. I got arrested and held at Regional Detention Centre. There was a problem with my bail. It was all a big misunderstanding. But then Christmas was coming, and I wanted to get Trace and the baby something special. She works so hard at the salon and – "

"And you're such a screw-up. So now you're working this crowd with Rollie the Roach? Don't bother to lie. You're lousy at it, and I can tell by your face that I'm right. What is the matter with you, teaming up with Rollie? He is the epitome of sleaze. He would steal from dying children. You're going down the tubes, Bunny. I can't believe you would let everyone down like this."

"I got no choice, Camilla. He's got something on me."

"Oh, come on. Who doesn't?"

"This is kind of serious. This would get me hard time. Two years plus a day, and I'll be in Kingston. I might need you to help me on that one."

I held up my hand. "Don't prejudice me. I don't want to talk about it. Just tell me about Rollie before he wipes out every wallet on the Hill."

"Well, he needed a partner for here tonight. We just got separated in the crowd. There's a lot of people, eh? Tonya wanted to come, but I told her it was too cold for the baby. If she saw me with Rollie, she'd go ballistic."

"I'm going ballistic myself. Rollie's going to get arrested tonight. You can be a partner with him for that."

Bunny blanched. "No. No. no no. If he sees us talking, he'll think I ratted him out and he'll roll over on me for that other thing that we're not talking about. They don't call him Rollie for nothing. I never should have talked to him at the RDC. We were just waiting by the pay phone and got to shooting the shit. He seemed harmless. You'd think you could trust a fellow prisoner."

"You might at that. Where are you meeting him?"

"Oh no. I'm not going to – "

"Oh yes, you are, Bunny."

"But you're a legal-aid lawyer. You can't turn on him."

"What are you talking about? I can turn on both of you."

"Are you sure, Camilla? What about client privilege?"

"Don't make me laugh. How many wallets did you get?"

"That was my first."

"Take it from the top, Bunny." The good thing about having represented Bunny on one too many occasions was that I can always tell if he's lying.

Bunny tried the truth. "Just that one. It felt kind of creepy: that old lady, and then she gave me the twenty. I should really stick to art. I don't have the heart to do this."

"Or you could even just get a job and try to keep it. Crazy idea, I know, but ..." I felt so hot under the collar during this conversation that I forgot the temperature was dropping.

Bunny grabbed my arm and pleaded, "I won't be able to get a job if I'm in the pen. Rollie will – "

"Get arrested. I'm calling the cops."

"I think, Camilla, if you check the code of ethics, you'll see that you can't really do that to a client. You could be reported to the Law Society of Upper Canada."

"Are you on crack? Because that's just plain insane."

"No, it isn't. I had a lot of time to read in the RDC. They got a library and law books, too. Up-to-date criminal code and digests. Everything."

"Digest this." I snapped open my phone. "I'm calling my brother-in-law."

"He's with the Ottawa force. Ottawa doesn't have jurisdiction here. It's RCMP on the Hill. Federal."

"I'm impressed, Bunny, that you know so much about my family circumstances and about police jurisdictions. Obviously, imprisonment has been good for you. Think of how much more you can learn in Kingston."

Bunny paled and swayed. Of course, I couldn't imagine how long he'd last doing hard time. And he was my favourite client ever.

"I can't go back. I'll die, Camilla. And think about Tonya and the baby. Think about – "

"Why don't you think about how you got yourself in this situation?"

"It's not my fault. You don't know how easy it is when you're with some people to get pulled over to the dark side. Like Rollie."

"The dark side? Oh Bunny, you're such a poet."

"But I don't want to be there. I'm going straight now. This is a lesson to me, for sure." Bunny stopped and blinked. "Except Rollie has got me stuck. I'm trapped. You know?"

I snapped the phone closed. "Here's a deal. Where are you meeting him? Tell me right now."

Behind Bunny, Alvin stood listening to the entire conversation with his mouth hanging open. Luckily, it was too cold for flies.

Bunny gulped. "Behind the Centre Block. By the edge of the Hill, near where the stray cats are. We're supposed to connect and sort everything out, plan the next step. He tosses the stuff over the fence into the bushes, in case he gets made, he won't have much on him. He can climb up from the bike path and pick it up after. But if you show up, he'll know I ratted him out. He probably saw me talking to you."

That was true enough.

And Rollie was more than just a small-time crook. He was a vicious and unpredictable small-time crook. Bunny knew that, and so did I.

Alvin headed away from us, striding purposefully. That's never good. "Come back here, Alvin," I yelled. "I may need your assistance with this situation." But I was too late. He, too, had melted into the crowd. It's so hard to get good help these days.

Bunny shuffled from foot to foot, a pathetic vision of anxiety. Of course he was Bunny and still good-looking. Any woman but me would have taken pity on him. I glanced around looking for an RCMP vehicle. Of course, it was too dark and they were too far away.

Twenty minutes later, the politicians were still droning, and I was still lecturing Bunny. Blah blah blah.

Up in front of the Centre Block, choirs launched into Christmas carols, and politicians took the mike and made muffled comments.

Small children began to cry. Alvin moved forward, seeking political guidance or something. The light show was in full flow, with the purple against the front face of the Centre Block and the Peace Tower changing to blue, then to snow flake patterns.

"Promise me, Bunny, that you mean it this time."

"I promise. Anything."

At that moment, with the choirs in the background, a hundred thousand lights bloomed, cutting the dark, raising spirits. A sea of bodies parted, and Alvin emerged. As scary as that was, I thought it might be good news. He was wearing a triumphant grin, but no scarf. I couldn't see a bulge in his pocket either, indicating that my scarf was gone, too. He did have an expensive maroon jacket slung over his arm.

Alvin leaned over and whispered in my ear, "Rollie would love to apologize for his threat, but I'm afraid he's tied up at the moment."

"Really?" I said, feeling a smile break out. "Did he put up a fight?"

Bunny turned white.

I said, "Did he recognize you?"

Alvin shook his head.

"Ah. But he knows it wasn't Bunny who, um . . . ?"

"Pretty sure."

"Where's your scarf, Alvin?"

"What you don't know won't hurt you, Camilla. Isn't that what Rollie told you?"

"Hmm. Remind me not to ask where my scarf is, too."

"The lights are on, and Rollie's nowhere near home."

I flicked open my cell phone and keyed in a number. "I've changed my mind about that Christmas gift exchange, Merv," I said. "You'll find a thoughtful present in back of the Parliament Buildings in the bushes. And Merv? You better hurry before your gift gets cold."

I snapped the phone closed. "Time you were home yourself, Bunny," I said.

As Bunny skittered off through the crowd, I said, "You know, sometimes I can really understand going over to the dark side."

"There is a certain appeal," Alvin said.

"Welcome back, Alvin."

"You, too. Do you think they'll be able to convict Rollie on anything?"

"Not a chance. Get him on parole violation maybe. Or revoke his bail if he's on bail. Cramp his style this year."

"Better than nothing," Alvin said. "I feel bad about the scarf. I'll make you another one."

"Don't worry about it, Alvin," I blurted.

"Maybe with neon this time. You want me to drop off this jacket to the Snowsuit Fund?"

Sometimes the Christmas spirit just warms the soul.

"Great idea. Happy holidays, Alvin."

"And to you, Camilla."

Christmas Eve on the Drink Train

By Andrew Pyper

From where they found him on Christmas Eve morning you could see his house across the field, close enough to make out the underbellies of cloud sliding across his windows. There'd been some snow the night before but nothing serious, a windless spooling of flakes that wouldn't have prevented a fellow from seeing his porch light across a dozen rows of plowed-under beans. This left the police with the obvious: Glenn Altman had fallen asleep on his way home after a few drinks and died of exposure at least an hour or two before dawn. It happens.

Although the authorities were intrigued by the fact that Mr. Altman was known to have recently won a substantial amount of money in the provincial lottery and that the winning ticket couldn't be found, they were forced to conclude the non-existence of foul play. It was funny – sad if you happened to know the guy – but unremarkable. Some people around town chose to call it "ironic" and others would nod gravely whenever they heard the word, though neither its users or nodders were entirely sure what it meant.

Glenn Altman (milk-truck driver until his father died of a "thing in his brain" and he inherited, then sold, the family farm) had lived his entire life in Perth County, Ontario. The last 30 years of this life had been spent in Sebringville, the kind of town common to the area, one without a good reason to be there at all: the meeting of concession roads on the flat tongue of land midway between Toronto and Windsor. Why there, at *those* roads? It was a place that quietly celebrated – if it celebrated anything – its arbitrariness. A trace of defiance in the windowless community centre, the brick-faced main street with rooftops of varied heights to simulate gentle hills. And the outcast Sebringvilla, the tavern separated from the rest of town by two snow-drifted lots.

This is where Glenn Altman did his drinking five nights out of seven before the divorce, six nights afterwards. The music was the oldies station in Listowel, Ontario, the carpet smelled like a shut-in's bed sheets and the menu was limited to pickled eggs turned green in a jar of brine. There was no justification to drink in such a place unless it was your *life*. But it did boast the novelty of a model railway screwed into the top of the bar. A stretched-out oval that took a Canadian National diesel, six freight cars and red caboose from the coffee machine, past the draft taps, around the egg jar and back again.

The Sebringvilla's regulars call it the Drink Train. The wait is never long for an "All aboard!" or elbow-pumping "Woo-*woo*!" This evening, however, the mood is more jaunty than usual. It's almost Christmas, for one thing. For another, the lottery winner is among them.

"Blue," Glenn Altman says to the pickled eggs. And in a moment, a bottle pimpled with condensation wobbles his way in a hollowed-out tanker car. He picks it up on the way by and brings it to his lips before his eyes have adjusted to the darkness, so that all he senses is a yeasty kiss.

"Figured where you're going to spend it all yet there, Glenn?

This is Ernie, a permanent shadow against the wall next to the coffee machine. He had only one arm to lift the bottles of Ex to his lips, the other having been devoured by a thresher 20 years earlier. But the arm that stayed with him managed the task with such efficiency the empties soon collected before him like bowling pins. There had once been a wife in Ernie's situation – as there had been for most of the Sebringvilla's men – but she'd left him not long after his arm did. "Mine's gone down to the city," he'd announce whenever anyone mentioned a departed beloved, as though she'd only gone shopping for the day and would be back in time to fry him a chop for dinner.

"Ernie, I am still thinking on that," Glenn answers him. "But you know, after the taxman gets through with me, I doubt I'll have enough to buy new shoes."

"Don't give me that. I bet you could buy the whole damn Hush Puppies factory."

"Now there's an idea."

A suede-faced woman makes her way in through the charcoal light of the open doorway and finds her spot at the bar.

"Hey there, Tammy," Glenn says, lifting his beer an inch in salute.

"Well if it isn't our boy the millionaire," she says too loudly for the room's dimensions, as though her intended audience was still sitting outside in her truck.

"It's got to be someone, doesn't it?"

"Yes, sir. But it sure as hell woulda been nice if it hadda been *this* someone!"

Tammy laughs. The same every time: 14 identical *ha's* that pounded all listeners into grimacing submission.

"Another?" Ron the bartender asks Glenn when Tammy has completed her sequence.

"I think I'll have a snort of the good stuff," Glenn says.

Ron wears a neck brace. When he moved to town from Ingersoll eight years ago (divorce, custody loss) he arrived suffering the effects of whiplash, which were apparently yet to leave him. The once-white cotton turned nicotine orange under his chin.

"And for you, Tam?" he asks.

Tammy corkscrews her finger into the air and Ron takes this to mean a Silk Tassel and Coke. When he's finished he places their drinks on freight cars.

"Woo-*woo*" Ernie hoots from out of the shadows.

Unfortunately, Tammy finds this funny enough to shell the room with her laughter once more. This gives Glenn Altman time to think about recent developments.

There was winning the lottery, of course. But that was the least of it. The wife wanted him back, which was altogether more surprising. Whatever happened to Steve, the retired real-estate guy she moved in with after she left? He didn't ask and she didn't say, except to note that "things are quiet" in the townhouse where she now lived, one of those Tudor jobs on the outskirts of Kitchener that Glenn had once glared at from his truck all night.

She'd heard about the money. He knew she was calling because she figured he might be rich and he didn't blame her for a second. Glenn Altman was comfortable with forgiving, having been literally forgiven himself over the course of his adult life. And he missed her. The stout space she took up in the rooms of their permanently unfinished house. The Germanic face capable of sudden, violent smiles.

He pretends he's wearing a watch: twists his wrist to give the bones there a good squint. Quarter past a birthmark. Time for another drink.

And here it comes. A Southern Comfort-and-orange sloshing its way to him on the flatbed meant for plastic sticks of timber.

"Cheers there, Ronald."

"Not a problem."

Tammy's laugh has now turned into a throat-clearing that takes a full minute to grind to a halt. Through the smoke Glenn notices a flush of colour in her cheeks.

"Now, tell me Mr. Altman," she says. "What *are* you planning on doing with your winnings? And don't hem and haw with me now."

"Tammy, I honestly do not know."

"A vacation?"

"A vacation from *what*?" Ron says, filtering his words through the stuffing of his neck brace.

"A trip would be nice." Glenn allows, ignoring him. "But where would I go?"

The bar pauses in collective consideration, a spinning globe in each of their heads.

"Anywhere you'd like, I would think," Tammy answers for all of them.

Glenn glances at his friends and knows what they've been saying about him around town. Knows even if he hasn't actually heard a whisper.

See old Glenny Altman there? Guy went and won the pick 'n' win jackpot, didn't he?

Horseshoe way us his ass.

Couldn't have happened to a nicer drunk.

He's aware of the rumours but does nothing to settle them with the truth. Why tell them if it would only end in disappointment? Not his, but theirs. Despite their head-shaking shows of envy he knows they *like* thinking their town is deserving of an instant millionaire. There seemed little point in relating the phone call he made to the lottery offices in Toronto where the man in charge of award distribution informed him he was the winner of $3,450.27. Not nearly enough to play a reformed Scrooge to all those he'd neglected and denied over the years. But enough to ease a man's troubles for a time.

Too bad he lost the damn ticket. He's still going through the mental motions of correcting himself – it's only *temporarily misplaced* – but he knows better. It's gone. Bye-bye. And though it gives him a stabbing cramp in his bowels to think of it, he's certain he burned the thing. *Burned* it! Emptied his pockets onto the kitchen table one night and in the morning grabbed yesterday's mail and threw it all into the belly of his wood stove. It was long after he touched a match to the kindling that he wondered where a safe place to stash his riches would be. Slapped at his pockets. Slid his fingers through the barren slots of his wallet. Scrambled around on hands and knees like a hound trying to pick up a scent. Not a thing.

He'd sat at the kitchen table after that, thinking about crying. Played the game of trying to remember the last time he had. His mother's funeral, probably. At the very same table with his wife on the other side and a bottle of Crown Royal standing between them. Fourteen years ago. And now he'd burned the goddamn ticket and he wondered if a few tears might be called for. But in the end he decided the stakes were too small for such a show. How could you mourn something you never really had in the first place?

"How're you doing there, Glenny?" Ron is asking him, and for a moment Glenn thinks the question is directed at his emotional state. But of course Ron is only inquiring after the condition of the empty glass before him.

"I could be finer," Glenn replies, blinking back what he tells himself is cigarette smoke. Ron sends another down the rails.

"Ever hear from your Helen?" Tammy asks him. Helen being Glenn Altman's ex.

"From time to time."

"She still with that used-car fella?"

"Real estate."

"*Real* estate then?"

"It's not something I ask about, Tammy."

"She heard about your good news?"

"I wouldn't know."

"Well *I* could make a bet on that."

Tammy is about to launch another carpet bombing of laughter but decides against it, screwing a cigarette between her lips instead.

"Mine's gone down to the city," Ernie says.

Later, the ones who had to be home for dinner begin to show up. Having survived the deadly hour of family time, their eyes stare out at the blinking wreaths in the windows with an equal measure of guilt and relief.

The drink train picks up steam at the bar.

"What do you wanna hear, Glenny?" one of them calls out from next to the juke box.

All eyes turn to Glenn. What will the lottery winner's musical selection be this evening?

"Well sir, a little Nat King Cole is always nice this time of year."

In a moment the room is warmed by the gooey string intro to *White Christmas*.

"How're you *really* doing, Glenn Altman?" Tammy whispers into his ear. Behind him, close.

"Feeling no pain," he answers, and realizes it's true. Perhaps, after all this time, pain had been judged an excessive punishment for such minor crimes as his.

Tammy slides her hands down to his elbows. He's not certain if she's ever touched him before, but he suspects not.

"Care for a dance?" she whispers again.

"Dance?"

"It's what I said."

"Well now."

He looks down at his glass as though it had told a joke at his expense. "Let's have a go then, Miss," he says finally.

They move into the centre of the room unaware that they are holding hands. Gentle and chest-high in the manner of 18th-century aristocrats. Both of them awaiting the inevitable wolf whistle to meet the spectacle the two of them are making, but it doesn't come.

"There now," Tammy says as much to herself as to him.

She smells good to him. A combination of all the daily smells he's grown used to – stale ash, rye, almost exhausted deodorant – along with an additional whiff of something womanly, unnamable. Something that even years of the kind of life that Tammy has lived couldn't entirely erase.

"You're a good dancer, you know that, Glenn Altman?"

"No, I did not," he says. But maybe she's right. He feels whole pounds of deep-fried frozen foods and nodules of arthritis lifting off him, leaving only smooth and efficient muscle.

"Hey there lovebirds, have ya gone deaf? The song's over," Ron laughs over his neck brace.

"Ah Jesus, I need a refreshment," Tammy says in a barky voice meant to cover her sudden embarrassment. Not that she'd been seen dancing with Glenn Altman long after the song ended, but by the pleasure she took in it. If it weren't so bung-headed she'd say that being moved across the floor by Big Glenn had made her feel young. Like a girl for God's sake. But somebody else's. A girl she never was even at the time.

"On me!" Glenn says as they make their way back to their stools, and he scans his nose through the murk to show that he means everybody. Makes a promise to do this sort of thing more often. Dance. Catch a little more sunlight before the day is done. Buy rounds for others without a thought about the price.

There is a feeling with Glenn Altman now that only days ago he believed would never visit him again: of being in the middle of things, a name upon the lips of others, a man of not altogether shameful note moving upright through the chilled air of the world. He has no thoughts of the future. It's good enough in the now, this blessing of money he doesn't actually have and love he doesn't wholly deserve.

He throws his drink down his throat while raising his thumb at Ron, a wordless spike of good fortune acknowledged, and soon another round is coming his way down the tracks.

A Migrant Christmas

by Jane Rule

Harry wasn't the one in the family who had a principle against doing what everyone else did. It was his wife, Anna, who liked to be out of sync with everyone else, whether for buying a house or starting a family; so Harry never seemed to have either the problems or the pleasures his friends did, both his children and his mortgage years younger. Mike's son was dealing dope before Joey had tried a cigarette behind the garage, and Al's daughter was in danger of pregnancy before Sally learned to read.

"Well, it gets worse before it gets better," Al philosophized. "The best thing about kids is that they grow up and leave home."

"Joyce and I have an even better solution. We're growing up and leaving home first. We're going to Mexico for January," Mike announced.

It wasn't just that Joey and Sally were too young to leave alone. Harry frankly couldn't imagine a holiday without them. Even the year Anna had talked them into going to Europe, Joey was less than a year old and went everywhere on Harry's back. Harry still couldn't eat an ice cream cone without expecting a second tongue to help. He and Anna were far too old to take a holiday on their own and still be able to stop at every advertised snake pit and haunted house along the way. Harry would feel like a fool going into one of those child-sized motel swimming pools by himself, and he didn't suppose you ever took just your wife out for a hamburger even if, like Anna, she happened to love them.

No, he didn't envy Mike and Joyce their freedom from the children for a month, but he did envy them their winter holiday. Wouldn't it be really good for Anna and the kids to have at least a couple of weeks out of the rain sometimes tipping to snow, in the winter sun? They wouldn't have to drive all the way to Mexico. Anna was good with languages, so good it had been sometimes hard for Harry not to feel unmanned by her confident handling of their lives all the time they were on the continent. Her stomach was as admirable as her tongue. She hadn't taken one Lomatil in the months they were in Europe. There were weeks when Harry ate nothing else. Montezuma's revenge, and therefore, Mexico, had no part in Harry's daydream.

"People in wheelchairs take winter holidays," Anna said over after-dinner coffee at the kitchen table while the children made a quarrelsome game of the dishes.

"Mike and Joyce don't even have a golf cart," Harry protested.

"Oh, it's because Mike and Joyce . . ."

"It is not. It is nothing of the kind. I want to do just what they're not doing. I want to take the kids along, go when we can all enjoy it together."

"What about school?" Joey asked.

"Might keep you out of trouble for a while after you get back," Anna suggested.

Their problem with Joey was that he was too good in school, his patience more often tested than either his mind or imagination.

"Then you like the idea?" Harry asked, encouraged.

"Could I take Petey?" Sally asked.

"I don't think birds are allowed to cross the border," Harry said.

It was one of those remarks that sent all three others into rounds of laughter, which mildly puzzled Harry.

"It's – like – birds, Dad," Joey then said kindly. "Going south. Petey could migrate in his cage."

Mike had already taken January off, and the office was too short-staffed for Harry to have a holiday at the same time.

"Go for Christmas," his boss said.

"All right," Anna agreed.

"We aren't going to miss Christmas, Sally," Harry explained. "Everywhere is Christmas."

"Will it snow?"

"No. We'll probably go swimming on Christmas day, just the way they do in Australia."

"Can we cut our own tree?"

"It will be a cactus. Now, look, you guys, the point is something different, all right?"

"Christmas isn't exactly boring the way it is," Joey said.

"It's time they travelled," Harry said later when the children had gone to bed. "They're in a rut already."

"Well, kids are conservative about greed, that's all," Anna said. "They don't want to get out of the range of Santa Claus. You can understand that."

"Since it's Christmas, do you think, just this once, we might try for reservations?"

"No," Anna said. What she had refused to do all through

crowded Europe, she was not about to agree to in the sparsely populated southern desert.

"If there's no room at the inn?"

"We stay in the stable. Anyway, who but a family of nuts goes away for Christmas?"

"Jews. Every Jew I know is trying to get his kids away from Christmas."

"Happy Hanukkah," Anna said and yawned.

The only elaborate preparations Harry tried to make were those for Sally's canary, but, though he called every office from embassy to customs, he could get neither Canada nor the United States to object to taking Petey with them. The bird had as much right to go south as they did.

"You don't even want a certificate from the vet?" Harry asked, incredulous.

"Not even proof of citizenship."

Harry finally resorted to reasoning with Sally. "What if the weather confuses him? What if he begins to molt?"

But Sally, at five, could be as implacable as her mother.

"The bird," Anna reminded Harry, "was your idea in the first place."

Harry had one of those clairvoyant moments about the trip, his idea in the first place, during which impossible-to-imagine responsibilities and problems would fall to him to bear and solve. How he wished it had been Anna's suggestion against which he could raise all that might be impractical and ominous.

Joey, once he'd brought home his first book about the desert, was Harry's enthusiastic ally.

"There are rattlesnakes and flash floods," Joey promised them all. "And much better earthquakes than we ever have."

He didn't scare Anna, who was a fatalist, but he terrified Sally with stories of carnivorous birds and aggressive cacti.

"You know, you can't treat a cactus like a tree, Dad," Joey explained. "They're more like porcupines." And to Sally he said, "You don't even have to touch some of them to make them shoot their quills at you."

"We're going to be picking grapefruit and oranges off the trees," Harry said. "We're going to be lying in the sun. We're going to be swimming and playing golf and tennis."

"I don't know how, most of those," Sally said.

"I'll teach you."

In the spirit of their escape from winter, Harry tried to curse their first snow, which fell only several days before they were to leave, but with the new snow tires he'd bought for mountain driving, he had no trouble getting home, and the kids were out on the hill with garbage can lids having a lovely time.

"This is going to be cake-and-eat-it year," Harry said confidently.

"It's hard to look out the window and then pack shorts and bathing suits," Anna said.

She did not go on to compare the experience with daffodils on the Christmas dinner table, of which she didn't approve.

"I've told them we're not hauling all presents down there and back. We'll have a second Christmas when we get home, all right?"

"I guess so," Harry said.

It was not practical, of course, with limited room in the car, with customs, but he was not sure, come the day itself, how he'd be Santa Claus without presents.

"Well, one each," Anna said, modestly relenting.

Petey was the only one to get his present early, a travelling cage a foot square with a light-tight cover.

"It's not just to shut him up at night," Anna explained. "It's to keep him from getting car sick."

"Do birds get car sick?" Harry asked, incredulous.

"They don't get seasick," Joey said, "or gulls wouldn't ride on the ferry boats."

"Is Petey going to throw up?" Sally asked.

"How about leaving him home?"

"Just because I get car sick, you don't leave me home," Sally answered indignantly.

It snowed again the morning they were to leave, but nobody minded, and Harry presented them all with new plaid lap robes for the occasion.

"I wanted to get beach towels," he confessed, "but there weren't any around this time of year."

The children were warmly settled in the back seat, cool can between them in which Anna had packed all they needed for breakfasts and lunches along the way, Petey in his covered cage on top of that. Anna was in front with her knitting.

"We're off," Harry said, as the wheels spun for a second before the new tires grabbed and sent them in a jolt out of the driveway.

Harry had planned three days for the trip. At the end of the first, he wondered if they'd ever get there at all. It had taken them twelve hours to get to Portland. He sometimes hadn't been able to see more than fifteen feet in front of him, and patches of ice made braking no option, as the huge double trailer trucks jack-knifed across the road testified.

"Wow, look at that!" Joey would exclaim, peering through the snow veil. "Is it going to blow up, do you think, Dad?"

Sally thought it wasn't fair not to let Petey see something of the trip, but, when she uncovered him and found him huddled in the corner of the tiny cage, his feathers fluffed out like a winter overcoat, she didn't have to be told to cover him again.

"Is he going to die?" she asked every fifteen or twenty minutes.

They hadn't dared to stop for lunch, not only because they might have frozen to death, but because there was no sure way off the road. The others ate, but Harry managed no more than half a sandwich and a couple of swigs of Anna's vegetable soup which sat, a sour fist of fear, in his stomach for the rest of the day. He couldn't even eat the hamburgers he finally managed to buy them after they were safely installed in a Portland motel.

If the heat had worked, if the ice machine hadn't kept him awake most of the night, Harry might have been tempted to suggest they hole in there until the storm – or winter – was over.

"We ought to be out of this in another day," Anna said reassuringly.

"Mike and Joyce *fly* to Mexico," Harry said grimly.

"We're doing what they're not doing," Anna reminded him.

Half way through Oregon, the snow turned to rain, but at Grant's Pass it was snowing again, and Harry was told by the motel manager that both roads into California were closed.

"For how long?"

There was no way of telling. This motel was, at least, warm, but it wasn't until the next afternoon during the seventh game of Monopoly that the sun finally came out and Petey began to sing. Though they had paid for a second night, Harry decided right after dinner, when he heard the roads were open, to leave at once. It would be the hardest part of the trip for Sally, the road twisting down out of the mountains, and this way she might sleep through it. After she threw up her dinner at a snow-narrowed turn out, she did, and Harry resisted taking up her question about the distressed bird. As they crossed the California border, they slowed to go through the inspection station where they had to give up the mandarin oranges they'd forgotten to declare at the international border. It seemed to Harry another symbolic deprivation of their Canadian Christmas.

"I thought there were orange and grapefruit trees in California," Joey said, peering out at the dark evergreen forests so like what they had left behind.

"There will be, son," Harry said determinedly.

At dawn, the first miracle of the trip occurred. There on either side of the road were the promised orange and grapefruit groves, bright with fruit lovelier than ornaments on a Christmas tree, acres and acres of them.

"Look," Joey said, "there's fruit on the ground. Could we ... ?"

"Waste not, want not," Anna said to Harry who was always dubious about anything that might not be law abiding.

So he stopped and they all got out and picked up oranges which were more fragrant and tasted sweeter than any Harry remembered since his childhood. So peacefully euphoric was he to have brought his family safely out of the winter storms of the north to this amazing morning that he said aloud what he had nearly decided not to mention.

"Old Carl lives in Bakersfield."

Anna did not respond.

"Who's old Carl?" Sally asked.

"A friend of mine," Harry said, preparing to regret his remark.

Carl was the sort of friend you had until you got seriously enough involved with a woman to introduce them and within moments of seeing Carl in a woman's eyes, even the most tolerant sort of woman, you wondered what you had ever seen in him at all, for he was fat, loud, and stupid. Yet, because Harry hadn't seen Carl in ten years, his memory went back to those times before Anna when Carl had been one of Harry's gang of to-hell with-it college buddies, willing to go to any game, movie, night club, on any drunk, willing to take his car and spend his money.

"He's married now. He's got kids," Harry said. "Might just give him a call, stop for a drink on our way through, since it's Christmas time."

Anna still didn't comment. Joey was watching her; then he turned to his father and shrugged. "It's okay with me."

Carl was, indeed, delighted to hear Harry's voice on the phone, gave him instructions in confused detail about how to get to the house, told him to come for a drink, come for dinner, spend the night, whatever.

"We are not going to impose on that man's poor wife," Anna began.

"Of course not," Harry agreed. "We'll just drop in and say hello."

"Could we have a cookie?" Sally asked.

"If you're offered one," Anna said.

"They'll probably be coconut," Joey suggested brightly; he loved coconut, and Sally wouldn't touch it.

It was one of the dozen times a day the strategically placed cool can kept marginal peace with Petey functioning as a sort of one-bird UN force.

When they arrived at the door, Carl opened it and said, much less enthusiastically than on the phone, "Come in and all, but my wife says to tell you the boy has mumps, so if your kids . . . "

"I've had the mumps," Joey said.

"Sally, darling," Anna said. "You'll have to wait in the car. We'll only be a few minutes."

Sally's face filled up with tears like a glass at a tap.

"You don't want to be sick for Christmas."

"There isn't going to be any Christmas," she wailed.

"Look, maybe we better make it another time," Harry began.

"At least, come in and see the tree," Carl said. "Otherwise, I'm stuck here with my mother-in-law all afternoon."

"I heard that, Carl!" shouted a deep, sexless voice from inside the room. "It's a question of who's stuck with who."

At the sound of that voice, the tears began to drain out of Sally's face.

"I *think* I've had mumps," Joey said.

"Look," Harry said, "both of you go back to the car, all right? We won't be long."

He and Anna were back in twenty minutes.

"What did the tree look like?" Sally demanded.

"Just like a tree," Harry said, "cluttering up the living room."

"Were there presents?"

"Were there cookies?"

"Mostly there were sick kids and crabby relatives."

"Was the lady inside a witch?"

"More or less," Harry said. "Now, aren't you glad we're not having a Christmas like that?"

"We don't have crabby relatives," Sally said.

"How fat do you suppose that guy is?" Joey said.

"Even fatter than I remembered," Harry said.

Though he was promising himself not to remember anything on his own before Anna again ever, he was also feeling modestly smug about his own decent shape, his good-looking and agreeable wife, his healthy children. "Poor old Carl. Some people are born to make other people feel good."

"Good?" Anna asked.

"Well, better," Harry clarified.

On the outskirts of town, he found a motel with a kidney-shaped pool, and he slept in the California sun while Anna and the children played in the water.

The next day in Palm Springs, they all did some secretive Christmas shopping.

"Let's get the kids a piñata," Anna suggested. "We're nearly at the Mexican border."

Once they had taken advantage of the stores, Harry was restless to be on their way.

"You mean, this isn't where we're going?" Anna asked.

"You don't want to stay here, do you?" Harry asked, surprised.

"Where else is there?"

"The state park. Borrego Springs. It has everything Palm Springs has except Palm Springs."

Not until they were leaving town and Anna began to sing carols did Harry realize she'd been resigning herself to a week in that rich resort town where private guard services protected the mostly deserted houses of celebrities, where the chief conversation among the locals seems to be skin cancer, and the tourists complained about the prices of flowered trousers. Harry had not spoken of Borrego Springs before because he wanted to seem spontaneous while being prepared. They would be in the real desert in a little community with, nevertheless, plenty of tourist accommodations, well before dark on Christmas Eve.

As they all sang together *We Three Kings*, Harry heard Sally's high, sweet version of "of Oreo Tar." His cookie-obsessed daughter did not get in the way of his fantasy that they could be that new breed of agnostic wise men still following a star across the badlands in the delicate winter light to a simple place, to a yearly miracle.

"Wow!" Joey said. "Did you see that sign? 'This Road Is Subject to Flash Floods'!"

Each time they dipped into a dry wash, Joey looked in vain for the rushing water. Then he saw a road runner with a snake's tail hanging out of its beak.

"Those big ones look like they're on fire," Sally said as they passed twelve-foot-high ocotillos, their bare, viciously thorned limbs tipped by fragile red bloom.

Anna's hand rested on Harry's thigh. "I like the ones with halos," she said, nodding to crowns of bright thorns.

Then there before them, nearly at the foot of western mountains, as bare of vegetation as a dinosaur's hide, was the oasis of Borrego Springs, green with golf courses, punctuated by date palms.

The two motels near the stores were full. The next three didn't take pets or children.

"No children?" Harry asked each time. "You've got to be kidding. And the bird's in a cage."

He drove them back into the centre and found a real estate office.

"I'm willing to rent a house if I have to," Harry explained, trying to sound reasonable.

"To have children in it, you'd have to buy one," the sales man explained. "Even then you couldn't buy one at any of the clubs."

"What are you, paranoid about school taxes or something? Didn't Proposition Thirteen take care of that?"

"This is a retirement community and an adult resort."

"You could camp in the park," a gas station attendant suggested. "There's no objection to kids in the park."

"It gets down to forty degrees," Harry protested. "We've got nothing with us but lap robes."

"I'd say your best bet is to go back to Palm Springs or over to San Diego."

"We want to stay here."

Sally was staring out the window watching a white-haired woman pedal a giant tricycle up the street.

"This is a funny place," she said. "She isn't really children, is she?"

"There aren't any children," Joey explained

"Did they die?"

"They aren't allowed."

Harry got a list of every place in the valley that offered accommodation. He stood putting dimes into the pay phone as if it were a slot machine.

"Surely, on Christmas Eve you'd make an exception," he'd try. Then exasperated, he'd begin to shout, "Children have rights, too, you know!"

"Harry," Anna finally said, "I think we better get out of here."

"I'm starving," Joey said. "Are kids allowed to eat here?"

"There's that little Mexican restaurant," Anna said. "How about some tacos, and then we'll drive over to the ocean."

The place was jammed. They had to stand to wait their turn and were finally seated at a table for ten, otherwise occupied by aging couples.

"What are people doing, eating out on Christmas Eve?" Harry whispered angrily to Anna. "They ought to be at home with their grandchildren."

But Anna was exchanging friendly greetings with the old man next to her.

"Nice to see a couple of kids," he was saying. "I said to my wife – this is Rachel, my wife – funny place with no kids around, quiet as the grave."

"Oh, Sam, don't exaggerate. There are children right next door to us. We're renting. We just come down from Oregon for a month," she confided to Anna, "and renters can't have children, but owners are allowed to have grandchildren visit."

"It's unnatural!" Harry said.

When Sam and Rachel heard the dilemma that faced these Canadian visitors, they were as irate as Harry and agreed that it was not only unnatural but un-American, and they would do something about it.

"Listen," Sam said. "We've got plenty of space, twin beds in the spare room, a second bathroom, big fold-out bed in the living room."

"But children aren't allowed," Harry reminded him.

"We'll just smuggle them in," Rachel decided. "When we finish here," she continued in a lowered voice, "we'll put the children in our car under a blanket. Then a little while later, you come along . . ."

"What about Petey?" Sally asked.

"We have a canary," Harry said glumly.

"If we can smuggle a couple of kids, who's worried about a canary?"

"But you could get evicted," Harry reminded them.

"So that's the end of the world?" Sam asked.

"You're wonderful," Anna said, "Thank you."

Once the plan was approved, all six of them took their parts with elaborate seriousness. Harry insisted on paying the whole bill while Rachel and Sam took the children and hid them under their own lap robes on the back seat of their large and impressive American car.

"God, I hope they're not kidnappers," Anna said suddenly as the old couple drove off.

"You're the one who agreed!" Harry shouted, rushing to their own car.

When Anna got in beside him, she was laughing. Then she said, "I'm sorry about being so dumb about making reservations."

"I would have settled for a stable if I could have found one."

They found the car parked in the carport of number 131 in the mobile home park, and they found the children in the living room, eating cookies. Harry put Petey in his covered cage on top of the television set.

"They'll think it's on TV," Rachel said, "whatever noise we make. As long as we keep the curtains closed, and the kids stay off the screened porch."

Anna helped Rachel make up the guest room beds and then settled the children while Harry accepted a drink and a look around, never having been inside these giant Kleenex boxes on wheels before. "Come say goodnight," Anna called.

"Dad," Sally said, "you said Christmas was everywhere."

"And so it is," Harry said, smiling at his clean, comfortable children as safely settled as they might have been with grand-parents.

"I don't see any tree. I don't see any presents."

"Well, older people, on their own, sometimes . . ."

"The thing is, Sally," Anna interrupted. "Sam and Rachel are Jewish, and Jewish people don't celebrate Christmas."

"Jewish people don't believe in Santa Claus?" Sally asked. "I don't really either, but everybody can pretend."

"Jews don't believe in Jesus," Joey said.

"Neither exactly do we," Anna said. "There are a lot of different ways to believe in kindness and hope and love. There'll be surprises in the morning. Just don't worry about it."

Out in the living room where Rachel was making up their bed, another worried conversation had obviously taken place.

"Rachel says we can make a tree out of palm fronds," Sam explained. "And . . ."

"You mustn't go to any trouble," Anna protested. "We came away partly to get away from all the elaborate fuss Christmas gets to be. We're not really believers either."

At that moment, they heard the voices of carolers outside the door, mostly wandering old voices with one true soprano, singing of a child born to Mary, and they all went out to listen.

"We're not all that much Jews either," Sam said as they went back into the house. "Anyway, there's no real way to get away from Christmas, not with kids in the house."

The courteous argument turned into the joy of finding palm fronds in the desert moonlight for the men, baking for the women. It was nearly as late as it always got at home when Sam and Rachel finally retired to their bedroom, leaving Harry and Anna to sleep in the splendor of a room-high tree of palm fronds, decorated with dozens of freshly baked and brightly frosted cookies, presents for everyone stacked underneath it, Harry's gift to

Anna and hers to him re-labelled for Sam and Rachel, the piñata hanging over the breakfast table.

Harry woke at dawn, for a moment uncertain where he was until he saw the tree, and he was very glad that he had a wife who believed in miracles rather than reservations, that Christmas would be as secret and illicit as it had been in the beginning, for the sake of the children. He got up and opened the curtains just a crack. Then he took the cover off Petey and let him sing. Outside a mocking bird in the ocotillo answered that caged, illegal carol.

Making Spirits Bright

by Michelle Berry

They are down south and it's hot and the little kid is digging in the sand and singing, "Here comes Santa Claus, here comes Santa Claus, right down Santa Claus lane." He looks up from his hole. He looks up from where the water is streaming into his hole in the sand and he says, "How's it go again, Mommy? What comes next?"

"Something about his reindeers," the mommy yawns. She is sitting on a lounge chair in the sun. Her leather skin is everywhere, pushing out of her bikini, her blond hair almost translucent. She is painting her nails fire-engine red. "Something about Mrs. Claus, maybe?" the mommy says logically. "Maybe something more about the lane where he lives?"

"No," shouts the dad. He is back a bit, in the shade of a beach umbrella, his arms and legs covered. His feet are bare, though, and later, when he's getting ready for the Christmas Eve Dinner Dance in the hotel, he won't be able to put socks on over his burned and peeling skin. "Reindeers. It's definitely reindeers."

It's the first holiday the mommy's been on since she had the little boy. The first holiday in the sun. They went skiing last year, but the little boy was three then and afraid of the snow, so she sat with him in the lodge while the father went up and down the slopes all day and sat in the bar all night. The mommy has a tanning bed at home though, so thankfully she looks like she's always on holiday. The little boy has become an expert at shutting the giant roof of the bed over his mother and then playing quietly on the floor while she lies still and lets the tanning lights do their trick. At the grocery store, the women all say, "Where've you been now? You're always going somewhere."

It's Christmas Eve and the beach is deserted. The little boy moves sand with a shovel into the hole he's just dug. The mommy looks up. She can't believe it. Her boy digs and digs a hole, working so carefully for so long, and then he fills it up and starts again. She can't believe it. The mommy doesn't understand her little boy any more than she understands her husband. He just sits and watches and waits. But waits for what, the mommy cannot tell. And it doesn't matter, really, that she doesn't understand her boy. But it matters quite a bit that she doesn't understand the dad.

"Nixon and Blixen," the dad shouts. "That's how it goes. Dancing on the lane."

"Nixon? Sweetie, not Nixon," the mommy says. She giggles.

"Vixen?"

The little boy starts singing again, "Here comes Santa Claus right down Santa Claus lane. Nixon and Blixen and all the reindeers pulling on the rein."

"That's right, pumpkin!" The mommy smiles. "That's just about right! What a smart boy I have."

"He learned it in school," the dad shouts. "They must have

taught that to him in school."

The mommy sighs. Every day back home, she takes the little boy to school in the mornings and then picks him up at lunch. He spends the afternoon with her. He plays. She tans. Sometimes they bake cookies. What does he know about what the little boy does in school? What does the dad know about it?

"I'm hungry," the little boy says. "All this singing and digging makes me hungry."

The mommy tries to pull a bag of carrots from her beach bag, but her nails are still wet and so she picks up the beach bag with her toe and tosses it towards the boy. It lands in his new hole.

"It's wet, it's wet," the dad shouts. "Get it out."

The mommy sighs and rises from her chair. She gingerly plucks the bag up from the hole and opens it up. She takes out some carrots.

"I don't want carrots," the little boy says. "I hate carrots." The water is so blue that it hurts the mommy's eyes. She shades her eyes with her hands, her fresh painted fingernails shining brightly. He's four years old, she says to herself. "There's cookies in the bottom of the bag, honey. If you can find them, you can have them." The little boy dives towards the beach bag.

"He'll ruin his dinner," the dad shouts. At dinner, the little boy will sit before his plate of roast beef and look at it. He'll look at it until he swears he can see it move.

She'll sit in front of the TV and miss watching her husband try to dance on his burned, sockless feet at the Christmas Eve Dinner Dance.

The little boy eats the cookies. Occasionally he looks at his dad while he's chewing. The dad looks at him.

The mommy turns toward the dad. "I'm going for a swim," she says. "It's hot." The dad nods.

"Will you watch him?"

"Sure," the dad says. "Sure I'll watch him." The dad puts his eyes on the little boy and doesn't take them off. He stares at the little boy until he is sure he can see right through him and to the water and to his wife, swimming in the water, her leather skin looking somehow healthy when it's wet, and then past her to the end of the horizon where he stares and stares, looking right through the body and bones of his son.

The mommy swims.

The little boy digs.

The mommy's hair flows out behind her in the water. She can feel it around her shoulders, around her neck. Later, after the little boy is in bed, after his screaming fit in the restaurant, after they've watched a bit of TV and the mommy will wonder where the dad is, the mommy will take a bath and she'll remember when her hair flowed out behind her in the sea.

"Are you sure he comes here?" the little boy says quietly.

"What?" the dad shouts.

"Santa Claus, are you sure he comes here?"

"To the beach?"

"No, to the hotel."

"Yes, I'm sure. I've told you a million times. He'll come here."

"But there's no fireplace."

"Speak up, boy."

"There's no fireplace."

"He can walk through the door," the dad shouts. "He can walk straight through it without hurting himself. Don't be ridiculous. He doesn't need a fireplace."

"But there's no tree."

"What?"

"There's no tree."

"What are you shouting about?" the mommy shouts from the water. "You're both shouting."

"He doesn't need a tree. He can put the presents on the floor," he says. "Why are you shouting?"

"The boy thinks that Santa won't come," the dad says.

"He'll come," the mommy says, bending down and touching her little boy's head. "He told me he would. In the mall, last Tuesday, when I was buying this nail polish," she holds out her fingers, "he told me himself he'd come down here and give you presents."

"Oh," the little boy says. Not for a minute does he believe that the Santa in the mall is the one who can walk through doors. "Here comes Santa Claus, here comes Santa Claus, right down Santa Claus lane," he sings.

"What about Jingle Bells?" the dad shouts. "I'm sick of that lane song. Where would Santa have a lane? The North Pole? The North Pole has no lanes. Just snow. Right?"

"Why don't you come over here?" the mommy says. "Why are you shouting so much?"

The dad puts his hands up to his temples. He massages them. This is the look he likes when he is tired of the mommy and her ways, when he is tired of her leather skin, of the white-blond hair, of the way she calls the little boy by pet names, honey and bunny and poopsy and pumpkin. He rubs his temples. The dad also uses this look when he's at especially important meetings with especially important clients and when they are discussing especially important things. This happens often.

And later, down at the beach, after the Christmas Eve Dinner Dance at the hotel, when's he's hobbling around on his burned feet in the sand with his voluptuous dance partner, the dad will use this look again. He'll use it to impress her and she'll like it and she'll say, "Oh, do you have a headache? Your poor man," and she'll touch his hands, which are touching his temples, and his feet won't hurt any more.

The mommy will float in her bathtub with her hair streaming out and she'll think about the sea she can hear through the open window. The waves crashing against the sand.

And the little boy will lie in bed at just about this time, willing Santa Claus to melt through his door and take him away. Take him back home. Where there's a tree and a fireplace. He is sure Santa doesn't put the presents on the floor, but he can't remember last year. Last year, he was only three.

"Here comes Jingle Bells, here comes Jingle Bells," the little boy sings.

"No, no, no, no, no."

"He can sing it just about any way he wants to sing it, can't you, poopsy?" the mommy says.

"Doesn't he learn anything at that school? What do they teach him there?"

The little boy continues to dig.

The mommy sits back down on her chair. Her wet skin glistens.

The dad massages his temples.

"You know," the mommy begins. "If you would just ..."

"Don't you start with me," the dad shouts. "Don't start."

"Dashing through the snow," the little boy sings loudly. Very loudly. He sings it so loudly that he drowns out the dad and the mommy. He drowns out the sea and the waves crashing and the gulls swooping wildly in the air. He drowns out the sun even and everything seems dark suddenly. "On a one-horse open sleigh."

"Well," the dad says. "You know that one, don't you? You know that one well. I told you they taught him something in that school. I told you he was learning something."

"Merry Christmas," the mommy says. She scoops up some sand, willing it to stick to her fingernail polish. But the fingernail polish is dry, it's been dry for a while, and so the sand rolls off the glossy red paint and into her lap.

Much later, after the dad comes back from his walk with his dance partner, after the mommy has had her nice, soothing bath, after the little boy has fallen asleep on the floor, propped up beside the door and after all is done and not said, then the presents are laid on the floor in a haphazard pile and the stockings are rested against a chair leg and someone big and jolly slowly makes his way through the door and out into the night. The dad nestles tight next to the mommy in bed and both of them listen to the little boy's breathing coming snore-like through the hotel walls and into their room.

"Merry Christmas to you too," the dad shouts at the mommy.

"O'er the fields we go," the little boy sings, "laughing all the way. Ha. Ha. Ha. Bells on cocktails ring, making spirits bright . . ."

"Cocktails?" the mommy interrupts. She giggles. "Oh, bunny, that's perfect. What a perfectly lovely idea."

The dad laughs.

The family packs up their belongings and moves sluggishly through the sand together toward their hotel. The little boy rests his hand in his mother's hand, and she wraps her fire-engine red nails around his palm. The dad carries the shovel and bucket and beach bag. His feet are stinging. They are feeling tender.

"Cocktails," the mommy murmurs. "What a perfectly lovely idea."

Angel with a Cowbell

by Roy MacGregor

S ip.
   Puff. Puff-puff.
Puff-puff-sip.
Puff-puff-puff.
Sip . . .
. . . dot. Dash. Dot-dash. Dot-dot. Dash-dot. Dot . . .
". . . Trust this finds you well, dear Elaine."

Seven final words and Stanley Thornton was beat. Puffed out –
and sipped out. Done. He had been writing since 7:00 a.m. Again
unable to sleep. When the morning nurse came in to turn him
over, he had asked to get up, and once up and washed and fed,
he had asked the nurse to roll his computer over, and here it was,
almost noon, and he had done nothing all the morning long but

write, yet another time, to Elaine. Four hours at the keyboard, four hours sipping and puffing and resting. And yet, if he printed what he had written out, perhaps it would run three pages. Three pages. It wasn't as if he had been hard pressed for words. The words came to him easily. It was the vowels and consonants he had trouble with.

A puff for a dot, a sip for a dash. Five puffs for a 'p', two puffs, two sips and two more puffs for a simple period. Communication among humans had gone from grunts and gestures to instantaneous transmission, and yet here was Stanley Thornton trying to marry Morse code to a computer modem in order to get a message to someone he had never met nor spoken to. He was sitting at a machine that could transmit data at 14,400 chunks of information per minute, and yet he, Stanley Thornton, worked at approximately 32 letters a minute: dash-dot-dot . . . dot-dash . . . dash-dash . . . dash-dot. Damn. He sometimes thought he could sense his computer waiting on him, arms folded impatiently, one foot tapping in annoyance.

He was writing again to Elaine. It was, according to his file records, the 19th time he had written to her in less than seven months. Nearly three letters a month. This was on the verge of getting serious. He had no idea what she looked like. He knew her e-mail address, and he knew, from her letters back, that she lived in a small town outside Ottawa with her parents, her sister Charmaine, a dog and two cats. He knew that she was 33. He was 32. He knew that she had a job at the House of Commons (she didn't say what she did). He knew she worried about the country, had cried watching *The Remains of the Day*, secretly read the grocery-line tabloids, loved spring, and was crazy about the Montreal Canadiens.

He was a Leafs fan. Always had been. Always would be. He wore a Leafs sweater most days in winter, his old number – 8 – on the back with his name, Thornton, stitched above the number in striking white. He liked to kid her about the 1967 series when the Leafs had stunned the more-talented Habs; she liked to kid him that it was the last and would remain the last time the Leafs had won the Stanley Cup.

They had met by accident. He had been scanning the community discussion section on Freenet, and his eye had been caught by a simple notice thrown into the millions of bytes that pass through every day. "Help!" she had written. "Can anyone out there get me out of here?"

He had loved the idea: trapped on a bulletin board. Unable to go anywhere, unable to leave, the microchip as deserted island. He had sat all morning wondering if he should contact her. He could help. He had one of the best computer systems in town, certainly the best, by far, of all the outfits he had seen in the Algonquin Facility, where he had been living since the accident. The Dukes, his old team, had chipped in to set him up with everything he would ever need: computer, colour monitor, internal modem and fax, tube adapter for Morse-code control. Ted Larsen, his old centre man, who was now running the best computer store in Pembroke, had set it up and brought in an expert from the States to teach Stanley how to use the Morse-code system. Sip-puff-puff-puff. Puff-puff. Puff . . . puff-puff. Puff-puff. Sip-puff. Sip-sip-puff . . . B-O-R-I-N-G.

It had taken him two years to get to this point, but at least now he could work the machine, get into his files and access the various networks. He loved browsing: others had shopping malls, he figured, he had the bulletin boards and various networks to scour for interest. For a long while he had been part of an extensive hospital group that ran all the way from Fresno, California, to Saint John, New Brunswick, each member in rehabilitation, and every one of them anxious to find someone who understood.

Understood . . . It struck Stanley as a ridiculous notion. Why waste time searching for someone who understands when he could not understand himself? He had bailed out after a month of chit-chat, and signed off permanently. Not interested.

But Elaine's call for help interested him. Her question had seemed so sweet, so innocent, so helpless. He had written back – puffing and sipping into his tube, the words slowly forming, the codes quickly accessing – and he had made contact. His first communication was simply a note: he said who he was, how long he had been involved with Freenet and the Internet, how he would be glad to help. She wrote back saying she was having trouble working her way through the complicated menus, having trouble knowing where to go to get what she wanted – whatever that was. She called herself a Luddite and a Techno-nerd. He liked that. She needed him.

He stayed up half that next night working on a long letter. It amounted to a sort-of *Cole's Notes* to getting and staying on and getting off of the information highway. It was clear and concise; when you sip and puff every single letter, you learn to be concise. He sent it off to her. She wrote back to him with thanks, telling him a bit about herself.

And that's how it began. And this is how it appeared to be ending. He had started to tell her more and more about himself. He told her about his family and his home, about his brothers and sister and about the things he liked. He talked about books and movies and video games and celebrities and sports heroes and politicians. He talked about fishing and poison ivy and how he was afraid of electrical storms ("I'm not," she wrote back).

Through letter after letter he had proceeded to lay out his life story, always stopping just short. He had told her about the year he failed in elementary school, about the dogs he had owned, about the places he had travelled. He spent nearly three full letters talking about the sports he had played. He told her about the swim team and about the year he played lacrosse and the high-school volleyball team (City champions!) and all about the best ski hills in Eastern Ontario and Western Quebec.

But mostly he talked about hockey. His game. He told her about starting out in novice, and about the little goaltender who forgot to go to the bathroom before his father suited him up and who ended up flooding the ice before the game was half over. He told her about the year the rep coach came to watch the house league, and how the rep coach had come and talked to his regular coach and then to his father and then had come and asked him if he'd like to join the team for a tournament in Arnprior. He had, and he had never looked back. Leading scorer in pee wee, The Quebec Pee Wee Tournament. All-star in bantam, Midget, Juvenile, a couple of years in Junior C.

And he told her all about his championship jacket. The colours – teal green and black – and the raised crests, and how the crest over the heart said Regional Champs, Senior Hockey. He did not tell her that he had never worn it.

He told her about the final series against the team from Renfrew, and how it had gone back and forth – the home-town team winning, then losing on the road – until it had all come down to that final game for the championship. He had scored in the first period, a lucky goal that had really been a pass that happened to scoot into the net off a defenceman's skate. The other team had scored. Then his team got two, the opposition got two and then – midway through the third period – he had the break-away that ended up deciding the championship.

He told her he had been named Most Valuable Player of the playoffs. He told her that they had eventually retired his sweater, and that it was now on show behind glass in the front hallway of the community centre.

None of it had been a lie. He did not tell her how the break-away ended, but it was a fact that this moment had decided the outcome. The last thing he remembered clearly was the sound of old Mrs. Humphrey's cowbell, the frantic clanging filling the rink as he shot ahead with the roar of the home-town crowd. The bell was ringing for him. He was old Mrs. Humphrey's favourite player. She even wore a button with his face on it – Stanley Thornton in full uniform, set to shoot, staring out with determination – and for two seasons now, she had announced when Stanley had possession of the puck with a loud, rhythmic clanging of the cowbell. The other teams despised it and often brought air horns to attempt to drown her out. But it never worked. When Mrs. Humphrey's bell sounded, it meant Stan The Man Thornton had the puck, and the enemy was under siege. It was the perfect musical accompaniment for his breakaway.

Mrs. Humphrey's bell was ringing when he went down. He had been tripped from behind, and when his feet went out, his head shot straight and uncushioned into the boards. When the game resumed – minutes later? Hours later? Days later? He wasn't sure – his team had been awarded a penalty shot which had resulted in a goal, which was the goal that decided the game. His penalty shot. His goal. The senior championship.

Only he hadn't taken the shot. His sweater had been retired because no one else would ever dare wear it, not after what had happened.

On the wall of his room in the Algonquin Facility was the team photo, taken moments after the championship trophy had been awarded. His teammates – Ted Larson front and centre – were surrounding it, some of them lying on the ice, some of them kneeling, some of them standing with their hands on the shoulders of those kneeling, young men, mostly in their 20s and some in their early 30s, all in the prime of life. It was a photograph that is taken a thousand times a year in this country, from the novice house-league championship to the Stanly Cup. Only this photograph was unlike all others. In this photograph, no one is smiling.

Stanley could not tell Elaine that he would soon count a full decade of his life spent in a wheelchair. He could not tell her that he had no movement from his neck down. He could not tell her that his letters took all day, every day, not that they were dashed off when he had time from his busy schedule. Dashed off . . . such a strange phrase for him. He could not tell her that he preferred to sign his letters "Stan" rather than "Stanley" because it took five fewer puffs and one less sip. Dash. Dot. Dot-dot . . . dot-dot.

Ted Larsen felt like a sneak. It was none of his business and he knew it, but he couldn't help himself. Every couple of weeks, just as he had ever since the accident, he dropped in to the Facility to spend some time with his old winger. Usually it was just to drop off a rented video or a hockey magazine or a new computer game, but sometimes it was to fiddle with Stanley's set-up. Because of his business, Ted had become the local computer expert to family and friends and now, thanks to a lifelong friendship with Stanley Thornton, to the entire computer operation at the Algonquin Facility.

Three months earlier, Stanley Thornton's hard drive had started to go wonky. Ted had taken the computer off for a few days and returned it in perfect condition, but to work on the hard drive he had first bled the files off onto several disks for safe keeping, made the adjustments, and then put all the files back. It was a simple procedure, routine, but in doing so Ted Larsen had ended up with all of Stanley Thornton's files copied to disks, which now lay on the desk in front of him. Normally he would have erased the files on the disks – but this time he hadn't.

Why had he snooped? He didn't know. He thought, at first, that he was dimply checking on his old friend to find out how he was doing, and in some way, that was true. Stanley Thornton's progress had been extraordinary, and if anything spoke to that miracle, it was the material gathered on these disks. Stanley was taking college courses with the cooperation of the local school's outreach program. A couple of students had volunteered to record lectures and transcribe notes to disk and bring the disks to Stanley. He was six courses into a social-work program, all done by correspondence. It might take him five years more, but he would eventually be a graduate.

If that wasn't a miracle, Ted asked, what was? Ted had been on the ice when it happened. He had, in fact, passed the puck ahead to Stan. He sometimes wondered if perhaps he himself was partly responsible, for he could have bumped the defenceman cutting across toward Stan, and it was this player who took Stan's feet out from under him. It would have held some risk – Ted could have been called for interference, meaning the breakaway would have been whistled down – but referees rarely call interference late in the third periods of important games. Now, comparing the risk of a penalty to what happened, there was no doubt in Ted Larsen's mind as to what he should have done.

Just consider what happened. When Stanley Thornton piled head first into the boards, his neck had snapped at the fourth cervical vertebrae. He had gone into convulsion. They had been so worried that they had brought the ambulance in through the Zamboni chute, loaded him on straight from the ice, and the ambulance had flown, lights flashing, back out the chute and straight to the Pembroke hospital.

Consider: a young man, then 23 years of age, in the prime of life, racing down the ice on skates one moment, racing off the ice in an ambulance the next. A young man who could, as they said, dance with the puck one minute, unable to move anything but his head and left shoulder the next. He went from a helmet to a halo, and from the halo to the wheelchair that he could operate by flexing his one working shoulder against a special pad fitted with sensors. It was, they said, a miracle that he was able to recover so much.

But why had Ted Larsen not been able to let it go at that? What compelled him to invade the privacy of his friend? He didn't know. All he knew was that he had started to scan through the files of Stanley's computer – cleaning up, he told himself at first – and had become more and more intrigued by this new life Stanley Thornton had created for himself through the Internet.

Ted not only had all the early letters that Stan had sent to Elaine, he had returned twice to "fiddle" with the computer – "I just want to see if maybe this communications program might be better suited to your modem" – and had deliberately, sneakily bled off the latest letters while he had been there. He now knew all about the stories Stan had been telling. And not telling. He knew about the lie concerning the hockey game.

Why had he done this? As a computer salesman and system installer, privacy was supposed to be a concern of Ted's. He knew all about passwords and security networks and viruses. But now he himself had become a lurker in his friend's system. A trespasser. Why?

He knew why. He felt responsible. Responsible for what had happened. Responsible for what happened after. He read on because he wanted to know how Stan would present the final game to someone who had not been there. He wondered at first if he would be blamed – "Of course, I would never have ended up in a wheelchair if my good friend, Ted Larsen, had done his job properly" – but his name hadn't even come up in any of the letters.

What had come up had been, in its own way, even more disturbing. Stan was lying to this wonderful woman who seemed more than willing to accept him for whoever he was – however he was. He had chosen a fantasy that did not involve the trip. He had scored the goal. He had seen his sweater retired. He was the local hero.

Ted felt an overwhelming urge to protect his teammate.

Now, nearly a decade after he felt he had first failed him.

"Mr. Stanley Thornton,
Mb238cFreenet.Carleton.CA

"My Dear Stan,

"Thank you for the wonderful letter of the 14th. I'm getting so I look forward to your letters more than anything else in the week. I like the idea of you writing every Wednesday and me answering every Sunday from now on, and I'll look forward to your Wednesday letter. I'll log on sometime around 7:00 p.m.

"Did you happen to see the movie, *Sleepless In Seattle*? I loved it. We're kind of like Sleepless in Pembroke and Sleepless in Ottawa. I love the way they talk to each other on the radio. It's kind of like us on the network. We don't even know what each other looks like!

"All I know about you is your age and that you have blond hair that you say is beginning to thin. But I don't know whether that means you look like Kevin Costner or Mr. Clean! Perhaps you should send a photograph so I can decide for myself.

"You never said whether or not you are still playing hockey. I imagine with all your courses and everything there's very little time for play, but a lot of people I know are playing late at night and I wondered if you were one of those – you know. "Every Thursday night, Stan and the boys get together for a little hockey and a few cold ones . . ." Are you still playing? I'd love to go to one of your games . . ."

Stanley Thornton had been staring at his computer screen for almost an hour. How could he tell Elaine the truth? He had conned her. He had lied to her. And now she wanted proof – she wanted to see him. Perhaps even see him play hockey. How would he ever get out of this?

Ted Larsen had an idea. He had been unable to sleep. He got up around 3:30 a.m., had gone downstairs, had made himself a big mug of hot chocolate, and he had sat staring at the back of a cereal box for nearly an hour when it came to him.

Why not let Stan live out his fantasy? It was his goal, after all, so why not let him enjoy it now, when he can. Look at how far he had already come. He was mobile. He was in college. He even had a girlfriend. So to speak. Electronically going steady, anyway.

Ted's first call had been to Rodney Chipperfield. He may as well begin with the most difficult one of all. If it fell apart there, there was little reason to go on. Rodney Chipperfield had been the player who had tripped Stanley Thornton. Now he was living in town and playing Sundays and Wednesdays with Ted's team in the "Gentlemen's League."

Ted knew how Rodney felt. Twice they had talked about it over beers after games. If Ted Larsen wished he had taken out the defenceman on that breakaway, the defenceman, Rodney Chipperfield, wished so much more passionately. If only Ted had taken Rodney's feet out from under him instead. If only it had been him crashing safely into his goaltender's pads, the puck already in the net, instead of Stanley Thornton going head first into the boards.

A fraction of a second. That is what had decided it for them all. Rodney Chipperfield had quit hockey for a long time after that game. He could not put up with the jeering and the insults.

They called him "Crippler." He could only play now, he told Ted, because now there was never anyone in the stands. And anyone of the ice knew: they all had had their own moments when something goes wrong so quickly, almost always without consequence. But they all knew how easily it could happen.

"You know what they call that play?" Rodney had said the first time they talked about it.

Ted wasn't following. "What play?"

"The trip – when I hauled down Stan Thornton."

"What do you mean?"

"A good penalty – that's what they call it. You hear it every Saturday on *Hockey Night In Canada*. I hear it every game I ever watch. A good penalty. What a hell of a thing to say."

They met at the car dealership where Rodney Chipperfield was in charge of leasing. He heard Ted out and thought the idea ridiculous.

"You want to finish that game?"

"Yes. For Stan Thornton. He needs to finish it."

"He's in a wheelchair."

"There's wheelchair sports."

"Not for hockey."

But Ted wouldn't stop. He had thought everything out: chains, even, for the tires, a contraption that would flick a puck ahead of the chair and could be controlled by Stan, a proper ceremony for the retirement of Stan's sweater. One that, this time, he could attend. A new team photograph.

"He wouldn't come," Rodney said.

"He'd come."

"Who'd rig up the wheelchair?"

"Paul Farley and Derek Houser run a machine shop. They were on the team. They could do it. It wouldn't have to be that complicated."

"And why me?"

"You have to be there. You were there when it happened."

"I caused it to happen – remember?"

"It was an accident."

"It still happened."

"Besides," Ted said. "This time it will be different."

"How?"

"I intend to take you out this time."

Stanley Thornton woke up to the fire alarm thinking it was old Mrs. Humphrey's cowbell: clang-clang-clang-clang-clang . . . He had burst from a sound sleep and, when he realized what it was, thought it must be the Christmas tree in the common room. But almost instantly there was an announcement – False alarm – and he had been unable to get back to sleep, the bell taking him back again to that last rush up the ice, that final drive toward the net.

He had never for a moment felt any bitterness toward the player who had dumped him. He would have done it himself had the tables been turned, had done it himself, in fact, many times. Taken a 'good' penalty. Stupid thing to say, he thought.

A couple of times Rodney Chipperfield had come and visited Stan. He had never come alone – always with a team-mate or a mutual friend, once with Ted Larsen – and the visits had never been very comfortable, but they had been important to both of them and both of them recognized that fact. They never talked about the trip – what could anyone say? – but in talking about everything else, Stanley's progress, Rodney's job, they had talked about nothing else, for the trip had become the point of departure for all that had since happened to both of them.

Stan figured he was up and may as well write Elaine. The

faster he got with his Morse code, the more he seemed to be writing her. This was the second letter in less than a week. This was getting serious. With his shoulder, he pressed the alarm for the nurse.

Elaine had suggested they try using the chat system. They could log on and then sort of talk back and forth, one asking a question, the other answering, almost like a telephone conversation conducted on a keyboard. He hadn't answered her on that point. She must have wondered. After all, they had met because he had presented himself as a bit of an expert with the Internet. If anyone should be suggesting they move on to another level, it should be him, surely. He wondered what she had thought about him not answering her question. Did she think he had just forgotten? Or did she suspect he was hiding something from her?

Stan felt he couldn't. He wasn't fast enough. He would be staring at the screen if they did what she wanted and her questions would be coming up about as fast as a person can type and his answer might take 15 minutes. Puff-puff-puff. Puff . . . puff. Puff . . . puff-puff. Puff . . . puff-puff. Puff-puff . . . puff-puff. Not a single sip in "S-O-R-R-Y." She would wonder what was wrong. And he would eventually have to tell her.

In a way, he liked living on the Internet. There was a certain beauty to it. A certain freedom. People could only see what he was thinking, and his brain was the last bit of prowess he had left in this body that chose to ignore everything he told it to do. She liked what she saw of him through the computer. Perhaps she'd run if she saw him through the doorway.

"Ms Elaine Boudrias,
Pw431cFreenet.Carleton.CA

"My Dear Elaine,

"Thanks for such a fine letter on Sunday. I've read it over two or three times and am very impressed by many of the insights you have. One day we'll have to talk at length – without typing!

"You asked about my hockey career after the championship. Well, I'd like to say I went on to play for the Toronto Maple Leafs and won the Conn Smythe Trophy when I led the leafs to a four-game play-off sweep of the Montreal Canadiens ("Na-na-na-na, na-na-na-na, heyhey-hey, na-na . . .") – but the truth is I did not. Senior champions was about as far as any of us got.

"Truth is, I haven't played much since. Oh, once in a while one of the guys like Ted Larsen – he was my centre – will call up about some ice time down at the old rink, and . . ."

They met at the Don Cherry sports bar. The waitress put together a few tables near the back, turned off the televisions and brought a tray of draft beer and diet cola for everyone. When they all had a drink, Ted Larsen laid out his plan.

They would give their old teammate, Stanley Thornton, the Christmas present of a lifetime. He told them about Stan's new love interest in Ottawa, and how he had met her through the computer the Dukes had all pitched in on. No one asked Ted how he knew, and he didn't tell them about the damaged hard drive and his discovery. What did it matter how he'd found out? The important point was that Stan was doing fine, and he had a new, significant friend.

Ted told them how he had rented the old rink for this Sunday night and he told them that Paul Farley and Derek Houser had been working on the stick for Stan's wheelchair, and that they figured it would work fine. He could shoot a puck. He could score his goal.

Terry Bartholomew, who rarely smiled, asked the question everyone was considering: "Why?"

"It's his dream," explained Ted. "It was his goal. It would have been his penalty shot if he could have taken it. All we're going to do is let him put it in the net."

"And that's going to make him walk?" Bartholomew asked.

"Of course it isn't. But it's going to show him that we all remember who won us that championship."

"We dedicated it to him," said one of the others.

"Sure we did – but he wasn't there. He has the picture up on his wall, but he isn't in it. We retired his sweater, but he wasn't there."

"Does he know about this?" Bartholomew asked. He no longer seemed so negative.

"No."

"Don't you think he should?"

"We want it all to be a surprise. We're going to have someone special in the audience for him. We think it's time they met."

Ted Larsen had no idea how he was going to talk Elaine into coming up to Pembroke for Stanley Thornton's big game. He figured he'd call and wing it, as he'd winged everything in life. He was 34, in good health, had a job – winging it had worked fine so far.

"Elaine Boudrias, please."

"I'm sorry?"

His first thought was that he had made a mistake. He had taken her address from one of the letters – she must have put it in hoping that Stan would send her a picture – and her father's name had been mentioned in another letter. He had taken the man's name and the address and simply gone through information. And now he had a wrong number.

"I must have the wrong number," he said.

"You want Elaine?"

"Yes – Elaine Boudrias. Does she live there?"

"Yes."

"Can I speak to her please?"

There was a pause. "Does she know you?"

What is this? Ted wondered. An over-protective mother? A snoopy sister?

"No, I'm calling for a friend – Stanley Thornton."

"You're Stanley Thornton?"

"No. No. I'm Ted Larsen. I'm a good friend of his. I just wanted to speak to Elaine for a moment about something we're planning for Stan."

"I see." Another pause. "Well, Mr . . ."

"Larsen."

"Larsen – there's something you must not know about Elaine."

When he heard, Ted thought he understood everything. Elaine was there but could not come to the telephone because she could not talk on it. Her job at the House of Commons was to do the sign language for the hearing impaired. If Stan had been attracted to Freenet and Internet because he would not be seen and judged, she had come to it so she could be heard without having to speak. She was probably as worried about actually meeting Stan as he was of meeting her. Her sister brought

Elaine to the phone and acted as go-between in a most unusual conversation. Ted told them about Stan – they didn't seem surprised; they said they knew there was something about him he was keeping to himself – and he told them about the plan to finish off the championship game the right way. The sisters loved the idea. They were anxious to meet Stan and they agreed to come up to Pembroke on the afternoon bus just before the game. They would have no trouble with getting away. Both worked on Parliament Hill and both were off for the Christmas break anyway. They would need a motel room to stay over, and would return to Ottawa the next day.

Ted picked them up at the downtown depot. They were obviously sisters, both dark and lively, both with the same childlike, charming smile. If there was a striking difference it was only to do with sound. The sister, Charmaine, was a talker; but so, too, was Elaine. Elaine, however, spoke with her hands, and Charmaine translated, the two so close and used to dealing with each other that, to Ted, the translation seemed instantaneous, Elaine's hand moving while Charmaine's voice read, with all the inflection and enthusiasm and humour that Charmaine possessed when she spoke for herself. They were a delight.

"What time's the game?" Charmaine asked aloud for her sister.

"Seven-thirty."

"Where's Stanley?"

Ted realized that Elaine was nervous, and the nervousness was captured perfectly in her sister's voice. Nervous and excited.

"Right after I drop you off, I pick him up."

"Are we allowed to cheer?" Charmaine asked.

"Of course. But just wait until we get him on the ice and he has the puck, okay?"

Charmaine's question hit him again. How could "we" cheer? Charmaine perhaps. But what could Elaine do? Perhaps Charmaine could shout for both of them. That seemed to be the way they worked together.

He dropped the women off at the motel just up from the rink, where he had already booked them a room. He wanted them at the rink before Stan arrived. Stan would have to know about the game before it began. The audience would hold the surprise.

Ted had made arrangements to pick Stan up at the Facility. He had told him they were going down to Ottawa to take in a junior hockey game at the Civic Centre. He would need the two hours they wouldn't be using on the drive down to rig up the chair and – though he hoped it wouldn't be necessary – to convince Stan to give it a try.

Ted felt an old familiar flutter in his stomach. The feeling he always had before a big game. A feeling he had almost forgotten.

"No."

"Why not?"

"I have no intention of making a fool of myself."

"Then we'll all be making fools of ourselves together. Half the guys are going to be there. Rodney Chipperfield is coming."

Stanley Thornton couldn't follow. His head was spinning. "Why would he come?"

Same reason you should come. Same reason I'm coming. We want you to see your face when your goal goes in."

Stanley shivered. He had always wondered what it would have felt like. He had the team photograph – him missing – none of them smiling. They looked like they had just lost the world, not won the championship.

"I never scored."

"It was your penalty shot."

"You took it."

"I took it for you. There was no way on earth that puck wasn't going in. I'm convinced even their goalie felt that way."

"It makes no sense."

"C'mon, Stan – why does everything have to make sense? We're bringing a photographer. We're going to take a new photo."

"What?"

"Yah – with you. MVP, Senior Championship."

Stanley did not know what to think.

"Would you want a picture with us all in it? Everybody smiling?"

"Maybe."

"Then let's go – what've you got to lose."

His dignity, for one thing. He could lose his dignity. And his mind. The way things were starting to spin on Stanley Thornton he did wonder if perhaps he was going crazy. This was nuts. But still, he let his mad friend get out the Facility van and he let him load him on and now they were headed down Main Street toward the rink. Stanley had been back dozens of times since the accident. But he'd never felt like this. His stomach was turning over. He had to laugh: not supposed to have any feeling below his shoulders, but he could feel a game coming on.

Everyone else was already there. Ted helped him wheel into the dressing room, and the sensation was overwhelming to Stan. He could smell their fetid equipment-perfume to long-time hockey players. He could hear, even before the door opened, the take-no-prisoners insults that are the great equalizer of a hockey dressing room. He could hear Lanny Dowbigging asking to borrow some shin-pad tape – still cheap, after all these years.

When the door opened, it did not open at all as Stan had imagined. He thought he would bring things to a halt.

He thought he would be invading, that they would stop, out of respect, and everyone would act sheepish and ask about him and centre him out and make him feel like he was some sort of imposition on them. But it didn't happen that way at all.

"You're 10 minutes late, Thornton!" a big voice said from behind the partition. It was Curly Simmons, their old coach. He looked around the corner and frowned at Stan. "You're fined one round of beer after the game." They cheered and threw towels at Stan. A couple of the guys moved over on the bench, and Ted wheeled him through the clutter and spun him around so he was sitting where he usually sat, between the goaltender, Sid Bartholomew, and the big defenceman, Serge Dumont. Dumont seemed slightly irritated that he had to move his equipment bag over. Just like always.

Paul and Derek came in with the electronic stick. It was remarkably simple: a stick blade attached to a metal plate, the plate hinged to another plate that fitted onto the front of his wheelchair, the hinge operated by a small electric device that was wired back up along the back of the chair and fitted to a pulse button they tucked in behind his shoulder.

"Shoot!" said Paul.

Stan leaned back hard on the little button. The stick swung quickly out, quickly back.

"Gunner!" someone shouted.

They were acting as if all this somehow made sense, when it so obviously didn't. But as Ted had said, what did it matter? It was Christmas.

They horsed around awhile on the ice before Stan got his shift. The Dukes played a little no-contact shinny against the Lumberjacks. Rodney Chipperfield was on the ice and only once did he acknowledge Stan's presence, and that was with a little nod and a slight smile as he passed by the exit where Stan sat waiting, behind the glass. They had opened up the glass display case in the hall and removed the retired No. 8 sweater and now Stan had it on. It even smelled the same as they had slipped it over his head. He had hockey gloves on. He had a helmet on. His tires had been wrapped with what looked like chicken wire. "Chains," Ted Larsen had called them, and chains they were.

When they got the score to 3-3, the score that they had reached in the third period of the championship, they came down and opened the big doors where the Zamboni usually came out and Ted Larsen helped start Stan out onto the ice. The last time he had been through these doors he had been in an ambulance. He was certain he could feel his stomach churn.

He came out with every player on the ice tapping his stick in salute. The fallen hero arisen. He tried his controls and the wheels spun, caught slightly, and he moved out slowly, slightly drifting past the net, and the Lumberjacks' goalie gave him a big swat on the rear of his chair as he passed him by. With Ted's help, he wheeled down to the other end. He tried to turn and look around as he moved down the ice, and he was sure he saw someone sitting in the stands, but he couldn't make out exactly who. They set up – a breakout pattern – in their own end, and one of the other players came and took hold of the chair's handles and began moving Stan down the ice as the Lumberjacks began skating backwards in defence.

Ted, of course, was carrying the puck, just as he had before the trip. He came out over the blue line, danced around one check, tucked the puck in between the legs of another player and burst over centre looking for Stan on his left. He passed, just as he had that night so many years ago, and the player helping Stan stopped the puck with his glove and set it onto the electric stick at the front of the chair. Small grooves on the blade kept the puck steady, and the player gave Stan one final push toward the opposition net and left him on his own.

He could hear the sounds of skates behind him. He didn't need to see to know what it was. It would be Rodney Chipperfield in full chase.

He could hear old Mrs. Humphrey's cowbell. Clang-clang-clang-clang . . . The same rhythm that had filled his ears that night just before . . . He couldn't believe the detail Ted and his teammates had gone to. They had even brought out old Mrs. Humphrey.

He heard a collision behind him and then, out of the corner of his eye, he caught sight of Rodney Chipperfield spilling by, a fallen Ted Larsen following. Both of them were laughing.

There was now nothing between Stanley Thornton and the net. The goalie was rapping his pads and wiggling out fast to cut off the angle. Stan instinctively pressed back on his controls and sped up, the chair catching, drifting slightly, and moving across the plane of the net.

It happened entirely by instinct. He could not even see the puck or the stick, but he knew by his eyes that the net was directly in front of him. He pushed back hard on the button. He saw nothing for a moment, then the puck emerged from below his knees, scooting along the smooth ice toward the net, the goaltender doing the splits, the puck cut off from sight until, a moment later, a red light flashed behind the sprawling goaltender, surprise somehow registering on his mask.

And then it began. The cowbell, the cheering, the whooping, the sticks tossed, the hugging, the spinning of Stanley Thornton's chair, the ruffling of hair, the slapping, the yelling, the tears.

It was as if the emotion had been piled up for all those years and now, suddenly, it had been released. Stan Thornton was crying. He wanted to cry. Needed to cry.

They were all in tears, including Rodney Chipperfield who

was lining up with his team-mates for the customary handshake. The two teams went down the line, each tapping each other, congratulating each other, no one acting as if Stanley Thornton was in anything but full uniform and accepting his due. Rodney Chipperfield gave him a special hug. The Lumberjack goaltender dropped the puck in his lap. His puck, his goal.

They lined up with the trophy for the team photo. Sticks sprawling out in front of them, helmets off, hair wet, all of them finally smiling. Stanley Thornton, MVP, winning goal scorer in the centre of it; Ted Larsen, who had set him up, beside him, his arm wrapped around Stan's head.

The cowbell sounded, a final salute.

"I thought old Mrs. Humphrey had died," Stan said to Ted.

"She did."

"Who brought the cowbell, then?"

"You'll find out in a minute."

On Christmas Eve: 1963

by Joan Finnigan

Dear Country Cousin:

Tonight, the night before Christmas, it is inevitable that my thoughts should turn to you. I think of you there on that wilderness farm with the road across the fields growing narrower, narrower in the vise of winter and not even the light of a neighbor to be seen in the distance, and I feel momentarily that I would gladly trade your clean stretch of stars for the gaudy insistent neons of my road here.

I think of how it will be in your house, shadowy with lamplight and warm with the heat of the stove, the cats curled up in the wood-box and the dogs on the mat by the door. You will be trying to get the last of your brood into their beds upstairs, and one, probably Jackie, the eldest, dreamer and watcher of wild birds, will be pressing his nose for the last time against the frosted pane, straining for a look at the sky, sensing it different tonight, full of expectations and mysteries.

It's many a year and event undreamed of that's gone by since you and I were his size, swallowed up in the great warm cocoon of our grandfather's house, pressing our noses against the bay windows of the big dining room, watching sleighs swing through the gate and into the yard. And what excitement as the buffalo robes disgorged the drivers and passengers, some uncles, some aunts, some cousins, perhaps our great blue-eyed giant of a grandfather returning from a Trip to Town!

They would cross the veranda and lift the latch on the kitchen door and enter like great fat furry bears and stomp their feet of snow. Such a stomping in those heavy boots! We stood, terribly small and wide-eyed, wondering if such stomping would not take them through the floor right into China. Looking back now I don't think it was necessary to shake the dishes in the cupboard like that at all, but I think it was a way of a man announcing his arrival back into the household. And then, too, in that county, Pontiac County, to be a good stomper was the earmark of a good dancer.

The horses, the carriage-shed, the house, the buffalo robes, even some of the people, are gone now, but in my mind the sleds have sprouted wings, still fly, glistening, graceful as swans, jingling through the wintry roads of my childhood journeys. Time has graciously embellished them with even greater magic than they had for me then. And I can't think of the sleigh rides I had through the white castles of the snow in the dark nights of the country without also thinking of the train up the Pontiac from Ottawa – the Push-Pull-and-Jerk I think they called it when they wrote its obituary several years ago and took it off the lines.

Many was the time this nose was pressed to the pane of that slow train winding along the Ottawa River into the dusk of the winter's evening. Many were my grave fears of missing the station, of the conductor going to sleep somewhere back on the mailbags and letting me miss my station and of my ending up in Mattawa with no grandfather or uncle walking the station platform to keep himself warm in the wait, no little black horse named May stomping her feet and tossing her head by the rail. But always he came, faithfully down the aisle, to a child lost behind the dusk and the glazed windows and sounded out my salvation by calling, "Shawville, next stop." I had had my bag clutched in my hand since Luskville, my hat and coat on since Quyon and there never was a racer at the starting-post so poised as I for the descent, the incredibly exciting descent down those train steps – I can see them yet, corrugated steel encrusted with ice – into the welcome of the waiting relative.

Then we would wrap ourselves up in the sleigh and take to the air and fly the snow-ways like a black bird, the clip-clop of the little horse beating out the rhythm of our wings. And we would beat our heavenly passage through the dark to the light of my grandmother's lamps, to the warm kitchen of her perennially ready suppers, to the great downy ticks of the high beds in the cold rooms and the house cracking and groaning as I fell like Alice in Wonderland down the long, long passage of sleep.

Somehow I can't think of all those mysterious things without remembering Joker.

Did you know, country cousin, that whenever the men came back from the lumber camps to the farm at Radford, that old collie would drop out of the winter's night onto their sleigh when they were yet many miles from home and had sent no word, indeed, could not send any word of their impending arrival? By some dog-mystique he knew that they had started out from the Rouge River, and he would begin his "incredible journey" and descend upon them like a wraith out of the night as they hurried through the last lap of their journey, still many miles from home. He did that for ten years, and he, too, has become in my mind a sort of inexplicable dog-spirit of uncanny devotion still abroad in our valley.

Remember all the days, too, we spent tugging toboggans to the hills or trekking along wintry roads to the houses of other cousins who always took us in, fed us and wrapped us up for the night. When you arrived by foot it was always implicitly, and, to me, mysteriously understood that you were "staying the night." There was no invitation issued; preparations were simply made for such an event, which was welcomed by the inhabitants of the farmhouse in the lonely days and nights of their cut-off winters.

And I cringe yet in memory of the "Time of the Wolf Tracks." Do you remember one day when we had gone to the farthest extremities of the farm in search of the highest hill? And there, out of sight of habitation and in the furious house of the wind I espied in the snow before our very eyes – wolf tracks! Nothing you could say could dissuade me from that conviction: not that they were Joker's tracks in the snow as he chased his old enemy, the groundhog; not that it was the neighbor Hanna's dog; nothing. They were wolf tracks, and without even so much as one slide down that long-sought hill, I forced you to turn back and head for the safety of the big house, to the spirit of warmth and light it exuded without central heating or electric lights.

Yes, spirit. That is what I am looking for as I write to you tonight, as my mind turns to your farm at the foot of the Brule Hill.

I know a very wise grandfather here who was asked by his grandchildren, "What is spirit?" And he answered this way: He held up his hand and blew his breath between his fingers upon their upturned faces.

"Can you see that?" he asked.

"No," came the reply.

"Can you feel it?"

"Yes," came the chorus.

"That is spirit, my children," he said.

Ah spirit! That is the thing I am seeking here in the city upon this Christmas Eve, and somehow I always have such a difficult time finding it here that I turn to thoughts of you, my country cousin, and, in the vicarious contemplation of the peace and beauty and tranquility in which you live, I seem to find what I am looking for.

I think perhaps other people find their minds turning like this upon a Christmas Eve, from the crowded turbulence of the city to the primitive peace of the country, seeking a spirit which is easier somehow to discover in your land, my country cousin, than in mine. But perhaps I am taking the easy way; perhaps being less than courageous. Perhaps I should look harder here, a greater struggle bringing a greater prize – at any rate, let me hear from you, how the spirit blew through your farmhouse beside the frozen lake on Christmas Eve, 1963.

Your city cousin,
Joan

The Unexpected Guest

by Mary Cook

The kitchen table was always set for dinner before we went to bed on Christmas Eve. The big pine table that sat against the west wall was stretched out as far as it would go. Days before Christmas, Mother would have taken the long, white linen cloth out of the trunk in the upstairs hall, and it would be washed, starched and ironed. This task took hours of her time, but as this was the most important meal of the entire year, everything had to be just perfect.

Although we didn't own a complete set of dishes, an effort was made to put out the very best we had. This meant matching up all those pieces we had collected from either Theatre Night in Renfrew or from the big bags of puffed wheat from Briscoe's General Store. Mother would put her best geranium in the centre of the table, and circle it with pieces of green cedar. The red broadcloth napkins, which were only used at that time of the year, were also used in the setting of the table.

It was my sister Audrey's and my task to set the table before we got ready for bed on Christmas Eve. Without fail, Father, who never took an interest at any other time, would hover over the table as if he alone was in charge of the Christmas dinner. He would instruct us to be sure to set an extra place at the end of the table. And then, as he did every year, he told us about the German custom his family had carried on as long as he could remember. They always set an extra place at the end of the table for an unexpected guest.

Father would say that we were blessed with an ample table, and if anyone came hungry, we could assure the visitor of a full plate. I always asked him if the guest ever showed up. Father would look very mysterious indeed, and say that we would never know for sure because sometimes the unexpected guest could not be seen.

That would send shivers right up my spine. Mother had little patience with Father's German folklore, but she indulged him at Christmastime, and by the time we went to bed, there would be the place at the head of the table for the unexpected guest.

One Christmas, when we came home from church, we could see from the end of the lane that someone was standing at our back door. As the sleigh got closer to the house we could see an old battered tapestry bag at her feet. Only when we rounded the corner at the summer kitchen did we recognize Father's old aunt. She was the one who came every fall to mend socks, knit mitts and sew buttons on our winter shirts, before going off to another relative's farm to help at sap time. We hardly ever saw her except during those few weeks late in the fall, but here she was, standing on our back stoop.

She was ushered in and welcomed like the much-loved aunt she was. The smells of the turkey cooking in the Findlay Oval met us when we opened the door, and the warmth of the kitchen was like a friendly arm reaching around us. When it came time to sit down at the ample Christmas table, Auntie was given the extra place at the end of the table which Audrey and I had set the night before.

As we all settled into our places, Father passed the back of my chair and ran his hand over my hair. In the softest voice, close to the ear, he said, "Sometimes the unexpected guest is someone we know."

Christmas Under a Pale Green Sky

by Barbara Novak

Santa Claus
North Pole, Planet Earth

December 1, 2054

Dear Santa,

Thanks for the laser camera you gave me last Christmas. It takes good 3-D pictures.

What I would like this year is some hockey equipment, especially skates and a hockey stick, more if possible.

The problem is nobody will be home at my house. We won't even be on Earth. My parents have to go to Borp for an intergalactic travel conference so they're taking my sister and me with them. We'll be staying at the Borp Holiday Inn Bubble Complex. It's supposed to be a nice place if you like to eat slow food which I don't. I only like fast food. But my dad says I have to go. Do you know what it's like on Borp? There is no snow, no ice, and no Christmas. Just food.

Yours truly,
Fenwick Lovington

"You've wasted your time, borple brain," said Trillium when she finished reading the copy Fenwick had stored on his computer. "Santa Claus has enough trouble getting around to all the girls and boys on Earth. He won't come all the way to Borp. It's not even in the Milky Way."

"He will, too!" Fenwick shut off his computer with an angry jab of his forefinger. The screen went dark. He didn't know which was worse: being on Borp for Christmas, or sharing a hotel room with his sister.

She leaned across the king-size bed and poked him in the ribs. "Besides, who plays hockey? It's an *archaic* sport! Why didn't you ask Santa for the video game?"

"Because I like the real thing." Ever since seeing some old cassettes of a guy named Gretzky play for the Edmonton Oilers way back in the 1980s, Fenwick had dreamed of being a hockey star when he grew up.

His sister snorted. "You can't even *walk* without tripping over your feet."

Fenwick thought longingly of his own bed in his own room in his own home on his own planet and felt tears sting his eyes. Tonight was Christmas Eve. What if Trillium was right? It was a long way to expect Santa to come, especially by sled.

Going over to the window, he leaned against the sill and looked over past the bubble to Borp proper, where the sun rarely set in the pale green sky. He could see that it was a pretty planet; it was just that he missed Earth. Directly below, three storeys down, a marble fountain sprayed thin jets of water almost as high as the window.

He swallowed hard, not wanting Trillium to see him cry. She was eleven. Once he'd believed he could catch up to her, but now he knew that no matter how old he was, he'd always be three years younger than Trillium.

"Didn't *you* ask Santa for anything?"

"Peace and goodwill among all creatures in the universe," she replied sweetly.

"Ha!"

"And a new video-phone," she added. "And some neon barrettes for my hair, and a subscription to *Seventeen* magazine."

Fenwick whirled around. "There! You see? Why would you have bothered asking Santa for anything if you didn't think he'd bring it to Borp?"

Trillium sighed impatiently. "I didn't ask him to bring it *here*. I explained that no one would be home and asked him to leave the stuff in the living room. And I left some cookies for him in the dispenser."

Fenwick wished he'd thought of that.

Just then there was a knock at their door. It was their parents, stopping by on their way to the convention.

"There's a party downstairs for the children who are staying at the hotel to meet some children from Borp," their mother told them.

"Some Eaties are there?" Trillium shrieked. "Oh, they're so cute!"

Fenwick groaned. The preparation and consuming of food was

of such importance on Borp that its inhabitants were called Eaties.

"What should I wear?" asked Trillium. "Is there dancing?"

"No, but there's some good food," said their father.

Fenwick perked up. "Fast food?"

His mother shook her head. "But try some, dear. You might like it. It's very wholesome. In the olden days, before MacDonalds, that's what we humans used to eat all the time."

Fenwick sighed. He knew all that. He knew about stoves and refrigerators and the preparation and cooking of food. He'd studied it on his computer and found the whole subject faintly disgusting. He would have given anything right then for a couple of Christmas turkey burgers from the food dispenser in their own kitchen.

His father placed a hand on Fenwick's shoulder. "I know this isn't how you'd like to spend Christmas," he said. "But if we refused to come to this convention then your mother and I would lose our jobs."

Fenwick nodded.

"The meeting will be over early," he continued. "We'll pick you up at the party as soon as we can so that we can all spend Christmas Eve together."

Their watches signalled the hour.

"We have to dash," said their mother, kissing the children goodbye.

"I'm not going," Fenwick announced as soon as their parents had left.

"You have to go," said Trillium.

"Why?"

"Because I'm going and I'm older and I'm supposed to be responsible for you."

"Goodbye," Fenwick said firmly. "Have fun."

"Fine. If you stay, I'll stay." Trillium strode across the room to their luggage and picked up her violin case. "You don't mind if I practice my violin for a few hours, do you?"

Seconds later the room was filled with the most terrible screeches and squawks.

"Stop!" Fenwick begged, his hands over his ears. "I'll go!"

Fenwick brightened when he saw the lobby glittering with Christmas decorations. A big plastic tree stood in one corner with a bright silver star sparkling at the top and a pile of colorful packages underneath.

"But I thought they didn't have Christmas on Borp," he said.

"This is an Earth hotel," Trillium reminded him just as a chorus of *O Come, All Ye Faithful* came blaring over the sound system.

"Look!" she cried, pointing to a jolly fat man with a white beard and a red suit who was ho-hoing his way in their direction, a big sack over his shoulder.

Fenwick's heart beat faster.

"Ho! Ho! Ho! And a Hairy Mismuch to you!"

His heart sank as he recognized the hollow-sounding voice of a computerized robot. Still, an electronic Santa was better than no Santa at all, and this one was offering him a candy cane.

As Fenwick reached out to take it, the Santa Claus robot cried, "Hairy Mismuch! Hairy Mismuch!" and plunged the candy into his own ear. "Ho! Ho! Ho!"

Trillium burst out laughing. Fenwick grumbled, "Someone better re-program that robot or it's going to cause serious damage."

Fenwick's chin rested glumly in his hand. His elbow was propped on the table at which he sat alone in the corner of the room, looking around at the party. There was Trillium, busy braiding an

Eatie girl's tentacles. Fenwick couldn't understand why everyone kept saying the Eaties were so cute. He thought they looked very peculiar with their glowing green skin (a sign of health in Borp), and their big eyes and pointy ears and extendable limbs. One was approaching him now, a plate of food in his rubbery hands.

"Bxvd zp ni qxprbu ggs pt, Borp?"

Fenwick quickly adjusted his automatic translator. "I beg your pardon?"

"Would you care for a fresh mushroom lovingly stuffed with Borp cheese? Asked the Eatie.

"No, thank you." But Fenwick quickly changed his mind when he saw the Eatie turn pale and begin to shrivel. He remembered how sensitive they were. And of course, it was a terrible insult to refuse food on Borp. "I'd love one," he said and was relieved to see the Eatie recover immediately.

He popped it into his mouth and swallowed fast, so he wouldn't have to taste it.

"Another?" asked the Eatie.

Fenwick ate this one slowly, nibbling discreetly around the edges.

"I don't suppose you have Christmas pudding pops here, do you?"

"Pops?" The Eatie shook his head. "Does not compute."

"No, I didn't think so."

"But I know all about Christmas," the Eatie said. "I did a project on it for planetary studies at school."

Fenwick had heard about schools from his grandfather, and he'd visited a model classroom in a museum once. In some ways the Eaties were very old-fashioned. If they still had schools, he thought, maybe they played hockey. "Do you have hockey here?" he asked.

"Hockey?" What does it taste like?"

Fenwick shook his head. "It's a game."

"A game! Like hot potato?"

"Not exactly," said Fenwick.

"Butter the muffin?"

"Do all your games have something to do with food?"

The Eatie nodded.

Fenwick began to explain to him about hockey. To his surprise, his new friend seemed very interested. He wanted to know where he could get some skates.

Before Fenwick could reply they were interrupted by the sound of an explosion in the lobby. Startled, they leaped to their feet and rushed out.

There, in a crumpled heap in front of a roaring fire in the fireplace, lay what remained of the Santa Claus robot. Wisps of smoke curled up like angel hair from the exposed wires, filling the lobby with the sharp odor of melted plastic.

Their feet crunched over broken candy canes as Fenwick and the Eatie pushed past the crowd of people and saw a man doubled over in pain near the robot, his face hidden in his hands.

"That's my dad!" cried Fenwick.

His mother looked up from where she knelt beside the groaning father. Fenwick ran into her arms.

The wail of a siren grew louder as an ambulance pulled up outside.

Fenwick, Trillium, and the Eatie sat quietly in the small waiting room of the bubble complex hospital while Mrs. Lovington described what had happened.

They had been on their way to meet the children when Mr. Lovington noticed the Santa Claus robot under the Christmas tree in the lobby stuffing the gifts into his sack. They thought it was strange, especially since those presents had been provided by the guests for their children. Mrs. Lovington wondered whether the Santa was preparing to hand them out personally. Then her husband pointed to the broken candy canes strewn all over the carpet. It seemed very suspicious indeed. In the meantime, the Santa began marching across the lobby toward the fireplace.

"Stop!" Mr. Lovington cried.

The Santa marched even faster. Mr. Lovington ran after him. The Santa swung his sack around and bashed Mr. Lovington in the nose. As he fell, he grabbed one of the Santa's boots, causing the robot to crash down to the floor where it exploded. But not before the sack went flying into the fire.

"Your father is a very brave man," said the hotel manager who had arrived while Mrs. Lovington was telling the story. "We're terribly sorry. We suspect it was a loose connection or a defective microchip. It's being checked out now."

"When can we see Dad?" Fenwick asked.

"You can see him now," said the doctor as he came into the waiting room. "It looks worse than it is. Fortunately, the only thing broken is his nose."

When Fenwick and Trillium saw their father lying under the white hospital sheet, his eyes ringed with ugly bruises, his face swollen and his nose covered with tape, they burst into tears.

"What an awful Christmas this is turning out to be for you," their father murmured. "I'm sorry about the presents."

"You could have been killed!" sobbed Fenwick.

Trillium sniffed. "We don't care about the presents."

"No!" Fenwick shook his head.

"Still," their father replied, taking their hands in his, "it's not a very nice way to spend Christmas, sitting around a hospital room in Borp."

"I have good news," said the doctor. "I've signed your release papers. You can all go back to the hotel."

The manager offered to have Christmas dinner sent up to their rooms, on the house.

The Lovington family looked at each other sadly. They all wished they were back on Earth.

"I have an idea," said the Eatie. "Will you excuse me? I want to phone home."

"What did he say?" asked Mr. Lovington, who wasn't wearing his automatic translator.

The Eatie's phoning home," Fenwick explained.

A moment later he returned. "It's all settled. You're invited to spend Christmas Eve at my house."

"Can we, Dad?" Fenwick asked, his eyes sparkling.

His father smiled. "I don't know. We'll have to wear space helmets outside the bubble, and I don't think mine will fit until this swelling goes down."

The hotel manager insisted on providing the whole family with expensive atmosphere adaptors so none of them would have to wear space helmets. And he offered them transportation as well.

"Then it's all settled," Mr. Lovington said, looking very pleased.

None of them had ever been to an Eatie home before. While still outside, Fenwick could smell a wonderful aroma, similar to that of turkey burgers but much richer.

The Eatie's parents greeted them at the door. Introductions were made and they were led into the living room. There, they gasped in astonishment. In the corner next to the window stood a beautiful Christmas tree sparkling with colorful lights and tinsel. Strings of popcorn and candy canes and gingerbread men hung on every branch. On the top perched an angel holding a silver star. Underneath the tree was a small pile of hay in which a doll lay, its eyes closed. Kneeling in front of it were the clay figures of Joseph and Mary.

"It's my project," said the Eatie. "For school, remember?"

Fenwick nodded, too overwhelmed to speak.

"I hope you got an A," said Trillium shyly.

The Eatie's eyes shone. "Is it accurate?"

"A real, old-fashioned Christmas!" exclaimed Mrs. Lovington, fingering one of the pine needles. "Look, children! A real tree!"

When Fenwik recovered his voice, he asked, "What's that delicious smell?"

"The rest of my project," said his friend, leading everyone into the kitchen, where the aroma was even stronger. They sat down to the best Christmas dinner any of them had ever tasted: roast turkey with stuffing and gravy, and roast potatoes and fresh cranberry sauce, glazed carrots, home-made sourdough bread with sweet, hand-churned butter, crisp salad, and hot Christmas pudding and mince-meat pies and shortbread cookies for dessert.

"I can't believe this is *slow food*," Fenwick said, helping himself to more turkey.

"I hope I'm not being rude," said Trillium, "but why are those socks hanging over the oven door?"

The Eaties laughed. "Because we don't have a fireplace!"

When Fenwick opened his eyes in the hotel room the next morning, the first thing he saw was a shiny new pair of skates and a hockey stock beside his bed.

Trillium was already up. She was sitting in the arm-chair next to the window flipping through a *Seventeen* magazine. A new pair of neon barrettes held back her hair. Beside her, on the table, sat her new video-phone.

"He came!" Fenwick cried. "Santa was here!"

Trillium grinned at him. "Have a look out the window."

Fenwick jumped out of bed and ran across the room. He looked outside and saw that the fountain had disappeared. In its place was a hockey rink enclosed in a clear plastic bubble of its own. Along the blue-line was written: *Merry Christmas Fenwick*.

A knock sounded at the door. Trillium opened it and in walked the Eatie, a pair of skates swinging from one hand, a hockey stick in the other. "I found these in my sock!" he said.

Fenwick threw his clothes on.

"Wait!" cried Trillium as the two were about to leave. "You forgot something."

She tossed her brother a small, heavy package wrapped in red paper and tied with a green ribbon. "Merry Christmas!"

Fenwick opened his gift, then gave his sister a big hug.

"Ahhhh!" said the Eatie, examining the present. "Licorice!"

"No," said Fenwick. "It's a puck."

"A what?"

"Come, I'll show you."

Green Gables Christmas

by L. M. Montgomery

Thermometer 5 below zero. A raging snowstorm to boot. Frost on window panes. Wind wailing in chimney. A box of white Roman hyacinths sending out alien whiffs of old summers.

My dear Mr. Weber,

When I received your last letter on October 29th, I said to myself, "For once I'm going to be decent and I'll answer this letter next week." What is more, I really meant it. Yet here it is December 22nd. Well, I couldn't help it, and that is all there is to it. I've been so busy – and so tired. I'm still the latter. I'd love to go to bed and stay there for a whole month, doing nothing, seeing nothing and *thinking* nothing. I really don't feel at all well – and yet there is nothing the matter with me. I've simply "gone stale." If you've ever experienced the feeling I'm sure of your sympathy. If you haven't, it's quite indescribable and I won't try to describe it. Instead I'll just pick up my notebooks, turn back to the entry of my last letter to you and discuss the jottings of any possibly interesting happenings since. I daresay the most of the letter will be about that detestable "Anne." There doesn't seem to be anything but her in my life just now and I'm so horribly tired of her, if it were not for just two things. One of these things is a letter I received last month from a poor little cripple in Ohio who wrote to thank me for writing "Anne" because she said it had taught her how to endure her long lonely days of imprisonment by just "imagining things." And the other is that "Anne" has gone through six editions and that must mean a decent cheque when pay day comes!

Well, it was September when I last wrote. We had the most exquisite autumn here this year. October was more beautiful than any June I ever remember. Couldn't help enjoying it, tired and rushed as I was. Every morning before sitting down to my typewriter I'd take a walk over the hill and feel almost like I should feel for a little while. November was also a decent month as Novembers go, but December has been very cold. Today as aforesaid has been a big storm. We are drifted up, have no mail, and were it not for my hyacinths I should feel inclined to stop being an optimist.

Well, I've done my duty by the weather, haven't I? Of course, one had to mention it. "Twouldn't be lucky not to."

WEDNESDAY, DEC. 23.

I hope *this* isn't going to last all winter – more storm and bitter frost. I *did* shovel snow as predicted – there's no one we can get to do this for us – it's all drifted back again. No mail still – and I'm ready to tear out my hair in handfuls!

Really, this has been a hard day. I haven't felt very well and am *tireder* than ever tonight. But I shall try to finish this letter – nay, I will *finish* it, even if I just have to *stop short*.

Yes, I want to see you settle down to some congenial work as soon as possible. Shake off as many of your metaphorical fleas as possible, resolve to *grin and bear* the unshakable ones, and *hoe in*. Nothing but steady, persistent labour will win in literature. *Dogged does it*. Why not try your hand on some essays on prairie life – the inwardness and outwardness of it, treating the subject delicately, analytically, *intimately*, exhaustively, and try your luck with William Briggs. Ten or twelve would make a book. Write on the prairie in all its aspects – by day, by night, in winter and summer, etc., etc., etc. Make each essay about three or four thousand words long and put all the airy fancy and thought into it that you can. Call the whole book *The Northern Silence* and write a title essay on that subject. Don't be in a hurry – write just when you feel in the mood for it.

EIGHT O'CLOCK

Here it is two hours later. A Christmas caller came in bringing a duck and a box of candy. (Write an essay on "Christmas on the Prairie" for your book!) It's really very hard to give good advice under such circumstances. But I was about through anyhow. Really, I'm in earnest. I think you could do it all right. There are many sentences and ideas in your various letters which could be worked admirably into such a series and if you decide to try it I'll copy them out and send them to you.

I must close now, for another caller has come and I do not expect to have any more spare time till after Xmas. I am enclosing the proof of the review that appeared in *National*. You may keep it. Also, as soon as I can get an envelope to fit it I'll send you a souvenir copy of my "Island Hymn," with music.

The best wishes of the season to you,

Yours very cordially,
L.M. Montgomery

Christmas at the Crompton

by David Cavanagh

Violet pulled her old green blanket more tightly around her, bunched her pillow behind her back, lit another Rothmans, took a sip of 5-Star rye and water, and continued to look at the snow falling past the street lamp outside her window. She liked the snow: the way it moved so silently and the silence it gave the street below. She would not enjoy the uneven, slippery footing on the sidewalk after the snowfall, but she wasn't worried about that tonight. She didn't plan to go out until the day after tomorrow, when things would open again. It was Christmas Eve, and Violet was settled in.

She lived in the back corner room on the top floor of the Crompton Hotel, two storeys above the bar. Had lived there for nearly twelve years. Every day about noon she made the rounds of the hurricane deck, which was what her friend Nobby called their floor in the "good ship Crompton." Nobby lived in the front corner room with the curtain blowing out the window, even in winter, and as self-designated captain of the ship he alternately terrorized, delighted, and took care of "his crew" with his pranks, outlandish singing, and constant small favors. Next to Cootsy, who lived two doors down, Nobby was the youngest on the floor. He was sixty-two, but most people thought he looked eighty-nine and acted seven. No one was quite sure of Violet's age, though they all teased her unmercifully to try to find out. Violet would just ignore them when they got in moods like that, call them fools, and sip on her beer.

There were five others living on the hurricane deck. Don and Rickshaw (so named because he loved harness racing), Peep, Ralph, and old Al, who was so fat he rarely left his room because he found the steep wooden staircase such torture. Every day Violet would visit the rooms, starting with Nobby's, and would tidy up a little, change the beds when they needed it, and generally make sure everybody was all right. In this way she worked off her eighty-dollar-a-month rent.

Some days she wouldn't be feeling well: kind of wobbly and upset in her stomach. Still she would make her way down the hall to Nobby's room and knock on his door.

"Who is it?" he'd bellow, even though he knew her knock. When she didn't answer, he'd open the door and feign surprise. "Oh my God, it's Maid Marion, come in, come in," offering her his only chair, an old stuffed leather one with a curved metal frame and wooden armrests. Violet could carefully sit down, resting the pile of clean sheets in her lap.

"How was your trip through the woods, fair lady?" Nobby would croak in a voice that sounded like a bag of stones poured over a washboard. "Did you notice old Cootsy didn't make it back to his hole last night? Ho. Ho." When he said "Ho. Ho." (which he did often), he breathed out each syllable distinctly, as if he were a diver getting ready to go under. "Maybe he got stuck in some other one. Pardon my Italian, fair damsel. So how are ya, old dear?"

"Not good today, Ian." Almost everybody called him Nobby, or Nob, maybe because his head was so bald and brown and tough, and as bald as a door handle. A few people called him "ya old buzzard," mostly with affection, though sometimes not. Only Violet called him Ian, his original name.

His voice would lower, "Well, don't worry about it, old sod. Just forget the beds for today. Twice a week's too often anyway." And they'd chat awhile, mostly about how the new owner of the hotel didn't treat them nearly as well as old Russ used to, but it didn't matter because "they'd outlast this new turk, the way he kept drinking up the profits of the bar." Then Violet would give Nobby a small smile and head back down the hall to the next room. Once she was inside and the door closed, Nobby would scuttle past and knock on all the other doors to tell the folks to take it easy on Violet, she wasn't feeling quite like the Queen Mother today.

Every night around midnight, after the rowdiest drinkers had gone away, Violet would come down to the bar, carefully sit at the little table near the front window, put her lighter and cigarettes on the table, and order two glasses of draft. Actually, she seldom had to order. The waiter would see her come in and bring her the beer. If Ned wasn't too drunk behind the bar, he would sometimes tell the waiter to say it was on the house. If he was in a mean mood, though, which was often, he would make some crack about the rooms she had cleaned that day, or didn't she think her liver was pickled enough already or some such thing. Violet wouldn't say a word but would light a cigarette, blow a long blue veil of smoke, and wait for her beer.

Usually, Nobby and Cootsy and a few others would join her and laugh and talk and sip beer. They never drank very much in the bar. Maybe they didn't want to be linked with the guzzlers who came in off the street. By closing time, one-thirty, Violet would always be back upstairs in her room. She would have another small drink, settle into bed and think for a while until she fell asleep.

But tonight was Christmas Eve, and the bar had closed at six so the staff could be with their families. Violet decided to go to bed early, not to sleep but to watch the steady snowfall, which always got her thinking. Usually her thinking floated above the steady murmur that filtered up from the bar. She found the drone comforting. In the bar itself the sounds were sharper, like glasses clinking. The voices rose and fell individually, filled with laughter, anger, boredom, the stories Violet had heard and overheard, learned from and lived with for years. Sometimes she was deeply tired of what she saw there, but mostly she loved the bar.

For her, bars were the most honest places around. The true churches of Canada, as Nobby would say. People confessed their sins there and their dreams, revealed their blackest and most beautiful and most petty sides. She felt that they came to the hotel to do their worship: to pour out their hatred for this life, and their love of it, their meanness and kindness, their failures and what they wished could be. She laughed at how stupid they could be, how stupid she could be, and inside wanted to cry at how good they all wanted to be. And all of it shared over slim, cool glasses of golden communion. She had lived in many towns and cities, and in many ways, but she knew that she had settled down on the top floor of the Crompton because everything she had ever seen happened every night right below her in the bar. When it came right down to it, there was nowhere else to go.

But tonight there was no sound. The only people in the hotel were the eight of them on this floor, the "permanents." Felt like Sunday, but different, too. Christmas Eve was always kind of strange. Silence on a Thursday night. Hard to get used to. At least the yeasty smell of beer, a hundred years of it, was still around. Incense. Hah. She took another sip of rye and thought that if the bar downstairs was the church, she and Nobby and Cootsy and the others must be – what? The statues? No, they moved around too much for that – must be the priests, and she must be a priest-ess. She liked that. She must remember to tell Nobby that one.

Her two-foot Christmas tree, plastic and gay with its little red lights and silver tinsel, winked at her from its spot on the high dresser that Ralph had painted white last month. Priests and Priestess. And what a bunch of holy terrors. Lord, how they teased her. Cootsy's gift was staring at her right now from beside the tree: a small stuffed penguin wearing a floppy green shawl and a wig of tight little curls and with a Rothmans hanging out of its mouth. The gift had surprised her. She hadn't gotten out to get anything for any of them. Suddenly she felt sad at the way the snow was beginning to pile up on the sill outside her window. It was going by the street lamp on a sharp slant now, too fast. She decided to get out of bed.

After going to the bathroom down the hall, she found herself at the top of the stairs, looking down into the dimness lit only by the small red exit light on the next landing. Moving along beside the shiny rubbed railing, she made her way down into the bar.

The yellow glow behind the bar, the Molson sign and the large red exit sign over the street door provided the only light. The heavy round tables were like old men stooped in the shadows. She went to her usual table and sat down. In the dark. No TV, no voices, no sound of glasses being washed behind the bar. Christmas Eve. The windows were frosted. The storm seemed far away. She liked the quiet, but she also felt very empty and small in the dark corner.

After a while she got up, went behind the bar and drew a glass of draft from the spigot. She could hardly reach it, but by hoisting herself a little with her elbow on the counter she managed. She walked carefully with the full glass back to her table, lit a cigarette, and took a sip of beer.

Her Christmas Eve party. A bar to herself. Stolen beer tasted good. If Ned ever saw her he'd wet his pants. Would suit him just fine, she thought, the big horse. The eight-foot tinfoil Merry Christmas over the bar made her laugh. She drained her glass and got up. This time she brought back two draft, her usual. "Thank you, Ned, bring them right over here. My table, Ned." She put a quarter tip on the table. "Next time take away the empties, Ned, or we'll find someone who will." She laughed a little. God, Violet, what are you doing stealing beer and talking to the air? "Merry Christmas, Violet," she toasted out loud and drained the glass.

A few minutes later she got up for two more draft, and a few minutes after that, two more. It began to be difficult to make the trip from the bar to her table, but she was damned if she would sit behind the bar on Ned's stool and slop down beer. She moved slowly back to her table, spilling some as she stepped down the one step between her table and the bar. "Damn." Lit another cigarette. Choked a bit, and took a big swallow of beer. She knew she was getting drunk. Knew she should be back in her room. Knew her room was the only place she was safe when she was like this. They'd laugh at her. She didn't mind the teasing of the bunch upstairs – they were like her, no better and in some ways worse off – but she wouldn't stand for anyone in the bar laughing at her. Ned laughing at her. The stuffed hog. She started to cry, the tears wetting her hand wrapped around the beer glass. The wrinkles. How did they ever get so wrinkled, she thought. Damn. Ned, you bugger. And knew that she was not just talking to Ned. He was just like her son – huge belly, mean, big voice – who lived in

Edmonton now. Hadn't talked to her for over eight years. Owned three trucks last time she'd heard. Made her cry to see how he hated his kids, his wife, her, the way he talked about racing the bohunks on the highway, the way he talked about her. Ned. Just like him. She got up. Got two more glasses of draft and a shot of rye from the bottles kept under the counter and put them all on a tray. Made it back to the table but knocked some of the empties on the floor as she put down the tray. She was crying hard now. "I'll clean it up, Ned. Damn you, I'll clean it."

"Oh my God, it's Mother Superior."

It was Nobby, standing in the doorway leading from the staircase, light from the Molson Golden sign glinting off his head. "Thought I heard something. What the devil are you doing down here on the poop deck?" When he saw her face, he just came over and sat down. He took her left hand. That surprised both of them. "Don't worry, Violet. It isn't worth it."

"I know, but sometimes I can't help it."

"I know, I know." Nobby leaned down and picked up the fallen glasses. He didn't ask what was wrong. It was the same with him some days. "What are you trying to do, make me work all through the birth of Our Lord?" It was Nobby's job to clean up the bar every morning before it opened. "Can I buy you a drink, Rapunzel?" Violet tried to grin and pointed to the empties on the table. Nobby moved behind the bar and brought back a trayful of beer. "Quite an idea you've got here. Don't move. I'll be right back."

He went to the bottom of the stairway and hollered Cootsy's name like a volley of cannon shots. Cootsy's head finally appeared at the top of the stairs.

"Ah, there you are. Alert the bridge, dear Coots. The Queen of Sheba's down here, and she's inviting everyone to a party on the poop. Ho. Ho. Tell them all to bring their stomachs and their dancing shoes."

It wasn't long before they all trooped down: Ralph, and Don, and Peep, and Rickshaw, carrying a transistor, and Cootsy, shaking his head and grinning like a chimp. "Oh Nobby, you've done it this time. Let's do it real Merry, 'cause we're gonna need a new home in the New Year."

"Never mind that, Cootsy old son, pass around some of this beer." And he handed him another trayful.

They were all awed by what was happening. All of them had, in one way or other, lived on the fringes of society for years, were used to being outcasts, even enjoyed it when things were going well: when their veterans' and old age pension came in, when Cootsy got a raise at Canadian Tire, when Rickshaw won at the track, or when they staged one of their frequent and complicated pranks, such as the day they moved all of Al's furniture into the big bathroom and stuffed his room from floor to ceiling with balled newspaper while he was out. They were used to themselves and to their lives, difficult or strange as they sometimes seemed, even to them, but they still relied on their routines, and they knew the boundaries that their outrageousness had to live within. They knew now that they were going beyond these bounds, drinking Ned's beer in his closed-up bar on Christmas Eve.

It made them hesitant at first, but also giddy. Soon they were hooting and drinking and telling old stories that had them in tears. Even old Al finally lumbered down the stairs to see what the commotion was about and in no time was holding forth, his mammoth rear spread across two chairs, about the time they flew Violet's underwear from the top of the TV antenna on the roof of the hotel. The flag of the good ships Lolly and Poop, Nobby called it at the time.

Rickshaw turned on the radio, and amid more trips to the bar they started dancing. Violet refused to dance but was tapping her feet and smiling through her cigarette smoke. Nobby told her she had beautiful hands, and kissed one of them. She shoved him away and shook her head at him the way she always did. Peep did a Spanish sword dance on the bar while they all clapped, and Nobby kept hopping all over the room, handing out beer and booming out, "Ho. Ho. Who has more fun that the poor people? Press on, press on, Lancelot." His last to Ralph, who was galloping toward the dartboard with Al's cane thrust out in front of him.

Everything would probably have been fine if Cootsy hadn't asked old fat Al to dance with him, and if Nobby and Cootsy and Rickshaw hadn't hauled Al to his feet against his protests. Soon Cootsy and Al were blimping around the room like a balloon blown up, turned loose and gone crazy, only in slow motion. Nothing was safe. Four hundred pounds of drunken enthusiasm knocked over tables, chairs, Nobby, just missed the color television, and finally fell against the crossbar handle of the street door.

Two things happened simultaneously. One was that Cootsy and Al disappeared from sight into the street. The other was that a shrill bell started clanging loud enough that even Violet stood up and stared, frozen with the others, at the once again closed door. It was the burglar alarm.

"Oh my God, we must be on fire. Abandon ship!" hollered Nobby and jumped behind the bar to find the switch to turn off the alarm. The bell clanged on and on. Most of the others were holding their ears and yelling at Nobby to hurry up and find the goddamn switch. Finally it stopped. They all looked at each other, wondering what next.

They didn't have to wait long. Cootsy and Al burst back into the bar, Al swearing himself hoarse and heading for a couple of chairs and Cootsy burbling and mumbling in a mixture of laughter and fear. It seemed a police car was heading their way down the main drag, red lights flashing. Cootsy had thought for a minute it was a Christmas tree coming to see what happened. Just then they heard the car pull up to the curb outside the door.

"Oh my God, the Gestapo," whispered Nobby and headed for the door. "This is it mates. See you in el hoosegow." And then, "Violet, quick. Go on upstairs."

Violet just sat down, pulled her shawl around her, took another sip of beer and reached for a cigarette. "Best party I've been to in years," she said, and waved him towards the door.

There was a knock, and Nobby called out, "Who is it?"

"Police. Who are YOU?"

Nobby opened the door and was greeted by the glare of a flashlight shone directly into his eyes. "Come in, gentlemen, come in, I didn't realize it was already noon."

Two large policemen, made larger by their winter parkas, came into the room and flashed their lights at Don and Ralph and Al and Peep and Cootsy and Rickshaw and the overturned chairs and tables and finally at Violet, sitting calmly smoking at her table in the corner. It was nearing midnight on Christmas Eve in a bar that had closed six hours ago, and there were about twenty empty and half-empty beer glasses on her table alone. "Hello, George, Paul. Won't you sit down?" She waved to two upright chairs at the next table.

Ralph pretended to faint over by the bar. Nobby just grabbed his head in both hands and looked on.

"What the hell's going on here, Violet?" the policeman called George said. So Violet explained. How she'd been up in her room, how she'd got feeling blue, since it was Christmas Eve, how she'd come down, how Nobby had heard her and come to help her out, how they'd all decided to have a party to cheer her up, and how things got a wee bit too merry, and how the door had tripped the alarm. It was quite a long story, and the two policemen just listened quietly.

When Violet was finished, the one called Paul said, "Does Ned Tanner know you're in here tonight?"

"I wouldn't think so," Violet said, and took a sip of beer.

Silence. And then finally Paul said, "Well, George, do you see any damage or signs of a break-in?"

"Nope," said George, "no sign of a break-in. Somebody better check that alarm. Must've shorted out."

"Guess so. Well, folks, too bad you have to work on Christmas Eve cleaning up the bar. Ned's kind of a mean bugger to make you work tonight. Hope it doesn't take too long. Have a good Christmas."

And they left.

"Oh my God, Mary Magdalene, you're a real Christmas bonus!" croaked Nobby, shaking his head.

Violet just raised her glass and smiled. "Who has more fun than the poor people, eh Nobby?"

'Tis Better to Give

by Al Roach

Clem had exactly two dollars left. All of his presents were purchased except for one. Did I want to go downtown with him on Christmas Eve to buy that one last gift?

We decided to save the nickel bus fare each way and walk from Walkerville. It was a beautiful evening: clear, snow on the ground, temperature hovering around ten degrees Fahrenheit. Our shadows walked along with us, first behind, then overtaking us and extending out in front as we passed each yellowish streetlight.

We reached the corner of Wyandotte and Ouellette, where in a field across the street, a sign proclaimed that a bank would be built there as a post-war project. Ouellette was alive with joyful last-minute shoppers.

We turned north and walked along the eastside toward the river. The wind was developing a bite and I adjusted the metal band over my brown fur earmuffs, drawing them closer to the sides of my head. My feet slipped on lumpy snow, hard-packed by hundreds of shoppers' boots.

"Where is this angel, anyway?" I asked.

"At Bartlet, Macdonald and Gow."

"It would be!" Almost to Sandwich Street (Riverside Drive)! I pulled my woolen jacket up tighter around my throat and leaned into the wind. We passed Meretsky and Gitlin Furniture, the Tea Garden Restaurant, John Webb Jewellers.

Despite wartime shortages, shop windows displayed a tempting variety of gifts "for her" and "for him", all competing for space with crossed Union Jacks, signs exhorting us to "Buy British" and purchase Dominion of Canada Victory Bonds, and others reminding us that "Loose Lips Sink Ships."

We approached the Fleetway Tunnel exit. Across the street was Liddy and Taylor Men's Wear, the store where Clem and I spent some of the dollars we earned, working Saturdays (for 40 cents per hour) at the A&P on Ottawa Street, to outfit ourselves for the return to school each fall.

We were surprised to see the newsstand at the tunnel exit open so late in the evening. The headlines were always the same in those days: success and disasters for the Allied armed forces on land, at sea and in the air, but inside, the comics were still there. War or no war, Li'l Abner was wrestling for a gun with the four-armed Mr. Armstrong, Brick Bradford was championing the weak against the strong, and Caps Stubbs remained the quintessence of boyhood.

In that festive season, all the papers, including *The Windsor Daily Star* and *The Detroit Times* were carrying Clement C. Moore's "The Night Before Christmas." And, assuring eight-year-old Virginia O'Hanlon that, yes, there is a Santa Claus, as they had done every year since the editorial first appeared in *The New York Sun* in 1897.

Light snow began to fall, powdering our hair and eyelashes, tickling our noses.

"What are you going to do with this angel, anyway," I asked.

"Put it on the top of the tree, of course. It's a beautiful white satin ornament with gold hair and all that. I'm going to put it up there tonight when everyone's asleep – a kind of surprise for my mother. She's wanted one since the cat got the old one last year. Top of the tree looks bare without an angel."

We crossed Park Street, passing the Prince Edward Hotel. Through the revolving doors and down the steps came a live angel in a white satin evening gown, Persian lamb coat and dangling silver earrings, her escort in black coat with velvet collar and fringed white silk scarf. They tiptoed their way (she holding her gown up with one dainty hand) over the icy sidewalk and into the waiting checkered cab.

There was to be a New Year's Eve dance in the Prince Eddy ballroom. Matti Holli's Orchestra. Three dollars per person. Clem and I would not be there. If we could scrape up the price of admission, we'd likely take our girlfriends ice skating at the arena "to the music of Ralph Ford at the electric organ."

Moments later we passed the Canada Building where Sid Tarleton and his St. Mary's Church Boys' Choir had made their annual appearance at 9 a.m. that day, leading the building's tenants in singing Christmas carols. An old tradition.

Across the street was the beautiful new building of Birks-Ellis-Ryri (successors to McCreery's). We remembered the original McCreery's Jewellery Store, located in the Prince Eddy.

A stubby little Sandwich, Windsor and Amherstburg Railway Ford bus crunched by, throwing dirty snow on our trouser legs. The Fords were among the first buses purchased after the streetcars were junked in 1939.

Ads in this day's *Star*, signed by W.H. Furlong, K.C., chairman of the S.W. & A., and F. X. Chauvin, vice-chairman, thanked Windsorites for their patience. The buses were badly overloaded, what with wartime workers and Christmas shoppers vying for standing room in the aisles. Maybe they should have kept the old reliable streetcars.

We passed Honey Dew Limited, which served the best orange drink in town, and looked across Ouellette at the sparkling windows of old established retailers, such as Burton the Tailor, Esquire Men's Shop, and George W. Wilkinson Limited. (Four decades into the future, these locations will be occupied by One Plus One Ladies' Wear, Jeanne Bruce Limited Jewellers and Chateau 333, respectively.)

In front of the five-storey Wilkinson's store ("Wilkinson's Shoes Wear like a Pig's Nose") stood a Salvation Army lass in her quaint bonnet with the big ribbon. Her little hand bell sounded somehow shy, matching her sad eyes.

An idea. "Why don't you give your two dollars to the Sally Ann?" I suggested. "It's Christmas Eve, you know."

"Bah! Humbug!" replied Clem in his best Dickens' manner. "Charity begins at home."

At the Palace, Cecil B. DeMille's The Sign of the Cross was playing. Starring Frederic March, Claudette Colbert, and Charles Laughton.

Across London Street (University), past Stuart Stores for Men, the Singer Sewing Machine Store, C.R. Wickens and Son Tobacconist and Gift shop, across Chatham Street, Wright's Butcher Shop, Grinnell's Music Shop (pianos, sheet music, radios, records), John A. Jackson Limited Men's Wear, the Star Restaurant, across Pitt Street, past the Canada Trust Company on the northeast corner.

As we went by the C.H. Smith Company store, we saw a small boy standing in front of Bartlet's, staring at something in the window. We recognized him; we'd seen him many times selling magazines to the drunks coming out of The Ritz and B.A. Hotels at Ouellette and Sandwich. He must have lived over one of the stores in those old run-down, three-storey brick buildings on Sandwich. Not exactly Willistead Crescent.

Shiny black hair. Big, staring brown eyes. He was looking at a black lace shawl with a $5 ticket on it. A lot of money in those days.

Clem's pace slackened, reduced to a crawl, and came to a stop. Silence. The boy turned as if to leave.

"Nice shawl, kid," said Clem.

A pair of brown eyes looked at him innocently. A bit perplexed.

"Uh huh." A pause.

"How much money do you have?"

Again the artless eyes stared at Clem, taking him in, registering no emotion. Another pause.

"Three dollars."

Three dollars, I thought. Three dollars earned the hard way. Long hours after school on that pavement in front of the two hotels, just up the hill from the old Detroit, Windsor, and Belle Isle Ferry Company dock. Long weeks, maybe months, of selling magazines at a profit of two cents per sale. Always thinking about the black lace shawl.

This, I decided, is going to be interesting. I leaned back against a lamp post to watch closely. "Think of that," I said. "He's two dollars short. Now that's quite a coincidence."

Clem gave me a why-don't-you-mind-your-own-damn-business look. Another pause. Clem looking at the boy. Boy looking back, wondering what was coming next. Me looking at Clem.

Finally: "Look, kid, take this two bucks and go in and buy the shawl and don't ask any questions."

A minute later we were looking into the store, watching the

perfumed saleslady wrapping the shawl in a Christmassy box. A pair of brown eyes watching her every move. Five-dollar bills scrunched up in a grubby hand resting on the sparkling glass counter.

Another minute later and he was out of the store, dashing around the corner and heading west on Sandwich Street. He disappeared into a south side doorway near Fifth Brothers Tailor Shop and the Taylor Furniture Company.

I thought a certain mother was going to be very happy on Christmas morning.

We turned back down Ouellette Avenue. In silence. We stopped at the traffic light at Chatham. The snow was falling heavier now, coating the scene in fresh holiday white. I looked sideways at Clem.

"I thought charity begins at home," I grinned.

"You can just shut up," he said.

But I couldn't get over the feeling that Clem would not need his satin angel. A far more substantial one would be shining down on him on Christmas morning.

Starry Starry Night

by Don Bailey

This morning I boarded a plane in Winnipeg and flew twelve hundred miles to sit on a chair next to the person in the bed beside me. It was a last-minute decision that upset the board and staff of the church where I am head honcho. They whined and wailed that the congregation would be upset by my absence. I didn't care. The truth is I don't care about anything. The last year of my life has been like living in a cave where the light is slowly diminishing, leaving me in the dark. I've come to offer comfort but also to seek the light.

I am not a person who acts on impulses, and the drama of using my influence as a clergyman to obtain a ticket for my son and me, claiming it was a life and death situation, the chaos of the airport, and the flight itself with many of the passengers drunk, expressing their emotional ambivalence towards the season by singing Christmas carols off key, has served to keep my mind off the purpose of the trip.

But now I am here. With my son. During the taxi ride from the terminal to my in-laws' Etobicoke home I was forced to face the fact that my actions are that of a man on the run. A man afraid to face certain truths about himself.

"This sure is a treat," the old man mutters. "You couldn't 've given us a better gift."

Joseph Edwin Bracknell, age 78, retired president of a discount shoe store chain he started himself from scratch. My father-in-law, grandfather to my son Mitchell, and father to my deceased wife, Bernice.

"People undervalue themselves," he says. "You get old and you realize the one thing you can't buy is time with the people you love."

He speaks with difficulty. The hospital bed he lies in is cranked up so he can watch the Christmas tree decorating going on in front of him. He has an IV going into each arm. One contains a solution to keep him from becoming dehydrated. The other feeds a steady flow of pain killer into his emaciated body.

Joe is dying. Three months after his daughter succumbed to cancer of the breast, his prostrate began acting up. It was removed but the surgeon said it was too late. Malignancy had set in and was deeply entrenched. Treatment would be useless.

No more fat Havana cigars or the daily half bottle of Crown Royale whiskey that functioned as a calming sedative to the explosive energy that drove him. He has lost sixty pounds from his six-foot frame and food is of little interest to him.

"Sometimes when I'm lying here alone I feel like I'm in the middle of a movie," he says. "I mean it's like a dream where I'm sitting in the audience with my family. It must be a long time ago because the kids are all young, and we're holding hands, touching each other at least even if it's just our legs rubbing up against the next person, but I'm up on the screen too. In the picture, looking out at myself and everybody else. And I know how the story's going to end and I want to tell those who are watching that the ending's kind of sad, but it's worth their while to watch. The trouble is I can't say anything except what's in the script. There's no way I can change anything."

"I don't understand Joe," I say.

"Me neither Jake. It's probably just the pharmaceuticals they're piping into me, making me see things."

"Joseph!" His wife, Nancy, shouts from the stepladder, "You're supposed to be resting."

She does not look our way but continues to hang the brightly colored glass balls on the huge scotch pine that reaches up to within six inches of the nine-foot ceiling.

"I'll get all the rest I need lying in the slumber room of Bardall's funeral home," he mutters. "After they run me through the walk-in barbecue they keep out back there won't be anything left of me but a pound and half of ashes that I want spread on the tomato plants in the Spring. Nothing like a little bone ash to pep up growing soil. Come August when those beefsteaks are as fat and juicy on the vine as I used to be, ripe for the picking, Nancy will be out there with her wicker basket gathering them up. And that night she'll have our sons over for dinner and I'll be reunited at the hearth of my family. In a manner of speaking. I just hope they remember my aversion to mayonnaise."

He chuckles by his mirth and erupts in a bubbling, choking manner as though an aquarium has been implanted in his chest.

"None of that morbid talk Christmas Eve," Nancy says. "We all know you're too stubborn to exit politely. Five years from now you'll still be laying in that bed pontificating on any subject that pops into your mind and I'll be up on this ladder, my joints as stiff as pig iron with this arthritis, probably slip, fall, break my neck, and be lying at your feet but you'll still be talking and won't even notice."

"You do your share pretty good too," he says.

"Have to," she replies. "A task assigned by God himself to remind you that there are others in the world beyond yourself. A fact you've always found easy to forget."

"I resent being reduced to the cross you have to bear," he says. "You seem to be implying that I'm not the sensitive man I imagine myself to be."

Mitchell smiles. He is twelve years old and has a strong affection for the concept that life is a series of re-runs of his favorite television situation comedy. Since my own parents died many years ago I have no models of grandparents other than Joe and Nancy to offer him. I am afraid he will misconstrue their banter as a form of mutual love and respect.

"Don't concern yourself Joseph," Nancy says, as she stretches precariously on the ladder, balancing on one leg to place another garish decoration on the tree. "Forty-seven years and I have very few splinter scars to show for my efforts."

Mitchell laughs out loud. He is quick to pick up on their stinging humor.

The doorbell rings.

"That'll be the boys," Nancy says as she climbs down the ladder. She is a handsome woman. I would guess she is in her late sixties, her white hair cut short and permed into a fluffy cap that bounces as she strides across the living room towards the front hall.

"The anointed heirs," Joe says. "Glory be, they finally made it. Without us sending out a search party too. Good thing those two weren't part of the wise men trio. We'd still be waiting for them to find the Christ child. One of them would be in a drug rehab

program and the other'd be taking an upgrading program in wisdom so he'd know what it was if it bit him on the ass."

Mitchell laughs loudly. He is sitting on the edge of the hospital bed with me next to him on a straight back chair, the theory
being that Joe won't have to raise his voice to talk with us. My son
takes his grandfather's hand in his own. He is the only grandchild.
Neither of his uncles are married or even have girlfriends they are
serious about. Joe has made it clear that he views Mitchell as the
only hope for the continuance of the family line. I worry that the
boy will be spoiled by the attention that is lavished on him and
the money he's liable to inherit.

Nancy stops in the hall and directs a fierce look at Joe. She
opens one of the French doors and shouts at him.

"You behave," she says. "Your sons may not have turned out
like you but that might be its own kind of blessing."

"Well disguised if you ask me," he says.

"At least when the time comes for them to retire their wives
won't have to put up with the chairman of the board calling in the
middle of the night begging for help to ease them out."

"Biggest mistake I made," Joe says. "Letting the company go
public. Don't know who was greedier, me or the stock holders. But
for different things. I wanted their capital to expand but they just
wanted to park their dough in a safe cove so they could collect
dividends into the twenty-first century. Spent all my time fighting
with them."

"And always got your way," Nancy says.

The doorbell rings but she doesn't move.

"No danger of those two ever having trouble with the board,"
he says. "I suppose with the voting block we still hold you could
demand seats for them on the board. I still own over forty per cent
of the company but the lawyers, bankers, and accountants would
fight it. The thing is neither one of them knows the difference

between cow slips and slippers. As far as wives are concerned, I don't think either one's got the energy to engage in the battle of the sexes."

"They're just slow starters," she says. "As long as I represent this family on the board, they'll have a place if they so choose."

The doorbell rings again and Joe releases a soft chuckle.

"Haven't even got the sense to try the door. Is it locked?"

"No," she says, moving to open it. "They were brought up to be polite. More than I can say for some others who are cluttering up the environment with their moaning about dying."

"I'm a sick man, Nancy and I've got the puncture marks to prove it."

"Well no dying tonight," she says. "You do and I'll be tempted to drag you out to the curb beside our blue box so you can be recycled with the tin cans."

Mitchell bounces on the bed in appreciation, laughing so hard the sound becomes locked in his throat. Nancy opens the door and her two sons enter. At the same moment the live-in registered nurse appears from the dining room, a glass of amber liquid in her right hand. She walks over to Joe's bed and checks the IVs. She pops a thermometer into the old man's mouth and takes his pulse as she waits for his temperature to register.

"Enjoying my rye Elsie?" Joe asks, as she completes her check of his vital signs.

"Smooth as an infant's behind," she says, taking a large gulp from the crystal glass that she then holds up to the light and admires.

"How 'bout pouring me one," he asks.

She releases a guttural chuckle and points to the two men entering the room.

"Your boys are here," she says. "You best be keeping your wits about you."

"Later then," he says, negotiating hard.

She tugs at the white material of her uniform that is as thick as tent canvas and hangs from her wide, middle-aged body like a protective tarpaulin.

"Perhaps when the tree's finished," she says. "A small one when the angel's put in place. To celebrate the season."

"We top our tree with a star," Nancy says.

"Whatever symbol suits you best," Elsie says with a shrug and saunters off towards the dining room where she will sit at the table in the dark, watching and listening as she nurses a glass of seasonal spirits.

Paul, the oldest of Joe's sons, enters the room briskly. He leans over the bed and plants a loud, wet kiss on his father's forehead.

"Geezus," the old man protests, "wait 'til I stop breathing before you start slobbering over me."

The younger son, Larry, who will be thirty-five his next birthday, squeezes out a laugh that is similar in sound to the steel wheels of a locomotive screeching to a halt.

Paul smiles painfully. Blonde, pale like his mother, he steps back from the bed and clasps his hands together in front of him, his thirty-eight-year-old face unlined by worldly concerns. A man committed to fierce politeness.

"I'm pleased to see you in such fine spirits, father," Paul says.

In his dark blue, three-piece suit he looks like an accountant and has the carefully controlled speech of a funeral director. I have tried during my fifteen years of being part of this family to warm to Paul, to connect with him, but some inadequacy within me has sabotaged this possibility. Although his name is biblical in its origins and therefore has some historical substance, the Paul holding his hand out to me is elusive, unrevealing. He makes me feel like a visitor from another planet.

"Good to see you Jake," he says. "Surprised but pleased."

His hand slides out of mine and stops in front of Mitchell who stands and grapples with it awkwardly.

"Hi Uncle Paul," the boy says.

"You've grown Mitchell."

"Yes," the boys answers.

"That's what kids do," Joe says. "You haven't seen him in almost a year. Don't be such a tight-ass, give the kid a hug."

Paul ignores his father's remark, removes his suit jacket, folds it carefully, and places it on the back of an upholstered chair. He turns towards me and we have eye contact for a second or two. His eyes make me think of two pools of murky brown mud that serve as cloudy windows so that it is impossible to know the inner rage I suspect he harbors. Both he and his brother exist on weekly allowances provided by their mother. She sends a weekly cheque to their landlords so they are assured of a place to live. Since neither brother has a car, she shops weekly for their groceries and delivers them to their apartments. When they need clothes, mother takes them on an excursion where she foots the bill and, for the most part, decides what they'll wear. I always wondered how their sister Bernice had turned out so differently. A rebel who depended on no one.

"I would have thought a clergyman would be in great demand to his congregation at this time of year," Paul says.

"I work in a team ministry," I reply. "Everyone else's taken holidays this year so I decided it was my turn."

"That's reassuring," he says. "When mother informed us you were coming I thought father's death was imminent. We only ever seem to see you at family funerals."

"Cute," Joe says. "Very cute Paul, but mean . . . No call for it . . . The medical profession has turned my body into an irrigation system and I've been ready to dry up and blow away for months now . . . They seem to believe that as long as I'm wet, I'll keep living. I feel like a patch of desert that the Israelis are trying to revitalize, pumping stuff into me at one end and collecting it at the other end. Speaking of which . . . Elsie! You gonna empty this bladder bag or let it run all over the carpet?"

"I checked it not ten minutes ago," she calls from the other room. "It's not even half full."

Larry, tall and thin in baggy jeans and a flannel shirt that hangs outside his pants, comes over to the bed and pokes at the plastic container being discussed.

"She's right Pop," he says. "Still plenty of room in the old piss bag."

Curious, Mitchell leans down to have a look. Nancy bustles over to the ladder next to the tree and scurries up to the last rung.

"Com'on boys," she says. "Your father's been waiting all night for you to come and finish the decorations."

"I'm taking a shower first," Larry announces. "Downstairs."

"Good idea," Joe says. "While you're down there have a look around for the garden shears. You find them, bring them up and I'll shorten that mop of hair by a foot or two."

The younger son laughs and pats his father gently on the shoulder.

"You haven't been paying attention," he says. "The sixties are back. Long hair is in again."

"You look ridiculous," his father says.

"Maybe," Larry says, "but then I guess so did Jesus. He was the first hippy. Right Jake?"

"And look what they did to him," I answer as a means of deflecting the question.

The old man releases a bubble of laughter.

"They nailed him good," he says. "Is that what you want Larry? A bunch of people come along and hammer you on to a cross?"

The smile on Larry's face collapses into an expression of dismay.

I think he imagines that these kind of exchanges with his father are all in good fun but Joe isn't joking. The old man festers with rage and resentment over the failure of his sons to follow the trail he has laid out for them.

But Larry is resilient. The smile returns to his face and he looks at his father with affection.

"You're right Pop," he says. "A person should have a reason for being weird. For me it's just a habit. Speaking of which, how is the church business these days Jake?"

Paul has joined his mother at the tree. She is hanging tinsel on the upper branches while he works on the bottom half.

"Finished for me," I say. "I put in my resignation for April."

"You're transferring to a new congregation?" Joe asks.

"I hope it's closer to Toronto," Nancy says. "That one time we visited you in Winnipeg was unbearable. So much cold can't be good for your health. My tulips were blooming the day we left here but when we stepped off the plane, a blizzard was blowing."

"I'm leaving the ministry."

Nancy cannot hide her surprise. She squats down and sits on the top step of the ladder.

"What're you going to do Jake?" she asks.

"My Dad's gonna get a nine-to-five job," Mitchell says. "Like all my friends' parents have. You know like a real job."

Everyone laughs but I sense an undercurrent of uneasiness.

"I haven't decided," I say. "All I know is that I want to do something different, something where I can see some tangible results that I think are worthwhile."

"What could be more satisfying than overseeing the spiritual lives of your flock?" Nancy asks. "I can understand wanting to change the location, God knows we'd be happier having you and Mitchell closer at hand . . . but to give up the whole thing . . . "

"I'm not a happy shepherd," I answer. "And anyway, the sheep are restless. Couples used to come to me for marriage counselling, now they're urging me to use the church to set up some kind of tax shelter so they can avoid income tax. They want my blessing on their decision to put their parents in nursing homes so they can get power-of-attorney and take control of the old folk's money before they spend it on foolishness like touring the country on a motorcycle. The visiting committee has me videotaping my sermons so shut-ins don't have to be picked up and lugged to the church Sunday mornings. We have a campaign to raise money to buy VCRs for any senior in the congregation who doesn't have one. Pretty soon I'll be able to FAX the service to everyone's home and no one will have to come to church."

"Sounds like you've let them shake your faith," Nancy says.

"Too heavy for me," Larry says as he clomps off towards the basement.

"Let's listen to what Jake has to say," Joe says.

"Perhaps, he's thinking of going into shoes," Paul says. "He might persuade our board to set up a charitable foundation to shoe the barefoot of the world. Reeboks for Russian waifs, Converse for cannibals. We could unload our mismatched sizes on Third World countries and the government would probably allow us a huge write-off. We could call it the Ministry of Soles."

I laugh.

"Not a bad idea," I say. "Sounds like a more honest hustle than what I'm doing now."

"Don't turn cynic on us Jake," Nancy says. "We've got enough of those around here to do us."

"What's that mean Dad? Mitchell asks.

"A cynic is a person who goes around bursting people's balloons because he hasn't got one himself," Joe says.

"My Dad's not like that," the boy says.

"No, he's not," the old man says, "but your grandmother is

worried about what he'll do when his job is finished in Winnipeg. Me too."

"I'll be fine," I say. "University of Toronto have offered me a teaching position in their theological department. Three courses a semester. Less work and more money."

"So you won't really be leaving the church," Nancy says. "Just doing something different. Well a change is good, healthy even. When will you start?"

"Next Fall but I haven't accepted it," I reply. "I'm still thinking about it. The other idea I had was to write a book about ministries in the inner city. All the churches I've worked for have been in the heart of the city and what I learned is that they're all dead. Some of them preserved beautifully, and visited weekly by all the faithful who live ten, fifteen miles away in the suburbs. But what about the people who live a block from the church, the students, the single mothers and their kids, the old people in small rooms cooking their margarine casseroles on hot plates? How come they don't attend and fill some of the space in the empty pews?"

"You can't expect people like that to keep a church going. They don't have the money and they have too many other problems to cope with. They're too busy surviving to have an appreciation for a good sermon. You should know that!" Nancy says. "If people drive in from the suburbs, ten, fifteen miles every week it just shows how committed they are. You should be happy they continue to be loyal."

"You're probably right," I say, "but twenty years ago when I was ordained I had this idea that our ministry was supposed to respond to the needy, heal the wounded, feed the masses . . . no one said anything about comforting the complacent."

"Well you're a fool if you think people are going to pay out money for a book that tells them their church is a corpse. People want good news, not bad. There's enough bad news going around for free."

She stands up on the ladder again and resumes hanging tinsel on the tree. Elsie sidles into the room with a triumphant grin on her face.

"He's doing it again," she says.

"What're you talking about?" Joe asks.

"Wacky tobacky," she says. "Number two son is toking up in the basement and blowing the smoke into the heating ducts."

"I can't smell anything," Nancy says.

Mitchell runs over to a heating vent on the floor, sprawls down, and puts his face against it. He breathes in deeply.

"Yup," he announces. "That's grass."

"How would you know?" I ask.

"Quite a few guys at my school smoke pot," he says. "Especially before math or science classes."

"You thought about private school for this boy?" Joe asks. "I'll be glad to pay the freight."

"That wouldn't do any good Grandpa," Mitchell says. "My hockey team plays against a private school and half their players get stoned before they go on the ice. They say it makes them calmer, helps them concentrate so they score more goals."

"Crap!" the old man bellows. "That stuff will rot your brain. You stay away from it Mitchell."

"I will," the boy says.

"Paul, go downstairs and speak to your brother. He knows I won't stand for that stuff in my house. If he has to use it, tell him to stick his head in the vent for the dryer. That way at least the smoke'll blow outside."

Paul puts his suit jacket back on and heads towards the basement. Nancy comes down the ladder and steps back to look at the tree. She then plugs in the Christmas lights and the tree gives off a shimmering multicolored glow.

"I think it's the best one we've ever had," she says.

———

"A beauty," Joe says. "But what about the star?"

"I'm going to make some eggnog first," she says. "Then we'll put it up."

"Can I help?" Mitchell asks.

"Of course," she says, and the two of them troop off to the kitchen.

"I might as well pitch in," Elsie says from the dark dining room.

"What about my drink?" Joe asks.

"In due time," Elsie replies as she too heads towards the kitchen.

Paul and Larry enter the living room through the French doors.

"We've gotta go," Paul says. "Larry's not feeling well. I've got a friend's car so I'll drive home."

"What's the matter?" Joe asks.

Larry takes his coat from the hallway closet and turns towards his father. "I just don't seem to be in the Christmas spirit," he says.

"Your mother'll be upset," Joe says. "We hardly ever see you."

"She sees lots of me," Larry says. "It's you and I that avoid each other. Saves us a lot of grief."

"Well speak to her before you leave."

"I'd rather not," he says. "She'll just try to talk me into staying."

He puts on his coat and heads towards the front door.

"You'll be coming back Paul?" Joe asks.

"I'll try," his son answers.

They open the door quietly and slip out into the cold winter night.

Joe and I sit quietly for a few moments. I feel embarrassed for the old man. He is too tired to express the anger I imagine he must feel. Suddenly he grabs my hand and squeezes it tightly. We can hear laughter coming from the kitchen.

"What's that Psalm about the shepherd Jake?" he asks.

"The Lord is my shepherd, I shall not want. He makes me lie down in green pastures; He leads me beside quiet waters. He restores my soul; He guides me in the path of righteousness for His name's sake . . . Even though I walk through the valley of death, I fear no evil; for thou art with me . . ."

"Yeah," he says. "That's the one. I've never been a religious person but one of the last times I saw Bernice . . . You were living out at the river house and she and I sat out on the lawn watching the stars come out . . . She was only a week from dying and I didn't have a clue what to say . . . I never felt so helpless. There was nothing I could do to fix the situation but she took my hand and recited that psalm . . . I think it was more to comfort me than her . . . And then she pointed up to the sky at the stars . . . She told me that stars were planets that had died but thousands of years later they were still burning . . . even the sun is a star . . . without them we'd be living in darkness. Before I got sick I'd always go walking at night and look up and the first star I saw always made me think of her . . . How do you remember her Jake?"

"I try not to Joe," I reply.

"Yeah, that's what I thought. Mitchell's the same. The two of you never mention her . . . It's not good for you Jake. Memories are like matches we strike to light up the gloom. I remember we stayed at this cottage one year and Bernice dragged me out of bed in the middle of the night to come outside with her to watch the fireflies. I thought she'd probably want to catch them and put them in jars. That's the kind of thing I did when I was a kid. But not her. She just wanted me to sit with her on the porch and watch these bugs flickering in the dark. She called them flying stars."

"I miss her terribly," I admit.

"I know you do," he says. "And the world's full of things that will remind you of her. Don't cut off your head and heart to your history, Jake. From what I saw, you and Bernice had your share of happiness. The future's just a black hole if you don't use those memories to blaze a new trail for you and Mitchell."

"Do I seem so unhappy?" I ask.

"You cover it up well," he says. "But quitting the church I think is your way of withdrawing from the limelight. You can hide out pretty good in a university. Get lost in the shuffle. Writing a book is even a better way of disappearing inside yourself."

"You're a pretty smart guy, Joe."

He smiles and grips my hand harder.

"Come work for me," he says. "We've got a store downtown that needs a manager. People need shoes as much as they need salvation."

"I'll think about it," I say with a smile.

"At least with shoes," he says, "you know whether the customer is satisfied or not before they leave the store. There's a certain gratification in that Jake."

"I can see that," I say.

"So you'll do it?" he asks eagerly.

"Maybe when we come in April, I'll try it. For a few months anyway."

"Good," he says. "You won't regret it Jake. A couple of months in the store and we can move you up. A year or two and you could be running the operation. Take a load off Nancy."

Suddenly I feel alarmed. This is not why I came. I have no desire to run a footwear empire. Being this close to Bernice's family will be too painful. For both Mitchell and me.

"Listen Joe, this would just be a temporary thing. I can't imagine myself filling your shoes, which it sounds to me like you want me to do."

He laughs softly.

"Filling my shoes . . . yes I guess that's it."

"I couldn't," I say. "Paul and Larry should be the ones."

"I'll leave that up to you," he says, his voice growing fainter. "Right now I've got to have a nap."

His eyes close and his breathing becomes shallow. In a minute or two his hand grows limp in mine. I am still holding it when Nancy, Mitchell, and Elsie enter the room. My son is carrying the punch bowl of eggnog which he sets on a table. Else has two glasses of whiskey.

"Time for the star to go up," Nancy announces, and then she looks around the room. "Where are the boys?"

"Larry was feeling sick," I say. "Paul drove him home."

"Oh," says Nancy. It's always been a tradition for one of the children to place the star. Bernice did it when she was small. And then the boys."

"I'll do it," Mitchell volunteers.

Nancy hands him the star while Elsie puts down the two glasses of whiskey on the bedside table and checks Joe's vital signs. She says nothing but removes the old man's hand from mine and places it gently across his stomach. She picks up her own glass and hands the other one to me.

Mitchell is at the top of the ladder where he places the large silver star carefully on the peak of the tree.

"That's beautiful!" Nancy exclaims. "Look Joe, isn't the star lovely."

"He's asleep," I say.

She glances over at him and smiles. Then she heads to the punch bowl and ladles out a cup of egg nog which she raises in the direction of the tree.

"It's never truly Christmas for me," she says, "until the star's in place."

Mitchell fills a cup and we all join in a silent toast.

The Wounded Christmas Choirboy

by David Watmough

The week that my little Cousin Terence joined our parish church choir was the time that Uncle Bill's dog, Skip, got caught in the grasscutter up to Tretawn Farm and had to have his leg amputated. It was also the week that Uncle Jan, Mother's older brother, retired from the blacksmith's forge he had worked for all those years and his son, Wilfrid, came back from St. German's and took the smithy over.

But what makes me remember that last week in June, 1943 in Cornwall so precisely wasn't really to do with the blacksmith's shop in St. Tudy, to which I rode our farm horses for shoeing all year round; nor was it the image of that marvelous rabbiter, Skip, now reduced to one back leg when digging out a rabbit or rat in the hedge; but the unpleasant feel of my nose out of

joint at Sunday Mass or Evensong when the old hags of our parish nudged each other and muttered over the new presence of
Terence – and ignored me.

In choirboy terms Master Terence Menhenniot was indubita-
bly a pin-up job. I had been what in our village of St. Keverne, the
elders grudgingly conceded as "a 'andsome little bugger" as I had
first set out down the Norman aisle in cotta and cassock at the age
of ten. But Terence's looks were of a wholly different order.

Setting aside such ancillary factors as my being now thirteen,
at the end of my chorister's tether, as it were, and with a couple of
pimples to declare with my breaking voice that my ethereal days as
a soprano were rapidly on the wane, eight-year-old Terence with
his golden curls, had instantly turned our bevy of worshippers who
were invariably inspired by malice towards mankind in general, and
hatred of our High Church Vicar in particular, into besotted fans.

I suppose the situation was inevitable. For the past three years
our twenty-member choir had found it progressively difficult to
sustain its dozen boys, and what new faces Father Trewin had
managed to dragoon into service had provided no competition
for me. With their ruddy faces, straight hair, oafish manners, and
squawking voices it was perfectly clear that our parish priest lay
more emphasis on the presence of an adequate number of small
boys in starched surplices and black cassocks than on their vocal
support of the six farmers, the sexton, and the schoolmaster who
provided the tenor and bass contributions to our assembly.

But in the Norman church tower, that strange place with the
furry ends of the bell-ropes looped like caterpillars over our heads,
and the broad slate flagstones of the floor littered with owl and
bat droppings, I glumly watched Terence Menhenniot prepare
for his debut in the procession to the choir stalls at the far end
of the church, with all the self-conscious diligence of a Duse or
Bernhardt. And in his poise and confidence as he arranged his

cotta over the cassock, and fitted the ruff at his neck – all articles of ecclesiastical apparel, which I knew he had never worn before in his life – I recognized both a consummate competitor for the eye of the congregation and a winner to boot.

And so it was. Mrs. Trebilcock, whose whisper was as loud as her reputation for venom was extensive, spoke across the aisle to Mrs. Harry Hoskyns – right after the first two pairs of little boys had passed her pew. "My, that Terence is a proper treat you! 'Tis lovely to have a chile as fetchin' as that one – specially after they other buggers."

I had no doubt, of course, as to the identity of "they other buggers." Only the previous Sunday I had overheard her in the church porch, telling Mr. Nankivell, who farmed the Glebe, how stuck up all we Bryants were, and how boys like Rob Pengelly, Tom Purdue, Will Carthew, and me, with our reputations, shouldn't be allowed in the choir at all. "Sex fiends, they be, Mr. Nankivell. A disgrace to St. Keverne if ever there was!" And her thin mouth had slammed shut with the same moist slap mother made when putting up pounds of fresh butter on the cold shelves of the dairy.

I knew the old cow was referring to an unpleasant incident involving twelve-year-old Molly, Police constable Apse's daughter, who in a fit of remorse had admitted to mutual anatomical exploration with us four boys on top of Mr. Prouse's freshly made haystack. The woman's vicious attack had concluded by her remarking to Mr. Nankivell that we should be all sent packing from St. Keverne parish church – "cos they'm really nothin' but a pack of Methodies." The latter being an allusion to the fact that my Aunt Marjorie, after having told Father Trewin that she could see no reason why her five kids couldn't attend both the church and chapel Sunday School outings, had broken with the custom of most of the families in our hamlet of Churchtown and started joining the folks from up Trelill way, who heard uneducated lay preachers rant in the chapel every Sunday morning, instead of Holy Mass.

Unfortunately, Terence Menhenniot's fan club didn't end with vile Mrs. Trebilcock and her sycophantic cronies – nor was it stimulated only by such ulterior motives as the Bryant hatred which animated her. Father Trewin, who definitely wasn't one of your child molestors (like the Parson over Rough Tot way, who was always fiddling with his boy scouts), could be seen from his special stall across from us in choir positively simpering over the beauteous newcomer.

And when it transpired, at the very first practice, that my little cousin couldn't even sing on pitch, let alone carry a tune in his head, Father Trewin simply told him not to worry and that it would all come right later, if he persisted.

Then there were those men in the choir who patently favored him over the likes of Rob, Tom, Will, and me, and never watched him with the suspicion and mistrust which they seemed to think wholly in order for the likes of us who were somewhat older and certainly finer vocalists.

The situation didn't improve as Sundays and Greater Feasts passed with the Church's Calendar and those rare but fiscally profitable occasions such as important weddings or the funerals of local notables, which all warranted the choral forces of the Parish Church of St. Keverne and the Blessed Virgin Mary – to give it its full, if rarely used, title.

Each time would see young Terence faithfully present, his curly locks as gorgeous as ever, his peaches and cream complexion unblemished, and those wide grey eyes wed to that kissable cupid's bow ever raised in dutiful supplication towards the lowered check of authority: innocence ever at the ready to repay experience.

In the words of the scriptures which we read and sang "*and the flesh of the child waxed warm*" and like King David (of whom we knew much and with whom *I* liked to identify) young Terence "*was ruddy and beautiful.*" Moreover, Terence did develop his singing

abilities as Father Trewin had prophesied, and by the end of his first
year in the choir his slightly husky, alto voice could soar beyond that
of any of us, and the sweetness and purity of it was so breathtak-
ingly distinctive that (I invariably noted with a scowl) the congregation would readily start to nudge one another and that Trebilcock
creature would immediately start her loud talking again.

I began to detest those days when I knew we would be singing
such old favourites of mine – because I'd always been given the
solos – as *I Know That My Redeemer Liveth* and *Lead Me Lord* for
my voice was but a croak and it was now 'golden boy' who warbled
to heaven – with or without the uncertain support of aged Miss
Clee at the organ.

Perhaps sensing that Terence was less than popular with his
fellow-choristers, the boy's mother, a thin woman named Muriel,
bean to attend each service at which her only child now sang.
She sat erect in the front pew, from where she could see him
most clearly and dreamily eye the lover of her life. For Muriel
Menhenniot, as my mother had told me once when I was com-
plaining about Terence's smug demeanor, had not borne her son
until she was forty-two and she and her railway-man husband
had despaired of ever becoming parents. That was the reason, my
mother asserted, why Terence was so initially spoiled at home –
although that excuse was later compounded by his mother's conviction that her golden-haired son was so delicate that he had to
be shielded from the more basic crudities of village life, such as
fraternizing with his coevals and even sharing the various chores
which were the lot of our Cornish childhood, regardless of gender,
parental wealth, or individual temperament.

So Terence was escorted twice each Sunday to church, just as
he was to choir practice on Wednesday evenings. He didn't go to
our village school (run by Mr. Oliver Bray who sang baritone)
but to a private one where the children wore cherry-red uniforms

and looked silly. And even that was not in Wadebridge, our local town, but north of us in Camelford where he took the National bus each day.

Then again, he never helped out at hay-making, corn harvest, or threshing when every youngster in the parish was pressed into service; nor was he ever to be seen collecting kindling for the copper and Monday's clothes-wash, up to Tregilderns cottage behind the fig bush, where the Menhenniots lived. Instead, if you please, he was given special voice lessons with Mrs. Wesley Jago, L.R.C.M., all the way up the coast road to St. Minver, which he attended in a big Austin car hired from Hawkey's of Port Isaac. The extravagance of that was so overwhelming that at least our family openly described it as sinful – even though we weren't Methodists, and thus obsessed with money matters.

I have referred to my cousin's smugness – and indeed, he did seem so complacent, so cheerfully expectant of the world's approbation, that there were times when I would gladly have given away my prize ferret, Sam, just to see Master Terence fall arse over tip in the mound of manure I steadily fed each Saturday morning after mucking out the stables. But I have to admit that, accompanying his conviction that the world loved him, even as it treasured his looks and his voice, was an odd kind of innocence. Then if old bitches like Mrs. Trebilcock, usually acidulous men like Oliver Bray, the baritone who sat behind me in the choir, and, of course, his own adoring parents, all turned into simpering idiots when discussing him or in his company, it was surely no surprise that the kid took an awful lot for granted.

But there my charity runs dry. Age did not improve him. One year after his entry into the choir he scarcely bothered to give us, his choral companions let alone his relatives, the time of day. By his tenth birthday he was not only dictating to a usually dictatorial Father Trewin what he wanted to sing as solos at each service, but had totally ignored our traditional seating in choir, which was based on seniority, and taken over the stall right opposite the vicar – without asking permission of any of us.

Terence's haughtiness was not confined to his activities in our church. That same summer he refused, via his mother, the regular invitation to my August birthday party, which I shared with my cousin Loveday, whose nativity was but two days from mine, and which most of our young relatives attended in the mowey where tressle tables were always erected for the outdoor feast.

In summary, I hardly feel that I am exaggerating when I say that by the time I had left the boys' section of the choir altogether and had become a mere passenger with the men while waiting to discover whether I was going to end up a baritone or a tenor, Terence Menhenniot, pretty-faced star chorister, was talking (or singing, rather) only to God!

I remember what was virtually my last exchange with The Brat (as my brother Jan and I had succinctly dubbed him). It was a Wednesday night in December: the special choir rehearsal, in fact, for the December 8th Feast of Our Lady – the observance of whose Immaculate Conception had been introduced into our parish by its current incumbent, Father Trewin. I had over-heard a recent conversation among some of our parish malcon-tents who objected to this rather exotic celebration. In church, just by the ancient granite font, and almost under the Great Seal of King Charles II given to those of St. Keverne for ral-lying to the restoration of the monarchy, I myself echoed their sentiments. "That there Immaculate Conception we'm having is really for Papists, you? 'Tidn'n exactly Church of England stuff, is it?"

But it was immediately obvious that The Brat had been well primed by the Vicar. "The Celtic Church is bravun older than Canterbury. We don't have to listen to they for what we can do and what us can't. After all, Davey, half of our saints they never heard on – including St. Keverne our patron!"

"I 'spose you got some special ole job to sing," put in Harry Purdue, my old friend Tom's younger brother. "That's why you'm a backin' of 'ee. Any ole sow-pig can see that! We b'aint born yesterday Terence Menhenniot. I bide you come only for the anthems and they descants."

"Our father says you b'aint here so much for the candlelight as the *limelight*," contributed a small boy who looked like a Cardew but I wasn't quite sure – now that there were so many of them with the ginger hair and freckles, about the place.

"I don't have to listen to none of 'ee," my cousin retorted hotly. "I'm sitting a choral scholarship if you did but know it. Then I shall be singing down to Truro Cathedral and in the choir school there. Shan't be sorry to shake the dust of this silly ole place off me feet, neither!"

And with that, plus a complementary toss of those curls which had turned a darker gold since he had first joined the choir, he sailed off in the direction of the church tower where all our music was untidily stacked and where the mice blithely chewed paper and left between our pages their pellets of digested pleasure.

The Feast of The Immaculate Conception of the Blessed Virgin Mary was duly celebrated according to the dictates of our parish priest, and went off without a hitch. How I loathed that fine-chiselled little face as I watched it stare up at the oak barrel-roofing of our church, as the sweet stream of sound spewed forth.

Afterwards, outside in the porch, where the Elizabethan stocks, in their wormholed antiquity, ranged the granite wall and from whose rafters rows of sleepy pipistrelle bats hung, amid a few terse and softspoken disapprovals of the service, I actually heard Muriel

Menhenniot sobbing her pleasure at the transporting joy her son's voice had just afforded her. And that Terence nearly having to be immaculately conceived himself! I wanted to vomit instead.

But fortunately I didn't and my iron self-control was very soon rewarded. We had no sooner gotten over the Immaculate Conception when we had to turn our attention to the Christmas festivities. Now that particular year what we call in our family our 'English cousins' were coming down from London to escape the Labor Government and the postwar shortages. It was what they called 'Austerity' up there and my mother felt that her sister and family would benefit from a bit of Cornish cooking and all the fresh farm and dairy produce that were available to us, as well as a few of the early vegetables from Penzance and The Scillies that would have cost the earth up to London.

Apart from the minor upheaval of stretching the resources of Polengarrow farm to contain ten people instead of the normal five, it also meant that my first cousin, Arthur, whom I had last seen as a baby, would be arriving. Well, he not only arrived, looking incredibly like a younger version of Terence to whom he was distantly related, but immediately asked whether he would be able to sing in our choir on Christmas morning, as he would have done in Wimbledon church had he stayed at home.

Although I wasn't minded to like small boys, let alone aid their requests, in this case I acted without hesitation. "I do know for a fact that we'm shorthanded down there," I told Arthur, "so I'll slip right down to the Vicarage on me bike and ask Father Trewin if he'll have on 'ee."

Just as I had expected, there was no prevarication from that quarter. In fact not only the Vicar, but everyone else with whom I spoke during those days leading up to the holidays, seem strangely elated at the prospect of young Arthur's presence in the chancel of St. Keverne Church. Unusual in that our villagers were disinclined to welcome strangers – even the kin of those who had lived among them for centuries, as had we Bryants.

At Christmastide in St. Keverne's Church that year we went full out. The rood screen was garlanded not only with the traditional evergreens, the holly and the ivy, but we even managed to scour the protected hedgerows and dells of the immediate countryside to yield a few early primroses and we also had some hardy roses from Uncle Joe Yelland's cottage with its secluded southern aspect, plus some usual winter jasmine from our farmhouse garden. The latter made a rich yellow frieze about the font and behind the altar of the Lady Chapel.

In 1947, I recall, we still had only candles and oil lamps for illumination as my Great Uncle Herbert didn't provide electricity (in memory of his wife) until the following year. But what with the sumptuous musical setting for Midnight Mass and the decorative efforts extending over three days by the women of the parish, even little Arthur, with all his London sophistication, was entranced with what he saw when the two of us entered the church the afternoon of Christmas Eve. We were there because our young visitor had asked if he might have a prior look at the music as he had been unable to attend earlier choir practices – a professional attention to detail, I duly noted, that far exceeded anything that Terence had ever demonstrated.

All my hopeful anticipations over Arthur were realized from the very moment the solemn procession of Christmas, including the blessing of the crib, wound us up and down the shadowy aisles to the words and tune of the hymn, *Adeste Fideles*. Not only did his animated face, bathed in the soft glow of oil lamps, yield an innocence and piety which made the overly familiar Terence look positively corrupt, but Wimbledon's soprano quite blotted out in range and sweetness the efforts of Master Menhenniot. And if it was thus in the opening hymn, it was ever more so as the

Liturgy unfolded. By the time we reached the Plainsong Setting of that lovely phrase from the Gradual, *"the dew of thy birth is of the womb of the morning,"* Terence had succumbed to the sulks and was silent while the rest of the boys gladly followed suit to allow the full force of Arthur's mastery of Gregorian chant, and ethereality of tone, to fill first the candle-bright choir stalls and sanctuary and then the great length of the nave itself. I looked quickly in the direction of Father Trewin, hoping that the priest was at least acknowledging that a greater than Terence had come among us and was gratified to observe the old man's eyes opening and closing in ecstasy. Leering by now in triumph, I turned to feast of the expressions of my fellow-choirmen: white heads and bald ones nodded in grave appreciation of the newcomer in our midst.

Nor was Arthur's devastating effect confined to those of us on the altar side of the rood screen. Out in the packed congregation, Cornish souls melted in the flow of such vocal beauty as my cousin from across the Tamar so felicitously bestowed. In the soft candlelight of the sanctuary Arthur Ingram's features held the delicacy of a Michelangelo sculpture as he soared in descant after descant and solo'd the Plainsong when the older music of the church usurped the more recent hymns.

Mrs. Trebilcock was seen to take a handkerchief from her large handbag and sob noisily into it and towards the end of the Eucharist – when the Wimbledon nightingale transported us finally on that wondrous and memorable night with the verses of *Once in Royal David's City* soaked in his own special purity – history in St. Keverne parish was made when, from isolated spots in the congregation, came the sound of enthusiastic clapping.

Wholly unnerved by the applause, a horrified Vicar gulped his blessing from the altar, and Miss Cleve, in panic (transmitted no doubt by her parish priest), laid too many digits upon the console, causing the organ to sound briefly like a ship's klaxon in a dense fog. The rest, I confess, was anti-climax.

Young Terrence, bud-mouth clamped tight, fairly bolted his exit in the final procession down the church to the belltower where we were routinely prayed over and dismissed. But that early Christmas morn Terence didn't linger longer than to yank off his cotta and tear at the multiple buttons of his cassock – as if the garment, too, were an offence not to be borne. Even as Father Trewin muttered a final Hail Mary, our erstwhile star of the choir stalls was pushing open the heavy oak door, tear-glistening eyes in a head held defiantly high.

I did not know then, of course, but he was never to sing in our choir again. In fact that was but the least of it for our toppled alto. For the next several days I put him quite out of mind as young Arthur and his relatives were our preoccupation. But after the Ingrams had left and the wintry rhythms of January had taken over, it gradually became apparent that not only was Terry now missing from choir practices and the Sunday services, but he was no longer to be seen anywhere in the village. I mentioned this to Mother who in turn informed me that when Father Trewin visited the Menhenniots to enquire after Terence, he was refused entry at Tregilderns cottage by the boy himself who began to scream and shout until the old priest turned sadly away.

I am sure that I would have thought a good deal less about Cousin Terence, now that he was no longer visible, had it not been for a distressing occurrence that March when his father met with a terrible accident at the entrance to the railway tunnel, just south of Port Isaac Road station. Severely mangled as a result of falling between the cars of a freight train, he was taken by ambulance to Tehiddy hospital where he survived for only three days. At the funeral down to St. Keverne, it was noted with shock and incredulity that a sobbing widow was unaccompanied by a mourning son. Muriel Menhenniot, almost hysterical in grief, relied on the succouring ministrations of old Mrs. Thethewey, her next door neighbor, and it was she who led the distraught woman out of the church before the Requiem was concluded.

After that there were many who presented themselves at the cottage behind the fig bush and fuchsia hedge to offer the two remaining Menhenniots their services. But none crossed the threshold. Either the black-clad Muriel or a progressively dishevelled Terence refused the world entry and shouted and screamed until obeyed. Eventually they were left alone. I recall talk of the district nurse visiting and even mention of a psychiatrist. But that is all rather vague by now. Certainly I never set eyes on Terence again during the remainder of his childhood and youth.

Whether the result of his savage fall from a stellar role in the choir, or the tragedy of his father's premature death, one can only speculate, but the fact remains that the Christmas of 1947 was virtually the last that Terence Menhenniot was seen beyond the confines of Tregilderns and its leafy garden.

It was in 1967 that Mother wrote to me in Vancouver, where I had settled some years earlier, and informed me that Muriel had recently passed on – Mother's letters were little more than St. Keverne obituary lists by this time – and that the stout, balding man who had stood alone as Chief Mourner at her burial service was none other than Terence. Immediately after the committal in the upper graveyard (where she lay flanked by her husband, Fred, and my second cousin Lewis) he left without exchanging a word with anyone save Ned Carhart, the stone mason, about a tombstone – presumably back to Tregilderns and its quiet behind that enormous fig bush.

One other snippet Mother added to her airletter. Terence was now a practiced ham radio operator and, according to village gossip, often stayed up all night talking via his microphone to people all over the world.

The Bird Feeder

by Donna Gamache

"Wind's getting up," Sadie said to herself, as she watched the fresh snow begin to drift across the driveway. "I better feed my birds, before it gets worse."

She struggled into her old grey parka, the one she'd brought from the farm. "I just might need that old coat," she told Tom when they moved here last September. "Even in the city, there will be outside chores."

She measured out a cup of bird seed from the small bag from the supermarket and mixed it with bread crumbs. The bird seed was expensive, but on Christmas Day the chickadees should have a treat, though she knew they'd prefer sunflower seeds, as she used to feed them on the farm.

Pulling on an old pair of Tom's rubber boots and tying a faded red scarf over her grey hair, she hurried out the back door. "Look like the Friendly Giant in these boots, don't I?" she muttered. "I should throw them out."

But it was comforting, somehow, to see a pair of men's boots just inside when you opened the door. Even though there was no longer a man to use them. And nobody would see her, except for the small dark-haired boy next door. Sadie saw him now, as usual, with his nose pressed to the window, watching her every move.

As she expected, the bird feeder was almost empty. It was the one they'd used for years on the farm, a glass-fronted box into which you poured the feed. A narrow slit at the bottom let the seeds seep slowly out as the birds ate them.

The feeder was a dull grey now. Tom had painted it a deep green in the beginning, but the paint long ago washed off. It was one of the things Tom planned to fix, after they retired to this little house. But nobody had expected Tom's retirement days to be so short.

"Still works just as well," Sadie assured herself aloud. "Maybe next summer I'll get it painted."

She had nailed the bird feeder to the clothes line pole. It wasn't quite where she wanted it. But without Tom to put in another pole, she made do with the one already there. And at least she could watch the birds from her kitchen table.

"The feeder should be higher, too, shouldn't it?" she said to the single chickadee that perched in the nearby maple tree watching her. "It would be safer for you." But she'd put the feeder as high as she could reach from the ground. These days she wasn't steady enough to hammer while standing on a chair or box.

She'd done her best, even nailed a sheet of old tin around the pole to keep down cats. That big grey one next door, especially. She'd yelled at it several times since she began putting out the bird feed. She yelled at the boy, too, last week. "Keep your cat out of my yard! Away from my birds!"

Funny, she used to like cats, on the farm. But a cat in the city meant trouble for her birds.

She'd startled the boy; she knew that by the way he grabbed the grey cat and rushed inside. She'd regretted her harsh tone, but maybe it would teach him to keep his cat at home. A nice looking boy he was, though, about seven or eight, Sadie thought, with big dark eyes and dark hair. If she'd ever had a son, she'd have liked him to look like that. But she and Tom never had a son, just one tiny daughter, after many years of trying. And she was stillborn.

"There, that'll do you for today," she said now to the waiting chickadee. "I've given you extra bird seed. It's Christmas, you know. Even birds get treats."

She held out her hand to the chickadee, a few seeds on the palm. He watched, tilting his black cap a little to one side, but he was not to be tempted. "Well, I'll give you a few more days to get used to me," Sadie said. "Maybe you'll come yet. I always got at least one bird to eat from my hand, at the farm."

She turned to go, glancing at the house next door as she did so. A curtain moved, and the small boy ducked behind it. Black head and eyes – almost like a chickadee too, Sadie thought, then laughed at herself. "Wonder what kind of bird he thinks *I* am? Old grey parka. Faded red scarf. And giant feet." She snorted. "Red-headed woodpecker, I guess."

She stamped her feet at the back door, then pulled it shut behind her. "Red-headed woodpecker," she said again, hanging up the parka. "Wouldn't I love one of those at my feeder. Or a nuthatch. That would be nice, too." She *had* seen a downy woodpecker a few times. The corner store butcher had given her a piece of fat which she strung in the maple, and the little woodpecker came for that. But not often. Usually there were just one or two chickadees.

"Remember all the birds we had on the farm," she said, pouring herself a cup of coffee from the pot on the stove. "Woodpeckers, sparrows, half a dozen chickadees at least, a couple of blue jays, and evening grosbeaks by the dozen."

She sat at the kitchen table and peered out the window at the feeder. Her bird book lay on a nearby shelf, but she hadn't needed it since coming to the city. "Bring the book," Tom had said. "There are lots of parks in the city. We can take walks there. I'm sure you'll see birds. And in the winter we'll have a feeding station. Birds like the city, too."

But Tom had missed out on that. They'd moved the first week of September, and used the second week to settle into the tiny house, decide what to keep, and what, for lack of space, to throw out. But by the third week, Tom was gone, felled by a sudden stroke. And Sadie had to adjust not only to life in the city, but also to life alone. She took no walks in the park.

Sadie flicked on the radio and Christmas music filled the kitchen. It didn't feel much like Christmas; she'd never been alone before. Always there was Tom, and two or three neighboring families in for Christmas dinner, since she and Tom had no relatives nearby. But those neighbors lived fifty miles away now. The neighbors here, Sadie barely knew.

The Waynes across the street had left last week, for Florida or Mexico, or somewhere. And the Johnsons next door, Sadie had spoken to only briefly. Mr. Johnson was a salesman, often away; Mrs. Johnson worked nights and slept days; and the chickadee boy with dark eyes was usually at school, or alone in his yard.

Sadie felt tears threatening and blinked hard. She mustn't give in to self pity. "I can manage alone," she assured herself. "I'll watch the Christmas shows on television, and eat my chicken."

She'd tried to decorate the house a little. The wreath they used on the farm was now nailed on her front door, and Christmas cards hung on a string across one wall. But sympathy cards still occupied the china chest, an incongruous mixture, Sadie knew.

The doorbell rang, jarring through the gentle Christmas music. It rang so seldom here, it startled Sadie. "Whoever can that be?"

She peered through the curtain before moving to open the door. "The chickadee boy! With a brown bag in his arms. What does *he* want?"

The bell rang again before she reached it. "I'm coming," she called. "Yes?" Her voice was sharp, she realized, and she smiled to soften the tone.

The boy hesitated. "I've – got a Christmas present for you," he managed. "Well, really it's for your birds." He held out the bag.

"Come in," Sadie said. "Don't stand there with the door open." The boy entered, lowering the heavy bag onto the floor.

"What is it?" she asked, unrolling the top. "Sunflower seeds!"

"We went to my uncle's farm yesterday," the boy blurted out. "I told him about your birds, the black and white ones. He gave me this from his granary. He grows sunflowers. Will your birds like these?"

Sadie smiled. "My birds will love them. The seed I get at the store isn't really what they want."

"What are they, your birds?"

"Chickadees. Black-capped chickadees. They're just like you, you know. Black cap and eyes. I call you the chickadee boy."

"My name is Todd," he said stiffly. "I'd better be getting home."

"Todd," Sadie nodded. "I thank you, Todd, for the present. My chickadees will love it." She closed the door, and watched him scurry down her driveway and back up his own.

"A present," she murmured. "*Real* birdfeed, this time." She carried the bag into the kitchen and set it on the counter, then glanced briefly outside. As she did, a grey and white streak ran head first down the maple tree, then flew quickly to the feeder and back to the tree. "A nuthatch! We hardly ever had those on the farm."

She watched him, marvelling at his ability to walk head down. "A nuthatch," she said again. "A second Christmas present. I'm sure he'll like sunflower seeds, too."

Abruptly, the telephone shrilled. "Yes?" she answered.

The voice was hesitant. "This is Fran Johnson. Next door, you know? Todd says he thinks you're all alone there. Would you join us for Christmas dinner? We'll be eating about one."

"I don't want to intrude," Sadie ventured.

"It's no intrusion." The voice was firmer now. "We'd love to have you. I should have called you sooner. Just never thought of you being alone there. Please come."

"Thank you," Sadie said, feeling a new lightness in her voice. "I'll come. One o'clock."

She put down the phone and looked out the window where the chickadee and nuthatch seemed to be taking turns at the feeder. "But first," she said, "I have to feed my birds."

Boxing Day

by Linda Svendsen

The morning after Christmas, I was in the kitchen picking at cold turkey and reading my new young adult book. It was called *Milestone Summer* and it was all about a teenage girl named Judy, whose father's death plunges the family into a colourful poverty. She's forced to become a thrifty interior decorator after school and meets Kent, a catch, who's conceited and sails. There were misunderstandings, there were barbecue and pool parties, and I couldn't put it down. It was set in California.

My mother came in scuffing her gift mules. "Is that your brother on the couch?" she asked.

"I didn't hear him come in," she said.

"I did."

"Late?" she asked.

"How late's late?" I said.

"Two."

"Yup."

"Under the influence?" she had to ask. I didn't say anything.

"I guess he was then," she said. She shook her head. "He won't be happy." *He* meant Robert, and my mother had just married him, although they'd been keeping company, laundry and bowling and meals and stuff, since she'd fled my father a few years back. Robert was twelve years her junior. Mom tucked in a towel around the turkey and took it away. "You've polished off all the dark, Adele. You know that, don't you?"

"Sorry," I said. "Like your mules?"

"I'll stretch them," she said. "They're a tad tight. How's the book?"

"Judy had to miss the regatta and Kent stormed off in a huff."

"That's life," Mum said. She wandered out and I heard her in the living room patiently saying, "Raymond. Raymond. Raymond," until she gave up.

I placed the book face down and looked out the window. The yard glared. On the west coast, in Vancouver, we weren't accustomed to snow. Like a long spell of fair weather in summer, it was unusual, worthy of attention and respect, an omen. I watched a tabby cat follow its breath across the white crust. Every few feet, the cat sank, then kept perfectly still and waited for fate. I couldn't tell if it was scared stiff or smart.

Sleep took him away. My brother Ray had a way of sleeping deep that made me jealous. His left eyebrow lifted in a kind of shrug and he smiled, as if privy to an epic starring his truly. I always wanted to see what he saw, do what he did, be where he was. He worked longshoring, was twenty-five to my eleven, and didn't act it. We also had two sisters, Joyce and Irene, who were married and no longer fun; Ray, Joyce, and Irene all shared the same father.

I tickled my brother's nose with a strand of tinsel. He turned to the cushion. "Cut it out," he said. I brushed his cheek. "Cease and desist, Adele, or you will die a slow, painful death." I stopped. He opened his eyes. "Merry X-mas," he said.

"That was yesterday," I said.

"Very funny."

"I'm not kidding," I said. "I'll tell you what I got, starting with my stocking – "

Ray sat up. "My pants? Where are they?"

"La-Z-Boy," I said.

"Fetch," he said.

I hopped up and brought his trousers over by a belt loop, so I wouldn't empty his pockets. He pulled them up and on. "Mum awake?" he asked. "The *hombre* of the house?"

"Mum's making the bed. Robert's making noise in the shower," I said. "Mum was worried about you. She called the RCMP to see if anybody who looked like you was in an accident."

Ray shook his head. "I'm indestructible," he said. "Where's Dallyce?"

"Texas."

"The girl," he said.

"What girl?"

"I'm losing my marbles," he said. He threw on his sweater, tapped his pocket for nicotine, dug into his jacket, and pulled out car keys on a red rabbit's foot. "Grab your coat," he said. "Let's go quick."

At the drug store Ray bought Mum everything, Evening in Paris, the shebang; Robert, Old Spice deodorant and swizzle sticks, erotic ones, with buttocks and breasts; our sister and their husbands, Black Magic chocolates, and stole all the ones with nuts when we got back to the Volkswagen. I chose Sea & Ski suntan lotion, which made you look Egyptian any season. It lasted longer than foundation. It didn't wash off. I wanted to fool kids at school and make them think I'd been somewhere. It was the only item Ray had to pay full price.

On the way home from the mall Ray said, "So."

"So?"

"So how's Mum doing? Okay?"

"I don't know," I said. "Ask her."

"You know the dirt. You're the only one home now. She and Robert still fight?"

I nodded.

"About?"

"You yesterday," I said. "How could you forget? You didn't even call."

"Long story." He braked for a yellow and we skidded over the traffic line into the intersection. A truck honked.

"Ice," I said, and he said, "Yeah, ice."

When Ray and I got back, a little whisper I'd never seen before, blonde and maybe thirty, sat at the kitchen table absorbed by Judy's life. Her hands seemed too tiny to hold my book.

"Where's my mother?" Ray asked her.

"Don't know. Nobody was here when I got up," she said. She sounded like she was coming down with something.

"They probably went next door for the open house," I said. "Then tonight we go to Irene's for turkey. It's her turn. We cooked yesterday."

Ray and the lady stared at each other. Then she said, "Lose your manners somewhere?"

Ray planted a kiss in her direction, in air. "Dallyce, this is

Adele," he said. "She's the baby of the family. Adele, Dallyce. She's my baby."

"Don't count on it," she said.

"That's the lay of the land, eh?" He opened the fridge door, bent, and disappeared. "Where did you finally crash?"

"Down in the rec room," Dallyce said.

"Comfy?"

"The Ritz it's not."

"Dream of me?" he asked.

"A little hairy," she said, which made him peek at her over the door. I wasn't sure she heard him right.

"Come back down with me and I'll serenade you on the piano. Then you can giftwrap for me."

"Thanks, but no thanks," she said.

Ray cracked ice cubes into a tumbler and poured two fingers of rye. "You both know where I am," he said.

I took off my jacket and hung it over my chair. Dallyce and I looked at each other across the table, and then we heard the opening bars of *Moon River*.

"My song," I said.

"He's not bad," she said.

"Yeah," I said. "You want coffee?"

Dallyce lit up. "Yes, please, thanks."

I filled the kettle and plugged it in. "So have you known my brother very long?"

"Since Christmas." She folded the top of a page in my book and closed it. "You could say I found him in my stocking. Literally."

"Sugar?" I said. "Milk?"

"Both."

We waited for the kettle to sing. "So do you do anything?" I said. "Work, I mean?"

"I teach."

"What?"

"I sub. Substitute. Science, French, P.E., you name it."

"Guidance is for the birds," I said.

I poured the hot water and Dallyce came over to doctor the brew. She wore a striped mini-skirt with matching top, something Tarzan's Jane might toss on in the jungle first thing. I looked down. "Hey, you've got the same mules as Mum. My stepfather got her a pair."

"Oh," Dallyce said. "They're hers. I didn't feel like squeezing into my boots." She stirred her coffee. "Ray says your mother's visited the altar a few times, eh?"

"Three."

"Three times."

"She's not exactly an Elizabeth Taylor," I said. "She's had it tough. It didn't work out with Ray's dad, and it didn't with mine."

"How's this one going?"

"Better."

"That's good." Dallyce put the mug down. "I was married once upon a time."

"Oh yeah?"

"Yeah. We got hitched on New Year's Day before the Polar Bear Swim. It was incredibly cold out so we stayed in the car and watched all the crazy gooseflesh make a mad dash for the sea." Dallyce lifted an edge of the towel, tore off some turkey, and ate. She also picked dark. She said, "It's not for everyone. Marriage."

When Mum and Robert trundled laughing up the driveway, Ray and Dallyce were still whispering and wrapping things in the rec room. I was reading, sprawled on the couch, under the tree lights. Robert, the big lug moose, stamped his boots on the front mat, then Mum the moose did. "It's below freezing," Robert said, opening the door. "Colder than a witch's tit."

"Here's my angel," Mum said. "Right under the tree."

"That's no angel," Robert said boisterously. "That's the brat."

"Don't call her that." Mum used her mock hurt voice.

"Why not?" Robert said. "That's what she is – the original brat."

"How was it?" I asked. "The open house?"

Mum slid off her coat and hung it up. "Nice to see the neighbours. I guess."

"Once a year is once too much." Robert lowered himself into the La-Z-Boy. "You wouldn't believe it, Adele. What the Strattons did. Should I tell her what the stupid Strattons did, dear?"

Mum floated back in. "Oh, I don't think she's really interested, hon."

"Sure she is."

"Not really." I pointed to my book. "Judy and Kent are on the brink."

"Hey," Robert stood, crossed to the couch, and crouched by me, his breath in my face. If I struck a match, the air between us would have lit. "And what are Judy and Ken on the brink of? Love? Hate? Wild sex? All three? Will there be a happy ending? Will anybody die? Who did it?"

"Don't torture her, Bob," Mum said.

"Am I torturing you, brat?"

"Yup."

Robert made a sad face, grabbed the last handful of peanuts from the dish on the coffee table, and sat back down.

"Where'd Ray get to?" Mum said. "His car's still – "

"Rec room," I said. "He's got a guest."

"Who?" Robert jumped up again.

"A school teacher."

"A school teacher!" Robert said. "Not a parole officer?"

"A school teacher," I said.

Robert strode into the hall and bellowed. "Raymond, bring

your teacher up and introduce her to your parents."

"He's irrepressible," I said.

Mum looked at me from across the room. "It wouldn't hurt for you to take an interest in what he has to say," she said gently. "After all, who's keeping a roof over your head? Who's putting presents under the tree?" And pointedly, "Peanuts in the dish?"

"I was only reading," I said.

"Who provided what you're buried in?" she said. "You know, he would give the shirt off his back for you kids. Does anybody ever think it hurts me to see him ignored?"

I closed my eyes. In the hallway, my brother introduced Dallyce to Robert. "My mother seems to have vanished," Ray said. "She tapped her magic mules together and went away."

"No, here I am," Mum said, and cleared her throat. "I'm right here."

Ray was ages in the upstairs john and Robert was verbal. He was warmed up. "Well, Dallyce. June – Ray's mother – and me – "

"I'm Adele's mother, too," Mum interrupted.

"Yes," Robert said, "June is Ray's and Adele's mother, and since we're being technical, Irene's and Joyce's mother, and what the hell, she's everybody's mother. Happy now?" he said.

"Happy," she said.

"Good. All right. What I was starting to say, Dallyce, was that June and I are what you could call a love match. I've been through a couple of tragic marriages I won't go into tonight. June here has suffered through two. Her first husband busted her heart running off with a Pacific Western airline stewardess, which would be the polite thing to call her. And Adele's Dad . . . " Here Robert glanced at me across the rec room. "Well, how would you tell the story, Adele?"

"I don't know," I said.

He looked at my mother. "How would you describe it, sweeter than honey?"

Mum twisted the glass in her hand. She looked tired. She needed lipstick. "Well, he didn't know how to show affection. You've probably met men like that, Dallyce."

"Sure," Dallyce said softly.

"With him it was always work, work, work," Mum said.

Robert got up to fix himself another drink. He was tall, with a voice big and capable as nature. He lowered it now. "Honey, in fact, wouldn't it be fair to say Adele might not even be here if you hadn't (pardon my being crass, Dallyce), got down to brass tacks? Correct me if I'm wrong."

Dallyce studied me hard as if I was coming and going before her very eyes. My mother nodded and said, "That's true." Then she looked at me and added, "But I would have had you anyway, Adele. Nothing could have stopped me."

"Of course," Dallyce murmured.

Robert went on. "June hoped the baby would save the marriage, you see."

"Right," Dallyce said.

"Now let's drop it," Mum said. "It's Boxing Day."

Ray came back in. "Why's everybody so serious? It's time to – ," and he sang, "*jingle bell, jingle bell, jingle bell rock.*"

"Your stepfather – " Dallyce began.

"Bob, please," Robert said. "And let me compliment you on your good taste, Ray." He gave a little nod Dallyce's way.

Dallyce nodded back. "Bob here was explaining how he and your mother got together and that marriage as an institution really works."

"Humbug," Ray said and made me laugh. "Let's party."

"Isn't he something?" Mum said to Dallyce.

I passed around the chips and garlic dip. Dallyce only took a few because she was on the mistletoe diet. Robert said she didn't need to lose. He said if Ray poured mercury into her, he could use her to tell the temperature. She said, "Your parents are terrific. They really are the Hosts with the Mostest."

I picked up the phone on the sixth or seventh ring. "What's going on over there?" Irene, my sister, shouted. "My bird's drying out in the oven."

"Ray's here," I said.

"Is he all right? Where'd he blow in from? Mexico?"

"Nowhere," I said. "He's okay."

Irene paused. "Were there words? From you know who?"

"No," I said. "Ray brought a girl."

"Who?"

"A teacher."

"Smart move," Irene said. "Well, round everybody up and get over here. We'll wait for you. Tell Ray to drive carefully, there's a lot of roadblocks, and don't you ride with him. Go with Mum." She paused. "What's that?"

"Everybody's singing carols."

"Who's everybody?"

"Mum, Ray, Robert, and Dallyce."

"Her name's Dallyce?"

"Yup."

"And what are you doing? Nose in a book? Don't say yup."

I hung up and Mum came upstairs and poked her head around the corner. Who was it?"

"Irene. She's holding the turkey for us."

"We better get going." Mum leaned closer. "Dallyce seems like a nice gal, doesn't she?"

"She's all right," I said.

"You don't like her?"

"I didn't say that," I said. "I said she's all right."

"Her skirt's short, though," Mum said. "Isn't it?" Then she rested her hand against my forehead. "Are you okay, hon?"

"A-1," I said.

She went back down and I went up to the bathroom. I locked the door and took off my blue corduroy jumper and white blouse and slip and underpants and navy blue knee socks. I clipped my bangs back with Mum's bobby pins. I gave the Sea & Ski a good shake, unscrewed the cap, poured lotion into my palm, and applied it thinly and evenly. It was cool. Across my forehead and cheeks, around my nose and lips and eyes, down my neck and shoulders and below, on any bit of me that might ever show. It was like getting into someone else's skin. I waited a few minutes for it to dry.

On the other side of the hill we lived on, there was only a sprinkle of snow. Enough to keep the plastic reindeer, strutting across lawns and roofs, and sleighs, from being ridiculous. It was already pitch dark. Mum wiped the windshield clear with her glove and Ray's VW tail lights blinked at us.

"She looks stupid," Robert said.

"She doesn't look stupid," Mum said. "Why do you keep saying that? She looks like she's just stepped out of a play. She looks made up."

"She looks stupid," Robert said. "Tell me why you did it."

"Don't say again I look stupid," I said.

"Well," he said, "you do."

"Enough," Mum said.

"She does. I'm just curious to know why a half-bright eleven-year-old would do such a stupid thing."

"I did it," I said, "because I wanted to pretend I'd been somewhere else."

"Oh," Robert said. "India?"

I didn't answer.

"Is this meant to criticize me as the breadwinner? Because we can't afford to take holidays like your friends?" Robert asked.

"You're going too far," Mum said.

"Am I?"

"Change the subject, Bob."

Ray made a quick left, Robert followed, then Ray picked up speed.

"That Dallyce seems pretty nice," Mum said. "Down to earth. Maybe she'll be the one."

"A teacher," Robert said. "He probably didn't meet her in the pub."

I piped up, "They met at a mutual friend's."

We drove in silence. Ray made another left, and then we did. The road was dark and bordered by open fields. I remembered my father had taken me to the pony rides there when I was little. I'd sat on the back of Hi Yo Silver, the oldest, most polite pony in captivity, and Dad had led us around, around, and around the winding sawdust path until the pony's bedtime. Now it was a new development.

Robert's signal kept ticking after the turn.

"Ray won't keep a girl like that, honey. A teacher and all. He's got to really shape up. Lay off the booze."

"You think she's better than him?"

He sighed loudly. "Why do you always twist my words, dear?" he asked.

"Am I twisting them, dear?"

"I think so, dear," he said. "What do you say in the back seat?"

"I'm not here," I said. Ray seemed to be going faster and leaving us behind. His tail lights shrank in the distance.

"Sometimes I get the feeling everyone's against me in this family," Robert said. "I really get that feeling." His voice shook.

"Here we go," Mum said. "Deck the halls. Tra la la la la. And do you know the feeling I get, dear?"

"No."

"I get the feeling you could really go for a young girl like that. Wearing bare legs up to there."

Robert glanced over at her. "Take that back," he said.

"Up to heaven," Mum said.

"You'll take that back," he said. Robert laid on the gas and we shot up the road.

Ray slowed, and signalled, and pulled into my sister's driveway. He was unfolding himself from the car, one foot on the ground, as we zipped by Irene's twinkling home. Dallyce must have been waiting for him to jog around and open her door. For a second, I could see what he saw. The Plymouth going dangerously fast; two ghosts in the front seat, my shadow behind.

"Take it back," Robert yelled, and pointed the car at a tall cedar on the side of the road. There was no way we weren't going to hit. We were going to hit. We were going to hit. Off the pavement, on the gravel shoulder, the car sang as Robert edged the wheel and pressed the brakes into a long scream. When the car stopped, our bodies kept travelling forward, then we snapped the few inches back into ourselves.

In the idling car we sat still. No one was hurt. The night was black outside us and the brights lit up the ice. The gauges on the dash glowed blue. He stared straight ahead, breathing rough. In that big cold quiet, she turned to him and kissed him, and kissed again, until she kissed him into kissing, kissing her back, until I couldn't hear the in, out, in again, of our breath.

Notes on the Authors

MARGARET ATWOOD is the celebrated author of *The Edible Woman*, *The Handmaid's Tale*, *The Robber Bride*, *Alias Grace*, and *The Blind Assassin*, which won the prestigious Booker Prize. She delivered *Payback: Debt and the Shadow Side of Wealth* as the Massey Lectures for 2008.

DON BAILEY published several award-winning poems, plays, and fiction collections during his lifetime. He wrote a biography of his dear friend, Margaret Laurence, entitled *Memories of Margaret*. A prominent member of the Winnipeg literary world, he died suddenly in 2003.

MICHELLE BERRY is the author of four novels, *What We All Want*, *Blur*, *Blind Crescent*, and *The Book Will Not Save Your Life*, which won the 2010 Colophon Award. Her short story collection *I Still Don't Even Know You* won the Mary Scorer Award and was shortlisted for the ReLit Award.

ROY BONISTEEL was the host of the long-running series *Man Alive* on CBC television. *There Was a Time* is his memoir of growing up in the Bay of Quinte region in Eastern Ontario.

DAVID CAVANAGH is a former resident of Eastern Ontario whose fiction appeared in the Kingston *Whig-Standard Magazine*. He who now lives in Vermont.

LESLEY CHOYCE lives at Lawrencetown Beach, Nova Scotia, where he surfs in the Atlantic Ocean. His book *An Avalanche of Ocean* was nominated for the Stephen Leacock Award. He is also a part-time instructor at Dalhousie University and founding director of Pottersfield Press.

MARY COOK has been delighting book readers and CBC Radio listeners for years with her remembrances of growing up on a family farm during the bittersweet years of the 1930s. She is the recipient of seven Actra awards and the author of several books, including *Liar, Liar, Pants on Fire!* and *Another Place at the Table*. She lives in Carleton Place, Ontario.

CHARLES de LINT is a celebrated fantasy author, folk musician, and book critic for *The Magazine of Fantasy & Science Fiction*. His works have been nominated for the prestigious Nebula Award and for the World Fantasy Award 17 times, winning in 2000 for his short story collection, *Moonlight and Vines*. He lives in Ottawa with his wife, artist, musician, and co-author MaryAnn Harris.

MARY ALICE DOWNIE is co-editor of the Amelia Frances Howard-Gibbon award-winning book *The Wind Has Wings* and the author of several children's and young adult books, including *A Pioneer ABC, Honour Bound, Danger in Disguise*, and the folktale *How the Devil Got His Cat*. She lives in Kingston, Ontario.

BRIAN DOYLE is a celebrated young-adult novelist whose stories are set in the Ottawa Valley. His book publications include *Angel Square, Easy Avenue, Uncle Ronald*, and *Covered Bridge*. *Angel Square* was made into a film directed by Ann Wheeler. He lives in Ottawa, Ontario.

MARIAN ENGEL published ten books of fiction during her lifetime, notably *Lunatic Villas* and *Bear*, which received the Governor General's Award. She also wrote two children's books: *Adventures of Moon Bay Towers* and *My name Is Not Odessa Yarker*.

JOAN FINNIGAN published poetry, short stories, screenplays, and oral histories about life in the Ottawa Valley, notably *The Best Damn Fiddler from Calabogie to Kaladar* and *Tell Me Another Story*. She was exceptionally proud of her poetry, selected in *The Watershed Collection*. She died in 2007.

DONNA GAMACHE has published three novels, *Sarah: A New Beginning, Spruce Woods Adventure*, and *Loon Island*, as well as non-fiction and poetry in rural newspapers. She lives in MacGregor, Manitoba.

DAVID HELWIG is the author of a host of novels, including *The Glass Knight, Old Wars, Of Desire,* and *Killing McGee*. Formerly a producer for CBC and a professor at Queen's University, he now lives in Prince Edward Island, where he has served as the poet laureate of the province. He is a Member of the Order of Canada.

MARGARET LAURENCE published many great works of fiction during her career, notably *A Jest of God, The Diviners,* and *The Stone Angel*. She died in 1987.

STEPHEN LEACOCK is the author of *Sunshine Sketches of a Little Town*, based on his childhood in Orillia, Ontario (aka Mariposa). He was the recipient of the Lorne Pierce Medal and the Governor General's Award. The Leacock Medal for Humour was established in his honour.

NORMAN LEVINE was born in Ottawa, Ontario, but spent most of his adult life in England. He published two novels and several collections of stories, including *Something Happened Here, The Ability to Forget,* and *From a Seaside Town*. He died in 2005.

ROY MacGREGOR is a columnist for *The Globe and Mail,* the author of the *Screech Owl* series of children's books, and a biographer of Tom Thomson. His penchant for hockey is clear in his book, *Home Team.*

ALISTAIR MacLEOD has published the short story collection *Island.* He won the International IMPAC Dublin Literary Award for his novel *No Great Mischief.* He divides his time between Windsor, Ontario, and Cape Breton, Nova Scotia.

MARY JANE MAFFINI has written several mystery series, including Ladies Killing Circle, starring Charlotte Adams and Camilla MacPhee. Her stories have also been published in *Chatelaine* and *Ellery Queen's Mystery Magazine.* A resident of Ottawa, she has won two Arthur Ellis awards for her short stories.

LUCY MAUDE MONTGOMERY is the creator of Anne of Green Gables, one of Canada's most endearing fictional characters in print and in film.

ALICE MUNRO has received the Man Booker International Prize for her literary achievement, as well as three Governor General's Awards. Her stories are typically set in Southwestern Ontario, where she still lives.

BARBARA NOVAK has published stories for children in *Miss Chatelaine* and *The Window of Dreams,* while her plays have been performed on stage and on CBC Morningside. She lives in London, Ontario.

ANDREW PYPER is the author of *Lost Girls,* which was selected as a Notable Book of the Year by *The Globe and Mail* and *The New York Times.* His second novel, *The Trade Mission,* was selected as a Top 10 Best Book of the Year by the *Toronto Star.* He was born in Stratford, Ontario.

AL ROACH was raised in Walkerville, Ontario, and wrote for *The Windsor Star* for more than 40 years. He is the author of two books on local history, *All Our Memories*, and *All Our Memories 2*.

PETER ROBINSON is best known for his award-winning crime novels, set in Yorkshire, England, featuring Inspector Alan Banks. The titles of his novels often echo popular music lyrics, such as *No Cure for Love*, *Piece of My Heart*, and *Friend of the Devil*. His novels have been translated into 20 other languages.

JANE RULE published several works of fiction during her career, notably *Lesbian Images*, *Inland Passage*, and *Memory Board*. She died in 2007.

ROBERT SERVICE lived in the Yukon for less than a decade but found the North especially inspiring, leading him to write such amusing narrative poems as "The Shooting of Dan McGrew" and "The Cremation of Sam McGee."

LINDA SVENDSEN is a Gemini-winning screenwriter and novelist, whose book *Marine Life* was awarded the Ethel Wilson Fiction Prize. She has also written the film adaptation of *The Diviners* by Margaret Laurence. She teaches creative writing at the University of British Columbia.

DAVID WATMOUGH is a Canadian playwright, short story writer, and novelist whose long list of publications include *Hunting with Diana*, *The Moor is Dark Beneath the Moon*, and his memoirs, *Myself Through Others*. He lives in Vancouver.

ERIC WRIGHT was born in England and now lives in Toronto. Four of his novels have been awarded the Arthur Ellis Award for Best Crime Novel, and *The Kidnapping of Rosie Dawn* was nominated for the prestigious Edgar Award. He has also received the Derrick Murdoch Award for lifetime contributions to Canadian crime writing.

Permissions and Acknowledgements

"A Christmas Story" by Roy Bonisteel is reprinted from *The Whig-Standard Magazine* by permission of the author.

"A Crow Girls' Christmas" by Charles de Lint and MaryAnn Harris is reprinted from *Muse and Reverie* by permission of the authors.

"A Migrant Christmas" by Jane Rule is reprinted from *Inland Passage* by permission of George Borchardt Inc.

"An Irish Jig" by Eric Wright is reprinted from *The Globe and Mail* by permission of the author.

"Angel with a Cow Bell" by Roy MacGregor is reprinted from *MacGregor's Family Christmas* by permission of the author.

"Big Blue Spruce" by Brian Doyle is reprinted from *The Globe and Mail* by permission of the author.

"Blue Christmas" by Peter Robinson is reprinted from *Best British Mysteries IV* and *Blood on the Holly* by permission of the author.

"Boxing Day" by Linda Svendsen is reprinted from *Northwest Review* by permission of the author and the Robin Straus Agency.

"Christmas Eve on the Drink Train" by Andrew Pyper is reprinted from *The Globe and Mail* by permission of the author.

"Christmas at the Crompton" by David Cavanagh is reprinted from *The Whig-Standard Magazine* by permission of the author.

"Christmas Under a Pale Green Sky" by Barbara Novak is reprinted from *Who and Why* by permission of the author.

"Green Gables Christmas" by Lucy Maude Montgomery is excerpted from *The Green Gables Letters from L.M. Montgomery to Ephraim Weber, 1905-1909*.

"Making Spirits Bright" by Michelle Berry is reprinted from *The Globe and Mail* by permission of the author.

"Never Smile Before Christmas" by Lesley Choyce is reprinted by permission of the author.

"On Christmas Eve: 1963" by Joan Finnigan is reprinted from *I Come from the Valley* by permission of the Estate of Joan Finnigan Mckenzie.

"One More Wiseman" by David Helwig is reprinted from *The Toronto Star* by permission of the author.

"Starry Starry Night" by Don Bailey is reprinted from the previous edition of *Best Canadian Christmas Stories in Prose & Verse* by permission of the Estate of Don Bailey.

"The Bird Feeder" by Donna Gamache is reprinted from *Our Family* by permission of the author.

"The Christmas Log" by Mary Alice Downie is reprinted by permission of the author.

"The Errors of Santa Claus" by Stephen Leacock is reprinted by permission.

"The Man with the Notebook" by Norman Levine is reprinted from *The Ottawa Citizen* by permission of Liepman AG Literary Agency.

"The Santa Claus Trap" by Margaret Atwood is reprinted from *The Weekend Magazine* by permission of the author.

"The Three Christmases" by Marian Engel is reprinted from *The Weekend Magazine* by permission of the Estate of Marian Engel.

"The Trapper's Christmas Eve" by Robert Service is reprinted from *The Collected Poems of Robert Service*.

"The Turkey Season" by Alice Munro is reprinted from *Moons of Jupiter and Other Stories* by permission of the author and the William Morris Agency.

"The Unexpected Guest" by Mary Cook is reprinted from *My Mind's Eye* by permission of the author.

"The Wounded Christmas Choirboy" by David Watmough is reprinted from *Vibrations in Time* by permission of the author and the Robert Drake Agency.

"'Tis Better to Give" by Al Roach is reprinted from the *Windsor Star* by permission of the Estate of Al Roach.

"To Everything There Is a Season" by Alistair MacLeod is reprinted by permission of the author and McLelland & Stewart.

"Turning on the Christmas Blights" by Mary Jane Maffini is reprinted by permission of the author.

"Upon a Midnight Clear" by Margaret Laurence is reprinted from *The Weekend Magazine* by permission of the Estate of Margaret Laurence.